O9-ABF-814

Throughout his life, **Robert Louis Stevenson** (1850–94) was plagued by ill health, which interrupted his formal education at Edinburgh University. Pursuing the life of a bohemian during his twenties and thirties, he traveled around Europe and formed the basis of his first two books, *An Inland Voyage* (1878) and *Travels with a Donkey* (1879). Stevenson gained his first popular success with *Treasure Island* (1883). *Dr. Jekyll and Mr. Hyde*, which sold 40,000 copies in six months, and *Kidnapped* appeared in 1886, followed by *The Black Arrow* in 1888.

Dan Chaon is the author of a novel, *You Remind Me of Me*, and two short story collections, *Fitting Ends* and the 2001 National Book Award Finalist *Among the Missing*. His work has appeared in numerous magazines, including *Story*, *Ploughshares*, and *TriQuarterly*, as well as *Best American Short Stories* and *The Pushcart Prize 2000*. The recipient of numerous prizes and honors, he teaches at Oberlin College.

DR. JEKYLL
AND
MR. HYDE

Robert Louis Stevenson

With an Introductory Essay by
Vladimir Nabokov
and a New Afterword by
Dan Chaon

A SIGNET CLASSIC

SIGNET CLASSIC
Published by New American Library, a division of
Penguin Group (USA) Inc., 375 Hudson Street,
New York, New York 10014, USA
Penguin Group (Canada), 10 Alcorn Avenue, Toronto,
Ontario M4V 3B2, Canada (a division of Pearson Penguin Canada Inc.)
Penguin Books Ltd., 80 Strand, London WC2R 0RL, England
Penguin Ireland, 25 St. Stephen's Green, Dublin 2,
Ireland (a division of Penguin Books Ltd.)
Penguin Group (Australia), 250 Camberwell Road, Camberwell, Victoria 3124,
Australia (a division of Pearson Australia Group Pty. Ltd.)
Penguin Books India Pvt. Ltd., 11 Community Centre, Panchsheel Park,
New Delhi - 110 017, India
Penguin Group (NZ), cnr Airborne and Rosedale Roads, Albany,
Auckland 1310, New Zealand (a division of Pearson New Zealand Ltd.)
Penguin Books (South Africa) (Pty.) Ltd., 24 Sturdee Avenue,
Rosebank, Johannesburg 2196, South Africa

Penguin Books Ltd., Registered Offices:
80 Strand, London WC2R 0RL, England

Published by Signet Classic, an imprint of New American Library,
a division of Penguin Group (USA) Inc.

First Signet Classic Printing, October 1987
First Signet Classic Printing (Chaon Afterword), September 2003
10 9 8 7

"The Strange Case of Dr. Jekyll and Mr. Hyde" copyright © The Estate of
Vladimir Nabokov, 1980.
Reprinted by permission of Harcourt Brace Jovanovich, Inc.
Introduction copyright © Dan Chaon, 2003
All rights reserved

℃ REGISTERED TRADEMARK—MARCA REGISTRADA

Library of Congress Catalog Card Number: 2003041504

Printed in the United States of America

Without limiting the rights under copyright reserved above, no part of this
publication may be reproduced, stored in or introduced into a retrieval system, or transmitted, in any form, or by any means (electronic, mechanical,
photocopying, recording, or otherwise), without the prior written permission
of both the copyright owner and the above publisher of this book.

If you purchased this book without a cover you should be aware that this
book is stolen property. It was reported as "unsold and destroyed" to the
publisher and neither the author nor the publisher has received any payment
for this "stripped book."

The scanning, uploading, and distribution of this book via the Internet or via
any other means without the permission of the publisher is illegal and punish-
able by law. Please purchase only authorized electronic editions, and do not
participate in or encourage electronic piracy of copyrighted materials. Your
support of the author's rights is appreciated.

Contents

"The Strange Case of Dr. Jekyll and Mr. Hyde"*

Vladimir Nabokov

"Dr. Jekyll and Mr. Hyde" was written in bed, at Bournemouth on the English Channel, in 1885 in between hemorrhages from the lungs. It was published in January 1886. Dr. Jekyll is a fat, benevolent physician, not without human frailties, who at times by means of a potion projects himself into, or concentrates or precipitates, an evil person of brutal and animal nature taking the name of Hyde, in which character he leads a patchy criminal life of sorts. For a time he is able to revert to his Jekyll personality—there is a down-to-Hyde drug and a back-to-Jekyll drug—but gradually his better nature weakens and finally the back-to-Jekyll potion fails, and he poisons himself when on the verge of exposure. This is the bald plot of the story.

First of all, if you have the Pocket Books edition I have, you will veil the monstrous, abominable, atro-

---

*Editor's note: In 1948 Vladimir Nabokov was appointed Associate Professor of Slavic Literature at Cornell University, where he taught Russian Literature in Translation, and Masters of European Fiction. For the next ten years he introduced undergraduates to the delights of great fiction, including *Dr. Jekyll and Mr. Hyde*, in fifty-minute classroom lectures. In 1980 his notes were collected by Fredson Bowers and published by Harcourt Brace Jovanovich as *Lectures on Literature*, from which this essay has been reprinted by permission.

cious, criminal, foul, vile, youth-depraving jacket—or
better say straitjacket. You will ignore the fact that
ham actors under the direction of pork packers have
acted in a parody of the book, which parody was then
photographed on a film and showed in places called
theaters; it seems to me that to call a movie house a
theater is the same as to call an undertaker a mortician.

And now comes my main injunction. Please completely forget, disremember, obliterate, unlearn, consign to oblivion any notion you may have had that
"Jekyll and Hyde" is some kind of a mystery story, a
detective story, or movie. It is of course quite true
that Stevenson's short novel, written in 1885, is one
of the ancestors of the modern mystery story. But
today's mystery story is the very negation of style,
being, at the best, conventional literature. Frankly, I
am not one of those college professors who coyly
boasts of enjoying detective stories—they are too
badly written for my taste and bore me to death.
Whereas Stevenson's story is—God bless his pure
soul—lame as a detective story. Neither is it a parable nor an allegory, for it would be tasteless as either. It has, however, its own special enchantment if
we regard it as a phenomenon of style. It is not only
a good "bogey story," as Stevenson exclaimed when
awakening from a dream in which he had visualized
it much in the same way I suppose as magic cerebra-
tion had granted Coleridge the vision of the most
famous of unfinished poems. It is also, and more
importantly, "a fable that lies nearer to poetry than
to ordinary prose fiction."* and therefore belongs to
the same order of art as, for instance, *Madame Bovary*
or *Dead Souls*.

*Nabokov states that critical quotations in this essay are drawn
from Stephen Gwynn, *Robert Louis Stevenson* (London: Macmillan,
1939). Ed.

There is a delightful winey taste about this book; in fact, a good deal of old mellow wine is drunk in the story: one recalls the wine that Utterson so comfortably sips. This sparkling and comforting draft is very different from the icy pangs caused by the chameleon liquor, the magic reagent that Jekyll brews in his dusty laboratory. Everything is very appetizingly put. Gabriel John Utterson of Gaunt Street mouths his words most roundly; there is an appetizing tang about the chill morning in London, and there is even a certain richness of tone in the description of the horrible sensations Jekyll undergoes during his *hydizations*. Stevenson had to rely on style very much in order to perform the trick, in order to master the two main difficulties confronting him: (1) to make the magic potion a plausible drug based on a chemist's ingredients and (2) to make Jekyll's evil side before and after the hydization a believable evil.

[Here Nabokov quoted from "I was so far in my reflections . . ." through "mankind, was pure evil," pp. 105–108.]*

The names Jekyll and Hyde are of Scandinavian origin, and I suspect that Stevenson chose them from the same page of an old book on surnames where I looked them up myself. Hyde comes from the Anglo-Saxon *hyd*, which is the Danish *hide*, "a haven." And Jekyll comes from the Danish name *Jökulle*, which means "an icicle." Not knowing these simple derivations one would be apt to find all kinds of symbolic meanings, especially in Hyde, the most

*Editor's note: Throughout his lecture, Nabokov quoted extensively from the novel. For this essay, we provide the beginning and the ending passages that he quoted, with the corresponding page numbers from this edition.

obvious being that Hyde is a kind of hiding place for
Dr. Jekyll, in whom the jocular doctor and the killer
are combined.

Three important points are completely obliterated
by the popular notions about this seldom read book:

1. Is Jekyll good? No, he is a composite being, a
   mixture of good and bad, a preparation consist-
   ing of a ninety-nine percent solution of Jekyllite
   and one percent of Hyde (or *hydatid* from the
   Greek "water" which in zoology is a tiny pouch
   within the body of man and other animals, a
   pouch containing a limpid fluid with larval tapeworms in it—a delightful arrangement, for the
   little tapeworms at least. Thus in a sense, Mr.
   Hyde is Dr. Jekyll's parasite—but I must warn
   that Stevenson knew nothing of this when he
   chose the name.) Jekyll's morals are poor from
   the Victorian point of view. He is a hypocritical
   creature carefully concealing his little sins. He
   is vindictive, never forgiving Dr. Lanyon with
   whom he disagrees in scientific matters. He is
   foolhardy. Hyde is mingled with him, within
   him. In this mixture of good and bad in Dr.
   Jekyll, the bad can be separated as Hyde, who
   is a precipitate of pure evil, a precipitation in
   the chemical sense since something of the composite Jekyll remains behind to wonder in horror at Hyde while Hyde is in action.
2. Jekyll is not really transformed into Hyde but
   projects a concentrate of pure evil that becomes
   Hyde, who is smaller than Jekyll, a big man, to
   indicate the larger amount of good that Jekyll
   possesses.
3. There are really three personalities—Jekyll, Hyde,

and a third, the Jekyll residue when Hyde takes over.

The situation may be represented visually.

Henry Jekyll
(large)

Edward Hyde
(small)

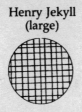

But if you look closely you see that within this big, luminous, pleasantly tweed Jekyll there are scattered rudiments of evil.

When the magic drug starts to work, a dark concentration of this evil begins forming

and is projected or ejected as

Still, if you look closely at Hyde, you will notice that above him floats aghast, but dominating, a residue of Jekyll, a kind of smoke ring, or halo, as if this black concentrated evil had fallen out of the remaining ring of good, but this ring of good still remains: Hyde still wants to change back to Jekyll. This is the significant point.

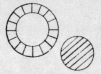

It follows that Jekyll's transformation implies a concentration of evil that already inhabited him rather than a complete metamorphosis. Jekyll is not pure good, and Hyde (Jekyll's statement to the contrary) is not pure evil, for just as parts of unacceptable Hyde dwell within acceptable Jekyll, so over Hyde hovers a halo of Jekyll, horrified at his worser half's iniquity.

The relations of the two are typified by Jekyll's house, which is half Jekyll and half Hyde. As Utterson and his friend Enfield were taking a ramble one Sunday they came to a bystreet in a busy quarter of London which, though small and what is called quiet, drove a thriving trade on weekdays. "Even on Sunday, when it veiled its more florid charms and lay comparatively empty of passage, the street shone out in contrast to its dingy neighbourhood, like a fire in a forest; and with its freshly painted shutters, well-polished brasses, and general cleanliness and gaiety of note, instantly caught and pleased the eye of the passenger.

"Two doors from one corner, on the left hand going east, the line was broken by the entry of a court; and just at that point, a certain sinister block of building thrust forward its gable on the street. It was two storeys high; showed no window, nothing but a door on the lower storey and a blind forehead of discoloured wall on the upper; and bore in every feature, the marks of prolonged and sordid negligence. The door, which was equipped with neither bell nor knocker, was blistered and distained. Tramps slouched into the recess and struck matches on the panels; children kept shop upon the steps; the schoolboy had tried his knife on the mouldings; and for close on a generation, no one had appeared to drive away these random visitors or repair their ravages."

This is the door that Enfield points out to Utterson with his cane, which was used by a repugnantly evil man who had deliberately trampled over a running young girl and, being collared by Enfield, had agreed to recompense the child's parents with a hundred pounds. Opening the door with a key, he had returned with ten pounds in gold and a cheque for the remainder signed by Dr. Jekyll, which proves to be valid. Blackmail, thinks Enfield. He continues to Utterson: "It seems scarcely a house. There is no other door, and nobody goes in or out of that one but, once in a great while, the gentleman of my adventure. There are three windows looking on the court on the first floor; none below; the windows are always shut but they're clean. And then there is a chimney which is generally smoking; so somebody must live there. And yet it's not so sure; for the buildings are so packed together about that court, that it's hard to say where one ends and another begins."

Around the corner from the bystreet there is a square of ancient, handsome houses, somewhat run to seed and cut up into flats and chambers. "One house, however, second from the corner, was still occupied entire; and at the door of this, which wore a great air of wealth and comfort," Utterson was to knock and inquire for his friend, Dr. Jekyll. Utterson knows that the door of the building through which Mr. Hyde had passed is the door to the old dissecting room of the surgeon who had owned the house before Dr. Jekyll bought it and that it is a part of the elegant house fronting on the square. The dissecting room Dr. Jekyll had altered for his chemical experiments, and it was there (we learn much later) that he made his transformations into Mr. Hyde, at which times Hyde lived in that wing.

Just as Jekyll is a mixture of good and bad, so Jekyll's dwelling place is also a mixture, a very neat symbol, a very neat representation of the Jekyll and Hyde relationship. . . . In a bystreet, corresponding to another side of the same block of houses, its geography curiously distorted and concealed by an agglomeration of various buildings and courts in that particular spot, is the mysterious Hyde side door. Thus in the composite Jekyll building with its mellow and grand front hall there are corridors leading to Hyde, to the old surgery theatre, now Jekyll's laboratory, where not so much dissection as chemical experiments were conducted by the doctor. Stevenson musters all possible devices, images, intonation, word patterns, and also false scents, to build up gradually a world in which the strange transformation to be described in Jekyll's own words will have the impact of satisfactory and artistic reality upon the reader—or rather will lead to such a state of mind in which the reader will not ask himself whether this transformation is possible or not. Something of the same sort is managed by Dickens in

Bleak House when by a miracle of subtle approach and variegated prose he manages to make real and satisfying the case of the gin-loaded old man who literally catches fire inside and is burnt to the ground.

Stevenson's artistic purpose was to make "a fantastic drama pass in the presence of plain sensible men" in an atmosphere familiar to the readers of Dickens, in the setting of London's bleak fog, of solemn elderly gentlemen drinking old port, of ugly faced houses, of family lawyers and devoted butlers, of anonymous vices thriving somewhere behind the solemn square on which Jekyll lives, and of cold mornings and of hansom cabs. Mr. Utterson, Jekyll's lawyer, is "a decent, reticent, likeable, trustworthy, courageous and crusty gentleman; and what such people can accept as 'real,' the readers are supposed also to accept as real." Utterson's friend Enfield is called "unimpressionable," a sturdy young businessman definitely on the dull side (in fact it is this sturdy dullness that brings him and Utterson together). It is this dull Enfield, a man of little imagination and not good at observing things, whom Stevenson selects to tell the beginning of the story. Enfield does not realize that the door on the bystreet which Hyde uses to bring the cheque signed by Jekyll is the door of the laboratory in Jekyll's house. However, Utterson realizes the connection immediately, and the story has started.

Although to Utterson the fanciful was the immodest, Enfield's story leads him, at home, to take from his safe Jekyll's will in his own handwriting (for Utterson had refused to lend the least assistance in the making of it) and to read again its provision: "not only that, in the case of the decease of Henry

Jekyll, M.D., D.C.L., L.L.D., F.R.S., etc., all his possessions were to pass into the hands of his 'friend and benefactor Howard Hyde,' but that in case of Dr. Jekyll's 'disappearance or unexplained absence for any period exceeding three calendar months,' the said Edward Hyde should step into the said Henry Jekyll's shoes without further delay and freed from any burthen or obligation, beyond the payment of a few small sums to the members of the doctor's household.'' Utterson had long detested this will, his indignation swelled by his ignorance of Mr. Hyde: "now, by a sudden turn, it was his knowledge [from Enfield's story of the evil small man and the child]. It was already bad enough when the name was but a name of which he could learn no more. It was worse when it began to be clothed upon with detestable attributes; and out of the shifting, insubstantial mists that had so long baffled his eye, there leaped up the sudden, definite presentment of a fiend.

" 'I thought it was madness,' he said, as he replaced the obnoxious paper in the safe, 'and now I begin to fear it is disgrace.' "

Enfield's story about the accident starts to breed in Utterson's mind when he goes to bed. Enfield had begun: "I was coming home from some place at the end of the world, about three o'clock of a black winter morning, and my way lay through a part of town where there was literally nothing to be seen but lamps. Street after street, and all the folks asleep— street after street, all lighted up as if for a procession and all as empty as a church. . . ." (Enfield was a stolid matter-of-fact young man, but Stevenson, the artist, just could not help lending him that phrase about the streets all lighted up, with the folks asleep, and all as empty as a church.) This phrase starts to grow and reecho and mirror and remirror itself in dozing Utterson's head: "Mr. Enfield's tale went by before his mind in a scroll of lighted pictures. He would be aware of the great field of lamps of a nocturnal city; then of the figure of a man walking swiftly; then of a child running from the doctor's; and then these met, and that human Juggernaut trod the child down and passed on regardless of her screams. Or else he would see a room in a rich house, where his friend lay asleep, dreaming and smiling at his dreams; and then the door of that room would be opened, the curtains of the bed plucked apart, the sleeper recalled, and lo! there would stand by his side a figure to whom power was given, and even at that dead hour, he must rise and do its bidding. The figure in these two phases haunted the lawyer all night; and if at any time he dozed over, it was but to see it glide more stealthily through sleeping houses, or move the more swiftly and still the more swiftly, even to dizziness, through wider labyrinths of lamplighted city, and at every street corner crush a child and leave her screaming. And still the figure had no face by which he might know it; even in his dreams, it had no face."

Utterson determines to search him out; at various hours when he is free, he posts himself by the door, and at last he sees Mr. Hyde. "He was small and very plainly dressed, and the look of him, even at that distance, went somehow strongly against the watcher's inclination." (Enfield had remarked: "But there was one curious circumstance. I had taken a loathing to my gentleman at first sight.") Utterson accosts him and after some pretexts he asks to see Hyde's face, which Stevenson carefully does not describe. Utterson does tell the reader other things, however: "Mr. Hyde was pale and dwarfish, he gave an impression of deformity without any nameable malformation, he had a displeasing smile, he had borne himself to the lawyer with a sort of murderous mixture of timidity and boldness, and he spoke with a husky, whispering and somewhat broken voice; all these were points against him, but not all of these together could explain the hitherto unknown disgust, loathing and fear with which Mr. Utterson regarded him. . . . O my poor old Harry Jekyll, if ever I read Satan's signature upon a face, it is on that of your new friend."

Utterson goes around to the square, rings the bell, and inquires of Poole the butler whether Dr. Jekyll is in, but Poole reports that he has gone out. Utterson asks whether it is right that Hyde should let himself in by the old dissecting-room door when the doctor is out, but the butler reassures him that Hyde has a key by the doctor's permission and that the servants have all been ordered to obey him. " 'I do not think I ever met Mr. Hyde?' asked Utterson.

" 'O, dear no, sir. He never *dines* here,' replied the butler. 'Indeed we see very little of him on this side of the house; he mostly comes and goes by the laboratory.' "

Utterson suspects blackmail, and determines to help Jekyll if he will be permitted. Shortly the opportunity comes but Jekyll will not be helped. " 'You do not understand my position,' returned the doctor, with a certain incoherency of manner. 'I am painfully situated, Utterson; my position is a very strange—a very strange one. It is one of those affairs that cannot be mended by talking.' " He adds, however, "just to put your good heart at rest, I will tell you one thing: the moment I choose, I can be rid of Mr.

Hyde. I give you my hand upon that," and the interview closes with Utterson reluctantly agreeing to Jekyll's plea to see that Hyde gets his rights "when I am no longer here."

The Carew murder is the event that begins to bring the story into focus. A servant girl, romantically given, is musing in the moonlight when she perceives a mild and beautiful old gentleman inquiring the way of a certain Mr. Hyde, who had once visited her master and for whom she had conceived a dislike. "He had in his hand a heavy cane, with which he was trifling; but he answered never a word, and seemed to listen with an ill-contained impatience. And then all of a sudden he broke out in a great flame of anger, stamping with his foot, brandishing the cane, and carrying on (as the maid described it) like a madman. The old gentleman took a step back, with the air of one very much surprised and a trifle hurt; and at that Mr. Hyde broke out of all bounds and clubbed him to the earth. And next moment, with ape-like fury, he was trampling his victim under foot and hailing down a storm of blows, under which the bones were audibly shattered and the body jumped upon the roadway. At the horror of these sights and sounds, the maid fainted."

The old man had been carrying a letter addressed to Utterson, who is therefore called upon by a police inspector and identifies the body as that of Sir Danvers Carew. He recognizes the remains of the stick as a cane he had presented to Dr. Jekyll many years before, and he offers to lead the officer to Mr. Hyde's address in Soho, one of the worst parts of London. There are some pretty verbal effects, particularly of alliteration, in the paragraph: "It was by this time about nine in the morning, and the first fog of the season. A great chocolate-coloured pall lowered over heaven, but the wind was continually charging and routing these embattled vapours; so that as the cab crawled from street to street, Mr. Utterson beheld a marvelous number of degrees and hues of twilight; for here it would be dark like the back-end of evening; and light of some strange conflagration; and here, for a moment, the fog would be broken up, and a haggard shaft of daylight would glance in between the swirling wreaths. The dismal quarter of Soho seen under these changing glimpses, with its muddy ways, and slatternly passengers, and its lamps, which had never been extinguished or had been kindled afresh to combat this mournful reinvasion of darkness, seemed, in the lawyer's eyes, like a district of some city in a nightmare."

Hyde is not at home, the flat has been ransacked in great disorder, and it is clear that the murderer has fled. That afternoon Utterson calls on Jekyll and is received in the laboratory: "The fire burned in the grate; a lamp was set lighted on the chimney shelf, for even in the houses the fog began to lie thickly; and there, close up to the warmth, sat Dr.Jekyll, looking deadly sick. He did not rise to meet his visitor, but held out a cold hand and bade him welcome in a changed voice." In response to Utterson's question whether Hyde is in concealment there, " 'Utterson, I swear to God,' cried the doctor, 'I swear to God I will never set eyes on him again. I bind my honour to you that I am done with him in this world. It is all at an end. And indeed he does not want my help; you do not know him as I do; he is safe, he is quite safe; mark my words, he will never more be heard of.' " He shows Utterson a letter signed "Edward Hyde" which signifies that his benefactor need not be concerned since he has means of escape on which he places a sure dependence. Under Utterson's questioning, Jekyll admits that it was Hyde who had dictated the terms of the will and Utterson congratulates him on his escape from being murdered himself. " 'I have had what is far more to the purpose,' returned the doctor solemnly: 'I have had a lesson—O God, Utterson, what a lesson I have had!' And he covered his face for a moment with his hands." From his chief clerk Utterson learns that the hand of the Hyde letter, though sloping in the opposite direction, is very like that of Jekyll. " 'What!' he thought. 'Henry Jekyll forge for a murderer!' And his blood ran cold in his veins."

Stevenson has set himself a difficult artistic problem, and we wonder very much if he is strong enough to solve it. Let us break it up into the following points:

1. In order to make the fantasy plausible he wishes to have it pass through the minds of matter-of-fact persons, Utterson and Enfield, who even for all their commonplace logic must be affected by something bizarre and nightmarish in Hyde.

2. These two stolid souls must convey to the reader something of the horror of Hyde, but at the same time they, being neither artists nor scientists, unlike Dr. Lanyon, cannot be allowed by the author to notice details.

3. Now if Stevenson makes Enfield and Utterson too commonplace and too plain, they will not be able to express even the vague discomfort Hyde causes them. On the other hand, the reader is curious not only about their reactions but he wishes also to see Hyde's face for himself.

4. But the author himself does not see Hyde's face clearly enough, and could only have it described by Enfield or Utterson in some oblique, imaginative, suggestive way, which, however, would not be a likely manner of expression on the part of these stolid souls.

I suggest that given the situation and the characters, the only way to solve the problem is to have the aspect of Hyde cause in Enfield and Utterson not only a shudder of repulsion but also something else. I suggest that the shock of Hyde's presence brings out the hidden artist in Enfield and the hidden artist in Utterson. Otherwise the bright perceptions that illumine Enfield's story of his journey through the lighted, empty streets before he witnessed Mr. Hyde's assault on the child, and the colorful imaginings of Utterson's dreams after he has heard the story can only be explained by the abrupt intrusion of the author with his own set of artistic values and his own diction and intonation. A curious problem indeed.

There is a further problem. Stevenson gives us the specific, lifelike description of events by humdrum London gentlemen, but contrasting with this are the unspecified, vague, but ominous allusions to pleasures and dreadful vices somewhere behind the scenes. On the one side there is "reality"; on the other, "a nightmare world." If the author really means there to be a sharp contrast between the two, then the story could strike us as a little disappointing. If we are really being told "never mind what the evil was—just believe it was something very bad," then we might feel ourselves cheated and bullied. We could feel cheated by vagueness in the most interesting part of the story just because its setting is so matter of fact and realistic. The question that must be asked of the work is whether Utterson and the fog and the cabs and the pale butler are more "real" than the weird experiments and unmentionable adventures of Jekyll and Hyde.

Critics such as Stephen Gwynn have noticed a curious flaw in the story's so-called familiar and commonplace setting. "There is a certain characteristic avoidance: the tale, as it develops, might almost be one of a community of monks. Mr. Utterson is a bachelor, so is Jekyll himself, so by all indications is Enfield, the younger man who first brings to Utterson a tale of Hyde's brutalities. So, for that matter, is Jekyll's butler, Poole, whose part in the story is not negligible. Excluding two or three vague servant maids, a conventional hag and a faceless little girl running for a doctor, the gentle sex has no part in the action. It has been suggested that Stevenson, 'working as he did under Victorian restrictions,' and not wishing to bring colours into the story alien to its monkish pattern, consciously refrained from placing a painted feminine mask upon the secret pleasures in which Jekyll indulged."

If, for instance, Stevenson had gone as far as, say, Tolstoy, who was also a Victorian and also did not go very far—but if Stevenson had gone as far as Tolstoy had in depicting the light loves of Oblonski, the French girl, the singer, the little ballerina, etc., it would have been artistically very difficult to have Jekyll–Oblonski exude a Hyde. A certain amiable, jovial, and lighthearted strain running through the pleasures of a gay blade would then have been difficult to reconcile with the medieval rising as a black scarecrow against a livid sky in the guise of Hyde. It was safer for the artist not to be specific and to leave the pleasures of Jekyll undescribed. But does not this safety, this easy way, does it not denote a certain weakness in the artist? I think it does.

First of all, this Victorian reticence prompts the modern reader to grope for conclusions that perhaps Stevenson never intended to be groped for. For instance, Hyde is called Jekyll's protege and his benefactor, but one may be puzzled by the implication of another epithet attached to Hyde, that of Henry Jekyll's favorite, which sounds almost like *minion*. The all-male pattern that Gwynn has mentioned may suggest by a twist of thought that Jekyll's secret adventures were homosexual practices so common in London behind the Victorian veil. Utterson's first supposition is that Hyde blackmails the good doctor— and it is hard to imagine what special grounds for blackmailing would there have been in a bachelor's consorting with ladies of light morals. Or do Utterson and Enfield suspect that Hyde is Jekyll's illegitimate son? "Paying for the capers of his youth" is what Enfield suggests. But the difference in age as implied by the difference in their appearance does not seem to be quite sufficient for Hyde to be Jekyll's son. Moreover, in his will Jekyll calls Hyde his "friend and benefactor," a curious choice of words perhaps bitterly ironic but hardly referring to a son.

In any case, the good reader cannot be quite satisfied with the mist surrounding Jekyll's adventures. And this is especially irritating since Hyde's adventures, likewise anonymous, are supposed to be monstrous exaggerations of Jekyll's wayward whims. Now the only thing that we do guess about Hyde's pleasures is that they are sadistic—he enjoys the infliction of pain. "What Stevenson desired to convey in the person of Hyde was the presence of evil wholly divorced from good. Of all wrongs in the world Stevenson most hated cruelty; and the inhuman brute whom he imagines is shown not in his beastly lusts, whatever they specifically were, but in his savage indifference" to the human beings whom he hurts and kills.

In his essay "A Gossip on Romance" Stevenson has this to say about narrative structure: "The right kind of thing should fall out in the right kind of place; the right kind of thing should follow; and . . . all the circumstances in a tale answer one another like notes in music. The threads of a story come from time to time together and make a picture in the web; the characters fall from time to time into some attitude to each other or to nature, which stamps the story home like an illustration. Crusoe recoiling from the footprint [*Emma smiling under her iridescent sunshade; Anna reading the shop signs along the road to her death*], these are the culminating moments in the legend, and each has been printed on the mind's eye for ever. Other things we may forget; . . . we may forget the author's comment, although perhaps it was ingenious and true; but these epoch-making scenes which put the last mark of [artistic] truth upon a story and fill up, at one blow, our capacity for [artistic] pleasure, we so adopt into the very bosom of our mind that neither time nor tide can efface or weaken the impression. This, then, is [the highest,] the plastic part of literature: to embody character, thought, or emotion in some act or attitude that shall be remarkably striking to the mind's eye."

"Dr. Jekyll and Mr. Hyde," as a phrase, has entered the language for just the reason of its epoch-making scene, the impression of which cannot be effaced. The scene is, of course, the narrative of Jekyll's transformation into Mr. Hyde which, curiously, has the more impact in that it comes as the explanation contained in two letters after the chronological narrative has come to an end, when Utterson—alerted by Poole that it is someone other than the doctor who for days has immured himself in the laboratory—breaks down the door and finds Hyde in Jekyll's too-large clothes, dead on the floor and with the reek of the cyanide capsule he has just crushed in his teeth. The brief narrative passage between Hyde's murder of Sir Danvers and this discovery merely prepares for the explanation. Time passed but Hyde had disappeared. Jekyll seemed his old self and on the eighth of January gave a small dinner party attended by Utterson and his now reconciled friend, Dr. Lanyon. But four days later Jekyll was not at home to Utterson although they have been seeing each other daily for over two months. On the sixth day when he was refused admission he called on Dr. Lanyon for advice only to find a man with death written on his face, who refused to hear the name of Jekyll. After taking to his bed Dr. Lanyon dies within a week, and Utterson receives a letter in the doctor's hand marked not to be opened before the death or disappearance of Henry Jekyll. A day or two later, Utterson is taking a walk with Enfield, who once again enters the story, and in passing the court on the bystreet they turn in and converse briefly with an ill-looking Jekyll sitting in the window of his laboratory, an interview that ends when "the smile was struck out of [Jekyll's] face and succeeded by an expression of such abject terror and despair, as froze the very blood of the two gentlemen below. They saw it but for a glimpse for the window was instantly thrust down; but that glimpse had been sufficient, and they turned and left the court without a word."

It is not long after that episode that Poole comes to see Mr. Utterson and the action is taken that leads to the forced entry. " 'Utterson,' said the voice, 'for God's sake, have mercy!'

" 'Ah, that's not Jekyll's voice—it's Hyde's!' cried Utterson. 'Down with the door, Poole!'

"Poole swung the axe over his shoulder; the blow shook the building, and the red baize door leaped against the lock and hinges. A dismal screech, as of mere animal terror, rang from the cabinet. Up went the axe again, and again the panels crashed and the frame bounded; four times the blow fell; but the wood was tough and the fittings were of excellent workmanship; and it was not until the fifth, that the lock burst and the wreck of the door fell inwards on the carpet."

At first Utterson thinks that Hyde has killed Jekyll and hidden the body, but a search is fruitless. However, he finds a note from Jekyll on the desk asking him to read Dr. Lanyon's letter and then, if he is still curious, to read the enclosed confession, which Utterson sees is contained in a bulky sealed packet. The narrative proper ends as Utterson, back in his office, breaks the seals and starts to read. The interlocking explanation contained in the narrative-within-a-narrative of the two letters concludes the story.

Briefly, Dr. Lanyon's letter describes how he received an urgent registered letter from Jekyll requesting him to go to the laboratory, to remove a certain drawer containing various chemicals, and to give it to a messenger who would arrive at midnight. He secures the drawer (Poole had also had a registered letter) and returning to his house examines the contents:

> [Here Nabokov quoted excerpts from ". . . when I opened one of the wrappers . . . through "upon the table," pp. 97–100. In this passage, Lanyon has retrieved the potion, and Hyde, as messenger, has come to get the potion he so desperately needs. Hyde mixes the potion in front of Lanyon.]

Lanyon is invited to withdraw, or to remain if he is curious so long as what transpires will be kept secret "under the seal of our profession." Lanyon stays. " 'It is well,' replied my visitor. 'Lanyon, you remember your vows: . . . And now, you who have so long been bound to the most narrow and material views, you who have denied the virtue of transcendental medicine, you who have derided your superiors—behold!'

> [Here Nabokov continued, quoting from "He put the glass . . ." through "murderer of Carew," pp. 101–102.]

Dr. Lanyon's letter leaves quite enough suspense to be filled in by "Henry Jekyll's Full Statement of the Case" which Utterson then reads, bringing the story to a close. Jekyll recounts how his youthful pleasures, which he concealed, hardened into a profound duplicity of life. "It was thus rather the exacting nature of my aspirations than any particular degradation in my faults, that made me what I was, and, with even a deeper trench than in the majority of men, severed in me those provinces of good and ill which divide and compound man's dual nature." His scientific studies led wholly towards the mystic and the transcendental and drew him steadily toward the truth "that man is not truly one, but truly two." And even before the course of his scientific experiments had "begun to suggest the most naked possibility of such a miracle, I had learned to dwell with pleasure, as a beloved daydream, on the thought of the separation of these elements. If each, I told myself, could be housed in separate identities, life would be relieved of all that was unbearable; the unjust might go his way, delivered from the aspirations and remorse of his more upright twin; and the just could walk steadfastly and securely on his upward path, doing the good things in which he found his pleasure, and no longer exposed to disgrace and penitence by the hands of this extraneous evil. It was the curse of mankind that these incongruous faggots were thus bound together—that in the agonised womb of consciousness, these polar twins should be continually struggling. How, then, were they dissociated."

We then have the vivid description of his discovery of the potion and, in testing it, the emergence of Mr. Hyde who, "alone in the ranks of mankind, was pure evil." "I lingered but a moment at the mirror: the second and conclusive experiment had yet to be attempted; it yet remained to be seen if I had lost my identity beyond redemption and must flee before daylight from a house that was no longer mine; and hurrying back to my cabinet, I once more prepared and drank the cup, once more suffered the pangs of dissolution, and came to myself once more with the character, the stature and the face of Henry Jekyll."

For a time all is well. "I was the first that could plod in the public eye with a load of genial respectability, and in a moment, like a schoolboy, strip off these lendings and spring headlong into the sea of liberty. But for me, in my impenetrable mantle, the safety was complete. Think of it—I did not even exist! Let me but escape into my laboratory door, give me but a second or two to mix and swallow the draught that I had always standing ready; and whatever he had done, Edward Hyde would pass away like the stain of breath upon a mirror; and there in his stead, quietly at home, trimming the midnight lamp in his study, a man who could afford to laugh at suspicion, would be Henry Jekyll." The pleasures Jekyll experiences as Mr. Hyde, while his own conscience slumbered, are passed over without detail except that what in Jekyll had been "undignified; I would scarce use a harder term," in the person of Hyde "began to turn toward the monstrous. . . . This familiar that I called out of my own soul, and sent forth alone to do his good pleasure, was a being inherently malign and villainous; his every act and thought centered on self; drinking pleasure with bestial avidity from any degree of torture to another; relentless like a man of stone." Hyde's sadism is thus established.

Then things begin to go wrong. It becomes harder and harder to return to Jekyll from the person of Hyde. Sometimes a double dose of the elixir is required, and once at the risk of life, a triple dose. On one occasion there was total failure. Then one morning Jekyll woke up in his own bed in the house on the square and lazily began to examine the illusion that somehow he was in Hyde's house in Soho.

[Here Nabokov quoted from "I was still so engaged . . ." through "I had awakened Edward Hyde," p. 112.]

He manages to make his way to the laboratory and to restore his Jekyll shape, but the shock of the unconscious transformation goes deep, and he determines to forsake his double existence. "Yes, I preferred the elderly and discontented doctor, surrounded by friends and cherishing honest hopes [observe the alliteration in this passage]; and bade a resolute farewell to the liberty, the comparative youth, the light step, leaping impulses and secret pleasures, that I had enjoyed in the disguise of Hyde."

For two months Jekyll persists in this resolution, although he does not give up his house in Soho or Hyde's smaller clothing that lies ready in his laboratory. Then he weakens. "My devil had been long caged, he came out roaring. I was conscious, even when I took the draught of a more unbridled, a more furious propensity to ill." In this furious mood he murders Sir Danvers Carew, stirred to rage by the old man's civilities. After his transports of glee as he mauls the body, a cold thrill of terror disperses the mists.

[Here Nabokov quoted from "I saw my life to be forfeit. . ." through "clasped his hands to God," p. 116.]

With a sense of joy Jekyll sees that his problem is solved and that he dare never again assume the form of the wanted murderer Hyde. For several months he lives a life of exemplary good works, but he was still cursed with duality of purpose and "the lower side of me, so long indulged, so recently chained down, began to growl for license." In his own person, for he can never again risk Hyde, he begins to pursue his secret vices. This brief excursion into evil finally destroyed the balance of his soul. One day, sitting in Regent's Park, "a qualm came over me, a horrid nausea and the most deadly shuddering. These passed away, and left me faint; and then as in its turn faintness subsided, I began to be aware of a change in the temper of my thoughts, a greater boldness, a contempt of danger, a solution of the bonds of obligation. I looked down; my clothes hung formlessly on my shrunken limbs; the hand that lay on my knees was corded and hairy. I was once more Edward Hyde. A moment before I had been safe of all men's respect, wealthy, beloved—the cloth laying for me in the dining-room at home; and now I was the common quarry of mankind, hunted, house-less, a known murderer, thrall to the gallows." As Hyde he cannot return to his house, and so he is forced into the expedient of calling on Dr. Lanyon's help, described in the doctor's letter.

The end now comes with rapidity. The very next morning, crossing the court of his own house, he is again seized by the vertigo of change and it took a double dose to restore him to himself. Six hours later the pangs returned and he had to drink the potion once more. From that time on he was never safe and it required the constant stimulation of the drug to enable him to keep the shape of Jekyll. (It was at one of these moments that Enfield and Utterson conversed with him at the window on the court, a meeting abruptly terminated by the onset of a transformation.) "At all hours of the day and night, I would be taken with the premonitory shudder; above all, if I slept, or even dozed for a moment in my chair, it was always as Hyde that I awakened.

[Here Nabokov continued, quoting from "Under the strain of this . . ." through "heart to pity him," pp. 122–23.]

The last calamity falls when the provision of the special salt for his potion begins to run low; when he sends for a fresh order the first change of color occurred but not the second, and no transformation took place. Poole had testified to Utterson of the desperate search for another supply.

[Here Nabokov quoted from "All this last week . . ." through "returned Poole," pp. 83–84.]

Convinced at last that his first supply was impure, that it was the unknown impurity which gave efficacy to the draught, and that he can never renew his supply, Jekyll begins to write the confession and a week later is finishing it under the influence of the last of the old powders. "This, then, is the last time, short of a miracle, that Henry Jekyll can think his own thoughts or see his own face (now how sadly altered!) in the glass." He hastens to conclude lest Hyde suddenly take over and tear the papers to shreds. "Half an hour from now, when I shall again and forever reindue that hated personality, I know how I shall sit shuddering and weeping in my chair, or continue, with the most strained and fearstruck ecstasy of listening, to pace up and down this room (my last earthly refuge) and give ear to every sound of menace. Will Hyde die upon the scaffold? or will he find courage to release himself at the last moment? God knows; I am careless; this is my true hour of death, and what is to follow concerns another than myself. Here then, as I lay down the pen and proceed to seal up my confession, I bring the life of that unhappy Henry Jekyll to an end."

I would like to say a few words about Stevenson's last moments. As you know by now, I am not one to go heavily for the human interest stuff when speaking of books. Human interest is not in my line, as Vronski used to say. But books have their destiny, according to the Latin tag, and sometimes the destinies of authors follow those of their books. There is old Tolstoy in 1910 abandoning his family to wander away and die in a station master's room to the rumble of passing trains that had killed Anna Karenin. And there is something in Stevenson's death in 1894 on Samoa, imitating in a curious way the wine theme and the transformation theme of his fantasy. He went down to the cellar to fetch a bottle of his favorite burgundy, uncorked it in the kitchen, and suddenly cried out to his wife: what's the matter with me, what is this strangeness, has my face changed?—and fell on the floor. A blood vessel had burst in his brain and it was all over in a couple of hours.

What, has my face changed? There is a curious thematical link between this last episode in Stevenson's life and the fateful transformations in his most wonderful book.

DR. JEKYLL
AND
MR. HYDE

Story of the Door

MR. UTTERSON the lawyer was a man of a rugged countenance that was never lighted by a smile; cold, scanty and embarrassed in discourse; backward in sentiment; lean, long, dusty, dreary and yet somehow lovable. At friendly meetings, and when the wine was to his taste, something eminently human beaconed from his eye; something indeed which never found its way into his talk, but which spoke not only in these silent symbols of the after-dinner face, but more often and loudly in the acts of his life. He was austere with himself; drank gin when he was alone, to mortify a taste for vintages; and though he enjoyed the theater, had not crossed the doors of one for twenty years. But he had an approved tolerance for others; sometimes wondering, almost with envy, at the high pressure of spirits involved in their misdeeds; and in any extremity inclined to help rather than to reprove. "I incline to Cain's heresy," he used to say quaintly: "I let my brother go to the devil in his own way." In this character, it was frequently his fortune to be the last reputable acquaintance and the last good influence in the lives of downgoing men. And to such as these, so long as they came about his chambers, he never marked a shade of change in his demeanour.

No doubt the feat was easy to Mr. Utterson; for he was undemonstrative at the best, and even his friendship seemed to be founded in a similar catholicity of good-nature. It is the mark of a modest man to accept his friendly circle ready-made from the hands of opportunity; and that was the lawyer's way. His friends were those of his own blood or those whom he had known the longest; his affections, like ivy, were the growth of time, they implied no aptness in the object. Hence, no doubt, the bond that united him to Mr. Richard Enfield, his distant kinsman, the well-known man about town. It was a nut to crack for many, what these two could see in each other, or what subject they could find in common. It was reported by those who encountered them in their Sunday walks, that they said nothing, looked singularly dull, and would hail with obvious relief the appearance of a friend. For all that, the two men put the greatest store by these excursions, counted them the chief jewel of each week, and not only set aside occasions of pleasure, but even resisted the calls of business, that they might enjoy them uninterrupted.

It chanced on one of these rambles that their way led them down a by-street in a busy quarter of London. The street was small and what is called quiet, but it drove a thriving trade on the week-days. The inhabitants were all doing well, it seemed, and all emulously hoping to do better still, and laying out the surplus of their grains in coquetry; so that the shop fronts stood along that thoroughfare with an air of invitation, like rows of smiling saleswomen. Even on Sunday, when it veiled its more florid charms and lay comparatively empty of passage, the street shone out in contrast to its dingy neighbourhood, like a fire in a forest; and with its freshly painted shutters, well-polished brasses, and general cleanliness and gaiety of note, instantly caught and pleased the eye of the passenger.

Two doors from one corner, on the left hand going east, the line was broken by the entry of a court; and just at that point, a certain sinister block of building thrust forward its gable on the street. It was two storeys high; showed no window, nothing but a door on the lower storey and a blind forehead of discoloured wall on the upper; and bore in every feature, the marks of prolonged and sordid negligence. The door, which was equipped with neither bell nor knocker, was blistered and distained. Tramps slouched into the recess and struck matches on the panels; children kept shop upon the steps; the schoolboy had tried his knife on the mouldings; and for close on a generation, no one had appeared to drive away these random visitors or to repair their ravages.

Mr. Enfield and the lawyer were on the other side of the by-street; but when they came abreast of the entry, the former lifted up his cane and pointed.

"Did you ever remark that door?" he asked; and when his companion had replied in the affirmative, "It is connected in my mind," added he, "with a very odd story."

"Indeed?" said Mr. Utterson, with a slight change of voice, "and what was that?"

"Well, it was this way," returned Mr. Enfield: "I was coming home from some place at the end of the world, about three o'clock of a black winter morning, and my way lay through a part of town where there was literally nothing to be seen but lamps. Street after street, and all the folks asleep—street after street, all lighted up as if for a procession and all as empty as a church—till at last I got into that

state of mind when a man listens and listens and
begins to long for the sight of a policeman. All at
once, I saw two figures: one a little man who was
stumping along eastward at a good walk, and the
other a girl of maybe eight or ten was running as
hard as she was able down a cross street. Well, sir,
the two ran into one another naturally enough at
the corner; and then came the horrible part of the
thing; for the man trampled calmly over the child's
body and left her screaming on the ground. It sounds
nothing to hear, but it was hellish to see. It wasn't
like a man; it was like some damned Juggernaut. I
gave a view halloa, took to my heels, collared my
gentleman, and brought him back to where there
was already quite a group about the screaming child.
He was perfectly cool and made no resistance, but
gave me one look, so ugly that it brought out the
sweat on me like running. The people who had
turned out were the girl's own family; and pretty
soon, the doctor, for whom she had been sent, put
in his appearance. Well, the child was not much the
worse, more frightened, according to the Sawbones;
and there you might have supposed would be an
end to it. But there was one curious circumstance. I
had taken a loathing to my gentleman at first sight.
So had the child's family, which was only natural.
But the doctor's case was what struck me. He was the
usual cut and dry apothecary, of no particular age
and colour, with a strong Edinburgh accent, and
about as emotional as a bagpipe. Well, sir, he was
like the rest of us; every time he looked at my prisoner, I saw that Sawbones turn sick and white with
desire to kill him, I knew what was in his mind,
just as he knew what was in mine; and killing being
out of the question, we did the next best. We told the

man we could and would make such a scandal out of this, as should make his name stink from one end of London to the other. If he had any friends or any credit, we undertook that he should lose them. And all the time, as we were pitching it in red hot, we were keeping the women off him as best we could, for they were as wild as harpies. I never saw a circle of such hateful faces; and there was the man in the middle, with a kind of black, sneering coolness— frightened too, I could see that—but carrying it off, sir, really like Satan. 'If you choose to make capital out of this accident,' said he, 'I am naturally help-less. No gentleman but wishes to avoid a scene,' says he. 'Name your figure.' Well, we screwed him up to a hundred pounds for the child's family; he would have clearly liked to stick out; but there was something about the lot of us that meant mischief, and at last he struck. The next thing was to get the money; and where do you think he carried us but to that place with the door?—whipped out a key, went in, and presently came back with the matter of ten pounds in gold and a cheque for the balance on Coutts's, drawn payable to bearer and signed with a name that I can't mention, though it's one of the points of my story, but it was a name at least very well known and often printed. The figure was stiff; but the signature was good for more than that, if it was only genuine. I took the liberty of pointing out to my gentleman that the whole business looked apocryphal, and that a man does not, in real life, walk into a cellar door at four in the morning and come out of it with another man's cheque for close upon a hundred pounds. But he was quite easy and sneering. 'Set your mind at rest,' says he, 'I will stay with you till the banks open and cash the cheque

myself.' So we all set off, the doctor, and the child's
father, and our friend and myself, and passed the
rest of the night in my chambers; and next day,
when we had breakfasted, went in a body to the
bank. I gave in the cheque myself, and said I had
every reason to believe it was a forgery. Not a bit of
it. The cheque was genuine."

"Tut-tut," said Mr. Utterson.

"I see you feel as I do," said Mr. Enfield. "Yes, it's
a bad story. For my man was a fellow that nobody
could have to do with, a really damnable man; and
the person that drew the cheque is the very pink of
the proprieties, celebrated too, and (what makes it
worse) one of your fellows who do what they call
good. Black mail, I suppose; an honest man paying
through the nose for some of the capers of his youth.
Black Mail House is what I call the place with the
door, in consequence. Though even that, you know,
is far from explaining all," he added, and with the
words fell into a vein of musing.

From this he was recalled by Mr. Utterson asking
rather suddenly: "And you don't know if the drawer
of the cheque lives there?"

"A likely place, isn't it?" returned Mr. Enfield.
"But I happen to have noticed his address; he lives
in some square or another."

"And you never asked about the—place with the
door?" said Mr. Utterson.

"No, sir: I had a delicacy," was the reply. "I feel
very strongly about putting questions; it partakes
too much of the style of the day of judgment. You
start a question, and it's like starting a stone. You sit
quietly on the top of a hill; and away the stone goes,
starting others; and presently some bland old bird
(the last you would have thought of) is knocked on

the head in his own back garden and the family have to change their name. No, sir, I make it a rule of mine: the more it looks like Queer Street, the less I ask."

"A very good rule, too," said the lawyer.

"But I have studied the place for myself," continued Mr. Enfield. "It seems scarcely a house. There is no other door, and nobody goes in or out of that one but, once in a great while, the gentleman of my adventure. There are three windows looking on the court on the first floor; none below; the windows are always shut but they're clean. And then there is a chimney which is generally smoking; so somebody must live there. And yet it's not so sure; for the buildings are so packed together about the court, that it's hard to say where one ends and another begins."

The pair walked on again for a while in silence; and then "Enfield," said Mr. Utterson, "that's a good rule of yours."

"Yes, I think it is," returned Enfield.

"But for all that," continued the lawyer, "there's one point I want to ask: I want to ask the name of that man who walked over the child."

"Well," said Mr. Enfield, "I can't see what harm it would do. It was a man of the name of Hyde."

"Hm," said Mr. Utterson. "What sort of a man is he to see?"

"He is not easy to describe. There is something wrong with his appearance; something displeasing, something down-right detestable. I never saw a man I so disliked, and yet I scarce know why. He must be deformed somewhere; he gives a strong feeling of deformity, although I couldn't specify the point. He's an extraordinary looking man, and yet I really can name nothing out of the way. No, sir; I can make no hand of it; I can't describe him. And it's not want of memory; for I declare I can see him this moment."

Mr. Utterson again walked some way in silence and obviously under a weight of consideration. "You are sure he used a key?" he inquired at last.

"My dear sir . . ." began Enfield, surprised out of himself.

"Yes, I know," said Utterson; "I know it must seem strange. The fact is, if I do not ask you the name of the other party, it is because I know it already. You see, Richard, your tale has gone home. If you have been inexact in any point, you had better correct it."

"I think you might have warned me," returned the other with a touch of sullenness. "But I have been pedantically exact, as you call it. The fellow had a key; and what's more, he has it still. I saw him use it, not a week ago."

Mr. Utterson sighed deeply but said never a word; and the young man presently resumed. "Here is another lesson to say nothing," said he. "I am ashamed of my long tongue. Let us make a bargain never to refer to this again."

"With all my heart," said the lawyer. "I shake hands on that, Richard."

Search for Mr. Hyde

THAT EVENING Mr. Utterson came home to his bachelor house in sombre spirits and sat down to dinner without relish. It was his custom of a Sunday, when this meal was over, to sit close by the fire, a volume of some dry divinity on his reading desk, until the clock in the neighbouring church rang out the hour of twelve, when he would go soberly and gratefully to bed. On this night, however, as soon as the cloth was taken away, he took up a candle and went into his business room. There he opened his safe, took from the most private part of it a document endorsed on the envelope as Dr. Jekyll's Will, and sat down with a clouded brow to study its contents. The will was holograph, for Mr. Utterson, though he took charge of it now that it was made, had refused to lend the least assistance in the making of it; it provided not only that, in case of the decease of Henry Jekyll, M.D., D.C.L., L.L.D., F.R.S., etc., all his possessions were to pass into the hands of his "friend and benefactor Edward Hyde," but that in case of Dr. Jekyll's "disappearance or unexplained absence for any period exceeding three calendar months," the said Edward Hyde should step into the said Henry Jekyll's shoes without further delay and free from any burthen or obligation, beyond the payment of a few small sums to the members of the doctor's household. This document had long been the lawyer's eyesore. It offended him both as a lawyer and as a lover of the sane and customary sides of life, to whom the fanciful was the immodest. And hitherto it was his ignorance of Mr. Hyde that had swelled his indignation; now, by a sudden turn, it was his knowledge. It was already bad enough when the name was but a name of which he could learn no more. It was worse when it began to be clothed upon with detestable attributes; and out of the shifting, insubstantial mists that had so long baffled his eye, there leaped up the sudden, definite present-ment of a fiend.

"I thought it was madness," he said, as he re-placed the obnoxious paper in the safe, "and now I begin to fear it is disgrace."

With that he blew out his candle, put on a great-coat, and set forth in the direction of Cavendish Square, that citadel of medicine, where his friend, the great Dr. Lanyon, had his house and received his crowding patients. "If anyone knows, it will be Lanyon," he had thought.

The solemn butler knew and welcomed him; he was subjected to no stage of delay, but ushered direct from the door to the dining-room where Dr. Lanyon sat alone over his wine. This was a hearty, healthy, dapper, red-faced gentleman, with a shock of hair prematurely white, and a boisterous and de-cided manner. At sight of Mr. Utterson, he sprang up from his chair and welcomed him with both hands. The geniality, as was the way of the man, was somewhat theatrical to the eye; but it reposed on genuine feeling. For these two were old friends, old mates both at school and college, both thorough respectors of themselves and of each other, and what does not always follow, men who thoroughly enjoyed each other's company.

After a little rambling talk, the lawyer led up to the subject which so disagreeably preoccupied his mind.

"I suppose, Lanyon," said he, "you and I must be the two oldest friends that Henry Jekyll has?"

"I wish the friends were younger," chuckled Dr. Lanyon. "But I suppose we are. And what of that? I see little of him now.

"Indeed?" said Utterson. "I thought you had a bond of common interest."

"We had," was the reply. "But it is more than ten years since Henry Jekyll became too fanciful for me. He began to go wrong, wrong in mind; and though of course I continue to take an interest in him for old sake's sake, as they say, I see and I have seen devilish little of the man. Such unscientific balderdash," added the doctor, flushing suddenly purple, "would have estranged Damon and Pythias."

This little spirit of temper was somewhat of a relief to Mr. Utterson. "They have only differed on some point of science," he thought; and being a man of no scientific passions (except in the matter of conveyancing), he even added: "It is nothing worse than that!" He gave his friend a few seconds to recover his composure, and then approached the question he had come to put. "Did you ever come across a protégé of his—one Hyde?" he asked.

"Hyde?" repeated Lanyon. "No. Never heard of him. Since my time."

That was the amount of information that the lawyer carried back with him to the great, dark bed on which he tossed to and fro, until the small hours of the morning began to grow large. It was a night of little ease to his toiling mind, toiling in mere darkness and besieged by questions.

Six o'clock struck on the bells of the church that was so conveniently near to Mr. Utterson's dwelling, and still he was digging at the problem. Hitherto it had touched him on the intellectual side alone; but now his imagination also was engaged, or rather enslaved; and as he lay and tossed in the gross darkness of the night and the curtained room, Mr. Enfield's tale went by before his mind in a scroll of lighted pictures. He would be aware of the great field of lamps of a nocturnal city; then of the figure of a man walking swiftly; then of a child running from the doctor's; and then these met, and that human Juggernaut trod the child down and passed on regardless of her screams. Or else he would see a room in a rich house, where his friend lay asleep, dreaming and smiling at his dreams; and then the door of that room would be opened, the curtains of the bed plucked apart, the sleeper recalled, and lo! there would stand by his side a figure to whom power was given, and even at that dead hour, he must rise and do its bidding. The figure in these two phases haunted the lawyer all night; and if at any time he dozed over, it was but to see it glide more stealthily through sleeping houses, or move the more swiftly and still the more swiftly, even to dizziness, through wider labyrinths of lamp-lighted city, and at every street corner crush a child and leave her screaming. And still the figure had no face by which he might know it; even in his dreams, it had no face, or one that baffled him and melted before his eyes; and thus it was that there sprang up and grew apace in the lawyer's mind a singularly strong, almost an inordinate, curiosity to behold the features of the real Mr. Hyde. If he could but once set eyes on him, he thought the mystery would lighten and perhaps roll altogether away, as was the habit of mysterious things when well examined. He might see a reason for his friend's strange preference or bondage (call it which you please) and even for the startling clause of the will. At least it would be a face worth seeing: the face of a man who was without bowels of mercy: a face which had but to show itself to raise up, in the mind of the unimpressionable Enfield, a spirit of enduring hatred.

From that time forward, Mr. Utterson began to haunt the door in the by-street of shops. In the morning before office hours, at noon when business was plenty, and time scarce, at night under the face of the fogged city moon, by all lights and at all hours of solitude or concourse, the lawyer was to be found on his chosen post.

"If he be Mr. Hyde," he had thought, "I shall be Mr. Seek."

And at last his patience was rewarded. It was a fine dry night; frost in the air; the street as clean as a ballroom floor; the lamps, unshaken by any wind, drawing a regular pattern of light and shadow. By ten o'clock, when the shops were closed, the by-street was very solitary and, in spite of the low growl of London from all round, very silent. Small sounds carried far; domestic sounds out of the houses were clearly audible on either side of the roadway; and the rumour of the approach of any passenger preceded him by a long time. Mr. Utterson had been some minutes at his post, when he was aware of an odd, light footstep drawing near. In the course of his nightly patrols, he had long grown accustomed to the quaint effect with which the footfalls of a single person, while he is still a great way off, suddenly spring out distinct from the vast hum and clatter of the city. Yet his attention had never before been so sharply and decisively arrested; and it was with a strong, superstitious prevision of success that he withdrew into the entry of the court.

The steps drew swiftly nearer, and swelled out suddenly louder as they turned the end of the street. The lawyer, looking forth from the entry, could soon see what manner of man he had to deal with. He was small and very plainly dressed, and the look of him, even at that distance, went somehow strongly against the watcher's inclination. But he made straight for the door, crossing the roadway to save time; and as he came, he drew a key from his pocket like one approaching home.

Mr. Utterson stepped out and touched him on the shoulder as he passed. "Mr. Hyde, I think?"

Mr. Hyde shrank back with a hissing intake of the breath. But his fear was only momentary; and though he did not look the lawyer in the face, he answered coolly enough: "That is my name. What do you want?"

"I see you are going in," returned the lawyer. "I am an old friend of Dr. Jekyll's—Mr. Utterson of Gaunt Street—you must have heard of my name; and meeting you so conveniently, I thought you might admit me."

"You will not find Dr. Jekyll; he is from home," replied Mr. Hyde, blowing in the key. And then suddenly, but without looking up, "How did you know me?" he asked.

"On your side," said Mr. Utterson, "will you do me a favour?"

"With pleasure," replied the other. "What shall it be?"

"Will you let me see your face?" asked the lawyer.

Mr. Hyde appeared to hesitate, and then, as if upon some sudden reflection, fronted about with an air of defiance; and the pair stared at each other pretty fixedly for a few seconds. "Now I shall know you again," said Mr. Utterson. "It may be useful."

"Yes," returned Mr. Hyde, "it is as well we have met; and à propos, you should have my address." And he gave a number of a street in Soho.

"Good God!" thought Mr. Utterson, "can he, too, have been thinking of the will?" But he kept his feelings to himself and only grunted in acknowledgment of the address.

"And now," said the other, "how did you know me?"

"By description," was the reply.

"Whose description?"

"We have common friends," said Mr. Utterson.

"Common friends?" echoed Mr. Hyde, a little hoarsely. "Who are they?"

"Jekyll, for instance," said the lawyer.

"He never told you," cried Mr. Hyde, with a flush of anger. "I did not think you would have lied."

"Come," said Mr. Utterson, "that is not fitting language."

The other snarled aloud into a savage laugh; and the next moment with extraordinary quickness, he had unlocked the door and disappeared into the house.

The lawyer stood awhile when Mr. Hyde had left him, the picture of disquietude. Then he began slowly to mount the street, pausing every step or two and putting his hand to his brow like a man in mental perplexity. The problem he was thus debating as he walked, was one of a class that is rarely solved. Mr. Hyde was pale and dwarfish, he gave an impression of deformity without any nameable malformation, he had a displeasing smile, he had borne himself to the lawyer with a sort of murderous mixture of timidity and boldness, and he spoke with a husky, whispering and somewhat broken voice; all these were points against him, but not all of these together could explain the hitherto unknown disgust, loathing and fear with which Mr. Utterson regarded him. "There must be something else," said the perplexed gentleman. "There *is* something more, if I could find a name for it. God bless me, the man seems hardly human! Something troglodytic, shall we say? or can it be the old story of Dr. Fell? or is it the mere radiance of a foul soul that thus transpires through, and transfigures, its clay continent? The last I think; for, O my poor old Harry Jekyll, if ever I read Satan's signature upon a face, it is on that of your new friend."

Round the corner from the by-street, there was a square of ancient, handsome houses, now for the most part decayed from their high estate and let in flats and chambers to all sorts and conditions of men; map-engravers, architects, shady lawyers and the agents of obscure enterprises. One house, however, second from the corner, was still occupied entire; and at the door of this, which wore a great air of wealth and comfort, though it was now plunged in darkness except for the fanlight, Mr. Utterson stopped and knocked. A well-dressed, elderly servant opened the door.

"Is Dr. Jekyll at home, Poole?" asked the lawyer.

"I will see, Mr. Utterson," said Poole, admitting the visitor, as he spoke, into a large, low-roofed, comfortable hall, paved with flags, warmed (after the fashion of a country house) by a bright, open fire, and furnished with costly cabinets of oak. "Will you wait here by the fire, sir? or shall I give you a light in the dining-room?"

"Here, thank you," said the lawyer, and he drew near and leaned on the tall fender. This hall, in which he was now left alone, was a pet fancy of his friend the doctor's; and Utterson himself was wont to speak of it as the pleasantest room in London. But tonight there was a shudder in his blood; the face of Hyde sat heavy on his memory; he felt (what was rare with him) a nausea and distaste of life; and in the gloom of his spirits, he seemed to read a menace in the flickering of the firelight on the polished cabinets and the uneasy starting of the shadow on the roof. He was ashamed of his relief, when Poole presently returned to announce that Dr. Jekyll was gone out.

"I saw Mr. Hyde go in by the old dissecting-room door, Poole," he said. "Is that right, when Dr. Jekyll is from home?"

"Quite right, Mr. Utterson, sir," replied the servant. "Mr. Hyde has a key."

"Your master seems to repose a great deal of trust in that young man, Poole," resumed the other musingly.

"Yes, sir, he does indeed," and Poole. "We have all orders to obey him."

"I do not think I ever met Mr. Hyde?" asked Utterson.

"O, dear no, sir. He never *dines* here," replied the butler. "Indeed we see very little of him on this side of the house; he mostly comes and goes by the laboratory."

"Well, good-night, Poole."

"Good-night, Mr. Utterson."

And the lawyer set out homeward with a very heavy heart. "Poor Harry Jekyll," he thought, "my mind misgives me he is in deep waters! He was wild when he was young; a long time ago to be sure; but in the law of God, there is no statute of limitations. Ay, it must be that; the ghost of some old sin, the cancer of some concealed disgrace: punishment coming, *pede claudo*, years after memory has forgotten and self-love condoned the fault." And the lawyer, scared by the thought, brooded awhile on his own past, groping in all the corners of memory, lest by chance some Jack-in-the-Box of an old iniquity should leap to light there. His past was fairly blameless; few men could read the rolls of their life with less apprehension; yet he was humbled to the dust by the many ill things he had done, and raised up again into a sober and fearful gratitude by the many he had come so near to doing, yet avoided. And then by a return on his former subject, he conceived a spark of hope. "This Master Hyde, if he were studied," thought he, "must have secrets of his own; black secrets, by the look of him; secrets compared to which poor Jekyll's worst would be like sunshine. Things cannot continue as they are. It turns me cold to think of this creature stealing like a thief to Harry's bedside; poor Harry, what a wakening! And the danger of it; for if this Hyde suspects the existence of the will, he may grow impatient to inherit. Ay, I must put my shoulders to the wheel—if Jekyll will but let me," he added, "if Jekyll will only let me." For once more he saw before his mind's eye, as clear as transparency, the strange clauses of the will.

Dr. Jekyll Was
Quite at Ease

A FORTNIGHT LATER, by excellent good fortune, the doctor gave one of his pleasant dinners to some five or six old cronies, all intelligent, reputable men and all judges of good wine; and Mr. Utterson so contrived that he remained behind after the others had departed. This was no new arrangement, but a thing that had befallen many scores of times. Where Utterson was liked, he was liked well. Hosts loved to detain the dry lawyer, when the light-hearted and loose-tongued had already their foot on the threshold; they liked to sit awhile in his unobtrusive company, practising for solitude, sobering their minds in the man's rich silence after the expense and strain of gaiety. To this rule, Dr. Jekyll was no exception; and as he now sat on the opposite side of the fire—a large, well-made, smooth-faced man of fifty, with something of a slyish cast perhaps, but every mark of capacity and kindness—you could see by his looks that he cherished for Mr. Utterson a sincere and warm affection.

"I have been wanting to speak to you, Jekyll," began the latter. "You know that will of yours?"

A close observer might have gathered that the topic was distasteful; but the doctor carried it off gaily. "My poor Utterson," said he, "you are unfortunate in such a client. I never saw a man so distressed as you were by my will; unless it were that hide-bound pedant, Lanyon, at what he called my scientific heresies. O, I know he's a good fellow—you needn't frown—an excellent fellow, and I always mean to see more of him; but a hide-bound pedant for all that; an ignorant, blatant pedant. I was never more disappointed in any man than Lanyon."

"You know I never approved of it," pursued Utterson, ruthlessly disregarding the fresh topic.

"My will? Yes, certainly, I know that," said the doctor, a trifle sharply. "You have told me so."

"Well, I tell you so again," continued the lawyer. "I have been learning something of young Hyde."

The large handsome face of Dr. Jekyll grew pale to the very lips, and there came a blackness about his eyes. "I do not care to hear more," said he. "This is a matter I thought we had agreed to drop."

"What I heard was abominable," said Utterson.

"It can make no change. You do not understand my position," returned the doctor, with a certain incoherency of manner. "I am painfully situated, Utterson; my position is a very strange—a very strange one. It is one of those affairs that cannot be mended by talking."

"Jekyll," said Utterson, "you know me: I am a man to be trusted. Make a clean breast of this in confidence; and I make no doubt I can get you out of it."

"My good Utterson," said the doctor, "this is very good of you, this is downright good of you, and I cannot find words to thank you in. I believe you fully; I would trust you before any man alive, ay, before myself, if I could make the choice; but indeed it isn't what you fancy; it is not as bad as that; and just to put your good heart at rest, I will tell you one thing: the moment I choose, I can be rid of Mr. Hyde. I give you my hand upon that; and I thank you again and again; and I will just add one little word, Utterson, that I'm sure you'll take in good part: this is a private matter, and I beg of you to let it sleep."

Utterson reflected a little, looking in the fire.

"I have no doubt you are perfectly right," he said at last, getting to his feet.

"Well, but since we have touched upon this business, and for the last time I hope," continued the doctor, "there is one point I should like you to understand. I have really a very great interest in poor Hyde. I know you have seen him; he told me so; and I fear he was rude. But I do sincerely take a great, a very great interest in that young man; and if I am taken away, Utterson, I wish you to promise me that you will bear with him and get his rights for him. I think you would, if you knew all; and it would be a weight off my mind if you would promise."

"I can't pretend that I shall ever like him," said the lawyer.

"I don't ask that," pleaded Jekyll, laying his hand upon the other's arm; "I only ask for justice; I only ask you to help him for my sake, when I am no longer here."

Utterson heaved an irrepressible sigh. "Well," said he, "I promise."

Plato
justice is not
giving each
his due

why is Hyde young
but Jekyll old?

The Carew
Murder Case

NEARLY A YEAR LATER, in the month of October, 18—, London was startled by a crime of singular ferocity and rendered all the more notable by the high position of the victim. The details were few and startling. A maid servant living alone in a house not far from the river, had gone upstairs to bed about eleven. Although a fog rolled over the city in the small hours, the early part of the night was cloudless, and the lane, which the maid's window overlooked, was brilliantly lit by the full moon. It seems she was romantically given, for she sat down upon her box, which stood immediately under the window, and fell into a dream of musing. Never (she used to say, with streaming tears, when she narrated that experience), never had she felt more at peace with all men or thought more kindly of the world. And as she so sat she became aware of an aged beautiful gentleman with white hair, drawing near along the lane; and advancing to meet him, another and very small gentleman, to whom at first she paid less attention. When they had come within speech (which was just under the maid's eyes) the older man bowed and accosted the other with a very pretty manner of politeness. It did not seem as if the subject of his address were of great importance; indeed, from his pointing, it sometimes appeared as if he were only inquiring his way; but the moon shone on his face as he spoke, and the girl was pleased to watch it, it seemed to breathe such an innocent and old-world kindness of disposition, yet with something high too, as of a well-founded self-content. Presently her eye wandered to the other, and she was surprised to recognize in him a certain Mr. Hyde, who had once visited her master and for whom she had conceived a dislike. He had in his hand a heavy cane, with which he was trifling; but he answered never a word, and seemed to listen with an ill-contained impatience. And then all of a sudden he broke out in a great flame of anger, stamping with his foot, brandishing the cane, and carrying on (as the maid described it) like a madman. The old gentleman took a step back, with the air of one very much surprised and a trifle hurt; and at that Mr, Hyde broke out of all bounds and clubbed him to the earth. And next moment, with ape-like fury, he was trampling his victim under foot and hailing down a storm of blows, under which the bones were audibly shattered and the body jumped upon the roadway. At the horror of these sights and sounds, the maid fainted.

It was two o'clock when she came to herself and called for the police. The murderer was gone long ago; but there lay his victim in the middle of the lane, incredibly mangled. The stick with which the deed had been done, although it was of some rare and very tough and heavy wood, had broken in the middle under the stress of this insensate cruelty; and one splintered half had rolled in the neighbouring gutter—the other, without doubt, had been carried away by the murderer. A purse and gold watch were found upon the victim: but no cards or papers, except a sealed and stamped envelope, which he had been probably carrying to the post, and which bore the name and address of Mr. Utterson.

This was brought to the lawyer the next morning, before he was out of bed; and he had no sooner seen it, and been told the circumstances, than he shot out a solemn lip. "I shall say nothing till I have seen the body," said he; "this may be very serious. Have the kindness to wait while I dress." And with the same grave countenance he hurried through his breakfast and drove to the police station, whither the body had been carried. As soon as he came into the cell, he nodded.

"Yes," said he, "I recognise him. I am sorry to say that this is Sir Danvers Carew."

"Good God, sir," exclaimed the officer, "is it possible?" And the next moment his eye lighted up with professional ambition. "This will make a deal of noise," he said. "And perhaps you can help us to the man." And he briefly narrated what the maid had seen, and showed the broken stick.

Mr. Utterson had already quailed at the name of Hyde; but when the stick was laid before him, he could doubt no longer; broken and battered as it was, he recognized it for one that he had himself presented many years before to Henry Jekyll.

"Is this Mr. Hyde a person of small stature?" he inquired.

"Particularly small and particularly wicked-looking, is what the maid calls him," said the officer.

Mr. Utterson reflected; and then, raising his head, "If you will come with me in my cab," he said, "I think I can take you to his house."

It was by this time about nine in the morning, and

alternating lighter / dark

the first fog of the season. A great chocolate-coloured pall lowered over heaven, but the wind was continually charging and routing these embattled vapours; so that as the cab crawled from street to street, Mr. Utterson beheld a marvelous number of degrees and hues of twilight; for here it would be dark like the backend of evening; and there would be a glow of a rich, lurid brown, like the light of some strange conflagration; and here, for a moment, the fog would be quite broken up, and a haggard shaft of daylight would glance in between the swirling wreaths. The dismal quarter of Soho seen under these changing glimpses, with its muddy ways, and slatternly passengers, and its lamps, which had never been extinguished or had been kindled afresh to combat this mournful reinvasion of darkness, seemed, in the lawyer's eyes, like a district of some city in a nightmare. The thoughts of his mind, besides, were of the gloomiest dye; and when he glanced at the companion of his drive, he was conscious of some touch of that terror of the law and the law's officers, which may at times assail the most honest.

As the cab drew up before the address indicated, the fog lifted a little and showed him a dingy street, a gin palace, a low French eating house, a shop for the retail of penny numbers and twopenny salads, many ragged children huddled in the doorways, and many women of many different nationalities passing out, key in hand, to have a morning glass; and the next moment the fog settled down again upon that part, as brown as umber, and cut him off from his blackguardly surroundings. This was the home of Henry Jekyll's favourite; of a man who was heir to a quarter of a million sterling.

An ivory-faced and silvery-haired old woman

opened the door. She had an evil face, smoother by hypocrisy: but her manners were excellent. Yes, she said, this was Mr. Hyde's, but he was not at home; he had been in that night very late, but he had gone away again in less than an hour; there was nothing strange in that; his habits were very irregular, and he was often absent; for instance, it was nearly two months since she had seen him till yesterday.

"Very well, then, we wish to see his room," said the lawyer; and when the woman began to declare it was impossible, "I had better tell you who this person is," he added. "This is Inspector Newcomen of Scotland Yard."

A flash of odious joy appeared upon the woman's face. "Ah!" said she, "he is in trouble! What has he done?"

Mr. Utterson and the inspector exchanged glances. "He don't seem a very popular character," observed the latter. "And now, my good woman, just let me and this gentleman have a look about us."

In the whole extent of the house, which but for the old woman remained otherwise empty, Mr. Hyde had only used a couple of rooms; but these were furnished with luxury and good taste. A closet was filled with wine; the plate was of silver, and napery elegant; a good picture hung upon the walls, a gift (as Utterson supposed) from Henry Jekyll, who was much of a connoisseur; and the carpets were of many plies and agreeable in colour. At this moment, however, the rooms bore every mark of having been recently and hurriedly ransacked; clothes lay about the floor, with their pockets inside out; lock-fast drawers stood open; and on the hearth there lay a pile of grey ashes, as though many papers had been burned. From these embers the inspector disinterred the butt end of a green cheque book, which had resisted the action of the fire; the other half of the stick was found behind the door; and as this clinched his suspicions, the officer declared himself delighted. A visit to the bank, where several thousand pounds were found to be lying to the murderer's credit, completed his gratification.

"You may depend upon it, sir," he told Mr. Utterson: "I have him in my hand. He must have lost his head, or he never would have left the stick or, above all, burned the cheque book. Why, money's life to the man. We have nothing to do but wait for him at the bank, and get out the handbills."

This last, however, was not so easy of accomplishment; for Mr. Hyde had numbered few familiars—even the master of the servant maid had only seen him twice; his family could nowhere be traced; he had never been photographed; and the few who could describe him differed widely, as common observers will. Only on one point were they agreed; and that was the haunting sense of unexpressed deformity with which the fugitive impressed his beholders.

Incident
of the Letter

IT WAS LATE in the afternoon, when Mr. Utterson found his way to Dr. Jekyll's door, where he was at once admitted by Poole, and carried down by the kitchen offices and across a yard which had once been a garden, to the building which was indifferently known as the laboratory or dissecting rooms. The doctor had bought the house from the heirs of a celebrated surgeon; and his own tastes being rather chemical than anatomical, had changed the destination of the block at the bottom of the garden. It was the first time that the lawyer had been received in that part of his friend's quarters; and he eyed the dingy, windowless structure with curiosity, and gazed round with a distasteful sense of strangeness as he crossed the theatre, once crowded with eager students and now lying gaunt and silent, the tables laden with chemical apparatus, the floor strewn with crates and littered with packing straw, and the light falling dimly through the foggy cupola. At the further end, a flight of stairs mounted to a door covered with red baize; and through this, Mr. Utterson was at last received into the doctor's cabinet. It was a large room fitted round with glass presses, furnished, among other things, with a cheval-glass and a business table, and looking out upon the court by three dusty windows barred with iron. The fire burned in the grate; a lamp was set lighted on the chimney shelf, for even in the houses the fog began to lie thickly; and there, close up to the warmth, sat Dr. Jekyll, looking deadly sick. He did not rise to meet his visitor, but held out a cold hand and bade him welcome in a changed voice.

"And now," said Mr. Utterson, as soon as Poole had left them, "you have heard the news?"

The doctor shuddered. "They were crying it in the square," he said. "I heard them in my dining-room."

"One word," said the lawyer. "Carew was my client, but so are you, and I want to know what I am doing. You have not been mad enough to hide this fellow?"

"Utterson, I swear to God," cried the doctor, "I swear to God I will never set eyes on him again. I bind my honour to you that I am done with him in this world. It is all at an end. And indeed he does not want my help; you do not know him as I do; he is safe, he is quite safe; mark my words, he will never more be heard of."

The lawyer listened gloomily; he did not like his friend's feverish manner. "You seem pretty sure of him," said he; "and for your sake, I hope you may be right. If it came to a trial, your name might appear."

"I am quite sure of him," replied Jekyll; "I have grounds for certainty that I cannot share with anyone. But there is one thing on which you may advise me. I have—I have received a letter; and I am at a loss whether I should show it to the police. I should like to leave it in your hands, Utterson; you would judge wisely, I am sure; I have so great a trust in you."

"You fear, I suppose, that it might lead to his detection?" asked the lawyer.

"No," said the other. "I cannot say that I care what becomes of Hyde; I am quite done with him. I was thinking of my own character, which this hateful business has rather exposed."

Utterson ruminated awhile; he was surprised at his friend's selfishness, and yet relieved by it. "Well," said he, at last, "let me see the letter."

The letter was written in an odd, upright hand and signed "Edward Hyde": and it signified, briefly enough, that the writer's benefactor, Dr. Jekyll, whom he had long so unworthily repaid for a thousand generosities, need labour under no alarm for his safety, as he had means of escape on which he placed a sure dependence. The lawyer liked this letter well enough; it put a better colour on the intimacy than he had looked for; and he blamed himself for some of his past suspicions.

"Have you the envelope?" he asked.

"I burned it," replied Jekyll, "before I thought what I was about. But it bore no postmark. The note was handed in."

"Shall I keep this and sleep upon it?" asked Utterson.

"I wish you to judge for me entirely," was the reply. "I have lost confidence in myself."

"Well, I shall consider," returned the lawyer. "And now one word more: it was Hyde who dictated the terms in your will about that disappearance?"

The doctor seemed seized with a qualm of faintness; he shut his mouth tight and nodded.

"I knew it," said Utterson. "He meant to murder you. You had a fine escape."

"I have had what is far more to the purpose,"

returned the doctor solemnly: "I have had a lesson—O God, Utterson, what a lesson I have had!" And he covered his face for a moment with his hands.

On his way out, the lawyer stopped and had a word or two with Poole. "By the bye," said he, "there was a letter handed in to-day: what was the messenger like?" But Poole was positive nothing had come except by post; "and only circulars by that," he added.

This news sent off the visitor with his fears renewed. Plainly the letter had come by the laboratory door; possibly, indeed, it had been written in the cabinet; and if that were so, it must be differently judged, and handled with the more caution. The newsboys, as he went, were crying themselves hoarse along the footways: "Special edition. Shocking murder of an M.P." That was the funeral oration of one friend and client; and he could not help a certain apprehension lest the good name of another should be sucked down in the eddy of the scandal. It was, at least, a ticklish decision that he had to make; and self-reliant as he was by habit, he began to cherish a longing for advice. It was not to be had directly; but perhaps, he thought, it might be fished for.

Presently after, he sat on one side of his own hearth, with Mr. Guest, his head clerk, upon the other, and midway between, at a nicely calculated distance from the fire, a bottle of a particular old wine that had long dwelt unsunned in the foundations of his house. The fog still slept on the wing above the drowned city, where the lamps glimmered like carbuncles; and through the muffle and smother of these fallen clouds, the procession of the town's life was still rolling in through the great arteries with a sound as of a mighty wind. But the room was gay with firelight. In the bottle the acids were long ago resolved; the imperial dye had softened with time, as the colour grows richer in stained windows; and the glow of hot autumn afternoons on hillside vineyards, was ready to be set free and to disperse the fogs of London. Insensibly the lawyer melted. There was no man from whom he kept fewer secrets than Mr. Guest; and he was not always sure that he kept as many as he meant. Guest had often been on business to the doctor's; he knew Poole; he could scarce have failed to hear of Mr. Hyde's familiarity about the house; he might draw conclusions: was it not as well, then, that he should see a letter which put that mystery to rights? and above all since Guest, being a great student and critic of handwriting, would consider the step natural and obliging? The clerk, besides, was a man of counsel; he could scarce read so strange a document without dropping a remark; and by that remark Mr. Utterson might shape his future course.

"This is a sad business about Sir Danvers," he said.

"Yes, sir, indeed. It has elicited a great deal of public feeling," returned Guest. "The man, of course, was mad."

"I should like to hear your views on that," replied Utterson. "I have a document here in his handwriting; it is between ourselves, for I scarce know what to do about it; it is an ugly business at the best. But there it is; quite in your way: a murderer's autograph."

Guest's eyes brightened, and he sat down at once and studied it with passion. "No sir," he said: "not mad; but it is an odd hand."

"And by all accounts a very odd writer," added the lawyer.

Just then the servant entered with a note.

"Is that from Dr. Jekyll, sir?" inquired the clerk. "I thought I knew the writing. Anything private, Mr. Utterson?"

"Only an invitation to dinner. Why? Do you want to see it?"

"One moment. I thank you, sir;" and the clerk laid the two sheets of paper alongside and sedulously compared their contents. "Thank you, sir," he said at last, returning both; "it's a very interesting autograph."

There was a pause, during which Mr. Utterson struggled with himself. "Why did you compare them, Guest?" he inquired suddenly.

"Well, sir," returned the clerk, "there's a rather singular resemblance; the two hands are in many points identical: only differently sloped."

"Rather quaint," said Utterson.

"It is, as you say, rather quaint," returned Guest.

"I wouldn't speak of this note, you know," said the master.

"No, sir," said the clerk. "I understand."

But no sooner was Mr. Utterson alone that night, than he locked the note into his safe, where it reposed from that time forward. "What!" he thought. "Henry Jekyll forge for a murderer!" and his blood ran cold in his veins.

Remarkable Incident of Dr. Lanyon

TIME RAN ON; thousands of pounds were offered in reward, for the death of Sir Danvers was resented as a public injury; but Mr. Hyde had disappeared out of the ken of the police as though he had never existed. Much of his past was unearthed, indeed, and all disreputable: tales came out of the man's cruelty, at once so callous and violent; of his vile life, of his strange associates, of the hatred that seemed to have surrounded his career; but of his present whereabouts, not a whisper. From the time he had left the house in Soho on the morning of the murder, he was simply blotted out; and gradually, as time drew on, Mr. Utterson began to recover from the hotness of his alarm, and to grow more at quiet with himself. The death of Sir Danvers was, to his way of thinking, more than paid for by the disappearance of Mr. Hyde. Now that that evil influence had been withdrawn, a new life began for Dr. Jekyll. He came out of his seclusion, renewed relations with his friends, became once more their familiar guest and entertainer; and whilst he had always been known for charities, he was now no less distinguished for religion. He was busy, he was much in the open air, he did good; his face seemed to open and brighten, as if with an inward consciousness of service; and for more than two months, the doctor was at peace.

On the 8th of January Utterson had dined at the doctor's with a small party; Lanyon had been there; and the face of the host had looked from one to the other as in the old days when the trio were inseparable friends. On the 12th, and again on the 14th, the door was shut against the lawyer. "The doctor was confined to the house," Poole said, "and saw no one." On the 15th, he tried again, and was again refused; and having now been used for the last two months to see his friend almost daily, he found this return of solitude to weigh upon his spirits. The fifth night he had in Guest to dine with him; and the sixth he betook himself to Dr. Lanyon's.

There at least he was not denied admittance; but when he came in, he was shocked at the change which had taken place in the doctor's appearance. He had his death-warrant written legibly upon his face. The rosy man had grown pale; his flesh had fallen away; he was visibly balder and older; and yet it was not so much these tokens of a swift physical decay that arrested the lawyer's notice, as a look in the eye and quality of manner that seemed to testify to some deep-seated terror of the mind. It was unlikely that the doctor should fear death; and yet that was what Utterson was tempted to suspect. "Yes," he thought; "he is a doctor, he must know his own state and that his days are counted; and the knowledge is more than he can bear." And yet when Utterson remarked on his ill-looks, it was with an air of great firmness that Lanyon declared himself a doomed man.

"I have had a shock," he said, "and I shall never recover. It is a question of weeks. Well, life has been

pleasant; I liked it; yes, sir, I used to like it. I sometimes think if we knew all, we should be more glad
to get away."

"Jekyll is ill, too," observed Utterson. "Have you
seen him?"

But Lanyon's face changed, and he held up a
trembling hand. "I wish to see or hear no more of
Dr. Jekyll," he said in a loud, unsteady voice. "I am
quite done with that person; and I beg that you will
spare me any allusion to one whom I regard as
dead."

"Tut-tut," said Mr. Utterson; and then after a considerable pause, "Can't I do anything?" he inquired.
"We are three very old friends, Lanyon; we shall not
live to make others."

"Nothing can be done," returned Lanyon; "ask
himself."

"He will not see me," said the lawyer.

"I am not surprised at that," was the reply. "Some
day, Utterson, after I am dead, you may perhaps
come to learn the right and wrong of this. I cannot
tell you. And in the meantime, if you can sit and talk
with me of other things, for God's sake, stay and do
so; but if you cannot keep clear of this accursed
topic, then in God's name, go, for I cannot bear it."

As soon as he got home, Utterson sat down and
wrote to Jekyll, complaining of his exclusion from
the house, and asking the cause of this unhappy
break with Lanyon; and the next day brought him a
long answer, often very pathetically worded, and
sometimes darkly mysterious in drift. The quarrel
with Lanyon was incurable. "I do not blame our old
friend," Jekyll wrote, "but I share his view that we
must never meet. I mean from henceforth to lead a
life of extreme seclusion; you must not be surprised,

nor must you doubt my friendship, if my door is often shut even to you. You must suffer me to go my own dark way. I have brought on myself a punishment and a danger that I cannot name. If I am the chief of sinners, I am the chief of sufferers also. I could not think that this earth contained a place for sufferings and terrors so unmanning; and you can do but one thing, Utterson, to lighten this destiny, and that is to respect my silence." Utterson was amazed; the dark influence of Hyde had been withdrawn, the doctor had returned to his old tasks and amities; a week ago, the prospect had smiled with every promise of a cheerful and an honoured age; and now in a moment, friendship, and peace of mind, and the whole tenor of his life were wrecked. So great and unprepared a change pointed to madness; but in view of Lanyon's manner and words, there must lie for it some deeper ground.

A week afterwards Dr. Lanyon took to his bed, and in something less than a fortnight he was dead. The night after the funeral, at which he had been sadly affected, Utterson locked the door of his business room, and sitting there by the light of a melancholy candle, drew out and set before him an envelope addressed by the hand and sealed with the seal of his dead friend. "PRIVATE: for the hands of G.J. Utterson ALONE, and in case of his predecease *to be destroyed unread*," so it was emphatically superscribed; and the lawyer dreaded to behold the contents. "I have buried one friend to-day," he thought: "what if this should cost me another?" And then he condemned the fear as a disloyalty, and broke the seal. Within there was another enclosure, likewise sealed, and marked upon the cover as "not to be opened till the death or disappearance of Dr. Henry Jekyll."

Utterson could not trust his eyes. Yes, it was disappearance; here again, as in the mad will which he had long ago restored to its author, here again were the idea of a disappearance and the name of Henry Jekyll bracketted. But in the will, that idea had sprung from the sinister suggestion of the man Hyde; it was set there with a purpose all too plain and horrible. Written by the hand of Lanyon, what should it mean? A great curiosity came on the trustee, to disregard the prohibition and dive at once to the bottom of these mysteries; but professional honour and faith to his dead friend were stringent obligations; and the packet slept in the inmost corner of his private safe.

It is one thing to mortify curiosity, another to conquer it; and it may be doubted if, from that day forth, Utterson desired the society of his surviving friend with the same eagerness. He thought of him kindly; but his thoughts were disquieted and fearful. He went to call indeed; but he was perhaps relieved to be denied admittance; perhaps, in his heart, he preferred to speak with Poole upon the doorstep and surrounded by the air and sounds of the open city, rather than to be admitted into that house of voluntary bondage, and to sit and speak with its inscrutable recluse. Poole had, indeed, no very pleasant news to communicate. The doctor, it appeared, now more than ever confined himself to the cabinet over the laboratory, where he would sometimes even sleep; he was out of spirits, he had grown very silent, he did not read; it seemed as if he had something on his mind. Utterson became so used to the unvarying character of these reports, that he fell off little by little in the frequency of his visits.

Incident at the Window

IT CHANCED ON Sunday, when Mr. Utterson was on his usual walk with Mr. Enfield, that their way lay once again through the by-street; and that when they came in front of the door, both stopped to gaze on it.

"Well," said Enfield, "that story's at an end at least. We shall never see more of Mr. Hyde."

"I hope not," said Utterson. "Did I ever tell you that I once saw him, and shared your feeling of repulsion?"

"It was impossible to do the one without the other," returned Enfield. "And by the way, what an ass you must have thought me, not to know that this was a back way to Dr. Jekyll's! It was partly your own fault that I found it out, even when I did."

"So you found it out, did you?" said Utterson. "But if that be so, we may step into the court and take a look at the windows. To tell you the truth, I am uneasy about poor Jekyll; and even outside, I feel as if the presence of a friend might do him good."

The court was very cool and a little damp, and full of premature twilight, although the sky, high up overhead, was still bright with sunset. The middle one of the three windows was half-way open; and sitting close beside it, taking the air with an infinite sadness of mien, like some disconsolate prisoner, Utterson saw Dr. Jekyll.

"What! Jekyll!" he cried. "I trust you are better."

"I am very low, Utterson," replied the doctor drearily, "very low. It will not last long, thank God."

"You stay too much indoors," said the lawyer. "You should be out, whipping up the circulation like Mr. Enfield and me. (This is my cousin—Mr. Enfield —Dr. Jekyll.) Come now; get your hat and take a quick turn with us."

"You are very good," sighed the other. "I should like to very much; but no, no, no, it is quite impossible; I dare not. But indeed, Utterson, I am very glad to see you; this is really a great pleasure; I would ask you and Mr. Enfield up, but the place is really not fit."

"Why then," said the lawyer, good-naturedly, "the best thing we can do is to stay down here and speak with you from where we are."

"That is just what I was about to venture to propose," returned the doctor with a smile. But the words were hardly uttered, before the smile was struck out of his face and succeeded by an expression of such abject terror and despair, as froze the very blood of the two gentlemen below. They saw it but for a glimpse for the window was instantly thrust down; but·that glimpse had been sufficient, and they turned and left the court without a word. In silence, too, they traversed the by-street; and it was not until they had come into a neighbouring thoroughfare, where even upon a Sunday there were still some stirrings of life, that Mr. Utterson at last turned and looked at his companion. They were both pale; and there was an answering horror in their eyes.

"God forgive us, God forgive us," said Mr. Utterson.

But Mr. Enfield only nodded his head very seriously, and walked on once more in silence.

The Last Night

MR. UTTERSON was sitting by his fireside one evening after dinner, when he was surprised to receive a visit from Poole.

"Bless me, Poole, what brings you here?" he cried; and then taking a second look at him, "What ails you?" he added; "is the doctor ill?"

"Mr. Utterson," said the man, "there is something wrong."

"Take a seat, and here is a glass of wine for you," said the lawyer. "Now, take your time, and tell me plainly what you want.

"You know the doctor's ways, sir," replied Poole, "and how he shuts himself up. Well, he's shut up again in the cabinet; and I don't like it, sir—I wish I may die if I like it. Mr. Utterson, sir, I'm afraid."

"Now, my good man," said the lawyer, "be explicit. What are you afraid of?"

"I've been afraid for about a week," returned Poole, doggedly disregarding the question, "and I can bear it no more."

The man's appearance amply bore out his words; his manner was altered for the worse; and except for the moment when he had first announced his terror, he had not once looked the lawyer in the face. Even now, he sat with the glass of wine untasted on his knee, and his eyes directed to a corner of the floor. "I can bear it no more," he repeated.

"Come," said the lawyer, "I see you have some good reason, Poole; I see there is something seriously amiss. Try to tell me what it is."

"I think there's been foul play," said Poole, hoarsely.

"Foul play!" cried the lawyer, a good deal frightened and rather inclined to be irritated in consequence. "What foul play! What does the man mean?"

"I daren't say, sir," was the answer; "but will you come along with me and see for yourself?"

Mr. Utterson's only answer was to rise and get his hat and greatcoat; but he observed with wonder the greatness of the relief that appeared upon the butler's face, and perhaps with no less, that the wine was still untasted when he set it down to follow.

It was a wild, cold, seasonable night of March, with a pale moon, lying on her back as though the wind had tilted her, and a flying wrack of the most diaphanous and lawny texture. The wind made talking difficult, and flecked the blood into the face. It seemed to have swept the streets unusually bare of passengers, besides; for Mr. Utterson thought he had never seen that part of London so deserted. He could have wished it otherwise; never in his life had he been conscious of so sharp a wish to see and touch his fellow-creatures; for struggle as he might, there was borne in upon his mind a crushing anticipation of calamity. The square, when they got there, was full of wind and dust, and the thin trees in the garden were lashing themselves along the railing. Poole, who had kept all the way a pace or two ahead, now pulled up in the middle of the pavement, and in spite of the biting weather, took off his hat and mopped his brow with a red pocket handker-chief. But for all the hurry of his coming, these were not the dews of exertion that he wiped away, but the moisture of some strangling anguish; for his face was white and his voice, when he spoke, harsh and broken.

"Well, sir," he said, "here we are, and God grant there be nothing wrong."

"Amen, Poole," said the lawyer.

Thereupon the servant knocked in a very guarded manner; the door was opened on the chain; and a voice asked from within, "Is that you, Poole?"

"It's all right," said Poole. "Open the door."

The hall, when they entered it, was brightly lighted up; the fire was built high; and about the hearth the whole of the servants, men and women, stood hud-dled together like a flock of sheep. At the sight of Mr. Utterson, the housemaid broke into hysterical whimpering; and the cook, crying out "Bless God! it's Mr. Utterson," ran forward as if to take him in her arms.

"What, what? Are you all here?" said the lawyer peevishly. "Very irregular, very unseemly; your mas-ter would be far from pleased."

"They're all afraid," said Poole.

Blank silence followed, no one protesting; only the maid lifted up her voice and now wept loudly.

"Hold your tongue!" Poole said to her, with a ferocity of accent that testified to his own jangled nerves; and indeed, when the girl had so suddenly raised the note of her lamentation, they had all started and turned towards the inner door with faces of dreadful expectation. "And now," continued the but-ler, addressing the knife-boy, "reach me a candle, and we'll get this through hands at once." And then he begged Mr. Utterson to follow him, and led the way to the back garden.

"Now, sir," said he, "you come as gently as you can. I want you to hear, and I don't want you to be heard. And see here, sir, if by any chance he was to ask you in, don't go."

Mr. Utterson's nerves, at this unlooked-for-termination, gave a jerk that nearly threw him from balance; but he recollected his courage and followed the butler into the laboratory building through the surgical theatre, with its lumber of crates and bottles, to the foot of the stair. Here Poole motioned him to stand on one side and listen; while he himself, setting down the candle and making a great and obvious call on his resolution, mounted the steps and knocked with a somewhat uncertain hand on the red baize of the cabinet door.

"Mr. Utterson, sir, asking to see you," he called; and even as he did so, once more violently signed to the lawyer to give ear.

A voice answered from within: "Tell him I cannot see anyone," it said complainingly.

"Thank you, sir," said Poole, with a note of something like triumph in his voice; and taking up his candle, he led Mr. Utterson back across the yard and into the great kitchen, where the fire was out and the beetles were leaping on the floor.

"Sir," he said, looking Mr. Utterson in the eyes, "was that my master's voice?"

"It seems much changed," replied the lawyer, very pale, but giving look for look.

"Changed? Well, yes, I think so," said the butler. "Have I been twenty years in this man's house, to be deceived about his voice? No, sir; master's made away with; he was made away with eight days ago, when we heard him cry out upon the name of God; and *who's* in there instead of him, and *why* it stays there, is a thing that cries to Heaven, Mr. Utterson!"

"This is a very strange tale, Poole; this is rather a wild tale, my man," said Mr. Utterson, biting his finger. "Suppose it were as you suppose, supposing Dr. Jekyll to have been—well, murdered, what could induce the murderer to stay? That won't hold water; it doesn't commend itself to reason."

"Well, Mr. Utterson, you are a hard man to sat-isfy, but I'll do it yet," said Poole. "All this last week (you must know) him, or it, whatever it is that lives in that cabinet, has been crying night and day for some sort of medicine and cannot get it to his mind. It was sometimes his way—the master's, that is—to write his orders on a sheet of paper and throw it on the stair. We've had nothing else this week back; nothing but papers, and a closed door, and the very meals left there to be smuggled in when nobody was looking. Well, sir, every day, ay, and twice and thrice in the same day, there have been orders and complaints, and I have been sent flying to all the wholesale chemists in town. Every time I brought the stuff back, there would be another paper telling me to return it, because it was not pure, and another order to a different firm. This drug is wanted bitter bad, sir, whatever for."

"Have you any of these papers?" asked Mr. Utterson.

Poole felt in his pocket and handed out a crum-pled note, which the lawyer, bending nearer to the candle, carefully examined. Its contents ran thus: "Dr. Jekyll presents his compliments to Messrs. Maw. He assures them that their last sample is impure and quite useless for his present purpose. In the year

18—, Dr. J. purchased a somewhat large quantity from Messrs. M. He now begs them to search with most sedulous care, and should any of the same quality be left, to forward it to him at once. Expense is no consideration. The importance of this to Dr. J. can hardly be exaggerated." So far the letter had run composedly enough, but here with a sudden splutter of the pen, the writer's emotion had broken loose. "For God's sake," he added, "find me some of the old."

"This is a strange note," said Mr. Utterson; and then sharply, "How do you come to have it open?"

"The man at Maw's was main angry, sir, and he threw it back to me like so much dirt," returned Poole.

"This is unquestionably the doctor's hand, do you know?" resumed the lawyer.

"I thought it looked like it," said the servant rather sulkily; and then, with another voice, "But what matters hand of write?" he said. "I've seen him!"

"Seen him?" repeated Mr. Utterson. "Well?"

"That's it!" said Poole. "It was this way. I came suddenly into the theatre from the garden. It seems he had slipped out to look for this drug or whatever it is; for the cabinet door was open, and there he was at the far end of the room digging among the crates. He looked up when I came in, gave a kind of cry, and whipped upstairs into the cabinet. It was but for one minute that I saw him, but the hair stood upon my head like quills. Sir, if that was my master, why had he a mask upon his face? If it was my master, why did he cry out like a rat, and run from me? I have served long enough. And then . . ." The man paused and passed his hand over his face.

"These are all very strange circumstances," said

Mr. Utterson, "but I think I begin to see daylight. Your master, Poole, is plainly seized with one of those maladies that both torture and deform the sufferer; hence, for aught I know, the alteration of his voice; hence the mask and the avoidance of his friends; hence his eagerness to find this drug, by means of which the poor soul retains some hope of ultimate recovery—God grant that he be not deceived! There is my explanation; it is sad enough, Poole, ay, and appalling to consider; but it is plain and natural, hangs well together, and delivers us from all exorbitant alarms."

"Sir," said the butler, turning to a sort of mottled pallor, "that thing was not my master, and there's the truth. My master"—here he looked round him and began to whisper—"is a tall, fine build of a man, and this was more of a dwarf." Utterson attempted to protest. "Oh, sir," cried Poole, "do you think I do not know my master after twenty years? Do you think I do not know where his head comes to in the cabinet door, where I saw him every morning of my life? No, sir, that thing in the mask was never Dr. Jekyll—God knows what it was, but it was never Dr. Jekyll; and it is the belief of my heart that there was murder done."

"Poole," replied the lawyer, "if you say that, it will become my duty to make certain. Much as I desire to spare your master's feelings, much as I am puzzled by this note which seems to prove him to be still alive, I shall consider it my duty to break in that door."

"Ah, Mr. Utterson, that's talking!" cried the butler.

"And now comes the second question," resumed Utterson: "Who is going to do it?"

"Why, you and me, sir," was the undaunted reply.

"That's very well said," returned the lawyer; "and whatever comes of it, I shall make it my business to see you are no loser."

"There is an axe in the theatre," continued Poole; "and you might take the kitchen poker for yourself."

The lawyer took that rude but weighty instrument into his hand, and balanced it. "Do you know, Poole," he said, looking up, "that you and I are about to place ourselves in a position of some peril?"

"You may say so, sir, indeed," returned the butler.

"It is well, then, that we should be frank," said the other. "We both think more than we have said; let us make a clean breast. This masked figure that you saw, did you recognize it?"

"Well, sir, it went so quick, and the creature was so doubled up, that I could hardly swear to that," was the answer. "But if you mean, was it Mr. Hyde? —why, yes, I think it was! You see, it was much of the same bigness; and it had the same quick, light way with it; and then who else could have got in by the laboratory door? You have not forgot, sir, that at the time of the murder he had still the key with him? But that's not all. I don't know, Mr. Utterson, if you ever met this Mr. Hyde?"

"Yes," said the lawyer, "I once spoke with him."

"Then you must know as well as the rest of us that there was something queer about that gentleman—something that gave a man a turn—I don't know rightly how to say it, sir, beyond this: that you felt in your marrow kind of cold and thin."

"I own I felt something of what you describe," said Mr. Utterson.

"Quite so, sir," returned Poole. "Well, when that masked thing like a monkey jumped from among the chemicals and whipped into the cabinet, it went down my spine like ice. O, I know it's not evidence, Mr. Utterson; I'm book-learned enough for that; but a man has his feelings, and I give you my bible-word it was Mr. Hyde!"

"Ay, ay," said the lawyer. "My fears incline to the same point. Evil, I fear, founded—evil was sure to come—of that connection. Ay truly, I believe you; I believe poor Harry is killed; and I believe his murderer (for what purpose, God alone can tell) is still lurking in his victim's room. Well, let our name be vengeance. Call Bradshaw."

The footman came at the summons, very white and nervous.

"Put yourself together, Bradshaw," said the lawyer. "This suspense, I know, is telling upon all of you; but it is now our intention to make an end of it. Poole, here, and I are going to force our way into the cabinet. If all is well, my shoulders are broad enough to bear the blame. Meanwhile, lest anything should really be amiss, or any malefactor seek to escape by the back, you and the boy must go round the corner with a pair of good sticks and take your post at the laboratory door. We give you ten minutes, to get to your stations."

As Bradshaw left, the lawyer looked at his watch. "And now, Poole, let us get to ours," he said; and taking the poker under his arm, led the way into the yard. The scud had banked over the moon, and it was now quite dark. The wind, which only broke in puffs and draughts into that deep well of building, tossed the light of the candle to and fro about their steps, until they came into the shelter of the theatre, where they sat down silently to wait. London hummed solemnly all around; but nearer at hand, the stillness was only broken by the sounds of a footfall moving to and fro along the cabinet floor.

"So it will walk all day, sir," whispered Poole; "ay, and the better part of the night. Only when a new sample comes from the chemist, there's a bit of a break. Ah, it's an ill conscience that's such an enemy to rest! Ah, sir, there's blood foully shed in every step of it! But hark again, a little closer—put your heart in your ears, Mr. Utterson, and tell me, is that the doctor's foot?"

The steps fell lightly and oddly, with a certain swing, for all they went so slowly; it was different indeed from the heavy creaking tread of Henry Jekyll. Utterson sighed. "Is there never anything else?" he asked.

Poole nodded. "Once," he said. "Once I heard it weeping!"

"Weeping? how that?" said the lawyer, conscious of a sudden chill of horror.

"Weeping like a woman or a lost soul," said the butler. "I came away with that upon my heart, that I could have wept too."

But now the ten minutes drew to an end. Poole disinterred the axe from under a stack of packing straw; the candle was set upon the nearest table to light them to the attack; and they drew near with bated breath to where that patient foot was still going up and down, up and down, in the quiet of the night. "Jekyll," cried Utterson, with a loud voice, "I demand to see you." He paused a moment, but there came no reply. "I give you fair warning, our suspicions are aroused, and I must and shall see you," he resumed; "if not by fair means, then by foul—if not of your consent, then by brute force!"

"Utterson," said the voice, "for God's sake, have mercy!"

"Ah, that's not Jekyll's voice—it's Hyde's!" cried Utterson. "Down with the door, Poole!"

Poole swung the axe over his shoulder; the blow shook the building, and the red baize door leaped against the lock and hinges, A dismal screech, as of mere animal terror, rang from the cabinet. Up went the axe again, and again the panels crashed and the frame bounded; four times the blow fell; but the wood was tough and the fittings were of excellent workmanship; and it was not until the fifth, that the lock burst and the wreck of the door fell inwards on the carpet.

The besiegers, appalled by their own riot and the stillness that had succeeded, stood back a little and peered in. There lay the cabinet before their eyes in the quiet lamplight, a good fire glowing and chattering on the hearth, the kettle singing its thin strain, a drawer or two open, papers neatly set forth on the business table, and nearer the fire, the things laid out for tea; the quietest room, you would have said, and, but for the glazed presses full of chemicals, the most commonplace that night in London.

Right in the midst there lay the body of a man sorely contorted and still twitching. They drew near on tiptoe, turned it on its back and beheld the face of Edward Hyde. He was dressed in clothes far too large for him, clothes of the doctor's bigness; the cords of his face still moved with a semblance of life, but life was quite gone: and by the crushed phial in the hand and the strong smell of kernels that hung upon the air, Utterson knew that he was looking on the body of a self-destroyer.

"We have come too late," he said sternly, "whether to save or punish. Hyde is gone to his account; and it only remains for us to find the body of your master."

The far greater proportion of the building was

occupied by the theatre, which filled almost the whole ground storey and was lighted from above, and by the cabinet, which formed an upper storey at one end and looked upon the court. A corridor joined the theatre to the door on the by-street; and with this the cabinet communicated separately by a second flight of stairs. There were besides a few dark closets and a spacious cellar. All these they now thoroughly examined. Each closet needed but a glance, for all were empty, and all, by the dust that fell from their doors, had stood long unopened. The cellar, indeed, was filled with crazy lumber, mostly dating from the times of the surgeon who was Jekyll's predecessor; but even as they opened the door they were advertised of the uselessness of further search, by the fall of a perfect mat of cobweb which had for years sealed up the entrance. Nowhere was there any trace of Henry Jekyll, dead or alive.

Poole stamped on the flags of the corridor. "He must be buried here," he said, hearkening to the sound.

"Or he may have fled," said Utterson, and he turned to examine the door in the by-street. It was locked; and lying near by on the flags, they found the key, already stained with rust.

"This does not look like use," observed the lawyer.

"Use!" echoed Poole. "Do you not see, sir, it is broken? much as if a man had stamped on it."

"Ay," continued Utterson, "and the fractures, too, are rusty." The two men looked at each other with a scare. "This is beyond me, Poole," said the lawyer. "Let us go back to the cabinet."

They mounted the stair in silence, and still with an occasional awestruck glance at the dead body, proceeded more thoroughly to examine the contents of the cabinet. At one table, there were traces of chemical work, various measured heaps of some white salt being laid on glass saucers, as though for an experiment in which the unhappy man had been prevented.

"That is the same drug that I was always bringing him," said Poole; and even as he spoke, the kettle with a startling noise boiled over.

This brought them to the fireside, where the easychair was drawn cosily up, and the tea things stood ready to the sitter's elbow, the very sugar in the cup. There were several books on a shelf; one lay beside the tea things open, and Utterson was amazed to find it a copy of a pious work, for which Jekyll had several times expressed a great esteem, annotated, in his own hand, with startling blasphemies.

Next, in the course of their review of the chamber, the searchers came to the cheval-glass, into whose depths they looked with an involuntary horror. But it was so turned as to show them nothing but the rosy glow playing on the roof, the fire sparkling in a hundred repetitions along the glazed front of the presses, and their own pale and fearful countenances stooping to look in.

"This glass has seen some strange things, sir," whispered Poole.

"And surely none stranger than itself," echoed the lawyer in the same tones. "For what did Jekyll"—he caught himself up at the word with a start, and then conquering the weakness—"what could Jekyll want with it?" he said.

"You may say that!" said Poole.

Next they turned to the business table. On the desk, among the neat array of papers, a large envelope was uppermost, and bore, in the doctor's hand, the name of Mr. Utterson. The lawyer unsealed it, and several enclosures fell to the floor. The first was a will, draw in the same eccentric terms as the one which he had returned six months before, to serve as a testament in case of death and as a deed of gift in case of disappearance; but in place of the name of Edward Hyde, the lawyer, with indescribable amazement, read the name of Gabriel John Utterson. He looked at Poole, and then back at the paper, and last of all at the dead malefactor stretched upon the carpet.

"My head goes round," he said. "He has been all these days in possession; he had no cause to like me; he must have raged to see himself displaced; and he has not destroyed this document."

He caught up the next paper; it was a brief note in the doctor's hand and dated at the top. "O Poole!" the lawyer cried, "he was alive and here this day. He cannot have been disposed of in so short a space; he must be still alive, he must have fled! And then, why fled? and how? and in that case, can we venture to declare this suicide? O, we must be careful. I foresee that we may yet involve your master in some dire catastrophe."

"Why don't you read it, sir?" asked Poole.

"Because I fear," replied the lawyer solemnly. "God grant I have no cause for it!" And with that he brought the paper to his eyes and read as follows:

My Dear Utterson,—When this shall fall into your hands, I shall have disappeared, under what circumstances I have not the penetration to foresee, but my instinct and all the circumstances of my nameless situation tell me that the end is sure and must be early. Go then, and first read the narrative which

Lanyon warned me he was to place in your hands; and if you care to hear more, turn to the confession of
   Your unworthy and unhappy friend,
                                    HENRY JEKYLL.

"There was a third enclosure?" asked Utterson.

"Here, sir," said Poole, and gave into his hands a considerable packet sealed in several places.

The lawyer put it in his pocket. "I would say nothing of this paper. If your master has fled or is dead, we may at least save his credit. It is now ten; I must go home and read these documents in quiet; but I shall be back before midnight, when we shall send for the police."

They went out, locking the door of the theatre behind them; and Utterson, once more leaving the servants gathered about the fire in the hall, trudged back to his office to read the two narratives in which this mystery was now to be explained.

Dr. Lanyon's Narrative

ON THE NINTH of January, now four days ago, I received by the evening delivery a registered envelope, addressed in the hand of my colleague and old school companion, Henry Jekyll. I was a good deal surprised by this; for we were by no means in the habit of correspondence; I had seen the man, dined with him, indeed, the night before; and I could imagine nothing in our intercourse that should justify formality of registration. The contents increased my wonder; for this is how the letter ran:

                                                    10th December, 18—.
Dear Lanyon,—You are one of my oldest friends; and although we may have differed at times on scientific questions, I cannot remember, at least on my side, any break in our affection. There was never a day when, if you had said to me, "Jekyll, my life, my honour, my reason, depend upon you," I would not have sacrificed my left hand to help you. Lanyon, my life, my honour, my reason, are all at your mercy; if you fail me to-night, I am lost. You might suppose, after this preface, that I am going to ask you for something dishonourable to grant. Judge for yourself.

I want you to postpone all other engagements for to-night—ay, even if you were summoned to the bedside of an emperor; to take a cab, unless your carriage should be actually at the door; and with this

letter in your hand for consultation, to drive straight
to my house. Poole, my butler, has his orders; you
will find him waiting your arrival with a locksmith.
The door of my cabinet is then to be forced: and you
are to go in alone; to open the glazed press (letter E)
on the left hand, breaking the lock if it be shut; and
to draw out, *with all its contents as they stand*, the
fourth drawer from the top or (which is the same
thing) the third from the bottom. In my extreme
distress of mind, I have a morbid fear of misdirect-
ing you; but even if I am in error, you may know the
right drawer by its contents: some powders, a phial
and a paper book. This drawer I beg of you to carry
back with you to Cavendish Square exactly as it
stands.

That is the first part of the service: now for the
second. You should be back, if you set out at once
on the receipt of this, long before midnight; but I
will leave you that amount of margin, not only in
the fear of one of those obstacles that can neither be
prevented nor foreseen, but because an hour when
your servants are in bed is to be preferred for what
will then remain to do. At midnight, then, I have to
ask you to be alone in your consulting room, to
admit with your own hand into the house a man
who will present himself in my name, and to place
in his hands the drawer that you will have brought
with you from my cabinet. Then you will have played
your part and earned my gratitude completely. Five
minutes afterwards, if you insist upon an explanation, you will have understood that these arrangements are of capital importance; and that by the
neglect of one of them, fantastic as they must appear, you might have charged your conscience with
my death or the shipwreck of my reason.

Confident as I am that you will not trifle with this
appeal, my heart sinks and my hand trembles at the
bare thought of such a possibility. Think of me at
this hour, in a strange place, labouring under a blackness of distress that no fancy can exaggerate, and
yet well aware that, if you will but punctually serve

me, my troubles will roll away like a story that is told. Serve me, my dear Lanyon, and save

Your friend,

H. J.

P.S.—I had already sealed this up when a fresh terror struck upon my soul. It is possible that the post-office may fail me, and this letter not come into your hands until tomorrow morning. In that case, dear Lanyon, do my errand when it shall be most convenient for you in the course of the day; and once more expect my messenger at midnight. It may then already be too late; and if that night passes without event, you will know that you have seen the last of Henry Jekyll.

Upon the reading of this letter, I made sure my colleague was insane; but till that was proved beyond the possibility of doubt, I felt bound to do as he requested. The less I understood of this farrago, the less I was in a position to judge of its importance; and an appeal so worded could not be set aside without a grave responsibility. I rose accordingly from table, got into a hansom, and drove straight to Jekyll's house. The butler was awaiting my arrival; he had received by the same post as mine a registered letter of instruction, and had sent at once for a locksmith and a carpenter. The tradesmen came while we were yet speaking; and we moved in a body to old Dr. Denman's surgical theatre, from which (as you are doubtless aware) Jekyll's private cabinet is most conveniently entered. The door was very strong, the lock excellent; the carpenter avowed he would have great trouble and have to do much damage, if force were to be used; and the locksmith was near despair. But this last was a handy fellow, and after two hours' work, the door stood open. The press marked E was unlocked; and I took out the drawer, had it filled up with straw and tied in a sheet, and returned with it to Cavendish Square.

Here I proceeded to examine its contents. The powders were neatly enough made up, but not with the nicety of the dispensing chemist; so that it was plain they were of Jekyll's private manufacture: and when I opened one of the wrappers I found what seemed to me a simple crystalline salt of a white colour. The phial, to which I next turned my attention, might have been about half full of a blood-red liquor, which was highly pungent to the sense of smell and seemed to me to contain phosphorus and some volatile ether. At the other ingredients I could make no guess. The book was an ordinary version book and contained little but a series of dates. These covered a period of many years, but I observed that the entries ceased nearly a year ago and quite abruptly. Here and there a brief remark was appended to a date, usually no more than a single word: "double" occurring perhaps six times in a total of several hundred entries; and once very early in the list and followed by several marks of exclamation, "total failure!!!" All this, though it whetted my curiosity, told me little that was definite. Here were a phial of some tincture, a paper of some salt, and the record of a series of experiments that had led (like too many of Jekyll's investigations) to no end of practical usefulness. How could the presence of these articles in my house affect either the honour, the sanity, or the life of my flighty colleague? If his messenger could go to one place, why could he not go to another? And even granting some impediment, why was this gentleman to be received by me in secret? The more I reflected the more convinced I grew that I was dealing with a case of cerebral disease; and though I dismissed my servants to bed, I loaded an old revolver, that I might be found in some posture of self-defence.

Twelve o'clock had scarce rung out over London, ere the knocker sounded very gently on the door. I went myself at the summons, and found a small man crouching against the pillars of the portico.

"Are you come from Dr. Jekyll?" I asked.

He told me "yes" by a constrained gesture; and when I had bidden him enter, he did not obey me without a searching backward glance into the darkness of the square. There was a policeman not far off, advancing with his bull's eye open; and at the sight, I thought my visitor started and made greater haste.

These particulars struck me, I confess, disagreeably; and as I followed him into the bright light of the consulting room, I kept my hand ready on my weapon. Here, at last, I had a chance of clearly seeing him. I had never set eyes on him before, so much was certain. He was small, as I have said; I was struck besides with the shocking expression of his face, with his remarkable combination of great muscular activity and great apparent debility of constitution, and—last but not least—with the odd, subjective disturbance caused by his neighbourhood. This bore some resemblance to incipient rigour, and was accompanied by a marked sinking of the pulse. At the time, I set it down to some idiosyncratic, personal distaste, and merely wondered at the acuteness of the symptoms; but I have since had reason to believe the cause to lie much deeper in the nature of man, and to turn on some nobler hinge than the principle of hatred.

This person (who had thus, from the first moment of his entrance, struck in me what I can only describe as a disgustful curiosity) was dressed in a fashion that would have made an ordinary person laughable; his clothes, that is to say, although they were of rich and sober fabric, were enormously too large for him in every measurement—the trousers hanging on his legs and rolled up to keep them from the ground, the waist of the coat below his haunches, and the collar sprawling wide upon his shoulders. Strange to relate, this ludicrous accoutrement was far from moving me to laughter. Rather, as there was something abnormal and misbegotten in the very essence of the creature that now faced me— something seizing, surprising and revolting—this fresh disparity seemed but to fit in with and to reinforce it; so that to my interest in the man's nature and character, there was added a curiosity as to his origin, his life, his fortune and status in the world.

These observations, though they have taken so great a space to be set down in, were yet the work of a few seconds. My visitor was, indeed, on fire with sombre excitement.

"Have you got it?" he cried. "Have you got it?" And so lively was his impatience that he even laid his hand upon my arm and sought to shake me.

I put him back, conscious at his touch of a certain icy pang along my blood. "Come, sir," said I. "You forget that I have not yet the pleasure of your acquaintance. Be seated, if you please." And I showed him an example, and sat down myself in my customary seat and with as fair an imitation of my ordinary manner to a patient, as the lateness of the hour, the nature of my preoccupations, and the horror I had of my visitor, would suffer me to muster.

"I beg your pardon, Dr. Lanyon," he replied civilly enough. "What you say is very well founded; and my impatience has shown its heels to my politeness. I come here at the instance of your colleague,

Dr. Henry Jekyll, on a piece of business of some moment; and I understood . . ." He paused and put his hand to his throat, and I could see, in spite of his collected manner, that he was wrestling against the approaches of the hysteria—"I understood, a drawer . . ."

But here I took pity on my visitor's suspense, and some perhaps on my own growing curiosity.

"There it is, sir," said I, pointing to the drawer, where it lay on the floor behind a table and still covered with the sheet.

He sprang to it, and then paused, and laid his hand upon his heart: I could hear his teeth grate with the convulsive action of his jaws; and his face was so ghastly to see that I grew alarmed both for his life and reason.

"Compose yourself," said I.

He turned a dreadful smile to me, and as if with the decision of despair, plucked away the sheet. At sight of the contents, he uttered one loud sob of such immense relief that I sat petrified. And the next moment, in a voice that was already fairly well under control, "Have you a graduated glass?" he asked.

I rose from my place with something of an effort and gave him what he asked.

He thanked me with a smiling nod, measured out a few minims of the red tincture and added one of the powders. The mixture, which was at first a reddish hue, began, in proportion as the crystals melted to brighten in colour, to effervesce audibly, and to throw off small fumes of vapour. Suddenly and at the same moment, the ebullition ceased and the compound changed to a dark purple, which faded again more slowly to a watery green. My visitor, who had watched these metamorphoses with a keen eye, smiled, set down the glass upon the table, and then turned and looked upon me with an air of scrutiny.

"And now," said he, "to settle what remains. Will you be wise? will you be guided? will you suffer me to take this glass in my hand and to go forth from your house without further parley? or has the greed of curiosity too much command of you? Think before you answer, for it shall be done as you decide. As you decide, you shall be left as you were before, and neither richer nor wiser, unless the sense of service rendered to a man in mortal distress may be counted as a kind of riches of the soul. Or, if you shall so prefer to choose, a new province of knowledge and new avenues to fame and power shall be laid open to you, in this room, upon the instant; and your sight shall be blasted by a prodigy to stagger the unbelief of Satan."

"Sir," said I, affecting a coolness that I was far from truly possessing, "you speak enigmas, and you will perhaps not wonder that I hear you with no very strong impression of belief. But I have gone too far in the way of inexplicable services to pause before I see the end."

"It is well," replied my visitor. "Lanyon, you remember your vows: what follows is under the seal of our profession. And now, you who have so long been bound to the most narrow and material views, you who have denied the virtue of transcendental medicine, you who have derided your superiors—behold!"

He put the glass to his lips and drank at one gulp. A cry followed; he reeled, staggered, clutched at the table and held on, staring with injected eyes, gasping with open mouth; and as I looked there came, I thought, a change—he seemed to swell—his face became suddenly black and the features seemed to melt and alter—and the next moment, I had sprung to my feet and leaped back against the wall, my arm raised to shield me from that prodigy, my mind submerged in terror.

"O God!" I screamed, and "O God!" again and again; for there before my eyes—pale and shaken, and half fainting, and groping before him with his hands, like a man restored from death—there stood Henry Jekyll!

What he told me in the next hour, I cannot bring my mind to set on paper. I saw what I saw, I heard what I heard, and my soul sickened at it; and yet now when that sight has faded from my eyes, I ask myself if I believe it, and I cannot answer. My life is shaken to its roots; sleep has left me; the deadliest terror sits by me at all hours of the day and night; and I feel that my days are numbered, and that I must die; and yet I shall die incredulous. As for the moral turpitude that man unveiled to me, even with tears of penitence, I cannot, even in memory, dwell on it without a start of horror. I will say but one thing, Utterson, and that (if you can bring your mind to credit it) will be more than enough. The creature who crept into my house that night was, on Jekyll's own confession, known by the name of Hyde and hunted for in every corner of the land as the murderer of Carew.

HASTIE LANYON

Henry Jekyll's
Full Statement
of the Case

I WAS BORN in the year 18— to a large fortune, endowed besides with excellent parts, inclined by nature to industry, fond of the respect of the wise and good among my fellowmen, and thus, as might have been supposed, with every guarantee of an honourable and distinguished future. And indeed the worst of my faults was a certain impatient gaiety of disposition, such as has made the happiness of many, but such as I found it hard to reconcile with my imperious desire to carry my head high, and wear a more than commonly grave countenance before the public. Hence it came about that I concealed my pleasures; and that when I reached years of reflection, and began to look round me and take stock of my progress and position in the world, I stood already committed to a profound duplicity of life. Many a man would have even blazoned such irregularities as I was guilty of; but from the high views that I had set before me, I regarded and hid them with an almost morbid sense of shame. It was thus rather the exacting nature of my aspirations than any particular degradation in my fault, that made me what I was, and, with even a deeper trench than in the majority of men, severed in me those provinces of good and ill which divide and compound man's dual nature. In this case, I was driven to reflect deeply and inveterately on that hard law of life, which lies at the root of religion and is one of the most plentiful springs of distress. Though so profound a double-dealer, I was in no sense a hypocrite; both sides of me were in dead earnest; I was no more myself when I laid aside restraint and plunged in shame, than when I laboured, in the eye of day, at the furtherance of knowledge or the relief of sorrow and suffering. And it chanced that the direction of my scientific studies, which led wholly towards the mystic and the transcendental, reacted and shed a strong light on this consciousness of the perennial war among my members. With every day, and from both sides of my intelligence, the moral and the intellectual, I thus drew steadily nearer to that truth, by whose partial discovery I have been doomed to such a dreadful shipwreck: that man is not truly one, but truly two. I say two, because the state of my own knowledge does not pass beyond that point. Others will follow, others will outstrip me on the same lines; and I hazard the guess that man will be ultimately known for a mere polity of multifarious, incongruous and independent denizens. I, for my part, from the nature of my life, advanced infallibly in one direction and in one direction only. It was on the moral side, and in my own person, that I learned to recognise the thorough and primitive duality of man; I saw that, of the two natures that contended in the field of my consciousness, even if I could rightly be said to be either, it was only because I was radically both; and from an early date, even before the course of my scientific discoveries had begun to suggest the most naked possibility of such a miracle, I had learned to dwell with pleasure, as a beloved daydream, on the thought of the separation of these daydreams, on the thought of the separation of these elements. If each, I told myself, could be housed in separate identities, life would be relieved of all that was unbearable; the unjust might go his way, delivered from the aspirations and remorse of his more upright twin; and the just could walk steadfastly and securely on his upward path, doing the good things in which he found his pleasure, and no longer exposed to disgrace and penitence by the hands of this extraneous evil. It was the curse of mankind that these incongruous faggots were thus bound together—that in the agonised womb of consciousness, these polar twins should be continuously struggling. How, then, were they dissociated?

I was so far in my reflections when, as I have said, a side light began to shine upon the subject from the laboratory table. I began to perceive more deeply than it has ever yet been stated, the trembling immateriality, the mistlike transience, of this seemingly so soli body in which we walk attired. Certain agents I found to have the power to shake and pluck back that fleshly vestment, even as a wind might toss the curtains of a pavilion. For two good reasons, I will not enter deeply into this scientific branch of my confession. First, because I have been made to learn that the doom and burthen of our life is bound for ever on man's shoulders, and when the attempt is made to cast it off, it but returns upon us with more unfamiliar and more awful pressure. Second, because, as my narrative will make, alas! too evident, my discoveries were incomplete. Enough then, that I not only recognised my natural body from the

mere aura and effulgence of certain of the powers
that made up my spirit, but managed to compound
a drug by which these powers should be dethroned
from their supremacy, and a second form and countenance substituted, none the less natural to me
because they were the expression, and bore the stamp
of lower elements in my soul.

I hesitated long before I put this theory to the test
of practice. I knew well that I risked death; for any
drug that so potently controlled and shook the very
fortress of identity, might, by the least scruple of an
overdose or at the least inopportunity in the moment of exhibition, utterly blot out that immaterial
tabernacle which I looked to it to change. But the
temptation of a discovery so singular and profound
at last overcame the suggestions of alarm. I had long
since prepared my tincture; I purchased at once,
from a firm of wholesale chemists, a large quantity
of a particular salt which I knew, from my experiments, to be the last ingredient required; and late
one accursed night, I compounded the elements,
watched them boil and smoke together in the glass,
and when the ebullition had subsided, with a strong
glow of courage, drank off the potion.

The most racking pangs succeeded: a grinding in
the bones, deadly nausea, and a horror of the spirit
that cannot be exceeded at the hour of birth or death.
Then these agonies began swiftly to subside, and I
came to myself as if out of a great sickness. There
was something strange in my sensations, something
indescribably new and, from its very novelty, incredibly sweet. I felt younger, lighter, happier in
body; within I was conscious of a heady recklessness, a current of disordered sensual images running like a millrace in my fancy, a solution of the

bonds of obligation, an unknown but not an innocent freedom of the soul. I knew myself, at the first
breath of this new life, to be more wicked, tenfold
more wicked, sold a slave to my original evil; and
the thought, in that moment, braced and delighted
me like wine. I stretched out my hands, exulting in
the freshness of these sensations; and in the act, I
was suddenly aware that I had lost in stature.

There was no mirror, at that date, in my room;
that which stands beside me as I write, was brought
there later on and for the very purpose of these
transformations. The night, however, was far gone
into the morning—the morning, black as it was, was
nearly ripe for the conception of the day—the in-
mates of my house were locked in the most rigorous
hours of slumber; and I determined, flushed as I was
with hope and triumph, to venture in my new shape
as far as to my bedroom. I crossed the yard, wherein
the constellations looked down upon me, I could
have thought, with wonder, the first creature of that
sort that their unsleeping vigilance had yet disclosed
to them; I stole through the corridors, a stranger in
my own house; and coming to my room, I saw for
the first time the appearance of Edward Hyde.

I must here speak by theory alone, saying not that
which I know, but that which I suppose to be most
probable. The evil side of my nature, to which I had
now transferred the stamping efficacy, was less robust and less developed than the good which I had
just deposed. Again, in the course of my life, which
had been, after all, nine tenths a life of effort, virtue
and control, it had been much less exercised and
much less exhausted. And hence, as I think, it came
about that Edward Hyde was so much smaller,
slighter and younger than Henry Jekyll. Even as

good shone upon the countenance of the one, evil
was written broadly and plainly on the face of the
other. Evil besides (which I must still believe to be
the lethal side of man) had left on that body an
imprint of deformity and decay. And yet when I
looked upon that ugly idol in the glass, I was conscious of no repugnance, rather of a leap of welcome. This, too, was myself. It seemed natural and
human. In my eyes it bore a livelier image of the
spirit, it seemed more express and single, than the
imperfect and divided countenance I had been hitherto accustomed to call mine. And in so far I was
doubtless right. I have observed that when I wore
the semblance of Edward Hyde, none could come
near to me at first without a visible misgiving of the
flesh. This, as I take it, was because all human beings,
as we meet them, are commingled out of good and
evil: and Edward Hyde, alone in the ranks of mankind, was pure evil.

I lingered but a moment at the mirror: the second
and conclusive experiment had yet to be attempted;
it yet remained to be seen if I had lost my identity
beyond redemption and must flee before daylight
from a house that was no longer mine; and hurrying
back to my cabinets, I once more prepared and drank
the cup, once more suffered the pangs of dissolution, and came to myself once more with the character, the stature and the face of Henry Jekyll.

That night I had come to the fatal cross-roads.
Had I approached my discovery in a more noble
spirit, had I risked the experiment while under the
empire of generous or pious aspirations, all must
have been otherwise, and from these agonies of death
and birth, I had come forth an angel instead of a
fiend. The drug had no discriminating action; it was

neither diabolical nor divine; it but shook the doors of the prisonhouse of my disposition; and like the captives of Philippi, that which stood within ran forth. At that time my virtue slumbered; my evil, kept awake by ambition, was alert and swift to seize the occasion; and the thing that was projected was Edward Hyde. Hence, although I had now two characters as well as two appearances, one was wholly evil, and the other was still the old Henry Jekyll, that incongruous compound of whose reformation and improvement I had already learned to despair. The movement was thus wholly toward the worse.

Even at that time, I had not conquered my aversions to the dryness of a life of study. I would still be merrily disposed at times; and as my pleasures were (to say the least) undignified, and I was not only well known and highly considered, but growing towards the elderly man, this incoherency of my life was daily growing more unwelcome. It was on this side that my new power tempted me until I fell in slavery. I had but to drink the cup, to doff at once the body of the noted professor, and to assume, like a thick cloak, that of Edward Hyde. I smiled at the notion; it seemed to me at the time to be humourous; and I made my preparations with the most studious care. I took and furnished that house in Soho, to which Hyde was tracked by the police; and engaged as a housekeeper a creature whom I knew well to be silent and unscrupulous. On the other side, I announced to my servants that a Mr. Hyde (whom I described) was to have full liberty and power about my house in the square; and to parry mishaps, I even called and made myself a familiar object, in my second character. I next drew up that will to which you so much objected; so that if anything befell me in the person of Dr. Jekyll, I could enter on that of Edward Hyde without pecuniary loss. And thus fortified, as I supposed, on every side, I began to profit by the strange immunities of my position.

Men have before hired bravos to transact their crimes, while their own person and reputation sat under shelter. I was the first that ever did so for his pleasures. I was the first that could plod in the public eye with a load of genial respectability, and in a moment, like a schoolboy, strip off these lendings and spring headlong into the sea of liberty. But for me, in my impenetrable mantle, the safety was complete. Think of it—I did not even exist! Let me but escape into my laboratory door, give me but a second or two to mix and swallow the draught that I had always standing ready; and whatever he had done, Edward Hyde would pass away like the stain of breath upon a mirror; and there in his stead, quietly at home, trimming the midnight lamp in his study, a man who could afford to laugh at suspicion, would be Henry Jekyll.

The pleasures which I made haste to seek in my disguise were, as I have said, undignified; I would scarce use a harder term. But in the hands of Edward Hyde, they soon began to turn toward the monstrous. When I would come back from these excursions, I was often plunged into a kind of wonder at my vicarious depravity. This familiar that I called out of my own soul, and sent forth alone to do his good pleasure, was a being inherently malign and villainous; his every act and thought centered on self; drinking pleasure with bestial avidity from any degree of torture to another; relentless like a man of stone. Henry Jekyll stood at times aghast before the acts of Edward Hyde; but the situation was apart from ordinary laws, and insidiously relaxed the grasp of conscience. It was Hyde, after all, and Hyde alone, that was guilty. Jekyll was no worse; he woke again to his good qualities seemingly unimpaired; he would even make haste, where it was possible, to undo the evil done by Hyde. And thus his conscience slumbered.

Into the details of the infamy at which I thus connived (for even now I can scarce grant that I committed it) I have no design of entering; I mean but to point out the warnings and the successive steps with which my chastisement approached. I met with one accident which, as it brought on no consequence, I shall no more than mention. An act of cruelty to a child aroused against me the anger of a passer-by, whom I recognised the other day in the person of your kinsman; the doctor and the child's family joined him; there were moments when I feared for my life; and at last, in order to pacify their too just resentment, Edward Hyde had to bring them to the door, and pay them in a cheque drawn in the name of Henry Jekyll. But this danger was easily eliminated from the future, by opening an account at another bank in the name of Edward Hyde himself; and when, by sloping my own hand backward, I had supplied my double with a signature, I thought I sat beyond the reach of fate.

Some two months before the murder of Sir Danvers, I had been out for one of my adventures, had returned at a late hour, and woke the next day in bed with somewhat odd sensations. It was in vain I looked about me; in vain I saw the decent furniture and tall proportions of my room in the square; in vain that I recognised the pattern of the bed curtains

and the design of the mahogany frame; something
still kept insisting that I was not where I was, that I
had not wakened where I seemed to be, but in the
little room in Soho where I was accustomed to sleep
in the body of Edward Hyde. I smiled to myself,
and, in my psychological way, began lazily to inquire into the elements of this illusion, occasionally,
even as I did so, dropping back into a comfortable
morning doze. I was still so engaged when, in one
of my more wakeful moments, my eyes fell upon my
hand. Now the hand of Henry Jekyll (as you have
often remarked) was professional in shape and size:
it was large, firm, white and comely. But the hand
which I now saw, clearly enough, in the yellow light
of a mid-London morning, lying half shut on the
bedclothes, was lean, corded, knuckly, of a dusky
pallor and thickly shaded with a swart growth of
hair. It was the hand of Edward Hyde.

I must have stared upon it for near half a minute,
sunk as I was in the mere stupidity of wonder,
before terror woke up in my breast as sudden and
startling as the crash of cymbals; and bounding from
my bed, I rushed to the mirror. At the sight that met
my eyes, my blood was changed into something
exquisitely thin and icy. Yes, I had gone to bed
Henry Jekyll, I had awakened Edward Hyde. How
was this to be explained? I asked myself; and then,
with another bound of terror—how was it to be
remedied? It was well on in the morning; the servants were up; all my drugs were in the cabinet—a
long journey down two pairs of stairs, through the
back passage, across the open court and through the
anatomical theatre, from where I was then standing
horror-struck. It might indeed be possible to cover
my face; but of what use was that, when I was

•

unable to conceal the alteration of my stature? And then with an overpowering sweetness of relief, it came back upon my mind that the servants were already used to the coming and going of my second self. I had soon dressed, as well as I was able, in clothes of my own size: had soon passed through the house, where Bradshaw stared and drew back at seeing Mr. Hyde at such an hour and in such a strange array; and ten minutes later, Dr. Jekyll had returned to his own shape and was sitting down, with a darkened brow, to make a feint of breakfasting.

Small indeed was my appetite. This inexplicable incident, this reversal of my previous experience, seemed, like the Babylonian finger on the wall, to be spelling out the letters of my judgment; and I began to reflect more seriously than ever before on the issues and possibilities of my double existence. That part of me which I had the power of projecting, had lately been much exercised and nourished; it had seemed to me of late as though the body of Edward Hyde had grown in stature, as though (when I wore that form) I were conscious of a more generous tide of blood; and I began to spy a danger that, if this were much prolonged, the balance of my nature might be permanently overthrown, the power of voluntary change be forfeited, and the character of Edward Hyde become irrevocably mine. The power of the drug had not been always equally displayed. Once, very early in my career, it had totally failed me; since then I had been obliged on more than one occasion to double, and once, with infinite risk of death, to treble the amount; and these rare uncertainties had cast hitherto the sole shadow on my contentment. Now, however, and in the light of that morning's accident, I was led to remark that whereas,

Plato's city-in-speech

in the beginning, the difficulty had been to throw off the body of Jekyll, it had of late gradually but decidedly transferred itself to the other side. All things therefore seemed to point to this; that I was slowly losing hold of my original and better self, and becoming slowly incorporated with my second and worse.

Between these two, I now felt I had to choose. My two natures had memory in common, but all other faculties were most unequally shared between them. Jekyll (who was composite) now with the most sensitive apprehensions, now with a greedy gusto, projected and shared in the pleasures and adventures of Hyde; but Hyde was indifferent to Jekyll, or but remembered him as the mountain bandit remembers the cavern in which he conceals himself from pursuit. Jekyll had more than a father's interest; Hyde had more than a son's indifference. To cast in my lot with Jekyll, was to die to those appetites which I had long secretly indulged and had of late begun to pamper. To cast it in with Hyde, was to die to a thousand interests and aspirations, and to become, at a blow and forever, despised and friendless. The bargain might appear unequal; but there was still another consideration in the scales; for while Jekyll would suffer smartingly in the fires of abstinence, Hyde would be not even conscious of all that he had lost. Strange as my circumstances were, the terms of this debate are as old and commonplace as man; much the same inducements and alarms cast the die for any tempted and trembling sinner; and it fell out with me, as it falls with so vast a majority of my fellows, that I chose the better part and was found wanting in the strength to keep to it.

Yes, I preferred the elderly and discontented doctor, surrounded by friends and cherishing honest hopes; and bade a resolute farewell to the liberty, the comparative youth, the light step, leaping impulses and secret pleasures, that I had enjoyed in the disguise of Hyde. I made this choice perhaps with some unconscious reservation, for I neither gave up the house in Soho, nor destroyed the clothes of Edward Hyde, which still lay ready in my cabinet. For two months, however, I was true to my determination; for two months, I led a life of such severity as I had never before attained to, and enjoyed the compensations of an approving conscience. But time began at last to obliterate the freshness of my alarm; the praises of conscience began to grow into a thing of course; I began to be tortured with throes and longings, as of Hyde struggling for freedom; and at last, in an hour of moral weakness, I once again compounded and swallowed the transforming draught.

I do not suppose that, when a drunkard reasons with himself upon his vice, he is once out of five hundred times affected by the dangers that he runs through his brutish, physical insensibility; neither had I, long as I had considered my position, made enough allowance for the complete moral insensibility and insensate readiness to evil, which were the leading characters of Edward Hyde. Yet it was by these that I was punished. My devil had been long caged, he came out roaring. I was conscious, even when I took the draught, of a more unbridled, a more furious propensity to ill. It must have been this, I suppose, that stirred in my soul that tempest of impatience with which I listened to the civilities of my unhappy victim; I declare, at least, before God, no man morally sane could have been guilty of that crime upon so pitiful a provocation; and that I struck in no more reasonable spirit than that in which a sick child may break a plaything. But I had voluntarily stripped myself of all those balancing instincts by which even the worst of us continues to walk with some degree of steadiness among temptations; and in my case, to be tempted, however slightly, was to fall.

Instantly the spirit of hell awoke in me and raged. With a transport of glee, I mauled the unresisting body, tasting delight from every blow; and it was not till weariness had begun to succeed, that I was suddenly, in the top fit of my delirium, struck through the heart by a cold thrill of terror. A mist dispersed; I saw my life to be forfeit; and fled from the scene of these excesses, at once glorying and trembling, my lust of evil gratified and stimulated, my love of life screwed to the topmost peg. I ran to the house in Soho, and (to make assurance doubly sure) destroyed my papers; thence I set out through the lamplit streets, in the same divided ecstasy of mind, gloating on my crime, light-headedly devising others in the future, and yet still hastening and still hearkening in my wake for the steps of the avenger. Hyde had a song upon his lips as he compounded the draught, and as he drank it, pledged the dead man. The pangs of transformation had not done tearing him, before Henry Jekyll, with streaming tears of gratitude and remorse, had fallen upon his knees and lifted his clasped hands to God. The veil of self-indulgence was rent from head to foot. I saw my life as a whole: I followed it up from the days of childhood, when I had walked with my father's hand, and through the self-denying toils of my professional life, to arrive again and again, with the same sense of unreality, at the damned horrors of the evening. I could have screamed aloud; I sought with tears and prayers to smother down the crowd of hideous images and sounds with which my memory swarmed against me; and still, between the petitions, the ugly face of my iniquity stared into my soul. As the acuteness of this remorse began to die away, it was succeeded by a sense of joy. The problem of my conduct was solved. Hyde was thenceforth impossible; whether I would or not, I was now confined to the better part of my existence; and O, how I rejoiced to think of it! with what willing humility I embraced anew the restrictions of natural life! with what sincere renunciation I locked the door by which I had so often gone and come, and ground the key under my heel!

The next day, came the news that the murder had not been overlooked, that the guilt of Hyde was patent to the world, and that the victim was a man high in public estimation. It was not only a crime, it had been a tragic folly. I think I was glad to know it; I think I was glad to have my better impulses thus buttressed and guarded by the terrors of the scaffold. Jekyll was now my city of refuge; let but Hyde peep out an instant, and the hands of all men would be raised to take and slay him.

I resolved in my future conduct to redeem the past; and I can say with honesty that my resolve was fruitful of some good. You know yourself how earnestly, in the last months of the last year, I laboured to relieve suffering; you know that much was done for others, and that the days passed quietly, almost happily for myself. Nor can I truly say that I wearied of this beneficent and innocent life; I think instead that I daily enjoyed it more completely; but I was still cursed with my duality of purpose; and as the first edge of my penitence wore off, the lower side of me, so long indulged, so recently chained down, began to growl for licence. Not that I dreamed of resuscitating Hyde; the bare idea of that would startle me to frenzy: no, it was in my own person that I was once more tempted to trifle with my conscience; and it was as an ordinary secret sinner that I at last fell before the assaults of temptation.

There comes an end to all things; the most capacious measure is filled at last; and this brief condescension to my evil finally destroyed the balance of my soul. And yet I was not alarmed; the fall seemed natural, like a return to the old days before I had made my discovery. It was a fine, clear, January day, wet under foot where the frost had melted, but cloudless overhead; and the Regent's Park was full of winter chirrupings and sweet with spring odours. I sat in the sun on a bench; the animal within me licking the chops of memory; the spiritual side a little drowsed, promising subsequent penitence, but not yet moved to begin. After all, I reflected, I was like my neighbours; and then I smiled, comparing myself with other men, comparing my active goodwill with the lazy cruelty of their neglect. And at the very moment of that vainglorious thought, a qualm came over me, a horrid nausea and the most deadly shuddering. These passed away, and left me faint; and then as in its turn faintness subsided, I began to be aware of a change in the temper of my thoughts, a greater boldness, a contempt of danger, a solution of the bonds of obligation. I looked down; my clothes hung formlessly on my shrunken limbs; the hand that lay on my knee was corded and hairy. I was once more Edward Hyde. A moment before I had been safe of all men's respect, wealthy, beloved—

the cloth laying for me in the dining-room at home; and now I was the common quarry of mankind, hunted, houseless, a known murderer, thrall to the gallows.

My reason wavered, but it did not fail me utterly. I have more than once observed that, in my second character, my faculties seemed sharpened to a point and my spirits more tensely elastic; thus it came about that, where Jekyll perhaps might have succumbed, Hyde rose to the importance of the moment. My drugs were in one of the presses of my cabinet; how was I to reach them? That was the problem that (crushing my temples in my hands) I set myself to solve. The laboratory door I had closed. If I sought to enter by the house, my own servants would consign me to the gallows. I saw I must employ another hand, and thought of Lanyon. How was he to be reached? how persuaded? Supposing that I escaped capture in the streets, how was I to make my way into his presence? and how should I, an unknown and displeasing visitor, prevail on the famous physician to rifle the study of his colleague, Dr. Jekyll? Then I remembered that of my original character, one part remained to me: I could write my own hand; and once I had conceived that kindling spark, the way that I must follow became lighted up from end to end.

Thereupon, I arranged my clothes as best I could, and summoning a passing hansom, drove to an hotel in Portland Street, the name of which I chanced to remember. At my appearance (which was indeed comical enough, however tragic a fate these garments covered) the driver could not conceal his mirth. I gnashed my teeth upon him with a gust of devilish fury; and the smile withered from his face—happily for him—yet more happily for myself, for in another instant I had certainly dragged him from his perch. At the inn, as I entered, I looked about me with so black a countenance as made the attendants tremble; not a look did they exchange in my presence; but obsequiously took my orders, led me to a private room, and brought me wherewithal to write. Hyde in danger of his life was a creature new to me; shaken with inordinate anger, strung to the pitch of murder, lusting to inflict pain. Yet the creature was astute; mastered his fury with a great effort of the will; composed two important letters, one to Lanyon and one to Poole; and that he might receive actual evidence of their being posted, sent them out with directions that they should be registered. Thenceforward, he sat all day over the fire in the private room, gnawing his nails; there he dined, sitting alone with his fears, the waiter visibly quailing before his eye; and thence, when the night was fully come, he set forth in the corner of a closed cab, and was driven to and fro about the streets of the city. He, I say—I cannot say, I. That child of Hell had nothing human; nothing lived in him but fear and hatred. And when at last, thinking the driver had begun to grow suspicious, he discharged the cab and ventured on foot, attired in his misfitting clothes, an object marked out for observation, into the midst of the nocturnal passengers, these two base passions raged within him like a tempest. He walked fast, hunted by his fears, chattering to himself, skulking through the less frequented thoroughfares, counting the minutes that still divided him from midnight. Once a woman spoke to him, offering, I think, a box of lights. He smote her in the face, and she fled.

When I came to myself at Lanyon's, the horror of

my old friend perhaps affected me somewhat: I do not know; it was at least but a drop in the sea to the abhorrence with which I looked back upon these hours. A change had come over me. It was no longer the fear of the gallows, it was the horror of being Hyde that racked me. I received Lanyon's condemnation partly in a dream; it was partly in a dream that I came home to my own house and got into bed. I slept after the prostration of the day, with a stringent and profound slumber which not even the nightmares that wrung me could avail to break, I awoke in the morning shaken, weakened, but refreshed. I still hated and feared the thought of the brute that slept within me, and I had not of course forgotten the appalling dangers of the day before; but I was once more at home, in my own house and close to my drugs; and gratitude for my escape shone so strong in my soul that it almost rivalled the brightness of hope.

I was stepping leisurely across the court after breakfast, drinking the chill of the air with pleasure, when I was seized again with those indescribable sensations that heralded the change; and I had but the time to gain the shelter of my cabinet, before I was once again raging and freezing with the passions of Hyde. It took on this occasion a double dose to recall me to myself; and alas! six hours after, as I sat looking sadly in the fire, the pangs returned, and the drug had to be re-administered. In short, from that day forth it seemed only by a great effort as of gymnastics, and only under the immediate stimulation of the drug, that I was able to wear the countenance of Jekyll. At all hours of the day and night, I would be taken with the premonitory shudder; above all, if I slept, or even dozed for a moment in my chair, it was always as Hyde that I awakened. Under the strain of this continually impending doom and by the sleeplessness to which I now condemned myself, ay, even beyond what I had thought possible to man, I became, in my own person, a creature eaten up and emptied by fever, languidly weak both in body and mind, and solely occupied by one thought: the horror of my other self. But when I slept, or when the virtue of the medicine wore off, I would leap almost without transition (for the pangs of transformation grew daily less marked) into the possession of a fancy brimming with images of terror, a soul boiling with causeless hatreds, and a body that seemed not strong enough to contain the raging energies of life. The powers of Hyde seemed to have grown with the sickliness of Jekyll. And certainly the hate that now divided them was equal on each side. With Jekyll, it was a thing of vital instinct. He had now seen the full deformity of that creature that shared with him some of the phenomena of consciousness, and was co-heir with him to death: and beyond these links of community, which in themselves made the most poignant part of his distress, he thought of Hyde, for all his energy of life, as of something not only hellish but inorganic. This was the shocking thing; that the slime of the pit seemed to utter cries and voices; that the amorphous dust gesticulated and sinned; that what was dead, and had no shape, should usury the offices of life. And this again, that that insurgent horror was knit to him closer than a wife, closer than an eye; lay caged in his flesh, where he heard it mutter and felt it struggle to be born; and at every hour of weakness, and in the confidence of slumber, prevailed against him, and deposed him out of life. The hatred of Hyde for Jekyll was of a different order. His terror of the gallows drove him continually to commit temporary suicide, and return to his subordinate station of a part instead of a person; but he loathed the necessity, he loathed the despondency into which Jekyll was now fallen, and he resented the dislike with which he was himself regarded. Hence the ape-like tricks that he would play me, scrawling in my own hand blasphemies on the pages of my books, burning the letters and destroying the portrait of my father; and indeed, had it not been for his fear of death, he would long ago have ruined himself in order to involve me in the ruin. But his love of life is wonderful; I go further: I, who sicken and freeze at the mere thought of him, when I recall the abjection and passion of this attachment, and when I know how he fears my power to cut him off by suicide, I find it in my heart to pity him.

It is useless, and the time awfully fails me, to prolong this description; no one has ever suffered such torments, let that suffice; and yet even to these, habit brought—no, not alleviation—but a certain callousness of soul, a certain acquiescence of despair; and my punishment might have gone on for years, but for the last calamity which has now fallen, and which has finally severed me from my own face and nature. My provision of the salt, which had never been renewed since the date of the first experiment, began to run low. I sent out for a fresh supply and mixed the draught; the ebullition followed, and the first change of colour, not the second; I drank it and it was without efficiency. You will learn from Poole how I have had London ransacked; it was in vain; and I am now persuaded that my first supply was impure, and that it was that unknown impurity which lent efficacy to the draught.

About a week has passed, and I am now finishing this statement under the influence of the last of the old powers. This, then, is the last time, short of a miracle, that Henry Jekyll can think his own thoughts or see his own face (now how sadly altered!) in the glass. Nor must I delay too long to bring my writing to an end; for if my narrative has hitherto escaped destruction, it has been by a combination of great prudence and great good luck. Should the throes of change take me in the act of writing it, Hyde will tear it in pieces; but if some time shall have elapsed after I have laid it by, his wonderful selfishness and circumscription to the moment will probably save it once again from the action of his ape-like spite. And indeed the doom that is closing on us both has already changed and crushed him. Half an hour from now, when I shall again and forever reindue that hated personality, I know how I shall sit shuddering and weeping in my chair, or continue, with the most strained and fearstruck ecstasy of listening, to pace up and down this room (my last earthly refuge) and give ear to every sound of menace. Will Hyde die upon the scaffold? or will he find courage to release himself at the last moment? God knows; I am careless; this is my true hour of death, and what is to follow concerns another than myself. Here then, as I lay down the pen and proceed to seal up my confession, I bring the life of that unhappy Henry Jekyll to an end.

Afterword

Vladimir Nabokov starts his introduction to *Dr. Jekyll and Mr. Hyde* with an injunction, telling us that we should "completely forget, disremember, unlearn, consign to oblivion" any of our assumptions about this book. But it's hard to do, isn't it? Like Frankenstein's monster, like Dracula, like the Werewolf and the Mummy, Jekyll/Hyde is an icon of horror, a Halloween staple. Perhaps as children we even played pretend, acting out the drama of the mad scientist: holding the test tube bubbling with a noxious green liquid, which we drink; putting a hand to our throats as our mouths constrict, grimacing. We imagined the moment of transformation—perhaps thick hair sprouted; perhaps the skin turned a sickly color; perhaps the brow extended, apelike, and the lips sneered over crooked teeth. Probably we thrashed around, and something in the laboratory fell crashing to the floor, no doubt shattering dramatically. And then came the evil maniacal laughter.

If you were alive in the century that followed the publication of this novel, it's likely that you encountered the basics of Stevenson's story dozens upon dozens of times, even if you never touched the book itself. For more than a hundred years, it's been a part of the cultural air around us. There have been at least ninety films based upon the text, as well as many stage shows, comic books, jokes, media references, etc., so that the *idea* of Dr. Jekyll and Mr. Hyde is as much a piece of the collective unconscious as it is a book.

We probably first encountered a parody of the story as children—via Sylvester the Cat and Tweety Bird in the cartoon short "Dr. Jekyll's Hyde" or via an episode of the animated series *Pinky and the Brain.* Maybe we saw a comic film with Abbott and Costello (*Abbott and Costello Meet Dr. Jekyll and Mr. Hyde*) or Jerry Lewis (*The Nutty Professor*) or Eddie Murphy (*The Nutty Professor* remake). Maybe we saw the episode of TV's *Gilligan's Island* in which Gilligan dreams he has transformed into the murderous Hyde and bumps off the other castaways one by one.

As we grew up, we were no doubt at least vaguely aware of the imagery from Rouben Mamoulian's 1932 film version, even if we hadn't actually seen the movie. Fredric March won an Academy Award for his performance as Jekyll/Hyde, and it's *his* Hyde, rather than Stevenson's, who still exists most firmly in the public imagination—that face somewhere between that of an ugly street thug and that of a caveman, with a nasty crooked overbite and a disturbing shock of unkempt hair and gleefully malevolent eyes.

Still, decade after decade, subsequent generations of actors gamely took on the challenge of the role of the doomed Dr. Jekyll—from Spencer Tracy (1941) to Jack Palance (1968) and John Malkovich (1996). The part has been given twists over the years, and each era has often brought a new, "socially relevant" slant to the old story. We may have seen the solemnly Freudian Victor Fleming 1941 version, or the 1976 blaxploitation flick called *Dr. Black, Mr. Hyde,* in which the African-American protagonist (Bernie

Casey) is turned into a Caucasian who can't control his murderous impulses; or the 1995 *Dr. Jekyll and Ms. Hyde,* in which the doctor gets to find out what it feels like to be a beautiful woman and explore his sexuality. We may have attended a performance of the 1997 Broadway musical *Jekyll and Hyde* and emerged from the theater humming such tunes as "This Is the Moment" and "Murder, Murder."

Disremember, Nabokov says. *Consign to oblivion.* Is he serious?

Maybe he is. Actually, a contemporary reader coming for the first time to Robert Louis Stevenson's *Dr. Jekyll and Mr. Hyde* may, in fact, be surprised. It's not quite what one expects. It is a fragmented, quietly feverish little book—a *sneaky* book. It proceeds through indirection, doling out sly hints but leaving, for the most part, the sordid facts to the imagination.

We begin in a place that is unfamiliar to those who know the story only through rumor and cultural static. There is the introduction of the lawyer Utterson, "a man of a rugged countenance that was never lighted by a smile; cold, scanty and embarrassed in discourse; backward in sentiment; lean, long, dusty, dreary and yet somehow lovable." The word "somehow" is of course a problematic one for a writer—a word that often signifies nothing so much as the writer's lazy inability to be specific. Yet it is a word that will appear frequently throughout *Dr. Jekyll.* Utterson, we are told, is *somehow* lovable, and in this first sentence, the foggy, tentative, strangely lacunar tone of the book is established.

We continue on down the page, perhaps a little puzzled, walking along with these two stodgy, reserved men, Utterson and Enfield—"It was reported by those who encountered them in their Sunday walks, that they said nothing, looked singularly dull. . . ." They walk past a dingy neighborhood, "a by-street in a busy quarter of London," and pass by a certain door that Enfield recognizes, "connected in my mind," Enfield says, "with a very odd story."

Okay. Now we're getting somewhere. Out of their stiff conversation emerges a piece of *Dr. Jekyll and Mr. Hyde* that we probably remember vividly from the movies: The image of Mr. Hyde deliberately running down a young girl in the street, trampling over her. We may recall having seen this moment dramatized. We may believe that it happens in a vivid, specific scene.

But it doesn't. It comes obliquely, in conversation, and the scene isn't so much described as referred to. *Somehow. Something.* There are other oddities to the narration, as well. Enfield says he "was coming home from some place at the end of the world, about three o'clock of a black winter morning" when he saw the scene with Hyde and the little girl. An attentive reader pauses for a moment. What does that mean—*some place at the end of the world*? And what is a little girl doing "running as hard as she was able down a cross street" at three in the morning? Even in these first few pages, there is a shadiness, a subtle uncertainty that begins to cast doubt on the solidity of the narrative. We can sense a more honest version of the tale sliding along, unspoken, beneath the surface.

We never do find out what Enfield was doing walking through this part of town in the dead of night, a part of town where "a man listens and listens and begins to long for the sight of a policeman," and we never get a real, solid description of Hyde from Enfield, either: "There is something wrong with his appearance," he says, "something displeasing, something down-right detestable. I never saw a man I so disliked, and yet I scarce know why. He must be deformed somewhere. . . ."

Even at this early point, the reader may begin to notice a pattern of evasiveness emerging, the *something*s and *somehow*s leaving blurred spots in our vision, like the fog that hangs over the London of this story, the fog that, as Utterson observes, "even in the houses . . . began to lie thickly." The book is full of polite silences, fey suggestions. We never find out what might cause Utterson to brood "on his own past, groping in all corners of memory, lest by chance some Jack-in-the-Box of an old iniquity should leap to light there." Beyond the incident that Enfield describes, and the subsequent murder of Sir Danvers Carew— observed by a maidservant from a distant window and reported in the novel secondhand—we never do find out, exactly, what Jekyll *does* in the guise of Hyde. All those hours he spends "drinking pleasure with bestial avidity from any degree of torture to another; relentless like a man of stone" are left to the reader's own uneasy dreams.

The structure of *The Strange Case of Dr. Jekyll and Mr. Hyde* follows a path as indirect and elusive as its multiple narrative voices. With its obliquely recorded incidents, its eyewitness accounts and sealed confessions, it resembles nothing so much as a casebook—a collection of gathered clues, fragments, through which the clever detective may be able to intuit or project a complete narrative. Perhaps one of the most compelling aspects of this novel is that, in fact, there's so much left here for us to fill in, so many scenes that we can only imagine.

Such a structure creates fertile ground for allegory hunters, and there are indeed many convincing interpretations of the novel. It's easy to picture it as a Christian parable about original evil that exists within us all, or as an illustration of the Freudian concepts of Ego and Id, the manifestation of Victorian sexual repression and hypocrisy. We can call the story a fable of addiction, with a junkie Jekyll in the end "crying night and day for some sort of medicine," sending out to pharmacies for "pure" samples of his drug. We can see Hyde as representing an anxiety of the underclass, with his Soho flat and his "lean, corded, knuckly" hand. We can see it as a reflection of Victorian ideas about evolution, with Mr. Hyde as a throwback to the primitive, precivilized ape cousin that Darwin's theories had evoked in the late-nineteenth-century imagination ("The man seems hardly human," Utterson thinks upon his first meeting with Hyde. "Something trogloditic, shall we say?") The puzzlelike structure of the novel creates for readers a kind of Rorschach test, open to a variety of interpretations.

Yet allegory is only compelling if it helps to explain some hidden aspect of our daily lives. *Dr. Jekyll and Mr. Hyde* was lucky to dovetail so nicely with both the radical ideas of the nineteenth century, such as Darwin's theories, but also with Freud, and with the twentieth century's fascination with the landscape of the mind. "I hazard the guess," Dr. Jekyll writes in his confession, "that man will ultimately be known for a mere polity of multifarious, incongruous and independent denizens."

It also happened that Stevenson's novel coincided rather closely with a series of murders that continue, even to this day, to capture the public imagination.

*   *   *

The famous Jack the Ripper killings occurred in the Whitechapel area of London in the late summer and early autumn of 1888, two years after the publication of *The Strange Case of Dr. Jekyll and Mr. Hyde*. Depending on which authority you consult, the Ripper murdered between four and nine women. No one was ever charged with the crimes.

By 1888, Stevenson's story was well-known. There were at least two stage versions of *The Strange Case of Dr. Jekyll and Mr. Hyde* being performed in London that year, including a musical farce based upon the story, which opened on September third, at the Royalty Theatre, three days after the first murder.

It seems likely that the Ripper, whoever he might have been, would have been familiar with Stevenson's story. Perhaps he even identified. This is idle speculation, it's true. Still, it's hard not to feel a little uncomfortable as we read Jekyll's ecstatic descriptions of becoming Hyde; he is suddenly "conscious of a heady recklessness, a current of disordered sensual images running like a millrace in my fancy, a solution of the bonds of obligation, an unknown but not an innocent freedom of the soul." Accurate or not, this passage has become a touchstone in the popular conception of the mind of a serial killer.

Jack the Ripper was not the first serial killer, of course, but he was perhaps the first to be presented as one, the first to appear when the general population was literate enough to follow the story of his deeds through the papers, the first to appear in the now familiar context of sensational journalism. The Ripper seemed aware of his murders as a kind of performance, leaving his victims in plain sight, sending taunting letters to the press, apparently enjoying the worldwide stir his crimes were causing. The public followed the search for the killer the way they would have followed a serialized novel, waiting impatiently for the next installment.

Given their proximity in time and tone, it's probably not surprising that over the course of the twentieth century, popular representations of the Ripper have tended to resemble images of Dr. Jekyll/Mr. Hyde. The two stories have often gone arm in arm in the public imagination, and frequently even the details of the two have been recombined, mixed up. Many of the film versions of Jekyll/Hyde have included a prostitute character or two, for example—imported, apparently, from the Ripper legend. Conversely, most of the film versions of the Ripper story present the killer as a Jekyll-like gentleman, outwardly respectable—a split personality.

And then there is the iconic imagery itself. In both cases, we are frequently presented with a picture of a man in top hat and cape, a silhouette standing under a gaslit streetlight. We might see a certain type of urban street. A Cockney prostitute stands on a corner, a drunkard stumbles muttering into the gutter, and a horse-drawn carriage *clip-clops* along the street. The alleyways are dark. In both cases we imagine a gentleman transforming into a monster, lifting a walking stick or a surgeon's knife, slashing downward, brutally. Grinning.

Does the novel anticipate a murderer like Jack the Ripper? Does it have some prescient insight into psychopathology? Well . . . not exactly. For the most part, the novel is very much grounded in a Victorian sensibility. The prose can be stodgy and florid, the attitudes both prim and melodramatic. Yet at the same time, there are intimations here of particularly modern concerns, and it might be claimed that this book is among the first popular works to begin to articulate the sense of urban alienation that would later become one of the primary subjects of twentieth-century fiction.

Mr. Hyde could not exist without the modern city. He needs the anonymity of the masses, and he needs the newly gaslit streets, the flickering nighttime landscape of pubs and brothels and beggars, the urban underworld that would later transform into the world of film noir. He needs an expanse of amoral territory to slink through, just as Jekyll needs a society in which his disaffection can go unnoticed, a world in which most neighbors are strangers.

"Men have before hired bravos to transact their crimes," Jekyll says in his confession. "I was the first that ever did so for his pleasures. I was the first that could plod in the public eye with a load of genial respectability, and in a moment, like a schoolboy, strip off these lendings, and spring headlong into the sea of liberty. But for me, in my impenetrable mantle, the safety was complete. Think of it—I did not even exist!"

The pleasures and terrors of this "sea of liberty" are perhaps more apparent to contemporary people than they were to the Victorians who first encountered this passage in Stevenson's book. We know that yearning quite well, don't we? We know that desire to dissolve into another identity entirely, to be reborn, to be incognito, and for us—with our new ease of mobility, with the constraints of class and rank loosened, in an age of anonymity—for us, it's more possible than ever to "spring headlong into that sea of liberty." This could well be the mantra of our nomadic age, the privilege of the overpopulated and estranged. *I did not even exist!* Jekyll exults, and in this single phrase he summarizes the great social change that was to overtake the civilized world in the upcoming century.

For modern readers, the Jekyll/Hyde legend seems to speak particularly to our nervousness about the solidity of the self. Who is the "real" me? What is the persona that people know as "me"? We are more self-conscious about the ordinary public masks that we naturally put on to negotiate our way through social interactions and the ways in which those masks separate us from the people in our lives we are supposed to be close to. One of the commonplaces of contemporary life is that sense that it's very easy to have a secret life. We know the old story: someone comes in and kills his coworkers with a semiautomatic. A serial killer spends years murdering folks and burying them in the crawl space beneath his house, and then later his acquaintances and coworkers are quite surprised. He's described as "quiet," "a nice guy." No one suspected. It's a familiar story that leads us all the way back to Jekyll's double life.

I did not even exist!

I thought of all of this again recently at the local amusement park. My nine-year-old son and I were standing in line among hundreds of thrill seekers, waiting for our chance at a ride called Mr. Hyde's Nasty Fall, and we casually discussed the novel—though my son had neither read it nor seen any of the movies. Still, he recognized that hirsute ogre in the top hat and Victorian cape; he knew that the counterpart was called Dr. Jekyll. He remembered the basics of the story, though he didn't know where, exactly, he had learned them.

"Why would you drink that potion, if you knew that it was going to turn you into a monster?" I asked, and my son looked at me sidelong.

"But it would be fun, too," he said. "I mean, you could get away with anything."

"That's true," I said. My son is not afraid of these rides, as I am, and he leaned back in the carriage as we were strapped in by the costumed attendant, before we began to ascend to the top. The faux-Cockney voice of Mr. Hyde spoke to us through a loudspeaker. "Step right up," he said, as we slowly rose, ten feet, fifty feet, one hundred twenty-five feet into the air. "I have something very interesting I want to show you," the Mr. Hyde voice said. We came to a stop at the pinnacle of the ride. "What would it be like if the cable on this elevator were to suddenly break?" Mr. Hyde whispered. "We're thirteen stories in the air now." My son smiled at my nervousness. He was pleasantly curious to know what it would feel like to be pushed down an elevator shaft by a giggling sociopath, and we braced ourselves.

"Have a nice fall," the loudspeaker Mr. Hyde cackled, and my son and I plunged together, screaming.

—Dan Chaon

Selected Bibliography

PROSE WORKS BY ROBERT LOUIS STEVENSON

An Inland Voyage, 1878 travel book
Edinburgh: Picturesque Notes, 1879 travel book
Travels with a Donkey in the Cévennes, 1879 travel book
Virginibus Puerisque, 1881 essays
Familiar Studies of Men and Books, 1882 essays
New Arabian Nights, 1882 stories
The Silverado Squatters, 1883 travel book
Treasure Island, 1883 novel
More New Arabian Nights: The Dynamiter (with Fanny Van de Grift Stevenson), 1885 stories
Prince Otto, 1885 novel
Kidnapped, 1886 novel
The Strange Case of Dr. Jekyll and Mr. Hyde, 1886 novel
Memoir of Fleeming Jenkin, 1887 biography
Memories and Portraits, 1887 essays
The Merry Men and Other Tales, 1887 stories
The Black Arrow, 1888 novel
The Master of Ballantrae, 1889 novel
The Wrong Box (with Lloyd Osbourne), 1889 novel
In the South Seas, 1890 travel book
The Wrecker (with Lloyd Osbourne), 1892 novel
Catriona, 1893 novel
Island Nights' Entertainments, 1893 stories

The Ebb-Tide (with Lloyd Osbourne), 1894 novel
The Amateur Emigrant, 1895 travel book
Records of a Family of Engineers, 1896 biography
Weir of Hermiston, 1896 novel
St. Ives, 1897 novel
Our Samoan Adventure (with Fanny Van de Grift Stevenson), 1956 travel book
Cévennes Journal, 1978 travel book

ANTHOLOGIES

Collected Works of Robert Louis Stevenson. South Seas Edition. 32 vols. New York: Scribners, 1925.
Robert Louis Stevenson: Collected Poems. Ed. Janet Adam Smith. London: Rupert Hart-Davis, 1952.
The Letters of Robert Louis Stevenson. 8 vols. Eds. Bradford A. Booth and Ernest Mehew. New Haven, CT: Yale University Press, 1994.

BIOGRAPHY AND CRITICISM

Balfour, Graham. *The Life of Robert Louis Stevenson.* 2 vols. London: Methuen, 1901.
Bell, Ian. *Dreams of Exile: Robert Louis Stevenson, A Biography.* New York: Holt, 1993.
Calder, Jenni. *RLS: A Life Study.* London: Hamish Hamilton, 1980.
——, ed. *Stevenson and Victorian Scotland.* Edinburgh: Edinburgh University Press, 1981.
Chesterton, G. K. *Robert Louis Stevenson.* London: Hodder & Stoughton, 1927.
Daiches, David. *Robert Louis Stevenson and His World.* London: Thames & Hudson, 1973.
Eigner, Edwin M. *Robert Louis Stevenson and the Ro-*

mantic Tradition. Princeton, NJ: Princeton University Press, 1966.

Furnas, J. C. *Voyage to Windward: The Life of Robert Louis Stevenson.* London: Faber & Faber, 1952.

Hammond, J. R. *A Robert Louis Stevenson Companion.* London: Macmillan, 1984.

Mackay, Margaret. *The Violent Friend: The Story of Mrs. Robert Louis Stevenson.* New York: Doubleday, 1968.

Maixner, Paul, ed. *Robert Louis Stevenson: The Critical Heritage.* London: Routledge & Kegan Paul, 1981.

McLynn, Frank. *Robert Louis Stevenson: A Biography.* New York: Random House, 1994.

Noble, Andrew, ed. *Robert Louis Stevenson.* Totowa, NJ: Barnes & Noble, 1983.

Noble, Scott Allen. *Robert Louis Stevenson: Life, Literature, and the Silver Screen.* Jefferson, NC: McFarland, 1994.

Ricklefs, Roger. *The Mind of Robert Louis Stevenson.* New York: Arno Press, 1962.

Sandison, Alan. *Robert Louis Stevenson and the Appearance of Modernism.* New York: St. Martin's Press, 1996.

Smith, Janet Adam, ed. *Henry James and Robert Louis Stevenson: A Record of Friendship and Criticism.* London: Hart-Davis, 1948.

Swearingen, Roger G. *The Prose Writings of Robert Louis Stevenson: A Guide.* Hamden, CT: Archon. 1980.

SIGNET CLASSICS (0451)

Classics of
Good and Evil

The Picture of Dorian Gray: & Other Stories
by Oscar Wilde   526015

Perhaps one of the most famous stories in English
literature, this classic tale of good and evil has sent chills
down the spines of readers for over one hundred years. This
volume also contains the well-known allegories *Lord Arthur
Savile's Crime*, *The Happy Prince*, and *The Birthday of
the Infanta*.

Crime and Punishment
by Fyodor Dostoyevsky   527232

The struggle between traditional Orthodox morality and the
new "philosophical will" of the Eurocentric intellectual
class that sprouted in 19th century Petersburg are the potent
ideas behind this powerful story of a man trying to break
free from the boundaries imposed upon him by Russia's
rigid class structure.

Available wherever books are sold or at
signetclassics.com

S602

READ THE TOP 20 SIGNET CLASSICS

SIGNETCLASSICS.COM

Penguin Group (USA) Online

What will you be reading tomorrow?

Tom Clancy, Patricia Cornwell, W.E.B. Griffin,
Nora Roberts, William Gibson, Robin Cook,
Brian Jacques, Catherine Coulter, Stephen King,
Dean Koontz, Ken Follett, Clive Cussler,
Eric Jerome Dickey, John Sandford,
Terry McMillan, Sue Monk Kidd, Amy Tan,
John Berendt…

You'll find them all at
penguin.com

*Read excerpts and newsletters,
find tour schedules and reading group guides,
and enter contests.*

Subscribe to Penguin Group (USA) newsletters
and get an exclusive inside look
at exciting new titles and the authors you love
long before everyone else does.

PENGUIN GROUP (USA)
us.penguingroup.com

"The pages of ON THE ROAD tell us why Charles Kuralt is one of this nation's best journalists. He is eloquent and understanding, refreshing and in-focus."

THE SAN DIEGO TRIBUNE

★ ★ ★

"Mr. Kuralt sets the scene, then steps aside and lets his subjects do the talking. The voices ring true.... The stories give us glimpses into America that make us feel good about ourselves, no mean feat these days."

THE BALTIMORE SUN

"Kuralt seeks out that rare
American breed called
Unlikely Heroes."
DETROIT FREE PRESS

★ ★ ★

"His people are the heart and soul of America, and his stories
celebrate them—how they cling to their dreams, move to a
singular beat, and stare down adversity.... Gems of stories
about the uncommon common man."

THE ASSOCIATED PRESS

"Most of the small miracles that Kuralt unearths have to do with men and women dedicated to a craft, a goal, or a code of honor."

THE PHILADELPHIA INQUIRER

★ ★ ★

"A crazy quilt of America divided into nine thematic groupings reflecting, among other things, Kuralt's interest in unsung heroes, joshers, big dreamers, small-town life, popular culture, language, and disappearing technologies."

THE DENVER POST

On the Road

WITH

By CHARLES KURALT

Charles Kuralt

FAWCETT GOLD MEDAL • NEW YORK

A Fawcett Gold Medal Book
Published by Ballantine Books

Copyright © 1985 by CBS Inc.
Foreword and chapter introductions copyright © 1985 by Charles Kuralt

All rights reserved under International and Pan-American Copyright Conventions. This book, or parts thereof, may not be reproduced in any form without permission. Published in the United States by Ballantine Books, a division of Random House, Inc., New York, and simultaneously in Canada by Random House of Canada Limited, Toronto.

Designed by Helene Berinsky

Library of Congress Catalog Card Number: 85-6330

ISBN 0-449-13067-3

This edition published by arrangement with G. P. Putnam's Sons

Manufactured in the United States of America

First Ballantine Books Edition: October 1986
Sixth Printing: November 1989

Acknowledgments

In television news, you can't ever say "I" did a story. You always have to say "we." The reporter depends on the skill of others who set up the lights just so, make pictures, record sound, and edit tape. Making a book turns out to be much the same. I have depended heavily on Neil Nyren, editor and gentleman, for advice and consent, and upon several of my associates at CBS News for generous assistance. Of these, I wish to acknowledge, first and foremost, Bernard Birnbaum, an inspirational friend to me, and gadfly. Cathy Lewis and Steven Kaufman helped me enthusiastically with rechecking of facts and preparation of photographs, and Marcie Jacobs pitched in willingly where needed. These stories could never have been told in the first place, or told in this manner, without the contributions of Russ Bensley, Jimmy Wilson, Isadore Bleckman, Larry Gianneschi, Jr., Charles Quinlan, Tommy Micklas, Harold Gold, Louise Colon, Peter Freundlich, and many others who have had reason, down the years, to feel that the stories were as much theirs as mine. And I don't know what I'd have done without the patient help of Karen Beckers, who, by capably managing things in New York, freed me to go a-wandering.

Television journalism is no field to enter if you have intimations of immortality; one's best work vanishes at the speed of light, literally. To call some of it back from the ether and place it in the pages of a book is immensely satisfying, therefore, if only as evidence to some curious grandchild of what his grandfather did for a living. Note to that grandchild: I was lucky in the people I worked with.

Contents

3. POETS AND OTHERS 85

4. TALL TALES AND DREAMERS 131

6. PASSING THE TORCH 217

7. AMERICAN SUITE 257

8. HALLOWED GROUND 299

9. SEASONS 333

Foreword

I was a real reporter once, but I was not suited for it by physique or temperament. Real reporters have to stick their noses in where they're not wanted, ask embarrassing questions, dodge bullets, contend with deadlines, and worry about the competition. In my youth, I did all these things, while trying to figure out an easier line of work.

In 1966, I dropped by the office of the President of CBS News, Fred Friendly. "Why don't you let me wander around the country and do some feature stories?" I asked.

Fred Friendly was a hard-news man. He hated feature stories. "If you want to do feature stories," he said, "go do them in Vietnam." I had just returned from Vietnam and knew I didn't want to do that. "No thanks," I said. He sent me off to cover an expedition to the North Pole.

When I got back, I found that Fred Friendly had quit his job in a dispute over hard-news coverage. He had been replaced by Richard S. Salant. I went to see Salant. I asked, "Why don't you let me wander around the country and do some feature stories?" He was distracted by the work piled up on his desk. "All right," he said without looking up. "Keep the budget low." I got out of town before he could change his mind.

I haven't had an assignment from that day to this. For story ideas I rely on dumb luck and letters from viewers. I have moseyed back and forth across the country, pausing in every part of every state, with CBS paying all the bills. My bosses, preoccupied with coverage of politics, wars, and calamities, don't even know where I am. They don't *care* where I am.

I have tried to go slow, stick to the back roads, take time to meet people, listen to yarns, notice the country-side go by, and feel the seasons change. I have attempted to keep "relevance" and "significance" entirely out of all the stories I send back. If I come upon a real news story out there On the Road, I call some real reporter to come cover it.

I return to New York each weekend to work on *Sunday Morning*, a program I feel at home with. Two or three times I've left the road to anchor some other program for a period of weeks or months. It never worked out. People take one look at me on their television sets and know I'm not an anchorman. On the Road, there's an advantage to being fat and bald. The pig farmer in Illinois to whom I'm talking about his corn crop sees the lights and the camera and, never having been on television before, gets nervous. But then he sees me and thinks, "Well, if that fellow can look like that and talk the way he does, then I can just be myself." Which is what I'm hoping he'll be, of course.

Izzy and Larry help put people at their ease. Izzy is Isadore Bleckman, the On the Road cameraman for most of these years. Larry is Larry Gianneschi, Jr., the sound-man. Izzy and Larry are the best I've ever seen at shoot-ing great pictures and sound without intruding on the situation. They are good friends and I could pay them other compliments, but there is no greater compliment you can pay a professional camera crew than to say they do beautiful work without anybody much noticing how they do it.

We feel we have the best jobs in journalism. We are out there now, leaving the motel parking lot with the sun coming up. We have just plugged in the coffee pot. Izzy is driving the bus. Larry is in the back, tinkering with his gear. I am looking at the road map to figure out which way we'll go today. We have a story we're headed toward, but we hope we'll never get there; we hope we'll stumble across something more interesting along the way. There's a long road ahead of us, and we don't know where we'll be spending the night.

ON THE ROAD
WITH
CHARLES KURALT

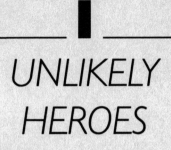

UNLIKELY
HEROES

F ifty miles down a dirt road in Wyoming one time, the old bus suffered two flat tires, which was one flat tire too many. We sat there for an hour wondering what to do about it before a rancher came along in his pickup truck. "Looks like you boys need some help," he said. He took us to a gas station on the highway, waited until the flats were fixed, drove us back to the bus, and helped us jack up the wheels and change the tires. By then it was getting dark. He said, "Nothing to do but take you boys home with me, I guess." His wife cooked us elk steaks for dinner, tucked us under warm quilts for the night, and sent us off full of flapjacks and sausage the next morning. Her husband followed us to the highway to make sure we didn't have any more flat tires. I don't know what he planned to do with those twenty-four hours, but he ended up giving most of them to some stranded strangers.

To read the front pages, you might conclude that Americans are mostly out for themselves, venal, grasping, and mean-spirited. The front pages have room only for defense contractors who cheat and politicians with their hands in the till. But you can't travel the back roads very long without discovering a multitude of gentle people doing good for others with no expectation of gain or recognition. The everyday kindness of the back roads more than makes up for the acts of greed in the headlines. Some people out there spend their whole lives selflessly. You could call them heroes.

The Free Doctor

(LINCOLN, MISSOURI)

It's not quite sunup yet in Lincoln, Missouri, but there's already a light in the window of Calamity Jane's Antique Shop, and the old store is full of people. They come early and take a number and take a seat. They're all waiting to see the doctor. To keep his expenses down, Dr. Richard T. Nuckles rents a little room in the back of Calamity Jane's. Here in these plain surroundings, he treats his neighbor's ailments. And he collects his fees.

★ ★ ★

DOCTOR: Okeydoke... three dollars all told.

   Three dollars, all told. Dr. Nuckles is not a high-priced doctor.

WOMAN: How much?
DOCTOR: One dollar. Plenty. Thank you ... Okay, a dollar.

   Dr. Nuckles charges you only for the medicine he dispenses. If he figures you can't afford it, then he doesn't charge you anything.

MAN: Sometimes we give him a tip, we get bighearted and give him a tip. [*Laughs*] Buy him a cup of coffee—
SECOND MAN: We feel ashamed.
MAN: Yeah—yeah, just kind of feel ashamed.

The doctor's fee is a dollar or two. Or three at the most. We're used to doctors on their way to becoming millionaires. I told Dr. Nuckles that I hardly knew what to make of him.

DOCTOR: I'm not in it for the money—I tell 'em I expect I could have been a millionaire long as I've practiced, if I wanted to. But I didn't want to. I ain't trying to be somebody good, I'm just trying to help my fellow man.

Much of his small income doesn't even go into the bank. It goes into the icebox. He is paid in buttermilk, and butter.

DOCTOR: Oh, my gracious, look at that. Boy! That looks good. What is it?
WOMAN: It's apple strudel—
DOCTOR: Apple strudel—
WOMAN: Without any sugar in it.

He is paid in apple strudel, and in the deep affection of people he has known and tended to all his life.

DOCTOR: I'll work on that all right. [*Laughs*]
WOMAN: I'll bring you some more next time.
DOCTOR: Thank you.
KURALT [*to doctor*]: Do you get a lot of produce?
DOCTOR: A lot of produce—I get everything. Fish, rabbit ... quail, duck, wild turkey, coon ... gooseberries, blackberries, pecans ... chicken—all of it, and I love it. It's better than what you could buy. I'd rather have it than money!

Dr. Nuckles does more than practice medicine. He doctors people. There's a difference.

DOCTOR: Pitting edema, pressure edema, they call it.
MAN: This leg is all right.

DOCTOR: Not as bad, no. When it's just in one leg, that shows it's not a general condition like your heart or your kidneys. If it was, it'd be both.

Richard T. Nuckles follows in the tradition of his father, who was a country doctor, and his uncle, who was a country doctor. We are all grateful for modern medicine, and grateful for modern doctors; we're less haunted by illness because of them. But still we feel the loss of men like Richard Nuckles. Back when America was a baby, bouncing west in the lap of history, it was doctors like Doc Nuckles who saw us through our fevers and set our broken bones and held our hands. They got, in payment, only what we could give. And they always gave more than they got. It's still that way in Lincoln, Missouri.

DOCTOR: I may not get all of you picked up, but I'll pick up part of you ... Now—I felt a few of 'em turn loose in there—

Complicated cases he may send to the hospital in Sedalia. But if you don't really need an operation, this doctor never recommends one.

DOCTOR: —And he's got some enlarged tonsils, and as he gets older, he won't have near as much trouble with 'em anyway, and I sure wouldn't take 'em out. He needs 'em. I think he needs 'em.

For this advice, since it was to do nothing, he charged nothing. Dr. Nuckles rents Calamity Jane's back room— she's really Jane Neeley—for seven dollars and fifty cents a week. Jane Neeley knows how much his patients need him.

JANE: This whole area is mostly retired people, and they're on a fixed income and everything keeps going up and up—
KURALT: Everything but doctor's fees.
JANE: Well, I think he lowers his. [*Laughs*]
KURALT [*to doctor*]: I wonder if other doctors don't sometimes get irritated with you.
DOCTOR: I'm sure they must. I'm sure they must, and I'm surprised I haven't heard from 'em. But I haven't so far—they might be gnashing their teeth—but I don't tell them what to charge, and they can't tell me what I can charge, so there you are. [*Laughs*]

When the waiting room is finally empty, Dr. Nuckles makes house calls. They're free, too. He's been doing this for forty-eight years, doctoring anybody who comes to him, for a dollar or two, or a mason jar of buttermilk, or a handshake of thanks. You'd think he'd be ready to hang up his black bag and sit in the sun somewhere. But he'll never do that.

DOCTOR: I don't know how to retire. I'm not a setter, I just can't set around and do nothing. I tell people that getting in a rocking chair is the worst thing they can do when they retire. If I even mention quitting out here, they just come to tears—and I don't know what they'll do when I quit. It's gonna be an awful jolt, the way some of these doctors are charging.

How many people are there who think all the time about the needs of others? And about their own needs, not at all? Well, here is one.

The Bicycle Man

Every kid in Belmont, North Carolina, seems to be riding a bike, and that's the story I want to tell you next. The one thing kids want, and parents want to be able to give them, is a bike. But here in this little town, as elsewhere, there are parents who just can't afford to do it. It hurt Jethro Mann to see kids growing up without bikes. See, *he* grew up without a bike.

★ ★ ★

JETHRO MANN: They didn't leave you a bicycle?
CHILDREN: No, no.

And so, while Jethro Mann knows he can't find the solution to everything that's wrong in the world, he decided he could do something about this.

MANN: Let's see if we can get one for you.
CHILD: All right.

In his garage, with broken bikes that he repaired, he started a sort of "lending library" of bicycles.

MANN: Somebody want to ride this bike?

Any kid can have one by just signing it out.

CHILD: Got a bike.
MANN: You're welcome.
CHILD: See y'all later.
MANN: Be careful.

Jethro Mann has about thirty-five of them now, all sizes, all fixed up by him.

KURALT: I notice they're all pretty careful to check 'em out.
MANN: Yes. We have a little system here. It's the honor system. If they fail to bring it back in this afternoon,

tomorrow they don't get to ride or they don't get to ride but a little while. [Laughs] So, they're pretty nice about bringing them back. And we try to use this as a learning situation for them, teach them how to be responsible for something, teach them that if they'll take care of other people's things they can't help but take care of their own. It works out pretty good.

Jethro Mann's garage is filled with parts of bicycles rescued from wrecked bikes or bikes thrown away by people who can afford to throw a bike away. And outside, his garage is a pile of thrown-away bikes waiting to be salvaged so some kid can have a bike to ride.

KURALT: Looks to me like you don't just repair bicycles; you *construct* bicycles here. [Laughs]
MANN: Well, that's about right. I buy bicycles—or I get them. Now, here's a little bicycle. This one is all together. This shows you what people throw away. The only thing this bicycle needs is a bolt here on the handlebars and two wheels and a chain on it. There's nothing wrong with it. This was an expensive bicycle.

Jethro Mann repairs the bikes for little kids, but this may be the most important part: he teaches little kids to repair the bikes for littler kids.

MANN: Let the air out now and mash it down a bit.

This is the strongest memory we carried away from Mr. Mann's garage: Keith Henderson, eleven, fixing a flat for Courtney Williams, six.

MANN: All right. You're in business. What do you say?
COURTNEY WILLIAMS: Thank you.
MANN: And you're welcome.
KEITH HENDERSON: You're welcome.

MANN: Turn it over for him. [*Laughs*] All right, sir. You have a good day.

Bicycle mechanics is not the only thing that is being taught here, as you can see.

MANN: I think a lot of times that politeness is a reflection. This is my way of thinking about it. Sometimes the children will treat you kind of the way you treat them. I found that to be true all along the way. And the things that we say to the children, we have to live up to. So, I find myself having to go pretty far out on a limb sometimes to provide when they come up and ask, because I already told them that if they ask in the right way, they'll get things. [*Laughs*]
So, it's a two-way thing. Mrs. Reid, who runs a store up here, said, "Mr. Mann," said, "You are doing a good job with the children." Said, "You have them correcting *me* now." Said, "If I ask them to do something and I don't say thank you, they'll say, 'You're welcome.'" [*Laughs*] So, I say, "Just keep it up." We're real proud.

Along toward suppertime every evening, the bicycles return. And the children who signed them out carefully sign them carefully back in. Jethro Mann has a full-time job, by the way, working for the state. He gives all his spare time to this. You can't get to know him without wondering whether you would have the patience to do what he is doing, or the money. I asked him if this didn't cost him most of his money.

MANN: Yes, a good bit of it. But I don't have many vices, so, this is about my only vice. [*Laughs*] I enjoy spending this that I would be spending on other things in a way that'll be helpful to somebody.

When it gets dark each night and the kids go home, Jethro Mann goes in for his own supper. But he'll be out here later, probably, working on the bicycles, as he does very often until one or two o'clock in the morning.

MANN: I look at it this way. I have had a pretty good life myself and I'm not apt to have very much more. But whatever I do have, I hope it will contribute to somebody else's welfare. And this is what I try to do.

[*Dog barking, children saying goodnight, going home*]

Good night, Mr. Mann.

Agatha Burgess

(BUFFALO, SOUTH CAROLINA)

The mill town of Buffalo, South Carolina, has a population of 1641. On the hill above it lives a woman who feels a kind of responsibility for the other 1640. Agatha Burgess is a widow-lady, as they say, who spends her day in the kitchen—all day. She's up every morning, cooking, at five o'clock.

BURGESS: I hit the floor and I come in here and I start working! I've got everything ready to go.

Her corn muffins have been well known to the town for more than fifteen years. After she puts the muffins in the oven, and checks the dressing for the turkey, she starts working on the biscuits. She does this every day. She feeds anybody who wants to come to her kitchen to eat. She doesn't make any money at it, and she doesn't care.

KURALT: When you were a young woman, did you have any idea that someday you'd be doing a thing like this?
BURGESS: Well, you know, I always wanted to be a person that lived by the side of the road, and be a friend to man. I have always wanted that. I've never wanted a big, fine home, I'm just satisfied like I am. I know you probably have a big, fine home—I don't want

your big, fine home—I'm glad you got it. And I can enjoy and just be happy that you have it. But me, I'm fine. Got what I want. I always get everything I want—but I know *what* to want!

She's done all this cooking, every day, five days a week, for fifteen years, all by herself. This one day, what with us getting in the way and all, she fell behind.

BURGESS: I believe you better stir my rice over there— I don't have time. See? I've got time for you now . . . Does it need water?
KURALT: I don't think so, Ms. Burgess.
BURGESS: Okay.
KURALT: Isn't this too much for one person to do, really?
BURGESS: That's why I'm asking you to do it!

It is not often in this world that you meet a person who could be called saintly. The word, however, fairly describes Agatha Burgess. She has assigned herself the daily duty of having meals on wheels prepared by eleven A.M. for fifteen local shut-ins, people she doesn't even know. They

pay, if they can afford it, two dollars a meal. You'll have to decide for yourself whether they get their money's worth.

BURGESS: This is peach cobbler.
MAN: Oh, it looks delicious.
BURGESS: I believe I'm giving this one turkey. And this is the rice, and this is the corn.
KURALT: It's fresh corn, huh?
BURGESS: Mm-hmm. And then the beans, and the gravy, the dressing, now corn muffin and the biscuit.
KURALT [*laughs*]: For two dollars, huh?

Volunteers come around to her house to put the meals on wheels and see that they are distributed into the community. All that happens by eleven o'clock in the morning. But Agatha Burgess's day is just beginning. By noon, cars and trucks start pulling up outside her house by the side of the road and people come in, all sorts of people. Mill workers and judges, and truck drivers, and the guy who runs the Ford agency, and they all crowd into Agatha Burgess's kitchen and dining room. She feeds anybody who comes to the door and she makes them feel welcome in the warmth of her two small rooms. She encourages them to fill their plates, to go back for seconds, if they wish. And for all this she charges $2.75. She knows that's too much for some people, and those people she doesn't ask for anything.

BURGESS: I'm not out to make money. I don't have any money, but I'm not making any money.
KURALT: Well, then, why do you keep doing it?
BURGESS: I love it. This guy asked me the other day, he said, "Miss Burgess, why don't you stop and rest?" I said, "What would I have to live for?" Wouldn't have anything to live for. Because these people coming every day, they mean so much to me. I just fall in love with people.

When the meal is over, when the last crumb of peach cobbler is finished, the guests put their money in a box on the side table, paying their own bills and making their own change. Isn't she afraid that people will steal from the box?

BURGESS: My sister told me, said, "One day you're going to be sorry. Somebody's going to rip you off." I said, "No. God's always took care of me." And I want to tell you one thing, if they bother that little box, He's going to take care of *them*! [*Kuralt laughs*] And He will. He'll get 'em.

She's been up since five o'clock. She's been doing this for fifteen years. She is eighty years old. When she finishes doing the dishes, she'll start her baking for tomorrow. She won't get out of the kitchen until ten o'clock tonight. She can't imagine living her life otherwise.

It all depends on what you want. What she always wanted was to live in a house by the side of the road and be a friend to man.

The North Platte Canteen

(NORTH PLATTE, NEBRASKA)

We came to North Platte to look for the place where a miracle happened, but time goes by. Urban renewal got here first. The old Union Pacific depot is gone, the station hotel is gone, and the seedy bars that used to line Front Street—but we knew this must be the place.

What brought us here was a letter from Nancy Green of Nantucket, Massachusetts. She wrote to me, "In 1944, my husband, Conrad Green, and I were crossing the United States in a troop train. He was going out on a Navy carrier from San Francisco as damage control officer. We boarded the train in Miami, and were three days with cold box lunches, not even coffee for breakfast, when the conductor told us at a stop to get off. We went into the train shed, which turned out to be filled with hot coffee and all kinds of hot food. When we tried to pay for it, they said no . . . I know I shall always remember the people of North Platte, Nebraska, with tremendous gratitude."

It is something worth remembering. Every day from 1942 to 1945, as many as ten thousand servicemen and women came through North Platte on the troop trains on their way to war. How many were there in all? Six million? Eight million? The people of North Platte and of the small towns around here—Elk Creek and Buffalo Grove and Lodgepole and Dry Valley—met every train, fed every soldier and sailor, and never sent a bill to anybody. That sounds impossible, but it happened. Jessie Hutchens and Edna Neid remember. They worked at the canteen side by side every day. And more intensely than anybody else,

Rose Loncar remembers. She was one of the original miracle workers.

★ ★ ★

ROSE LONCAR: We were sort of caught in the middle of the country. There was a war going on one side of us and on the other side of us, our boys were leaving, and here we sat, frustrated. We wanted to do something, too. So one day they were shipping our boys across, the boys from—where was it, 134th?

JESSIE HUTCHENS: National Guard.

EDNA NEID: The 134th.

LONCAR: The National Guard, and word got out that they were going to come through Nebraska. Well, Lordy, everybody that had anybody that knew anybody that was in the service was down at that station with cookies and candy and what have you. Waited all darn day, and the train comes in way late. And when the train came in, it wasn't our boys; it was the Kansas boys. So, after everybody was kind of over their sad, sunken feeling, they says, "Aw, to heck with it." So they gave the stuff to the Kansas boys, with hugs and tears and what have you, total strangers. And that's how the thing started.

KURALT: With all these thousands of soldiers and sailors coming through every day, what happened when you ran out of food?

HUTCHENS: We didn't!

LONCAR: I don't know—you have to go back to the Bible where He fed the multitude with five loaves of bread. So help me, Hannah, I don't know.

HUTCHENS: We never ran out.

LONCAR: We never said, "Now, sorry, we're all out." I remember one time when Stapleton community up north there—it was during pheasant season—they all organized a great big pheasant hunt, and let me tell you, they brought pheasants in dishpans, in bushel baskets—

NEID: Bushel baskets.

left: Rose Loncar, center: Jessie Hutchens, right: Edna Neid

LONCAR: —fried up. And this chairman, whoever was in charge, saved all the tail feathers. We had them in jars on the tables, and I tell you, it was just like Yankee Doodle Dandy. Every soldier had a feather in his hat when he left. It was just something else. But that was the least of it, though. It was the people. The people from these little towns like Hershey, Maxwell. I don't think there are six hundred people in Maxwell, but you'd think there was nine thousand when they came with their baskets of food and stuff. And as far as Colorado, and as far as the Kansas line. Those people—you can't describe them. People wouldn't believe it, but there's that kind of people in the country. That's Nebraska.

HUTCHENS: Everyone was involved.

LONCAR: I don't think there's a soul within two hundred miles around in this territory at that time that wasn't somehow or other giving, doing or something. North Platte couldn't have lasted one week working by itself.

NEID: We had a hundred and twenty-some towns.

LONCAR: As far west as almost to the Wyoming border.

NEID: From Arcadia, Ansley, Atkinson, Stromsburg, Brady...

KURALT: What kind of food did they bring?

LONCAR [*reading from one day's register*]: Eleven birthday cakes, nineteen cakes, fifty-seven and a half dozen cookies, eight pounds of butter, sixty-one eggs, twenty-seven pounds of coffee, fourteen quarts of salad dressing, eight quarts of relish, and seventy-three fried chickens. That's just a little town. And Mack, he had a Sunshine Dairy here. He'd be there with that little truck of his, and he'd have not one milk shake, he'd probably have fifty milk shakes sitting there ready to pass out to the boys.

And this one boy, Gene Slattery, he was about eleven years old. He'd go to all the farm sales, and when they were auctioning cattle, he'd get up there and take his shirt off his back and auction it off. Somebody'd buy it, and whatever he'd get—of course, he got his shirt back biggest share of the time. Now he's a married man with a family of his own; lives here in the neighborhood. But that was his war effort. Now I take a community about, oh, west of Ogallala. They came—what was it, Edna—once a month?

NEID: Big Springs.

HUTCHENS: I think it was the third Wednesday every month.

LONCAR: Their specialty was homemade pies, and their husbands made them big trays so they could just slide them in. They'd have pies of every description, of every flavor: cream, sour cream, raisin pie, apple pie, cherry—any kind of pie you'd believe. And every boy that went out of there had a slab of pie. Can you imagine a dignified officer running out there to catch his train with that big slab of pie in his hand and a grin on his face!

HUTCHENS: We served officers. It didn't make no difference how high nor how low the men were, we served them, and rank didn't mean nothing to us. We fed them all. Still hear from one, fellow that I got—yeah, I gave him a birthday cake, but I sure had a lot of fun kidding him, and I still hear from him.

KURALT: It wasn't his birthday?

LONCAR: No, they'd get conscience-stricken, they'd write back.

HUTCHENS: No. He said it was. He said it was George's and George wasn't able to get off the train, so he'd just take it. And so, he still signs his name "George" whenever he writes to me.

LONCAR: There was a woman who worked there. Her son had been reported missing in action, and she was kind of tense, you know, waiting, and it was quite some time after that she got word that he was actually killed in action. Well, she was a dear friend to all of us, and she went home, stayed for a couple of days. She couldn't stand it. She had to come back. She took her turn in her job, worked right along—but there was bunch of airmen came in one day. This lady was Officer of the Day that day, and they were all standing around the piano real happy singing "Here we go, off into the wild blue yonder," and she's right in there with them singing that song with the tears running down her face, never letting on to any of those boys what the song meant to her. It was really touching. Many tears have been shed, and I—I tell you I can still—I can still shed them talking about it.

KURALT: It sounds as if you not only gave things to them, they gave things to you.

ALL: Oh, yeah. They did. They gave us more than we gave them, really. A lot more. They gave us much, much more.

KURALT: Look at all those names signed so long ago.

HUTCHENS: Yes. They all wanted to register. Boy, they didn't want to leave without registering.

LONCAR: There's Ohio, Wisconsin, Virginia, New York—

NEID: Connecticut.

LONCAR: —Connecticut, ah, all over the world, all over

the world. England, France, Germany and—all over, all over, all over.

NEID: You know, Rose—

LONCAR: What?

NEID: —I thought what I did for some other mother's son, that perhaps somebody would do for mine. He was in Iceland. And I was hoping that somebody would be kind enough to give him something. And I felt that I got paid for everything that I did for the boys.

It's all gone. The place where it happened, where the women of North Platte worked such long hours serving those plates and washing those dishes, is just a freight yard now, like any other freight yard. The small homesteads out in the country where farmers slaughtered their prize cattle and the farm wives baked pies all day to keep the canteen going are indistinguishable from any other homesteads. And when she goes shopping downtown in North Platte, Rose Loncar is not recognized as a heroine who once organized the care and feeding of an American multitude. It has been more than thirty years, after all, and the brittle hope of World War II has given way to the disillusionment of other wars. But everybody should have one shining moment to remember, the boys smiling and waving good-bye, going off to war with their pockets full of cookies and pheasant feathers in their hats.

LONCAR: I'd like to hear from all of them. Every one of them that's listening to this, just to see how many of them really still remember. And I know we'd get letters, many, many, many, many letters all the time.

KURALT: You're talking about six or eight million men and women.

LONCAR: I hope so. I hope so. I hope so. And if they ever have occasion to come past through this country, to stop in. We're going to have a miniature canteen set up in the museum. And come by. I'll probably be out there and serve them a cup of coffee and a cookie again someday.

The Liberator of Bulgaria

(NEW LEXINGTON, OHIO)

You will walk a long way through a lot of small-town cemeteries before you find an inscription as unlikely as the one that's on a grave in New Lexington, Ohio: MAC-GAHAN, LIBERATOR OF BULGARIA. Who? Liberator of what? And if MacGahan liberated Bulgaria, what's he doing in Maplewood Cemetery?

The library isn't much help. Barbara Jones, the editor of the *Perry County Tribune*, has a book about MacGahan, *The Liberator of Bulgaria*, but nobody in town can read it; it is written in Bulgarian.

And unlikeliest of all, there are Bulgarian dancers in the streets of this little southern Ohio county seat. It's a Bulgarian-American festival. I put the key question to editor Barbara James.

★ ★ ★

KURALT: Are there any Bulgarian-Americans that you know of in this whole county?

BARBARA JAMES: In this whole county, I don't know of a single one.

And tell me, Mayor Otis Huffman:

KURALT: Are there any Bulgarian-Americans in Perry County?

MAYOR OTIS HUFFMAN: Not that I know of.

Then what's going on here? Well, the dancers have come from Pittsburgh and Toledo to honor one of the more amazing and least known heroes of history.

Januarius Aloysius MacGahan, son of a Perry County farmer, got restless back in the 1860s, as farm boys will, and went off to Europe with the notion of becoming a dashing and gallant foreign correspondent. He certainly succeeded in that. He witnessed the fall of the Paris Commune. He was pursued by Cossacks a thousand miles across the desert of Central Asia. He covered the Carlist revolution in Spain, and sailed with an expedition to the Arctic, was sentenced to death twice and twice escaped.

And then in 1876—and here we come to the dancing in the streets of New Lexington, Ohio—in 1876, MacGahan went off to Bulgaria. His reports to the *London Daily News* about Turkish atrocities against the innocent Bulgarians outraged Queen Victoria, galvanized Europe, and forced the reluctant Czar of Russia to send armies across the Danube to free the Bulgarians from the Turks.

Januarius Aloysius MacGahan, riding along, found

throngs of Bulgarians kissing his boots and throwing flowers in his path. A Buckeye farm boy had changed the map of the Balkans.

MAYOR HUFFMAN: These Bulgarians tell me that any town of any size over there has a monument in their square honoring MacGahan.

A Bulgarian scholar named Vatralsky came to New Lexington in 1900 to lay a wreath and make a speech. He said: "Bulgaria and Ohio will never forget Januarius Aloysius MacGahan." And Bulgaria didn't, apparently. But Ohio did.

Today New Lexington is trying to make up for all those years of neglecting the town's most illustrious native son. The plain people of Perry County have invited costumed strangers to come to town and are giving them a plain Perry County welcome even if the visitors don't know quite what to make of it.

After a procession to the cemetery, the local folks listened respectfully to a prayer for MacGahan, even though they couldn't understand a word of it. Some kids from town sang "Amazing Grace."

"I once was lost, but now I'm found"—the words of that old American hymn were just right for the day when the amazing hero of Bulgaria, the farm boy-journalist-liberator, Januarius Aloysius MacGahan, became what he always should have been, an Ohio hero, too.

Pauli Murray

[Church bells ringing]

At the old antebellum Chapel of the Cross in Chapel Hill, North Carolina, the bell is ringing out. Let it ring. This is a story about reconciliation and triumph. The triumph belongs to Pauli Murray, who has spent her whole life, in a sense, struggling toward the sound of that bell.

And the triumph belongs to this church, which has been standing here since 1848, long enough to have seen a lot of history.

This is a story of triumph, but it begins with pain and disgrace. It begins, to speak plainly, with a rape. The rape was committed in the days before the Civil War by a wealthy young North Carolina lawyer named Sidney Smith. His victim was a young slave woman. Nothing unusual about that in the sorry annals of slavery. But in this case the baby who was born, a beautiful octoroon child named Cornelia, was recognized by the white family.

Sidney Smith's sister, Mary Ruffin Smith, listened to her conscience. And her conscience told her that this child, born a slave, was also, after all, her niece. When the time came, Mary Ruffin Smith, the white slaveowner, brought Cornelia, the slave child niece, to this church to be baptized. The record says: "Baptized, 1854, December twentieth, five servant children belonging to Miss Mary Ruffin Smith." And among their names is listed:

"Cornelia, age ten."

[The choir sings]

On Sundays, Cornelia used to sit up there in the balcony during services, standing to sing with the rest of the congregation, "O God, our help in ages past, Our hope for years to come." She was twenty-one when the Union Army came through here and set her free. She married a black Union veteran from Pennsylvania, who built a house for them to live in. It was the house Pauli Murray grew up in. She is Cornelia's granddaughter, part black, part white, part American Indian, probably. Her grandmother taught her, as she grew up, to be proud of all those things and she never forgot.

She left the house to become a fighter for civil rights as long ago as 1938, to become a lawyer and a professor of law, poet and author. And then four years ago, at the age of sixty-two, to become something else. She entered the Episcopal Seminary to study for Holy Orders. Last January she was ordained the first black woman priest in the Episcopal Church.

Did I say black? She would say black and white. African and Irish. Today at the old Chapel of the Cross, at the very altar where her grandmother was baptized as a slave, the Holy Eucharist is to be celebrated for the first time by the Reverend Doctor Pauli Murray.

★ ★ ★

MURRAY: The Holy Gospel of our Lord Jesus Christ, according to Luke.
CONGREGATION: Glory be to thee, Lord Christ.

The Bible Pauli Murray is reading from belonged to her grandmother Cornelia. The lectern the Bible is resting on was given in the memory of the woman who owned Cornelia, Mary Ruffin Smith.

MURRAY: —And as ye would that men should do to you, do ye also to them, likewise.
RECTOR: Pauli, my dear sister in Christ.

The Rector of the Chapel of the Cross, the Reverend Peter James Lee, delivered his sermon today to Pauli Murray.

RECTOR: Those purple ribbons marking the place in your Bible recall another chapter in our common history. They came to you in 1944 with a box of flowers to mark your graduation from Howard University Law School, a gift from another Episcopalian, Eleanor Roosevelt. You are a woman. You are a Negro. That proud description for which you fought so valiantly and which you will not let passing fashion take from you. The Parish register of the Chapel of the Cross records your grandmother's baptism in an entry dated December twentieth, 1854, with these words. "Five servant children belonging to Miss Mary Ruffin Smith." Can those words now apply to each of us as we minister to the world and support one another? Is there a better description of the pilgrim people of Christ than servant children, who belong to one another?

MURRAY: The peace of the Lord be with you.

CONGREGATION: And also with you.

MURRAY [*to Kuralt*]: For me, what I was trying to communicate as I administered the bread was a lovingness for each individual who received the bread. And I went very slowly. Very often a priest may move right along the line. I didn't. I didn't care how long it took.

KURALT: Do you think your grandmother would have been pleased to have been there at that Communion service, maybe sitting in her old seat in the balcony and looking down on you holding Communion?

MURRAY: My grandmother was much closer than that. She was right behind me.

MAN: Welcome, sister.

MURRAY: And to you. [*To Kuralt*] I think reconciliation is taking place between individuals groping, reaching toward one another. And the six hundred people who packed that little chapel on Sunday were reaching out. I think this is what made it moving. It was not I as an individual. It was that historic moment in time, when I represented a symbol of the past, of the suffering, of the conflict, of one who was reaching out my hand, symbolically, and all of those behind me. And they were responding.

KURALT: Do you feel reconciled yourself with your own past? I mean, here all these crosscurrents of violence and pain of the South meet in you.

MURRAY: Yes, I know. I lived with it for sixty-six years. It's like riding wild horses. I am tempestuous. I am volatile. I have a tremendous amount of nervous energy. My friends say, "You wear out six people." I have a terrible temper, of which there is no worse. I am sensitive, aggressive, shy. I'm all these warring personalities, trying to stay in one integrated body, mind, and spirit. And there are days when I bless my ancestors. And there are other days when I look in the mirror and I say, "What hath God wrought!"

"In Christ there is no East or West," the old hymn goes, "in Him no South or North. But one great fellowship of love, throughout the whole wide earth." That is what Pauli Murray has been trying to say as civil rights struggler, lawyer, poet, and—here in this little chapel where her slave grandmother and her slaveowner great-great-aunt worshiped—as priest. She's been trying to say that there is no East or West, no North or South. That and one other thing: that there is no black or white, either.

MURRAY: I believe in reconciling the descendants of all the slaves and slaveowners of the South. And by now these genes have recirculated so that I suspect that if you put all the people of the United States end to end, according to true line blood relationship, we would all be in one long line. All of us. This is the fascinating thing about the South. Black, white, and red are related by blood and by culture and by history and by common suffering. And so what I am saying is look, let's level with one another. Let's admit we are related and let's get on with the business of healing these wounds. We're not going to heal them until we face the truth.

The Bird Lady

Every afternoon a frail old
woman leaves her house in a
modest block of St. Petersburg and pedals her tricycle
gallantly toward the city. She
wears a light smock, a straw
hat, and a beatific smile. And
wherever she goes, the birds
of St. Petersburg follow her.
Miss Esther Wright is known
as the Bird Lady.

All those years teaching school in Wisconsin, studying
art in Chicago, Miss Esther was seized by a divine dis-
content. She says she was not satisfied with her life. Now,
at seventy-five, she has found her career at last, and her
duty. It is to see that no living creature within the range
of her tricycle goes hungry even for a day.

★ ★ ★

MISS ESTHER WRIGHT: [*as she feeds a great flock of
birds*]: Everything gets hungry, rain or shine. [*Laughs*]
It's kind of a compulsion with me. It really is. I love
animals, just dearly. I feel so good with them. That's
the way to describe it. I feel good with them.

Miss Wright lives in poverty. Of her Social Security
payment, she pays two dollars a day for rent, less than

that for food. All the rest she spends on scraps for the cats and nuts for the squirrels and seeds for the birds.

WRIGHT: People think I'm crazy.

KURALT: Do they?

WRIGHT: Surely. Loony! And they treat me like that, too. In the beginning, people called the police. The police felt very friendly towards me, but they have to answer complaints. And they have to do their duty.

KURALT: What was the charge?

WRIGHT: Well, bird feeding. You see, that law is still on the books. But the judge was lenient. And all he did was to say, here it is in the book. And he read the city ordinance to me.

KURALT: About how you couldn't feed birds.

WRIGHT: That's right. But I had my birdfeed with me and I fed the birds on the way home.

No law of man can deter the Bird Lady now. Nor can people calling her names as she passes. Nor can traffic nor frailty nor threat of storm. Miss Esther Wright has found her role in life. And while she lives, she will play it.

[*Birds fly about her as she pedals down the street.*]

WRIGHT: I just keep on going. That's all. And I'm always glad I did. Sometimes I'm very weary. I make the trip and I'm glad I did it.

Mr. Misenheimer's Garden

(SURRY COUNTY, VIRGINIA)

We've been wandering the back roads since 1967, and we've been to a few places we'll never forget. One of them was on Route 10, Surry County, Virginia. We rolled in here on a day in the spring of 1972 thinking this was another of those little roadside rest stops. But there were flowers on the picnic tables. That was the first surprise.

And beyond the tables, we found a paradise, a beautiful garden of thirteen acres, bright with azaleas, thousands of them, and bordered by dogwoods in bloom, and laced by a mile of paths in the shade of tall pines. In all our travels, it was the loveliest garden I'd ever seen. It made me wonder how large a battalion of state-employed gardeners it took to keep the place up. The answer was it took only one man, and he was nobody's employee. Walter Misenheimer, a retired nurseryman, created all this in the woods next to his house, created it alone after he retired at the age of seventy. He was eighty-three when I met him and was spending every day tending his garden for the pleasure of strangers who happened to stop.

★ ★ ★

WALTER MISENHEIMER: I like people, and this is my way of following out some of the teachings of my parents. When I was a youngster, one of the things they said was, "If you don't try to make the world just a little bit nicer when you leave here, what is the reason for man's existence in the first place?" I have tried to give it to the state. The Parks Department says it is too small for them. The Highway Department says it is too big for them.

KURALT: What's going to happen to this place after you're gone?

MISENHEIMER: Well, I imagine that within a very few years, this will be undergrowth, or nature will take it over again.

KURALT: You mean, it's not going to survive?

MISENHEIMER: I doubt it.

KURALT: That's a terribly discouraging thing, isn't it?

MISENHEIMER: Well, that's the way I see it now.

We watched for a while as people enjoyed the beauty of Walter Misenheimer's garden. And we left, and a few years later somebody sent me a clipping from the Surry County paper. It said Walter Misenheimer had died. I wondered what would happen to his garden. I wondered whether the Virginia sun still lights the branches of the dogwood, which he planted there.

Well, it does. Some stories have happy endings. Walter Misenheimer's garden does survive, and so does his spirit, in Haeja Namkoong. It seems that she stopped by the garden just a few months after we did, eleven years ago.

HAEJA NAMKOONG: We slowed down and saw a sign and picnic tables and a lot of flowers blooming. We came to the picnic table, found a water spigot, helped ourselves, and we were sort of curious as to what this place was all about. Finally, we saw the old man sort of wobbling around and coming 'cross the lawn, saying "Hello," and just waving to us to stop. I guess he was afraid we were going to leave.

To please the old man, and herself, Haeja Namkoong stayed the afternoon with him, walking in his garden. It made her remember, she says, something she wanted once.

HAEJA: I grew up in a large city in Korea, and I have never really seen rice grow. I always dreamed about living in the country, about a small, little cabin in the wilderness, with lots of flowers. That's what I dreamed about, but I guess that was just childhood dreams.

When the sun went down that day, the young woman said good-bye to the old man and headed home to Boston, but the roadside Eden called her back. That is, Walter Misenheimer did. He phoned her, long distance, and asked her to come for a little while and help in the garden.

HAEJA: He was sort of pleading with me, "Please come down. Just help me for a couple of weeks."

A couple of weeks only, and then a few more, and then it was Christmas. Haeja Namkoong was twenty-six. She had no family. Neither did Walter Misenheimer and his wife.

HAEJA: From wildflowers to man-grown shrubberies, he taught me. I was interested in learning the whole thing. I was out here almost every day with him.

They became as father and daughter working in the garden, and in time Haeja Namkoong was married in the garden.

HAEJA: He was very proud to give me away. I guess he never thought, since he didn't have any children of his own, he would give someone away.

Brown earth was coaxed by the gentle old man into green growth and flowering red and pink and white. The earth rewards every loving attention it is paid. People repay such love, too, in memory.

HAEJA: I was very, very close to my mother. But other than my mother, I can't remember anyone that loved me so much and cared for me so much as Mr. Misenheimer.

The garden is still here. Walter Misenheimer died in 1979 and left it to Haeja Namkoong. She pays a caretaker, Ed Trible, to help keep it beautiful for anybody who passes by. Haeja and her husband and their children live in Richmond now, but they return on weekends to work in the garden.

HAEJA: So, knowing how much the garden meant to him, I want to keep it up and carry on.

Walter Misenheimer told me that he expected when he was gone the garden would soon be overgrown. He might have known better. His garden shows that something grows from seeds and cultivation. And if what you plant is love and kindness, something grows from that, too.

HAEJA: Look at this purple one.
CHILD: I like the red.
HAEJA: Aren't they pretty?

DIFFERENT
DRUMMERS

I love to read about the travels of those who wandered the country before me, de Tocqueville, Mark Twain, John Steinbeck, and all the rest. Each of them caught a little bit of the truth about America and wrote it down. Even the best of them never got it all into one book, because the country is too rich and full of contradictions. Newspaper columnists, on slow days, write columns about "the mood of America." That takes a lot of nerve, I think. The mood of America is infinitely complex and always changing and highly dependent on locale and circumstance. The mood of Tribune, Kansas, depends on whether that black cloud to the west becomes a hailstorm that flattens the wheat crop or passes harmlessly. The mood of Haines, Alaska, depends on whether the lumber mill is hiring. The mood of Altoona rises and falls with the fortunes of the high school football team. The mood of New York City is much affected by heat and rain and the percentage of taxis with their off-duty signs lighted at any given time. You can't get your thumb on America's mood. I never try.

Even the clearest-eyed observers of the country, like Alexis de Tocqueville, got into trouble by overgeneralizing. "As they mingle," de Tocqueville wrote, "the Americans become assimilated...They all get closer to one type." Right there, the great de Tocqueville stubbed his toe. The assimilation never came to pass; the "Melting Pot," so much written about, never succeeded in melting us. Americans are made of some alloy that won't be melted. To this day we retain a dread of conformity.

Henry Thoreau, who never traveled at all (except, as he said, "a good deal in Concord"), composed us a credo in 1854: "If a man does not keep pace with his companions, perhaps it is because he hears a different drummer. Let him step to the music which he hears...."

We admire de Tocqueville, but it was Thoreau we listened to.

The Horse Trader

(CUMBY, TEXAS)

Thanks to the Interstate Highway System, it is now possible to travel across the country from coast to coast without seeing anything. From the Interstate, America is all steel guardrails and plastic signs, and every place looks and feels and sounds and smells like every other place. We stick to the back roads, where Kansas still looks like Kansas and Georgia still looks like Georgia, where there is room for diversity and for the occurrence of small miracles.

I mean, you'd never have to slow down on Interstate 80 to let a herd of horses cross. Happens all the time on the country roads around Cumby, Texas. And since what we are looking for along the country roads are those old ornery virtues of cussedness and nonconformity, Cumby, Texas, is a pretty good place to start.

It's been said that if you have any affection for the Old West or a touch of larceny in your soul, or both, you'll get along fine with Ben K. Green.

★　★　★

BEN K. GREEN: That's the way about horses. One thing about having horses is that you'll always have a few gate and fence problems. They wouldn't feel good if they didn't cause you a little trouble now and then.
KURALT: Where did that little black horse come from?
GREEN: That's a stray. I don't know who she is or where

she came from. She showed up here in the pasture
a few days ago.

KURALT: She seems to be eating your oats all right.

GREEN: Yeah, and somebody will come along in a few
days that's missed her. They may have already missed
her and realized that the grass is good in the pasture
and they'll be a few days in finding her, you know.

KURALT: If you were trying to sell me that horse, what
would you find good to say about her?

GREEN: Well, I'd say she's a four-year-old and about fourteen hands high and would be ideal for a small rider,
or a kid. And she's a nice little short black mare with
small feet, and a pretty good pony. You know, something you'd be proud of.

KURALT: And about how much would you ask for a horse
like that?

GREEN: Oh, I'd ask a hundred and a half for her. I think
she's worth ninety dollars, but I'd be trying you, you
know. I doubt if she's got much breeding, but I
wouldn't tell you that.

KURALT: Now, suppose on the other hand you were trying to buy that little horse?

GREEN: Well, I'd say—I wouldn't be trying to buy her, but if I were—I'd say she's long-backed and short-shouldered and that her eyes didn't set out on the side of her head good enough and that she probably didn't have good enough feet to carry her weight and she had a short hindquarter. And just that I'd think she's a rather common kind of a horse that would be worth about sixty dollars. Now, would you rather I buy her from you or sell her to you? Huh?

KURALT: In your long career as a horse trader, did you ever get cheated?

GREEN: Oh, a million times. You get cheated all the time, and it sharpens you up, it's good for you. And while you're getting cheated, you're liable to learn a trick that you can use for maybe more than it cost you too. You know. But a man that's never been cheated trading horses didn't trade but once, you know.

We came away with the impression that it has been quite a while since anybody got the best of Ben Green in a horse trade. His neighbors all know about pickup trucks; Ben Green *knows* about horses.

The Carousel

(ROCHESTER, NEW YORK)

Dreamland Amusement Park is closed for the winter. Salt-water taffy stands are shuttered, no teenagers screaming on the roller coaster, the bumper cars all in their stalls, and at the merry-go-round, the exquisite carousel which has been right here since 1915, the horses are frozen in their classical posture, waiting for another spring.

But Dreamland is not deserted, not quite. In a basement woodshop, one man is working. He is George Long, the seventy-seven-year-old owner of the amusement park, and what he is doing is something nobody else in America is doing anymore. He is carving merry-go-round horses. It's as if this one man hasn't heard that the way you make merry-go-round horses these days is cast them out of aluminum or stamp them out of plastic or fiberglass. He is making horses for his carousel in the thoroughly obsolete way they were made by turn-of-the-century craftsmen, patiently, slowly, with basswood and chisel, and love.

★ ★ ★

KURALT: How long does it take you to finish a horse?
GEORGE LONG: From start to finish?
KURALT: Yes.
LONG: Must be probably eighty hours or so, including painting.

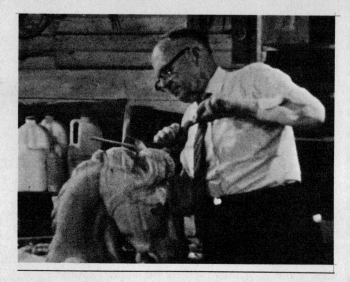

KURALT: Do you know anything about horses? Did you study the anatomy of the animal?

LONG: No, I haven't—only what I've seen on the merry-go-round year after year. Probably taken the ideas of the old carvers.

KURALT: What is there about the merry-go-round that seems to last down the ages? There's something appealing about it, must be.

LONG: I don't know. It's probably the age at which people ride. They never forget the experience of riding on the merry-go-round.

KURALT: Can you remember when you first rode the merry-go-round?

LONG: Oh, yes, yes. I remember when I tried to jump on, I was so small I couldn't get up to the platform so I just sat down and grabbed the horse's leg and rode around with her. [*Laughs*] It's a long time ago.

A modern metal merry-go-round horse can be stamped out in an hour. It takes George Long the better part of two weeks to make one. But his is a horse of a different color, and style, and craftsmanship. And after he applies that last of five coats of clear lacquer, his work is fit to take its place in the midst of a ring of other masterpieces created long decades ago by other masters, whose skill lives in him.

In George Long's office at Dreamland there hangs a photograph of a carousel which operated on this same spot in 1904, and in the center of the picture is the twelve-year-old ticket-taker of that year, George Long.

[*The carousel begins moving with music playing.*]

Sixty-six summers have passed since then. The children who rode then have grown up and had children of their own, who have also heard the music and reached out for the brass ring. And *those* children, now grown, bring their children back to the merry-go-round at Dreamland. It is a wondrous circle, and with George Long standing there watching the work of his hands fly by, you find yourself hoping that it goes on forever.

The Singing Mailman

(MAGOFFIN COUNTY, KENTUCKY)

[Sound of Moses Walters singing "What a Friend We Have in Jesus"]

Here on Cow Creek in Magoffin County, the postman doesn't ring twice—he doesn't even ring once. But nobody doubts when he's coming. That's Moses Walters, carrying the United States mail. Moses Walters rides a mule because a mule is the only conveyance that can be counted on to carry the mail and the mailman all the way to the end of Cow Creek. He sings because he just feels like singing. He's been riding a mule and singing, six days a week, since 1926, and the United States Post Office Department, which mostly rides around in red, white, and blue trucks, has long ago accustomed itself to the fact that on days when trucks are stuck in snowdrifts, the mail gets through on Cow Creek.

Moses Walters' day starts early at the post office in Hager, Kentucky, where he ties his mailbags on his mule, Julie. He has had several mules, and they've all been named Julie. Moses Walters is a man of inflexible routine.

The fewer changes in his life, the better he likes it. We would tell you how old he is, but he wouldn't tell us. He is old enough, he says, to keep his nose out of other people's business.

At ten minutes after eleven A.M., he arrives at the post office in Stella, Kentucky, and carefully ties Julie to the same fencepost. At Stella, he drops off some mail and picks up some more, part of it in cloth bags or "pokes."

★ ★ ★

KURALT: How do you tell the pokes apart?
WALTERS: Just by the looks of them, and I hang them on in order. They should brand them, or have their initials on them. That should be required, I think. Now this is the Reeds' poke out here. And this is the Adams'. And this is one of the Burtons', the Burton poke. This is Alsop poke.

Moses Walters would pause that long to talk, no longer. He carries more than pokes and packages; he carries a sense of mission, and he's not quite the anachronism you might think. We talked about that to Paul Smith, the rural delivery analyst of the regional post office.

KURALT: It comes as a surprise to me, and I think it will to most people, that there are still muleback routes in the United States Postal Service. How many of them are there?
SMITH: There are twenty-one now. This varies from time to time. In the spring, we look at the roads, and sometimes we take muleback routes out and then find that we have to put them back again when fall comes.
KURALT: Why do you have them at all?
SMITH: Well, this is a communications system for all the people. At one time all of our routes were muleback or horseback routes, and as the roads improved and vehicle equipment became better, we took them out

and put vehicles in. But still, there are some remote areas where we cannot serve the people with vehicles on a year-round basis, so we have to resort to mules.

Folks along Cow Creek wondered what in the world we wanted to take pictures of Moses for. For more than forty years, they have seen him every day, and heard the same hymns echoing behind him after he has passed. He's ordinary to them, so they have not stopped to consider that it takes a lot of people to make a country work, and that one of them might be an old man on a mule.

[*Moses Walters rides around a bend, singing.*]

Bricks

Ever wonder how bricks are made? Well, one way is the way the Pine Hall Brick and Pipe Company does it: twenty-five thousand fully automated bricks an hour. A quarter of a million a day.

There is another way, George Black's way. It requires no console with flashing lights, no machinery, no conveyor belts. It requires only a mule hitched up to a mud mill in his backyard in Winston-Salem, North Carolina, and the sure hands and certain knowledge of a master craftsman. George Black is ninety-two. He made his first brick just this same way in the year 1889.

★ ★ ★

BLACK: Well, I've been making bricks all these years and still going to make some more yet. Yes, siree. A little more sand in there.

KURALT: There is something ancient and elemental in this. For what other man can you think of who has made his whole life out of water and earth and fire?

BLACK [*in front of the R. J. Reynolds Tobacco Factory*]:
R. J. Reynolds come out on his horse—he rid a horse,
you know, all the time. And he come out and ordered
these bricks. His first order was five hundred thousand, and the next time he come out he ordered a
million. Yeah, yeah.

KURALT: That would be enough to scare me, I think.

BLACK: It gave a lot of us a whole lot of work. For a
dollar and a half a day. Yes, siree. Made six at a time.
Put them out on the board and put them in the kiln
and burned them.

KURALT: And ended up with a million and a half?

BLACK: Yep, yeah, that's what we ended up with. [*At the
Old Salem Restoration*] These bricks that we're
walking on, they was made around thirty-five or forty
years ago.

George Black was eleven years old when his father
died, and he and his brother, fourteen, had a talk.

BLACK: He said, "George, we're not going to get to go to school. We're going to have to work for our living." He said, "Let's learn the trade that'll make the most money out of work. That's what we're going to have to do. So we're not going to get to go to school." He said, "If we don't go to school, say if we stand up, haul ourselves up and make men out of ourselves, if we don't know A from B," he says, "we can make somebody call us 'Mr. Black' someday." So that's what we done. Yeah.

And now, at ninety-two, Mr. Black cannot take a walk in his hometown without seeing the work of his hands, the bricks he has made, one by one, for more than eighty years. They are here in this bank, there in that church, there in that school. The cornerstones record more than the construction of buildings. They speak the life of a man.

Misspelling

They say this is an age of conformity, but wherever we go, we keep finding refreshing evidence of individualism, even on the roadside signs. You know that no stuffy conformist painted this sign. PARK HEAR. It is spelled wrong, but it does tell you where to park: "hear"! MACHANIC ON DUTY. FRONT END REPAIRES. This mechanic may not be good at spelling, but he's probably fine at making "repaires." Anything which can be sold, we have found, can also be misspelled... ANTIQES... anything from antiques to souvenirs... SOUVINERS... especially souvenirs... SOUVENIERS. How *do* you spell souvenirs? SOUVENIRES. This is the American answer: just exactly as you please!

We have found our country's spelling to be horrible, and entirely excusable. ACERAGE FOR SAIL—we may

excuse this man because he's a farmer, not a school-teacher. RASBERIES—so is this man. SPEGHETTI AND PIZZA—and this man because he's probably from across the sea. BEER AVAILALBE HERE—and this man because, like as not, he was sampling his own product while he painted the sign. BAR DRINKS 55¢ ANEYTIME—that can blur anybody's memory of how to spell.

Some misspellings are quiet and private, like this one in the back room of an Oklahoma diner: BE CURTEOUS AND SMILE. Others are spectacular like this one in Oregon—[*huge lighted sign*] BAR AND RESTRUANT—and proclaim their error proudly for half a mile in every direction. HUNGARY? MARION'S SNACK SHACK 6 MILES. If you are hungary enough, of course, it doesn't matter much.

NO TRESSPASSING. We like the snappy rude signs. NO TRASPASSING. You get the idea. NO TRUSTPASSING. Keep out. NO BOATS ALOUD—silent boats okay, but no boats aloud.

The point about American spelling is that, however awful, it serves the cause of individualism, and serves the purpose. We read this one at a gas station in Tennessee: NO CONGRETATING ON THE DRIVEWAY. VIALTORS WILL BE PROSCUATED. Well, naturally we didn't congretate. Fearing proscuation, we paid for our gas and pulled right out of there and headed on down the road.

The Canoe Maker

(BIGFORK, MINNESOTA)

Watch Bill Hafeman, a jaunty man with a hawk feather in his hat, stride through the North Woods where he has been at home for sixty years, and think of Longfellow's "Song of Hiawatha."

> Thus the Birch Canoe was builded
> In the valley, by the river,
> In the bosom of the forest;
> And the forest's life was in it.

★ ★ ★

BILL HAFEMAN: Ah, it's a beautiful one.

Bill Hafeman came up here with his wife, Violet, in 1921 and built his first canoe with only a knife and an ax so they'd have some way of getting to Bigfork, the nearest settlement, fifteen miles down the river. Every canoe he built was a little better than the one before. Now he teaches his grandson-in-law, Ray Boessell, the craft of  which he has become the world's acknowledged master.

HAFEMAN: Now she's still lined up pretty good, pretty good.

He is eighty-three. He's faced down wolves and survived blizzards, and come to know the North Woods better than any other man alive. And all of that, somehow, goes into each canoe.

KURALT: Why did you pick such a lonely place to live, in the first place?

HAFEMAN: I wanted to live in a wild country like the Indians did. I thought, now that would be a free life. It'd be free. You could work as you wanted to and nothing holding you back. I didn't want to live in a city where you go to work by a whistle, come home by a whistle. I didn't like all that stuff. So I thought, "I'll go out to the woods and live in the woods." And we done it.

KURALT: It must have been pretty hard in the beginning up here, all alone?

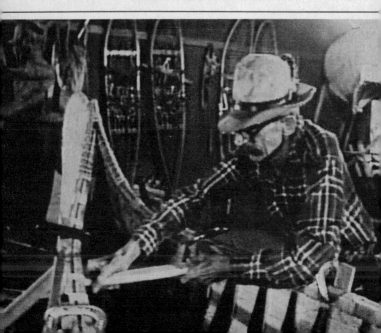

HAFEMAN: No, not too bad. Violet and I, we knew how to live—that is, to pick berries. There was everything growed here. This was really a Garden of Eden. Everything growed here. There was the wild rice for your grain, and there was the meat, venison, fish, berries, fruit. Oh, we had everything to live on. I'd shoot deer. A butcher would have starved to death in Bigfork. Everybody shot his own meat. So we got along that way.

By giving up the ease and comfort he and Violet might have had living in town, Bill Hafeman gained the long, satisfying peace of the woods and the knowledge of how to do things supremely well. He does it without nails or any hardware, the way Hiawatha did, with a result so beautiful it almost brings tears to your eyes.

> Thus the Birch Canoe was builded
> In the valley, by the river,
> In the bosom of the forest;
> And the forest's life was in it.
>
> All its mystery and its magic,
> All the lightness of the birch-tree,
> All the toughness of the cedar,
> All the larch's supple sinews;

HAFEMAN: Ah, she's a good one! Seams are tight. And it's a good job.

> And it floated on the river
> Like a yellow leaf in Autumn,
> Like a yellow water-lily.

Bill Magie

(MOOSE LAKE, MINNESOTA)

The problem with trying to tell you about Bill Magie, who lives up on Moose Lake in a comfortable shack with his old dog, Murphy—the problem is that his life has been too rich and gaudy to get it all in. So we'll leave out the part about his getting kicked out of Princeton for inviting Marilyn Miller of the Ziegfeld Follies to the junior prom, and the part about his friendship with F. Scott Fitzgerald and the Vanderbilt boys. How he came to the North Woods to be a guide is just too long a story. And we can't get into the time he guided Margaret Mead into the Boundary Waters Wilderness, or the time he took Knute Rockne and Grantland Rice on that long canoe trip back in the twenties. Just understand that if you want to know anything about the Minnesota-Ontario wilderness, Bill Magie's the man you have to ask.

★ ★ ★

KURALT: You know this country pretty well?

BILL MAGIE: I know it like a book. I'm the only man alive that's walked from Lake Superior to Lake of the Woods and carried a transit on his shoulder all the way, yeah, on the ice, yeah.

KURALT: Summertime or winter, you know it?

MAGIE: At wintertime, I know it like a book. I know it in summertime too. Wintertime is a hell of a lot of difference. Boy, you got to be rugged in the winter.

And I'm telling you, I often think how the hell I made it, I don't know how I did, but I made it. I was young then, I was in my twenties.

KURALT: Could I get you lost out here in these lakes?

MAGIE: Huh? No. You could tie me right-handed, blindfold me, and fly me into some lake and dump me off, I'll find my way back; damn right, and without any help either.

Magie on old age:

KURALT: There aren't very many people at the age of seventy-six who go around carrying canoes on their backs and going hundreds of miles in a canoe?

MAGIE: I had a woman, eighty-three, though; I guided her, and she lives in Vermont. And by God, she carried her canoe over one portage. It was a short portage, but she had to carry the canoe, so she could go on and say she carried the canoe, yeah.

Magie on death:

MAGIE: My doctor tells me, friends say, "For God's sake, Magie, take it easy or you're going to pop off over

there." And I said, no, when I die in the canoe country, that's where I want to die. I said they can carry me out feet first, and my son would come and get me.

KURALT: You're not afraid of rugged trips at seventy-six?

MAGIE: No, no, no. I'll make it another year anyway. [*Laughs*] Well, if you're going to die, you might as well die and get it over with. I don't want to do it like my father and mother. My mother was in the hospital six years, went in and out, in and out; father was in four years. I don't want that. If it's going to catch me, it's going to catch me on a portage—the old man, the old Reaper, the long portage to the happy hunting ground. [*Laughs*]

I asked him about the night he crawled inside a moose he had shot to keep from freezing, but it took him half an hour to tell the story... so we'll have to leave that out, too.

A Pioneer of the Road

(COVINA, CALIFORNIA)

ALICE HUYLER RAMSEY [*at the wheel of her car*]: These young people—they get a little smarty cat, you know, and they sneak in because they think it'll frighten somebody. Well, that's not my idea of good driving. They may be fast, but sooner or later, they're gonna catch it.

I went driving the other day with Alice Huyler Ramsey, who is ninety. Mrs. Ramsey has fixed opinions about driving. She ought to. She has been driving for seventy years. In 1909, at the age of twenty-two, with a certain determination shining in her eyes, Alice Huyler Ramsey became the first woman to drive a car across this country. She left New York's Broadway at the wheel of a Maxwell with three women passengers, and two months later, after a trip of 3800 miles on farm roads, through plowed fields and along Indian trails, she drove into San Francisco. The San Bernardino Freeway holds no terrors for a woman like that.

I have always found driving across this country to be an adventure. Alice Huyler Ramsey did it when it *was* an adventure.

★ ★ ★

KURALT: How did you find your way?
RAMSEY: Well, we had to find our way mostly by the telephone poles.

KURALT: The telephone poles?

RAMSEY: Yes, they had those all the way across the country, crude and not very tall, and we could usually suppose that the ones with the more wires went to a larger town. We thought that was good common sense. Once or twice we got mistaken. [*Laughs*]

In 1909, when Alice Huyler Ramsey drove across America, that was as good as highways got. Transcontinental motoring in 1909 required you to open and close a good many pasture gates, and, if you got stuck in the mud in Nebraska, you might hope for some friendly well-diggers to come along in a horse-drawn cart to give you a hand. That happened to her. If you had a flat tire, or what was just as likely, a broken axle, you had to know how to fix it. Alice Ramsey knew how.

KURALT: You must have been a pretty good mechanic, yourself.

RAMSEY: Well, for a girl, yes. [*Laughs*]

KURALT: But there you were, a young woman out in the automotive wilderness. Weren't you frightened sometimes?

RAMSEY: Well, I can only think of one time when we were a little bit scared. We rounded a little hill, and off to the right was a group of Indians riding bareback, with drawn bows and arrows, great big bows and arrows.

All of a sudden they wheeled to the left and came right toward us, and then my heart sort of went down in the bottom of the car, I think. Finally, in front of us, across the road, jumped a great big jackrabbit. They were hunting this poor jackrabbit with the bow and arrow, and they nonchalantly crossed the road ahead of us and paid no attention to us at all. [*Laughs*]

As surely as those earlier women who drove wagons down the Oregon Trail, Alice Huyler Ramsey was a pioneer. Alice Huyler Ramsey wanted to drive a car, and did, and still does. She drives across the country 'most every summer. She says there's nothing to it anymore.

The Croquet Player

(STAMPING GROUND, KENTUCKY)

We've met rich people while traveling around the country, and poor people, and lots of people in between. We've noticed that while there are classes in America, there isn't much of a class system. The rich are always willing to move over, make room for one more. For example, you probably think croquet is a game for aristocrats.

Croquet players drink champagne and eat caviar and sit under parasols on crisp, green lawns, you probably think. And summer in places like Newport and the Hamptons and Saratoga. Well, yes, that's true, as far as it goes. But it doesn't go far enough. It doesn't go as far as Stamping Ground, Kentucky, for instance, population six hundred and home to Archie Burchfield.

Archie Burchfield farms tobacco outside of Stamping Ground. What he's doing right now, though, is smoothing out his playing surface. It's not a country club lawn; it's good Kentucky dirt, but it's a croquet field and Archie Burchfield plays croquet.

★ ★ ★

BURCHFIELD: I started playing up at the Christian Church. All the fellows played up there, and one of them at the service station one day said, "You can't beat us in a game of croquet." And I said, "Well, I probably couldn't." And he said, "Come on down." So, I went down and they trashed me pretty good. I didn't get to play any and I didn't realize how hard it was. They put me behind the posts and they wouldn't give me a shot, and they laughed. I come home and I told my wife, Betty, I said, "Boy, those people really aggravated me." I said, "I'm going to get me a mallet and go back up there and practice."

He did. He practiced. You have to understand that Archie Burchfield is a determined man. We will pause for just a second here to let you read the back of his jacket.

Kentucky Croquet
State Champ

Singles	Doubles
1970	1973
1971	1976
1972	
1976	

Since that first time down at the churchyard Archie has become state champion many times over and, with his son Mark, a national doubles champion. And do not think of his brand of Kentucky croquet as tea-party croquet.

BURCHFIELD: I would say that our game is more—played for blood, I mean, we're all good friends and get along good, but once you walk over that line, it's everybody's out for theirself. And if they beat you without you hitting the ball, they will. They'll have no mercy on you whatsoever.

Playing this hardball croquet on the hard dirt of Stamping Ground, Kentucky, Archie Burchfield fell to dreaming about the clipped green lawns of Palm Beach, Florida—where, as he had heard, gentlemen of leisure and breeding contest for the club team championship of the United States Croquet Association. From Stamping Ground to Palm Beach is a very far wicket.

Just the same, Archie Burchfield decided to go have a look. And it was every bit as tony and blasé as he had imagined. The wealthy and illustrious competitors parked their cars at the Palm Beach Polo Club and entertained friends in their suites at The Breakers. Archie Burchfield of Stamping Ground, Kentucky, did not stay at The Breakers.

[Burchfield drives up to Paul's Motel.]

BURCHFIELD: The first time I came down to the Polo Club, why, I came over with a friend from over on the West Coast in a tractor trailer with twenty-two tons of lettuce. We parked out at the front gate, walked in, and the people at the gate didn't want to let us in. So, after talking awhile, they finally let us in. And still, we noticed that everybody didn't talk to us much. After playing awhile, we decided to go get something to eat. The lady told us, "They won't let you in the restaurant." And I said, "Why, ma'am?" She said, "Because the way you're dressed." And I said, "Oh." I said, "I'm sorry." I said, "What's wrong?" And she said, "You have to wear white clothes."

That sort of steamed Archie up. He went out and bought himself some white clothes to see if he couldn't put a little crack in the upper crust.

GAME COMMENTATOR: The world's leading croquet player, Mr. G. Nigel Aspinall from London. *[Applause]* Assisting him will be the president of the South African Croquet Association, Mr. Ian Gillespie. *[Applause]* Palm Beach's own, four times national singles champion, twice doubles champion. Mr. Archie Peck. Next, a growingly famous man from Stamping Ground, Kentucky, Mr. Archie Burchfield. *[Applause]*

At Palm Beach, Archie Burchfield found that while his

opponents all had long pedigrees and large bank balances, they still put on their white pants one leg at a time; they still had to hit the ball and run the wicket. And when the game started, Archie Burchfield felt right at home.

GAME COMMENTATOR: You might notice that Archie Burchfield taps his ball each time after he's hit it. He's more accustomed to playing on sand, and he knocks the ball to get the sand off it.

He also treated the Palm Beach Polo Club to its first Stamping Ground strategy.

BURCHFIELD [*to partner*]: I think the plan is to go down and rush black over where you can hit him, take off, get blue, throw blue to the other end and take shape. We got to hope like heck blue don't hit us, though.

He was up against the *crème de la crème* of international croquet, players of the sort who never have to worry about also getting in the tobacco crop. And Archie showed them a thing or two. He and a partner took on two of the best players in the world in an exhibition match, and beat their socks off. We wish we could say he also packed the National Club Team championship trophy into that lettuce truck and headed home to Stamping Ground. However, in a pressure-packed semifinal match, Archie Burchfield lost.

Never you mind! The polo ponies will be here next year. So will the champagne. So will the worldly stars of croquet. And since he already has the white clothes now, washed and folded and put away, and since he's beginning to enjoy himself at Palm Beach, Archie Burchfield will be back next year too. It's like he told his wife, Betty, after the first game with his cronies from the gas station. "Boy, those people really aggravated me. I'm going to get me a mallet and go back up there and practice."

The Pilot

(ROANOKE, TEXAS)

At the age of eighty, Edna Gardner Whyte thinks back on all the men in her life. Almost every one of them was an obstacle. They stood in the way of what she really wanted to do, but she did it anyway. She became a famous flyer. Today, she has a hangar where most people have a garage—no thanks to men. Take the year 1926, for example.

★ ★ ★

EDNA GARDNER WHYTE: The first three instructors I had told me to quit—I was going to kill myself. I knew I wasn't going to kill myself. I knew that I could learn to fly. If a man could do it, I could do it. They didn't want to solo me. They would just keep riding with me, ride with me, and wouldn't solo me, and I knew I could do it. The day he got out of that airplane, I sang all the way around the airport and came in and made a beautiful landing. I was so glad to get rid of him.

From that day to this, Edna Gardner Whyte has put in thirty thousand hours in the air, probably more than any other woman in the world—no thanks to men. One tried to turn her down for her pilot's license, though she had the highest score. Many turned her down for airline jobs, though she had the highest qualifications.

WHYTE [*flying craft; flying it upside down*]: When I get down near to eighty-five, I pull it up like this and I get . . .

[*Sound of passenger moaning*]

The man who is moaning in the background is CBS News cameraman Isadore Bleckman. He has just been put through a snap roll by a little old lady of eighty.

WHYTE: It's good for your veins: only two and a half g's. Want another one?
ISADORE BLECKMAN: Nope.

Such flying has earned Edna Gardner Whyte a roomful of trophies. Almost every one of them reminds her of some insult from a swaggering male pilot, with a white scarf and goggles. There was Maryland in 1934.

WHYTE: They put up a sign: PYLON RACE. $300 AND TRO-PHY. And so I thought, oh, I'm going to enter that, 'cause I'd be racing against men. I've always wanted to race against men, so badly.

They laughed at her. She went up in her Wright Whirl-wind J65 Aristocrat and beat their socks off—took their money and their trophy.

WHYTE: Next year, the same sign came out again: SUN-DAY AFTERNOON AT 3:00. MEN ONLY.

She never got mad; she got even.

WHYTE: This trophy here is Las Vegas to Philadelphia. It was in 1958 and it was a men's race. I was the only woman in it. They knew they had no worry from me. I was no competition. But we flew the race and I happened to come in first.

She has happened to come in first 123 times, judging from the trophies I could count and all the newspaper clippings with photographs of the pretty young woman in goggles. When Amelia Earhart handed her a trophy in 1937, she already had a lot more flying hours than Amelia Earhart had.

WHYTE: [*teaching young woman*]: Educate that hand to do that. Educate this hand to handle the throttle.

At eighty, she teaches flying. And her special pleasure is teaching young women like thirteen-year-old Sonya Henderson, making it easier for them than any man ever made it for her.

WHYTE: People ask me, do you regret not having any children? And I'll say, well, I feel like my students and my pilots are my children. I hope I can continue. I want to fly until after I'm a hundred, I really do. I want to keep flying races.
KURALT: Beating men.
WHYTE: Beating men.

Nickey, The Chicken Man

(HARTFORD, CONNECTICUT)

They say we're a plastic society, but I don't know. I keep running into characters. I knew some day I'd run into the one who could win the prize for stubbornness and survival against the odds. I think I've just found him. He's in an ugly little building on the corner of Columbus and Grove—Nickey, the Chicken Man.

★ ★ ★

NICKEY [*laughs*]: You realize I've been here over forty years? That's right. Matter of fact, this has been my life. I was born at the corner of State and Front, and I worked here the lifetime. Simple as that! [*Laughs*]

Dominic LaTorre has spent his whole life in the business of live chickens and survival. His little Connecticut Live Chicken Store survived the Depression, several floods, the war, and redevelopment. When the city tore down the old Italian neighborhood, Nickey LaTorre refused to go. When the city widened one of the streets that form his corner and took two-thirds of his store, he patched up the part that was left and refused to move. When the Travelers Insurance Company bought up the block for a fifteen-story, twenty-million-dollar office building, he refused to sell. When Travelers built around him, and the city of Hartford announced plans to widen the other street and tear down what was left of his building, he took them all to court. After many months, the Supreme Court of the State of Connecticut ruled that Nickey LaTorre had to go. The City of Hartford has the right to widen Grove Street any time it chooses.

KURALT: I guess they think it would be beautifying the city to get rid of this little building.

NICKEY: You call this beautification across the street? Those parking lots? Is that beautification? Over there, there used to be apartment houses with beautiful people living in them and all kinds of stores, right along, where you could buy anything you wanted. You could buy a fig for a nickel.

KURALT: They call it progress.

NICKEY: Progress is fine, where it's essential and where it's needed. I know many a people that were living down here and, when they got their notification to move, they were up in arms. They were happy here, because this was the little world of their own. They knew everybody. And there were all kinds of people living here—Italians, Polacks, Chinamens, colored—made no difference. We were one happy family.

KURALT: Why do they want to eliminate this business?

NICKEY: I think it's a thorn in the side of my friend, the Travelers Insurance Company. Now, the Council— our illustrious Council—decides that that street needs widening. There's traffic on that street from seven to about eight in the morning and from four to about four-thirty in the evening. The rest of the day, you could sit there and have a picnic and nobody'll bother you. The thing is Travelers doesn't want me here, because I'm a thorn in their side. Yet I've been here almost as long as they have. [*Laughs*] But the fact is that the City Council went along with, naturally, what "Mister Traveler" said. So they voted me down, right down the sewer.

The Travelers Insurance Company employs nearly ten thousand people in Hartford. Nickey LaTorre employs nobody but himself.

Fred C. Maynard—Executive Vice President of Travelers:

MAYNARD: Well, we tried to buy his property on a bona fide offer and at a reasonable price. And he exercised his right not to accept it. I regret that he feels that we've been out to get him. I don't feel that way at all, nor have I ever sensed any such attitude on the part of anybody who works for this company. I don't think we've been picking on Mr. LaTorre at all.

NICKEY: Travelers pays a million dollars in taxes to the City of Hartford. Don't forget, the $2300 a year I pay to the City of Hartford hurts me more than that million dollars that Travelers donates. Am I wrong or am I wrong?

MAYNARD: This company has been doing business at this

site for about a hundred and fifteen years, and as our business grew, the number of employees grew. We added one building and then another and another, till we reached the mid-sixties and it was apparent we were going to need a new building to house more employees to handle more business. We built our building and our people are down there working now. So is Mr. LaTorre.

NICKEY: This is Grove Street. When they built that building, they put that sidewalk in there, prior to any other mischievous thing at all. They said, "This guy isn't going to stay here. How is he going to buck us?"

But *they* are city planners and he is just Nickey, the Chicken Man. Sooner or later, they *will* widen Grove Street and Nickey LaTorre's stubborn holdout will be over. There will be nothing on the corner to show that there ever was such a thing as the Connecticut Live Poultry Store.

KURALT: So now you're just living on borrowed time?

NICKEY: So now I'm dying by the inches. I wish I knew where I stood. That's right. On borrowed time, as you say. Look at this place. I used to have a beauty parlor here at one time. But now I'm letting it go, for the simple reason that I don't know if I'm going to be here today or tomorrow or the next day. It's an aggravating situation.

KURALT: Do you think a bulldozer is going to come down Grove Street one of these days and—

NICKEY: Well, to tell you the truth, many a morning I come down that street there with my little pickup, and I don't expect to find the place. [*Laughs*] I don't expect to find the place because, you know, it's nothing, but to me it's a livelihood. Who's going to hire a guy like me at this stage of the game? I ought to become a bookie or a racehorse bettor.

In nearly half a century, surviving on this corner, Nickey

LaTorre, as you can tell, has developed his own philosophy about city planning. He thinks a city should be more than new buildings and widened streets.

KURALT: I notice that you wave to everybody who comes by. A lot of people know you.

NICKEY: Oh, man! As far as that goes, I'm a fixture on this corner. In the morning I'll say good morning to anybody. I have people come around this corner, and if they don't see me they'll rap on the window to catch my attention so they can wave at me. I've been here a long time, friend. I've been here an awful long time.

The Mayor of Duncan City

(HALL COUNTY, GEORGIA)

 We came to a country cross-roads in Hall County, Georgia, and found it a very well marked place. One sign points the way to Flowery Branch, Gainesville, Lake Lanier, Dawsonville, and Fairbanks, Alaska. That's not the only sign. Another, for example, shows the direction to Duncan's Creek Church, Auburn, Dacula, Winder, Highway 124, Disneyland, and Miami. There are seven signs in all, and the sign painter, Lucius Duncan, is not done yet. Somebody asked him the way to Stretch It, Texas, a few days ago, and he doesn't want to be asked that anymore. So he's adding Stretch It to one of the signposts. The problem is that Lucius Duncan's house is the only house around here. When people get lost, they knock on his door. At the age of seventy-eight, he decided enough is enough.

★ ★ ★

KURALT: Did you ask the county to put up signs?
LUCIUS DUNCAN: Yes, sir.
KURALT: What did they say?
DUNCAN: They couldn't do it; it'd bankrupt the county.

So he put up his own. He figures since he's the only man in Duncan City, that makes him the mayor. He is also, he says, the law west of the Mulberry, a little stream that meanders nearby, so he can set the speed limit and the speed limit is: [*Sign:* LET 'ER GO]"Let 'er go."

KURALT: You've lived here a long time.
DUNCAN: Sixty-five years.
KURALT: And people have been knocking on your door all those years?
DUNCAN: I have answered the door for sixty-five years, all times day and night. I only had six kids. I'd of had twelve or fifteen if I'd had the signs up fifty years ago. I'm going to sue the county for the loss of kids.

KURALT: Which you'd have had if you hadn't had to spend so much time answering the door.
DUNCAN: That's right, yeah. Yeah, yeah. [*Laughs*]

So, this is all a protest against the penny-pinching of the county. Mayor Duncan lives on three mail routes, and he has three mailboxes: one for checks, one for duns or bills, and one for love letters. He gets no love letters from the county commissioners. But now, at least he does have a well-marked corner.

DUNCAN: Yeah, that road goes to London, and that one to Hong Kong, thataway. [*Laughs*] That one there goes to Shake Rag and Honolulu, thataway.

Shake Rag and Honolulu. As we wandered over in the general direction of Shake Rag, Georgia, and Honolulu, Hawaii, I asked Lucius Duncan what travelers think of his signs.

DUNCAN: A lady stopped one day and said: "Whatcha putting up the signs for?" And I says, "Stop folks from asking questions." [*Laughs*] She said, "You go to hell!" [*Laughs*]
KURALT: Tell me the truth. Even with all these signs, are there sometimes people who stop and still ask directions?
DUNCAN: You know, it'd surprise you. There's lots of people can't read.
KURALT [*laughing*]: Is that a—
DUNCAN: That's a fact.

No sooner were the words out of his mouth than it happened.

DUNCAN: Where're you wanting to go?
VOICE: Duluth.
DUNCAN: Duluth? Follow that straight road to Buford.

Now that man was standing right beside a sign pointing the way he wanted to go.

DUNCAN [*to same traveler*]: Go to that straight road there to Buford. Follow that truck. Yes, sir. Get to Buford, you know where you're at. [*To Kuralt*] You see what I'm up against? He can't read.

So one more traveler got pointed in the right direction, one of thousands over the last sixty-five years. We got the impression Lucius Duncan, in spite of what he says, gets a kick out of being indispensable around here. We left him waiting for the next lost stranger. The mayor of all he surveys, at war with the county, but at peace with the world.

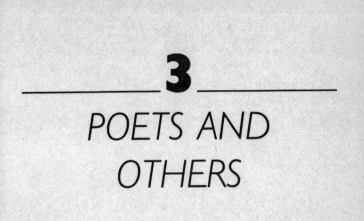

3

POETS AND OTHERS

*H*ardly a week goes by that I don't come across a poet at some country crossroads. I don't mean a writer of verse. I mean somebody who had inside of him such a love of something—farming, flying, furniture-making—and talks about it so lyrically and intensely, that in telling you about it, he makes you love it, too. If you take the time to listen, you can hear much unrhymed poetry in the air of America—in the singsong chant of the auctioneers, the jargon of the truckers on the CB radio, the bawdy jokes of construction workers, the lazy gossip of neighbors, the extravagant tale-telling of tipsy strangers in a bar—but clearest of all in the passionate accents of someone caught up in what he does for a living—or did for a living once.

The Poet of Steam

BYRD: Seaboard engine 60–41 calling Atkinson Yard office.

RADIO: Seaboard Atkinson Yard on.

BYRD: Bud, can we come through the crossover, please, sir?

RADIO: Okay to come through the crossover and into the main track.

BYRD: All right, here we go.

[*He reaches up and pulls the whistle cord and the whistle pierces the air.*]

Billy Byrd is that fabulous character from the American story, a locomotive engineer. From Madisonville, Kentucky, down through Mortons Gap to Hopkinsville and Guthrie, he has memorized every sidetrack, hill, and curve.

★ ★ ★

BYRD: This is a private crossing. I'm afraid that old farmer will come out there with a tractor or something, you know. I always look for him.

[*Train whistle*]

Billy Byrd is a master at running a big L&N diesel. It is well known on the railroad that nobody does it better.

But some men are born too late. Billy Byrd's hand is on the diesel throttle, but he left his heart back in the cab of the steam locomotive he ran when he was young. Look for Billy Byrd on his day off and chances are you'll find him in the yard of the Crab Orchard and Egyptian Railroad in Marion, Illinois. The CO&E still runs steam, the last working freight line to do so. And here, Billy Byrd, an old lover, comes to visit his old love.

BYRD: When they've got steam in them, they're just like they're alive. There's movement about them. The air pump's working, sounds just like they're breathing. Hear the thump, thump, thump, thump.

[*Train whistle, steam engine chugging, bell clanging*]

KURALT: It sounds to me like you'd like to climb back up in the cab of a steam locomotive, as in the old days, and do it all over.
BYRD: Best over-all job in the world. I'd rather have it than have President Reagan's job. [*Laughs*] Beautiful machine, beautiful machine.

[Bell ringing]

Now, it's not a real big engine, It's a small engine. But they were mainline engines, and they hauled the freight of this country. She and her sisters, that's what made this country what it is today. It was a sad sight for me and other fellows like me to see them leave, to think of the good they had done and were still capable of doing.

[Long blast of the whistle]

Make your blood turn cold, don't it?

[Train whistle; conductor calling "Board!"]

So deep does the passion for steam engines run in Billy Byrd that he went out and found one of his own. He keeps it parked beside his house in Madisonville, a marvelous Nichols and Shepard relic dating to 1919. And, as the

neighborhood dogs bark and the neighbors hold their ears, he regularly fires it up and drives it around town.

[*Steam tractor whistle*]

BYRD: You hear that stack out there? You hear it talking to you? Listen to that one. You're not going to get a gas engine to sound like that.

[*Steam engine chugging*]

It's always had a fascination for me. You can see everything. It's just the raw power and the feel of control of the engine in your hand, the power at your command. I just have always loved them. Ever since I was big enough to know anything, why, I knew I was born to run a steam engine. So, when the railroad dieselized, I had to get one that they couldn't take away from me, one that was my own.

Engineers of the steam locomotives which passed Billy Byrd's schoolyard in Adams, Tennessee, used to wave to him when he was a boy and even stop and give him rides on the engine. And there began this passion for steam trains and steam men that has burned in him lifelong. He became a steam locomotive engineer just about the time they started replacing the steam engines.

But he remembers those great machines. I stood there with Billy Byrd and listened to as beautiful a description as a man could ever give of the job he had once.

BYRD: Well, there was no thrill like having a good steaming locomotive with a tonnage train—you know, one up in good shape, good water, and good coal. And a moonlight night was the best time 'cause it would be light enough that you could see your valve motion and side rods and see your drivers turning over the big balance weights on the drivers, and see the fire dancing through the holes in the firebox door. Think of all the power that you had at your command and she was responding to your touch! She held no secrets from you! You lean on the armrest and see the smoke trail back over the train and see that headlight shining out there and hear that old girl talk to you in the language just you and she understood; go through the little towns; people would be sleeping; seemed like it was just you and she in a world all your own now.

[Train whistle]

Every working day, Billy Byrd takes the afternoon freight down to Guthrie, all the power of a modern diesel in his hand. And he is good at it and he does it by the book, observing the speed restrictions, blowing for the blind crossings. It is an honorable craft. But steam is poetry and Billy Byrd is a poet born too late.

[Bell ringing; steam locomotive whistle]

The Bridge Builders

(SAN FRANCISCO, CALIFORNIA)

Drive across the country and you find that hardly anybody makes anything. I think of my own friends and neighbors. One of them sells insurance, one of them takes pictures for a living, one's an actor, one's a lawyer—none of them makes anything. I talk on television. I don't make anything either. This may be the most fundamental change in the country. Years ago, nearly everybody in the cities made something—harnesses, wagon wheels, hats, violins. . . .

I've just spent a wonderful couple of days with some old guys who made something together. They started fifty years ago this year. That's what they made.

[*We see the Golden Gate Bridge.*]

There had never been a bridge like the Golden Gate Bridge, and there had never been a job like the job of building it.

★ ★ ★

ALFRED ZAMPA: The wind was sharp and the fog was cold, cold to the bone. But there was some beautiful scenery, too. Sometimes you'd be working above the fog—it was great. It was going to be one of the greatest things that ever happened, one of the Wonders of the World, I guess it was.

Fifty years ago, the Golden Gate Bridge wasn't here. There were serious doubts as to whether it could be put up to stay against the wild winds and tides of San Francisco Bay.

Alfred Zampa was one of those who volunteered to put it up to stay. He was an aristocrat of the construction trades, an ironworker, and he got top pay in hard times, eleven dollars a day.

ZAMPA: Hard times, the Depression. Oh, we didn't have much work, you know.

Al Zampa needed that job. To get it he had to get past the union business agent.

ZAMPA: Oh, the B-A says, "Well, it's all right. We're going to let you go out there. You make sure you vote for Roosevelt." I says, "Naturally. Who else am I going to vote for?" [Laughs]

Frenchy Gales was not an ironworker. He was a bus driver who had lost his bus driving job and who had never been up on anything higher than his garage roof.

FRENCHY GALES: We used to have to go from one cage to the other on a two-by-twelve plank up there, five or six hundred feet, no handrails or nothing on it. Believe me, it was hairy. [Laughs] I didn't like that. I had good long toenails on my feet by the time I got through.

Edward Souza was on a WPA project and looking for something that paid better. He knew building the Golden Gate Bridge was going to be more dangerous, and it was.

EDWARD SOUZA: I guess it was the challenge of myself against the bridge and the feeling that it had. The only time I ever got hit—well, I got hit out there. I went in the hospital for a couple of weeks. I looked up to see if anything was above me. I seen somethin'

Frenchy Gales

Edward Souza

Alfred Zampa

go by my light. It hit me in the mouth and busted all
my teeth out and bust my mouth.

KURALT: What was it?

SOUZA: It was either a rivet or a bolt. I'm sure it was a
rivet. But it didn't hit me square. If it'd hit me square,
it'd have gone right through my face. But it hit me
in a glancing blow.

Worst of all, of course, was losing your footing up there.
They said that was a ticket to hell, unless you hit the
safety net. They called that halfway to hell.

ZAMPA: Well, it was first thing in the morning, eight, eight
ten. It was wet and foggy and I stepped from that
beam and stepped down. If you go down straight you
won't slide. I went out too far, slipped, flipped three
times, and hit the net, and the net hit the ground at
the same time. It wasn't no ground; it was rocks.
And I bounced. I wasn't scared, because I thought
I was gonna bounce and then get up just like they
do in the circus, you know. I wasn't a bit scared
going down.

KURALT: But the net hit the rocks

ZAMPA: I hit the rocks and I bounced. The first one didn't
seem so hard, but when I come down the second
time—whoof!—that's when it hurt. [*Laughs*] Oh, I
had a hell of a time then.

KURALT: What happened to you?

ZAMPA: I cracked four vertebras in my back.

KURALT: How long were you in the hospital?

ZAMPA: Oh, I figure just about twelve weeks. But all the
time, my friends would come and see me and give
me a lot of bull. Says, "You know, Al, you might as
well start going out there selling shoestrings or something because you'll never make it. Your nerve's gone.
You'll never get out there." So, when I went out of
the hospital, I didn't go home. I went right out to the
bridge and walked all over that thing. I just wanted
to make sure. No problem.

KURALT: [*to Gales*]: Did you ever fall off?

GALES: No, I fell in the net once, in the back span, but—

KURALT: How did it happen?

GALES: Well, I was walking across one of the crossbeams, and I had a coil of wire. We were sizing the other wire with it. A gust of wind come, and I just went off backwards there and landed on my tail in the thing, and I was so scared I just stood there like a gopher in a hole. [Laughs]

KURALT: But did you hit the net?

GALES: Oh, yeah. The net was in already. Had a hell of a time to get out of that net, too. Boy, was I petrified. I'm not kidding you. No use lying about it. It sure scared the hell out of me when I felt that fall.

They all got scared, about as regularly as they got paid. One day, after the towers were up but before they were bolted firmly into place, an earthquake struck.

SOUZA: I guess we were about, I don't know, maybe six hundred feet up. I felt this kind of funny feeling, and I said this to a couple of my crew, I said, "There's something wrong here." We had a bucket of bolts, a five-gallon bucket about half full. We tied it to the middle rung of this ladder, and it acted like a pendulum, started to rock back and forth. When it started to hit each side of the cell, I said, "Let's get the hell out of here."

GALES: They had a railing around. We all got against the railing and the old thing would—[makes leaning motion] shifting, you know. And the guys would say, "Here we go!" [Laughs] And then she'd stop and kind of quiver and then go back the other way, just like that, about three or four times.

KURALT: And you went back to work after that?

GALES: Went back the next day and we had another one the next day, but not like that one. I wouldn't have gone within four miles of that thing if I knew it was going to do it again. I had all I wanted. A lot of guys were laying in the deck throwing up; old riggers too, scared to death.

That was June of 1935. The earthquake terrified a lot of brave men but killed nobody. The greater horror came later when a construction platform collapsed, carried the safety net down with it, and ten men down with the platform and the net into the ocean.

GALES: The tide was going out. All you could see was lumber and I saw one boat way out picking up two guys. One guy was alive and he was hanging on the other guy and the other guy was dead. He got killed in the fall, but this guy hung on to him. And then one guy, when it went down, grabbed ahold of one of the iron beams on the bridge, and he hung there, you know. They dropped a rope down to him. He had no part of that rope. He just hung on to that goddamn thing. He was a little Irishman, and he had a corncob pipe in his mouth and he didn't let go. Finally, they got a genuine rigger and dropped him down and tied a rope around him and jerked him up.

KURALT: Was he okay?

GALES: He was okay, and he went straight down the thing to the office and quit. He had enough.

Why didn't they all quit? What kept them pulling on their coveralls and packing their lunch buckets and climbing up there into the fog every day?

ZAMPA: I don't know. I just wanted to do things that everybody couldn't do. I felt it was a thrill. I loved it. In fact, you have to when you work on them bridges. My dad told me, "You're crazy," he says. "That's just for desperate men to do that." [*Laughs*] And I says, "Well, I know, but I like to do it." Oh, I was terrific. I could bite nails when I was young. Whew! I was terrific.

KURALT: These were pretty tough guys, weren't they?

GALES: Oh, man, you ain't kidding! Oh, hell, yes! Those ironworkers—in those days they couldn't get any insurance of any kind; life span was too short. Those guys lived hard and they liked to fight. They loved it. The bars in Sausalito, they used to have pretty good times all right, during the weekends. See, they only worked a forty-hour week on that bridge. So a weekend was a day of relaxation. My boss used to say—Monday morning when they walked behind you, sweating, you could smell that bourbon, you know—and he said, "Geez, if they could only put a still on their shoulders, they could get another pint during the day—sweat it out." [*Laughs*]

ZAMPA: Oh, we'd shoot dice and drink and raise hell, chase women or they'd chase us—because we had a lot of money, you know.

KURALT: And not many people had in those days.

ZAMPA: Oh, no. Geez, we were like rich men.

Some were killed instantly on the job . . . many, many more were maimed by lead poisoning and falling steel objects. The ones who were left each night climbed up there again the next morning. Remember, these were hard times.

ZAMPA: A hundred and fifty men down that tower, waiting for a job, waiting for us either to quit or fall off, right down the bottom of the tower. Hell, they'd cook beans and bacon butts in these five-gallon tins, you know . . . but fire there waiting all the time. They wasn't as cold as we were. I'd look down and see that fire going down there. Jesus . . .

KURALT: Can you believe that all that was fifty years ago?

ZAMPA: No, just like yesterday. Just like yesterday. I got my fingerprints all over that iron, I'll tell you.

SOUZA: Well, once in a while I come across the bridge and I look at those towers and look how high they are, yeah. And say, "I worked on that. I remember being up there." That's the feeling I get. It's a proud feeling.

Angler

(UPPER PENINSULA, MICHIGAN)

Judge John Voelker, Michigan Supreme Court, retired. In the wintertime he writes books. He wrote *Anatomy of a Murder* among others. In the spring and summer, every day of the trout season, he fishes for trout. John Voelker is an uncommon man, a man, you might even say, who is in revolt. It is bigness he is revolting against, the old and widely accepted idea of the bigger the better. John Voelker fishes only with the tiniest flies, tied to gossamer leaders, and fishes only for the smallest fish, the beautiful native brook trout which inhabit the ponds and streams of his beloved Upper Peninsula of Michigan. They are elusive circles in the water, but knowing they're there is enough for John Voelker, alone in the backwoods, a long way from the big buildings of the big cities of this big country.

★ ★ ★

VOELKER: Hey, a little one! Here is a tiny fish, maybe not big enough to keep legally, and I'm not going to keep him. I mean, imagine going out in a boat winching in fish. I guess there's a thrill in it, a lot of people do it. While it keeps a lot of pressure from this water, for which I'm thankful, there's a kind of a sadness in it. It's part of this bigness thing. And a ten-inch trout here on this tackle is like catching a five-pound rainbow. In fact, in a way, it's a little more difficult. Some of these guys use hawsers, you know; you could tow a tugboat with some of the gear that they use. [*Puts fish back*] He's going to make it. His feelings are hurt, but he'll make it.

Why do you do it? I asked him. Why do you spend every day fishing? "Well," he said, "I wrote it down once. I'll go find it and say it for you if you'd like." He did and we were glad he did.

VOELKER: I fish because I love to. Because I love the environs where trout are found, which are invariably beautiful, and hate the environs where crowds of people are found, which are invariably ugly. Because of all the television commercials, cocktail parties and assorted social posturing I thus escape. Because in

a world where most men seem to spend their lives doing what they hate, my fishing is at once an endless source of delight and an act of small rebellion. Because trout do not lie or cheat and cannot be bought or bribed, or impressed by power, but respond only to quietude and humility, and endless patience. Because I suspect that men are going along this way for the last time and I for one don't want to waste the trip. Because mercifully there are no telephones on trout waters. Because only in the woods can I find solitude without loneliness. Because bourbon out of an old tin cup always tastes better out there. Because maybe one day I will catch a mermaid. And finally, not because I regard fishing as being so terribly important, but because I suspect that so many of the other concerns of men are equally unimportant and not nearly so much fun. Amen

Hex Signs

(LENHARTSVILLE, PENNSYLVANIA)

Most farmers manage to keep witches out of their barns without the use of hex signs, but the Pennsylvania Dutch never believed in taking chances. So if you drive out through Lenhartsville or Fleetwood or Hamburg or Virginville, you can see old hex signs yet, fading now, some of them, but still up near the rooflines of the old barns, doing their jobs.

It is said that a good hex-sign painter can protect your barn from lightning and your cattle from disease and provide you with a perfect marriage, abundance, good luck, industrious children, food for your family, and rain for your crops. So naturally we went looking for such a man. And found him.

John Claypoole.

John Claypoole inherited his powers from the legendary old hex-sign painter Professor Johnny Ott. Twenty years ago John went up to the Professor and asked if he could share in the mysteries.

★ ★ ★

CLAYPOOLE: He said, "John, what the hell are you going to learn it for?" I said, "I'd like to learn it for a hobby." He said, "Hobby, hell, you're like all the rest of them, by God, you just want to make money." I said, "Yah, well, I wouldn't mind making money, but I don't expect to be as good as you." So I got a

little peeved about it and I started to walk off. And he says, "Yah, go ahead, bullhead, go ahead, walk away, be a damned sorehead." I said, "No, I'm not sore, just your attitude." He said, "Come on the hell back here, by golly, I'll teach you and see what you learn." I said all right.

KURALT: They tell me that some of Johnny Ott's hex signs seem to really work sometimes.

CLAYPOOLE: Oh yeah. One time, back in 1955, they had a big flood. He went fishing up on the Delaware, and one of the fellows up there he used to fish with wanted a hex sign for his barn. We were having a lot of drought at that time. He said, "Hey, Johnny," he said, "could you make a sign for rain?" John says, "Yeah, I'll make you the fertility hex sign. That'll bring a lot of rain, hang it out on your barn." So the guy hung it out on the barn. And right at that time we got that two- or three-million-dollar flood. The river overflowed and my God, it washed his barn away and every other darn thing. And the guy come back," he said, "Jesus cripes, Johnny," he says, "I didn't want the whole place to wash away. I wanted a little bit of rain, not to lose the barn and all." Johnny said, "You damned fool, you put it up but you forgot to take it in! You should have put it inside!" Oh, boy, he was a great one!

KURALT: What's the origin of hex signs?

CLAYPOOLE: The hex signs actually started back in Bible times. They have a religious significance. There was actually, from what I know, about seven signs. They came from the seven books of Moses. They were mostly stars, rosettes, wheels. The rosette is for good luck and good health—ward off disease, pestilence, and bring good luck. There is your black chain in the yellow field: the eternal chain of life to keep you together. Rosettes represent the big rosette window of your churches.

The coalico star—you'll see that down through the Lebanon Valley, Schuylkill County, Bucks County; you might see it in different colors, but the main color is purple with a dot in the center. It has very religious significance. The purple dot represents the robe Christ was crucified in. The white field in the background is purity and the black circle around the side always represents unity in Christ.

KURALT: There are a lot of Amish and Mennonites around

here, but they aren't the ones who make hex signs, are they?

CLAYPOOLE: No, the Amish are very wonderful people. Very plain. But hex signs, definitely not. They do not believe in any of that stuff. What they call the Gay Dutch—they're Lutheran, Catholic, Protestant Dutch—they are the type who have hex signs. They're all Pennsylvania Dutch, technically.... A lot of people come up and say, "Can you make me a hex sign to put a curse on somebody?" That's no way. I won't do it. In the first place, hex signs are not for that. Hex signs are good luck and good health and success. They are not for bad luck. A lot of people hear the word hex and they figure it's connected with witchcraft. It is not connected with witchcraft.

I had a party up in Uncasville, Connecticut, which is right outside of New London, and they asked me to make them a fertility hex sign. The guy had been married about five or six years and he said we just can't have no children. So I made them a fertility hex sign. This was about, oh, seven or eight years ago. He came back about five years later. He was in the area and he came back, he had the sign—it looked like it was worn a little bit—and he gave it to me and he said, "Here, pal, you can take this sign—and

jam it. I've had enough." I said, "What are you talking?" He said, "Boy, ever since I've had that thing,
all I got to do is look at my wife. She's pregnant,
pregnant, pregnant." I said, "Jeez almighty." I didn't
think I had the power. I didn't realize it would work.
So I kept the sign and later on I finished it off and
sold it to somebody else. I don't know if it's still
working or not.

John Claypoole sent us down the road to see some hex
signs which he had repainted on ancient barns. Along the
way we saw a multitude of starbursts and rosettes and
whirligigs and flowers. And I got to thinking. Pennsylvania Dutch *are* among the country's most successful
farmers, after all. And you hardly ever hear of witches
in their barns.

Be that as it may, we bought a hex sign, a rosette for
good luck, and hung it on the bus. That afternoon, coming
around a curve, a ten-ton truck just missed us. Missed
us, I say.

Of course, he might have missed us if we hadn't had a
hex sign.

Might have, I say.

Moonshiners

(GEORGIA, VIRGINIA, AND TENNESSEE)

Come all you booze buyers if you wanta hear
I'll tell you 'bout the kind of booze they make
   around here
Made way back in the swamps and the hills
Where there's a-plenty of moonshine stills.

Moonshine has been sung about, and sipped, and made
in the Appalachian Mountains ever since people began
calling these hard, beautiful hills home. White lightning
was made from the first, by settlers from England and
Ireland and Scotland; they and all their descendants have
known the uses of mashed corn.

★ ★ ★

HUBERT HOWELL: I might have broke the law here, I
   mean the state law, but I don't believe I broke God's
   law, no. I don't believe I did.

One drop will make a rabbit whip a bulldog
And a taste'll make a rabbit whip a wild hog.
Make a toad spit in a blacksnake's face
Make a hardshell preacher fall from Grace.

In his day, C. L. Radford was a real working moonshiner. He learned how from his daddy, which is the way
most people learned to make corn whiskey.

C. L. RADFORD: It comes out about a hundred and eighty proof. But you'd run it until it gets very weak and then you take the weak and mix it with the strong and you proof it down to about ninety proof, and then you drink it. It's still pretty strong then, it don't ¨ take that much to kinda set you down, you know.

If you follow the crest of the Blue Ridge down from Virginia to Georgia, you'll never be far from a whiskey still, right to this day. But you won't ever see one, unless you know how to find it. Frank Rickman knows how, and without much trouble he found us one. The owners weren't around to shake our hands when we got there. That was just as well. Moonshiners customarily do not welcome strangers to the premises.

FRANK RICKMAN: Now, I'd guess this still would hold about seventy-five or eighty gallons. Somewhere in that vicinity.

Frank Rickman knows how to find stills and judge their capacity because his father used to be sheriff here in Rabun County, Georgia, and lots of times he went along when his daddy found stills and broke them up. It was customary for the lawmen to have a sip or two, just to sample the product.

RICKMAN: We all used it for just a little boost, you know, Just pep you up a little and make you smile and make you feel a little better.

On the other hand there's Hubert Howell. He never acquired a taste for moonshine. He was never against making it, though. And he made a lot of it.

HOWELL: Whiskey is the worst thing that's ever been. But I always said, whiskey was made to sell, not to drink. A man's a damn fool for drinking it, I don't care who he is.

Hamper McBee

Hamper McBee doesn't moonshine anymore, but he admires a well-made copper pot as much as the next man. And the one he's looking at is identical to certain well-made copper pots that Hamper McBee recalls fondly.

HAMPER McBEE: This is a good little old still and it's light: you can move it. Now maybe, if the feds are after you or something, or they're close, or you think somebody's turning you up, hunters or something, you can just set a few mash barrels down in the creek, and you can just grab this little old still up and move it, you know, ain't that much trouble. Just take it apart, pick it up, go down the stream, and put it up again. You don't have all that trouble, see, the pot's light. Anybody could carry that pot. But you can make some good booze on this thing here. And I've drank enough to float a ship, I guess, out of it.

Maude Thacker is up in her eighties now. She doesn't look like a moonshiner—but when she was a little girl, growing up in the shadow of Hendricks Mountain in Georgia, she hauled mash and bran for her father's still. Her father made moonshine and music too, and he taught his daughter to do both.

MAUDE THACKER [*singing*]: "Ha, ha, you and me, little brown jug don't I love thee. Hee, ha, ha, you and me, little brown jug full of rye whiskey." That's all I know. [*Laughs*]

That may be all Maude Thacker knows of the song, but it's far from all she knows about moonshining. She knows you can't have a still without running water. There are three principles of whiskey-making: build on the little

Maude Thacker

Hubert Howell

branch of a big river, hide your still well, and make it portable.

THACKER: We'd just moved from one place to another, so they never did cut us down but one time. But one time they cut my daddy down. He was making brandy. And they cut him down.

The revenuers cut a lot of people down. But nobody much stayed cut down. The stills would grow back, like weeds. Really, they had to. In good times and in bad— and especially in bad— moonshine was a hill farmer's best cash crop.

You could make the dirt yield up just about enough to eat. But you couldn't make it yield money. For that, you had to fire up a still, get the corn mash to bubbling and steaming, and then cool the steam into moonshine. At the end of the great jumble of pipes and pots and barrels is the bit of pipe the liquor finally comes out of. That is called the money piece.

Even in the worst of times—during Prohibition and the Depression—the money piece worked wonders.

HOWELL: That was the best years of my life. It really was. The best years of my life. It was hard work, slavish work. But, you see, I enjoyed it. Because I was doing good. I know a lotta people thinks I wasn't now. Don't seem like I was. But I was a-feedin' lots of people that would've been hungry otherwise.

RICKMAN: It was make liquor or starve. Well, now, I don't care who it is, when he gets to where he'll starve, if he's honorable enough to make liquor instead of stealing, he's the man I'm interested in. He's the man that's wanting to do the right thing.

MCBEE: Lazy people don't make whiskey. No, there's too much work involved in it, especially when you've got an old still here that—way off in the woods, and you've got to pack all that stuff in there and back out. Then you're working scared, too, all the time, because hell, you don't know when they're gonna run in there and get you.

Often, the raiding lawmen are tipped off by paid informers. The mountain folk have an awful name for these informers. They call them reporters.

But even when the reporters do their reporting well, the lawmen still have the problem of chasing the moonshiners down.

Frank Rickman

MCBEE: Never been caught at a still in my life. But Lord, I've runned till my tongue was hanging out! And got away, thank God! But sometimes you don't. I know an old boy was running from the law one time, and he looked back to see how close they was to him, and he run into a big tree and knocked himself out and they had him handcuffed when he came to. I said, why, hell, they ain't close to you until they get their hands on you! You know? Ain't no need of looking back.

Making the whiskey was one thing. Moving it was something else. For that you needed a fast car. The man who drove the whiskey was called a tripper, and the car he loved to drive was a '39 Ford with a big V-8.

In those days, of course, the police cars didn't have radios. So a tripper could outrun the police. And when that failed, he could crash right through their roadblocks. Shade Radford remembers all that.

KURALT: How fast did you drive, at your fastest?

SHADE RADFORD: Well, just as fast as it'd run. Most of the time it was about a hundred miles an hour.

KURALT: On these mountain roads?

RADFORD: A lotta times, yeah. You had to.

KURALT: So the thirty-nine was a good model for transporting moonshine, huh?

RADFORD: I'd say it was the best. That was the best, more stabilized. You could maneuver it where you couldn't anything else hardly.

Whiskey is made for drinking, of course. But it's also made for healing. The folks here believe that if you take the right roots and herbs, and soak 'em in a jar of white lightning, what you end up with is good for what ails you. Maude Thacker's mother believed that, years ago.

MAUDE THACKER: She'd take a quart of whiskey, and take all kinds of herbs, like ginseng and rattleroot and mayapple, and put it all in that bottle and make us take a sip of it every morning. Shooo! It was bad! Bad ... [*Laughs*] It didn't taste like whiskey, it tasted like herbs. So—I didn't like it.

MCBEE: And a lot of old-timers used to mix ginseng root and poke root and stuff with it, what they call making 'em some bitters, you know, for their rheumatism and the arthritis, but the only way it helped them, I think, is when they kept increasing their dose. It didn't stop 'em hurting, but they didn't give a damn for hurting then, you know.

Moonshine isn't what it used to be. Industry has come to the mountains, offering real jobs, with real pay, and no worry about going to jail. Some of the moonshiners have walked away from their stills. But some never will. Earl Palmer guided us around these mountains, and he left us with this thought:

EARL PALMER: As long as the streams run cold, and the woods are thick, as long as there are hills that God made, and as long as there's a country, moonshine will always be made by someone or other. Handed down—there isn't any way to erase it from the mountain scene. No way.

Whiskey isn't the only thing that's been distilled in these hills. The people are a distillation too, a boiling down of good Scots-Irish stock, refined by mountain summers, and winters, and condensed by hard times. Their memories go a long way back, all the way back to when whiskey making was any man's right.

Up in the hills, somewhere, in some hollow by some trickling branch, a hickory wood fire is licking the bottom of a copper pot right now, making mash bubble and boil. It's a way to make steam drinkable, and corn a little more profitable, and life a little more tolerable. As long as the moon shines on the mountains, there'll be moonshiners in the hollows.

The Auctioneer

(FREDERICKSBURG, INDIANA)

If you don't actually *want* a tomahawk or an oxen yoke or an inlaid walnut plowboy with one broken leg, then the thing for you to do is to stay away from Fredericksburg, Indiana, on a Saturday night because, as everybody around here knows, Howard Strothers is quite a salesman.

★ ★ ★

STROTHERS: All right. Hey, here's that polo stick. All right, I want twenty-five dollars, will anybody give thirty? What'll you give for it?

That's Howard on the podium at Strothers Auction Barn, trying to sell a polo mallet.

STROTHERS: What'll you give for it? A dollar bill? I thought sure in the world somebody'd bid a half a dollar on that thing. Would anybody give a half dollar for it? Half a dollar? I bet there's not too many in here that's got one, and that's a good one, too. Fifty now, to bid seventy-five. Sold at that lady back yonder for half a dollar. I bet she's glad she's here.

He sold it to a lady who did not come here expecting to buy a polo mallet. Around Fredericksburg they say that nobody can sell things like Howard Strothers. His auction barn is a social center, a bargain basement, and the best show in town. People come from as far away as Rosebud and Paoli and Livonia just to see what Howard can sell tonight.

STROTHERS: How much, what'll you give? Dollar bill? Dollar-dollar-lemme-hear-a-dollar! Would you give a half a dollar for both of them? Thank you, ma'am, I knowed you'd bid directly. Fifty, now to bid seventy-five—fifty—seventy-five—now one. Dollar now, and a quarter. Now, I'd like to see you get them; they're real pretty.

Every couple of hours a subauctioneer takes over and Howard rests his voice. When we asked him about his salesmanship he admitted even he doesn't know how he does it, but he does it.

KURALT: What did you sell at first?
STROTHERS: Well, I sold a pie supper over at Bacon, Indiana. You know where Bacon is? You know where that's at? Well that's way down yonder in the hills, Bacon is. Bacon, Indiana.
KURALT: And you sold pies?
STROTHERS: Sold my first pie supper. The first selling I ever done was a pie supper in Bacon.
KURALT: How did the pies sell?
STROTHERS: Oh, I think they done pretty well. Got a quarter for some of them.
KURALT: What is the most unusual thing you've ever sold in your auction?
STROTHERS: Oh, I don't know, I think the most common thing that I ever sold in my life was a sack of rocks. I sold a sack of rocks down here one night. I think that's the most common thing I ever sold, but...
KURALT: How much did you get for the rocks?
STROTHERS: Oh, I don't know, maybe a dollar, maybe a half a dollar. I don't remember now, but I sold them anyway.
KURALT: Everything that comes in here moves out?

STROTHERS: Everything that they bring in here we try to sell it for some price. We never know what we're going to get, but we sell it.

Some in the audience come to buy, but most people are here for the sheer joy of listening to Howard Strothers grow lyrical over a common cream pitcher.

STROTHERS: You know when you go down in the morning to get your coffee and you've got no cream pitcher there and you have it in an old can or something, you know, and the hole gets stopped up and you have to go to punching around on it. You see, you get your little cream pitcher there and you just reach right over there and pour it in your coffee. It's awful nice that way! I'm atelling you that that's awful handy if you drink coffee. Well now, I'll tell you, get up in the morning and you'll be able to put—listen to me. You give thirty-five? Thirty-thirty-thirty-five, who'll say fifty cents?

Everything they say about Howard Strothers is true. We sat and watched him sell a bunch of bananas, a folding chair, a bolt of gingham, a flatiron, a flask, a hand-carved wooden chain, and a book on the stock market. Our sound engineer lost his gloves here tonight, and we have the uneasy feeling that Howard Strothers might have just disposed of them to the highest bidder.

STROTHERS: My, my. [*Holding up an adze*] Now listen, if you're going to split some, you know, shingles for your house, if you're going to split some shingles, if you roof is leaking you got to split you a few shingles, now right there's a necessity for shore. You *got* to have that to split shingles with. All right, what'll you give for it? A dollar bill, anybody? One dollar, quarter now, half. Oh, I'd like to see you get that. I know you need it.

The Gumball King

(OAKLAND, CALIFORNIA)

We've been worrying about the penny. The government says it would like to eliminate the penny on the grounds that it doesn't buy anything anymore. As usual, the government is overlooking something. You know how gumball machines work. If you want a red gumball, you put a penny in, give it a crank, and out pops a—pink gumball. But even a pink gumball is better than no gumball at all. Whither the penny gumball? Can it survive in a world in which everything else costs at least a dollar ninety-eight? That was the question that led us to turn in at the United States Chewing Gum Company, and we found we needn't have worried. The penny gumball lives—thanks, in part, to Uncle Al, the Kiddies' Pal.

[*Uncle Al blows a gumball bubble.*]

Until a few years ago, Al was nobody's uncle. He was merely Alan Silverstone, a successful New York investment banker who wore Brooks Brothers suits. Then he asked himself, "What would you really rather be?" And the answer came back clearly, "I would really rather be a Gumball King." Now he wears a blue tuxedo with a ruffled shirt, a red tie, and a top hat. The penny gumball has been good to Uncle Al.

★ ★ ★

"UNCLE AL" SILVERSTONE: Right here we have Purple Poppers. Purple Poppers are sour grape gumballs.

You can put 'em in your mouth and pop out a bubble with 'em. This is like a vintage grape from the Sonoma County wine country. If you take 'em and put a whole bunch of 'em down in a barrel and crush them with your feet, you can make bubble gum wine.

Alan Silverstone's world was once full of municipal bonds and mutual funds, pretty gray stuff. Color has come into his life—Purple Poppers and Orange Chews, Powies and Zowies and Puckeroos.

SILVERSTONE: Everybody chews gumballs, from little kids who are two, three years old—in fact that's their very first purchase; if you stop and think about it, when you were small, the very first thing you probably bought was a gumball for a penny out of a penny vending machine, and then you learned what the value of money was.

KURALT: One penny equals one gumball.

SILVERSTONE: Right. In fact, that's still true today; even after sixty, seventy years of gumballs, there is still the penny gumball.

KURALT: When you were a kid, were you a gumball fan?

SILVERSTONE: When I was a smaller kid—now I'm a big kid—my parents never let me chew gum, so I look upon this as the ultimate rebellion, making gum and chewing gum all day long.

Anytime Uncle Al wants a gumball, he just strolls through his gumball factory and picks one out. He has six million gumballs a day from which to choose, one and a half billion gumballs a year. He spends his day chewing gumballs and pulling legs.

SILVERSTONE: This is my newest invention—Fu Man Chews, chewable Chinese checkers. You play Chinese checkers with gumballs instead of marbles, and then the winner gets to chew up the loser's gumballs, just like this. [*Uncle Al takes a gumball.*] This is the game you can sink your teeth into.

As Alan Silverstone, he was just an investment banker. As Uncle Al, the Kiddies' Pal, he has become a happy man. His motto? A penny saved is a gumball denied. Uncle Al, by the way, is a millionaire. He got there one penny at a time. [*Uncle Al blows the ultimate bubble and ends with gum all over his face.*]

Mushrooms

(FILLMORE, ILLINOIS)

[*Sign*: NO MUSHROOMING. KEEP OUT]

This is a thoroughly remarkable sign, if you stop to think about it, and it raises the question: Is mushroom hunting really so widespread and tenacious an activity that people have to put up signs to prevent it? Well, we've done a little investigation into that subject in Central Illinois, and the answer is yes. Mushroom hunters will stop at nothing.

In this season they are tromping purposefully through every patch of woods, their own or somebody else's, from Peoria to Centralia. These people should really be doing something else, their spring planting or housecleaning. But for two precious weeks in mid-May, they do nothing much but walk in the woods and stare at the ground. For what? For a wrinkled fungus. Success, for such a man as Bonnie Branum, arouses emotions akin to ecstasy.

★ ★ ★

KURALT: What do you do with these things when you get them home?

BRANUM: Well, you clean them, first; you get all the bugs out of them that you can get out. Then you put them in saltwater and hope the saltwater kills the rest of them, and then whenever you fry them, why, what bugs are left, you just chew up, I guess.

It is said in the backroads village of Fillmore that people

in northern Illinois don't have any mushrooms and that people in southern Illinois are too cautious and superstitious to hunt them. Well, there's reason for caution. There are mushrooms in the woods that, with the merest nibble, will destroy your red corpuscles, paralyze your nervous system, and lead to delirium and death. But in central Illinois, even children know enough to pass up the deadly amanitas. They also pass up mushrooms they're not sure of, the scarlet cups, and mica caps, and go unerringly for what they call the sponges, the waxen, sculptured morel.

MAN: Look around.
GIRL: There's one!
MAN: Well, pick it up.
GIRL: I found one!

They find it in the leafmoldy soil of the woods and in old orchards and under young ferns. And they never tell where they find it. The legendary mushroomers of Fillmore, men like Pug Jerden and Buster Carter and Goog Flowers, will do anything for a neighbor, milk his cows, mow his hay, but tell their mushrooming grounds they will not. Neither will Jack Cole.

COLE: One thing about it, it's something that a child, an old person, a lady or a man, they don't have to give anybody any odds physically, they can all find mushrooms. Say it's a universal sport. And they're good eating, whether you've got milk teeth or store teeth. Oh, they taste good, there's no question about that. A mushroom cooked right is one of the best eating things there is now, that is all. If they're not cooked so good, they're still second best.

Once found, of course, they're cooked, and here taste enters in. Norval Prater likes his scrambled with eggs, so that's the way Wilda Prater does them. Denver Spears prefers them in breadcrumbs and butter, so Alice Spears goes through a lot of breadcrumbs and butter in mushroom season.

Morels have a wonderful, delicate taste, far better than those rubbery slices that come in a can. But we have learned a secret: Eating mushrooms, great as that is, is not as great as finding them. Ruth Alexander, on her way home from her woods or somebody else's, has found 584 in the last week. The news has spread. Her name is spoken with deference all over Montgomery County.

Morels are a miracle. They appear only for a few days, only in the spring, and since they defy cultivation, only in the wild. They are a gift from the woods. People around here accept the gift.

MAN: Oh, I found another one. Oh, my God, and is it a beauty!

SECOND MAN: Where, here?

MAN: Right here. Oh, look at that! It's pushing up the leaves. Look at that!

SECOND MAN: Oh, beautiful!

MAN: And it is a fresh one! We're going to have mushrooms tonight!

Oystering

(CHESAPEAKE BAY, MARYLAND)

Out here on the Chesapeake, they call it "drudging for arsters." But after a morning of it, I want to tell you something: Whatever you do for a living, it's not as hard as "drudging for arsters."

Five minutes after the gray, cold dawn, the crewmen of the *Robert L. Webster* hauled their first dredge, and went down on their knees on the deck to start culling marketable bluepoints from the undersized oysters and rocks and empty shells. When they've culled about fifty thousand—150 bushels—we get to go home.

Chauncey Wallace has been at this wordless, backbreaking work for fifty years, and the others in the crew are not far behind. They say this is a dying occupation. The wonder is that men have stayed at it for so long.

The boats are as old and tired as the men. Once there were two thousand skipjacks on the Bay; now there are thirty-three. A few of them—*Seagull, Martha Lewis, Geneva May*—are circling out here above Sharp's Rock with us, their crews also on their knees. And this is an easy day, one of the two days a week when the skipjacks

may use their powdered yawl boats to push them along. The rest of the time they have to sail, or stay in port. What with light winds and an oversupply of oysters, they've been mostly staying in port.

But it is not age or weariness that is decimating the last working sailboat fleet. It is a maze of government regulations that seem to favor the efficiency of the newer, faster powerboats that now operate everywhere on the Bay, taking oysters with hydraulic tongs.

When at last her day's work done, the *Robert L. Webster* raises her sails for the trip home, you get the sad feeling that you're watching the last performance of a long-running play. This old boat with her leg-o'-mutton rig and her clipper bow has gone oystering every year since she was built in 1918. But her captain, Eldon Willing, says she'll likely go oystering no more.

★ ★ ★

KURALT: If you quit, what will happen to this boat?
ELDON WILLING: If we don't sell her, we'll have to tie her to the wharf.

KURALT: Do you suppose the day of the skipjack is just about over?

WILLING: It won't be too long.

KURALT: That'll be a terrible pity, won't it?

WILLING: Yeah, they're graceful.

So says *Robert L. Webster*'s captain. And what says her crew? Sam Jones, who is just sitting down for the first time in nine hours:

KURALT: Two more years to go?

SAM JONES: Two more. I'll be sixty-five. Lord willing, I'm going to try to make it, start on the old-age pension. I'll just fidget then on land.

KURALT: Do you think you're going to miss oystering?

JONES: Yeah. I might get a boat of my own.

In another year, or two, or three, the last bushel of oysters will be swung over the side of the last skipjack, and the old cry will be heard for the last time: "One, two, three, four, tally."

WILLING: Tally.

An era will be over. These watermen will find other work ashore. Whatever work it is, it won't be as hard as "drudging for arsters."

Peace to the World

(LA CROSSE, WISCONSIN)

La Crosse, Wisconsin: busy little city on the Mississippi. Not many of the people going about their business on a snowy afternoon have any idea that, just at this moment, down the street and around the corner, they are being prayed for. And you, by the way, just at this moment, you are being prayed for, too.

A golden clock in the corner of the small chapel of Maria Angelorum ticks away the minutes and the hours and the days. And every minute, every hour, every day, two nuns kneel before the altar. [*Two nuns are heard reciting prayer in unison.*] The clocks chime the hour. The two sisters end their prayer always with the same words, "Bring peace to the world." They leave the chapel, their places taken by others. The chain is never broken.

They are Franciscan Sisters of Perpetual Adoration. They have been praying *without interruption* for a hundred years! This began in 1878. Every hour of every day and night for a century, two sisters have been on their knees, side by side, always praying for the same thing—for an end to sickness and hunger, for an end to social injustice, for wisdom in high places, for their city and their country, for their friends, for their enemies, for all people, including you and me—always ending, "Bring peace to the world."

Sister Mileta, a scholar and writer, historian of the St. Rose convent, first took her place in this chain of prayer in 1915—hundreds of thousands of hours ago.

★ ★ ★

KURALT: Aren't you slightly discouraged sometimes to think, for example, that you've been praying for world peace for a hundred years and there's been so little peace?

SISTER MILETA: Right. And we think the Lord must be discouraged, too, after all these years of wanting His kingdom to come and fill so many who are so far away. Yet discouragement, perhaps, should be a reason for still more fervent prayer, rather than for giving up.

KURALT: So you're just going to go on praying for another hundred years?

SISTER MILETA: Hopefully, yes. Hopefully, we can go on for another hundred years, and perhaps another hundred years, till the end of time.

"Till the end of time" is not an idea most of us think about very much, but we stayed around the chapel of Maria Angelorum long enough for the intention of these women to sink in. Bright sunshine gave way to soft snowfall, and day to night, and night to morning, and always the ticking clock, and always the angels looking down from the chapel windows, and always the two sisters on their knees. They mean to pray forever. That will depend on young novitiates, of course. There aren't as many as there used to be, so one of the things the old women pray for now is for young women to take their places.

[*Two nuns conclude prayer: "Bring peace to the world."*]

4

TALL TALES AND DREAMERS

*T*here's a lot more roar and gusto left in America than I would have expected when I started out to see the country. I didn't know I'd run into prospectors, moonshiners, gandy dancers, timber cruisers, yarn spinners, brawlers and boasters in such numbers. I was under the vague impression that the robust life drained out of the land a little while after the Andrew Jackson administration, and that the USA was now fairly pale and humorless, safely buttoned down. I was unprepared for all the big dreamers and outrageous undertakings, and I was surprised by how many Americans are still willing to look you right in the eye and tell you a whopper.

American Weather

Well, the sun was shining a few minutes ago, but now it looks like there's a big storm coming. Mark Twain, remarking on American weather, said one time that he sat in one place and counted 136 different kinds of weather inside of twenty-four hours. That may be an exaggeration. When it comes to the weather, Americans do tend to exaggerate. So, when we decided to do a national weather survey, we sought out only exceptionally truthful individuals like my friend Roger Welsch, a Nebraska tree farmer and keen observer of Nebraska weather.

★ ★ ★

KURALT: When the real dog days come, it does get hot in Nebraska.

ROGER WELSCH: I don't think there's any place hotter than Nebraska in the summer. Down here by the river, just not too far from us, it'll get so dry that the catfish will come up here to the house and get a drink at the pump. Yep, really. Yeah. And a lot of the farmers around here will feed their chickens cracked ice so they won't lay hard-boiled eggs.

Well you may laugh, but the hot weather leads to tragedy sometimes. Kendall Morse remembers what happened in Maine.

KENDALL MORSE: Oh, it was so hot here in Maine last

summer that one day—it was right in the middle of corn season, that corn was almost ripe—and it got so hot that the corn started to pop, and it popped and it went all over the place. And there was a herd of cows right next to that cornfield and they looked up and they saw that popcorn coming down like that. And cows are not very bright, of course. They thought it was snow. And every one of them idiot cows stood there and froze to death!

For Maine, of course, that was a hot day. Here's a Hoosier weather report from Charles Porter.

CHARLES PORTER: It was so hot here one day in Odon, Indiana, you could take a frozen hamburger patty out of the freezer, toss it up in the air, and when it came down it was cooked well done. But you had to be careful and not toss it up too high. If you did, it came back down burned. [Chuckles]

We went to Arizona in midsummer to ask Jim Griffith how he and his neighbors are holding up.

JIM GRIFFITH: It does get a little bit warm. Joe Harris says it usually gets so hot and dry in the summertime that he's got to prime himself before he can spit. And the dog's sort of wandering around at midnight trying to find some shade to lay down in. It does warm up a little bit, but you get used to it. It's been known, especially in this part of Arizona, to get so dry that the trees will follow the dogs around.

That's dry, all right. But right there in Nebraska, Roger Welsch's wife has to run their well through a wringer this time of year to get enough water to cook with. And the river gets low, of course.

WELSCH: They talk about frogs that would grow up to be three and four years old without ever having learned how to swim. And they'd have to, in the schools, you know, get little cans and put holes in the bottom and sprinkle water so that kids could see what it was and wouldn't panic the first time they saw it rain. They tell about one farmer who's out plowing one day and it started to rain, and the first drops that hit him shocked him so that he passed out. And to bring him to, they had to throw two buckets of dust in his face!

Oh, it's been a dry summer, but it sure was a wet spring. Don Reed remembers how wet it got in the Middle West.

DON REED: In Minnesota, the floods were so bad that the turtles crawled out of their shells and used the shells as rowboats.

PORTER: The raindrops were so big here one day, it only took one raindrop to fill a quart jar. [*Laughs*]

Big as those Indiana raindrops were, they weren't as big as some Ed Bell remembers from a Texas storm back in '73.

ED BELL: There was one place there that I noticed raindrops nearly as big as a number-three washtub and they formed a kind of a marching pattern coming straight down, one right behind the other, and it wore a hole in the ground that we used for a well. And ten years later, we are still drawing rainwater out of that well.

What rain they get in the Great Plains comes all at once, eight or ten inches in one day and that's it for the year. Every farmer has a little lane out to the highway and the rains on the plains fall mainly on the lanes.

WELSCH: Like this road of mine, there's some holes out here you can run set lines in and catch fish out of the road. And there's one farmer who talked about finally having to walk into town, because his wagon wouldn't get up his lane. So, he had to walk into town to get some groceries, and he found this huge puddle out in the middle of his road. And there was a nice hat floating around in the center. So, he reached out with his foot and kicked in this hat, and there was a guy's head under it. So, he got down on his hands and knees and he said, "Are you all right, stranger?" And the guy said, "Well, I guess so. I'm on horseback." [*Laughs*]

Wherever you got puddles like that, of course, you get mosquitos. I thought we had big mosquitos back home in North Carolina. My grandfather told me he saw a couple once the size of crows, and heard 'em talking about him. One of those mosquitos said, "Shall we eat him here or take him with us?" The other one said, "Well, we better eat him here. If we take him with us, the big guys will take him away from us." What surprised me was to learn that they grow mosquitos bigger than that out West.

JIM GRIFFITH: They get reasonably good-sized, not so big that you can't shoot 'em down with a scattergun. You know, you don't have to take a rifle to 'em, but they get pretty good-sized. But the really big ones are up in southern Nevada. There was one, I remember, it was in the papers at the time, there was one that come in to Nellis Air Force Base up there, and they filled it up with high-octane fuel before they realized that it had the wrong markings on it. And—
KURALT [*laughing*]: That was a big mosquito.
GRIFFITH: That was a good-sized mosquito, yeah. that was pretty good-sized.

I should mention again I'm not sure all these stories are true. Americans do lie sometimes. There was a fellow down home with such a reputation for lying that he had to have a neighbor come in to call his hogs. But if these aren't true stories, they're about as true as any other weather reports you're likely to hear.

In the middle of August, it's easy to forget how cold it was last winter. A friend of mine who lives in a cabin in Montana told me it was so cold there that the flame froze on his candle and he had to take it outside and bury it to get it dark enough to sleep. Sidney Boyum says it was cold in Wisconsin, too.

SIDNEY BOYUM: It was so cold here in Madison that a night crawler came out of the ground, mugged the caterpillar, stole his fur coat, and went back into the ground.

You know it's cold when you see something like that happen. In Maine, Joe Perham says it was an awful quiet winter.

JOE PERHAM: Well, it was so cold last winter up here in Maine that the words froze right in our mouths. That's right. We had to wait till spring to find out what we'd been talking about all winter.

The real old-timers remember a winter like that in Nebraska. They still talk about the blizzard of '88.

WELSCH: The worst part was the first day of spring, 'cause you couldn't hear yourself think, for all the rooster crows and train whistles that were thawing out. Another guy said, no, the worst part was milking, because he said it was so cold that when you milked, the milk would freeze before it hit the bottom of the bucket; and another guy said, well, they learned how to deal with that in their family. They'd milk with one arm out. They'd milk out over their arm until they had an armload of frozen squirts. And they'd tie that up with binder twine and put it up in the barn till their mother was cooking and she'd send them out for however many squirts the recipe called for. [*Laughs*]

Arizonans are not much troubled by cold weather, of

course. But that desert is about the *windiest* place I've ever been.

KURALT [*as gusts blow the sand*]: Does the wind always blow this way?

GRIFFITH: Well, no, Charles. About half the time it backs around and blows the other way. In the summertime, the west wind blows so darn hard that it causes the sun to set three hours later than it does in the wintertime.

KURALT [*to Welsch*]: I guess the wind blows here in Nebraska sometimes, huh?

WELSCH: All the time. They say one day the wind stopped and everybody fell down.

Ed Bell says they had a pretty good windstorm in Texas just this spring.

BELL: Folks, that was a wind! That wind blew and blew and blew. It just got harder and harder; blew the bark off the trees, blew all the feathers off of chickens, even blew the four tires off the old Model-T Ford; turned a bulldog wrong side out.

REED: A fellow in northern Wisconsin wrote that in 1976 they had a windstorm so bad that it stretched his telephone wires so far that when he called his neighbor across the street, he was billed $17.60 plus tax for long distance telephone charges.

PORTER: I was out in the front yard one day and we had a windstorm came through there. That wind was so strong, it blew a big iron kettle across the front yard so fast, the lightning had to strike it five times before it got a hit. [*Laughs*]

WELSCH: Easterners often notice that in Nebraska, unlike other parts of the country, there aren't wind vanes on the barns, 'cause what you normally do is look out and see which way the barn is leaning, and that will tell you which way the wind's blowing. But they do have a Nebraska wind directional teller, which is a post in the ground with a logging chain on the end, and then you just watch to see which way the logging chain blows to tell which way the wind's from. And you can tell the wind speed by how many links are being snapped off at the end. [*Laughs*]

Well, of course, you'd expect the wind to blow hard in Nebraska, because there's nothing between there and the North Pole but a couple of barbed wire fences. And if somebody leaves one of the gates open, then there's nothing to stop the wind, all the way down.

PERHAM: Wind? Well, the wind blew so hard here last night that the hen laid the same egg four times.

Laid the same egg four times. That was in Maine. This is Chuck Larkin, who lives in Georgia.

CHUCK LARKIN: I seen a chicken, just this afternoon, standing with her back to the wind, laid the same egg five times.

Five times in Georgia!

WELSCH: The other day someone told me that they had a chicken here that laid the same egg seven times.

Seven times in Nebraska!

GRIFFITH: Old Joe was raising chickens and first thing that happened was that he got 'em back the wrong way in the wind, and the old hen laid the same egg fourteen times over before she finally got it out.

Fourteen times in Arizona! I told you Arizona was the windiest place of all! But then, it's a pretty windy country, as you may have noticed.

The Prospector

The dream of gold dies hard. There are a few old dreamers who haven't quite given up, living in a few old towns that haven't quite fallen down. I'm in one now. It has a name, but we cannot tell you what it is. We promised not to.

★   ★   ★

PROSPECTOR: Well, it was a rip-roarin' an' snortin' good-goin' town at one time. There were just people, and more people and more people. But it's just dwindled and dwindled and dwindled and dwindled down— where now, in the wintertimes especially, there's only about eight or nine people stay here.

It is summertime now and the population has grown to maybe two hundred, enough people to keep the two taverns running. There are some reminders of the kind of place this used to be.

[*Sign over bar, reading:*
CHECK ALL FIREARMS WITH BARTENDER]

There is one living reminder. If you go a little way through town and take a turn to your right, you will meet the genuine article, a fourteen-carat, old-time prospector.

PROSPECTOR: Hey, you know, an ounce of gold is only a teaspoonful, and a teaspoon isn't very big. Well there's

four hundred dollars a teaspoonful. So, when you consider it and look at it in that angle and you get into a mine where you can pan gold out of her freely and you can grind it out of there freely, you get the gold fever. I don't care who you are. [*Laughs*] And that's what happens.

This man has a name, but we can't tell you that, either. He doesn't want to be bothered by a bunch of people who have no better sense than to be watching television when they could be mining gold. He staked out his mine in 1962. It's three miles away, uphill. And for all these years, he's been carrying buckets of rock downhill and then pounding the rock into powder in his backyard. He figures there's a million dollars of ore up there. Getting it down a bucket at a time is something else again. The trick is to wash away the crushed rock, leaving the heavier stuff behind. The heavier stuff is gold.

PROSPECTOR: I didn't get it very fine, but it'll show some gold. Oh yeah, that's a rich rock. [*Laughs*]

It doesn't look like much, tiny golden flecks in a pan. But if you pound and pan enough rock and purify the gold and collect a few months' work in one lump, it looks a little better.

PROSPECTOR: That's pure gold there. That's an ounce.

Four hundred dollars' worth of gold. But if you stop to think about it, that isn't much of a payoff for several months of work.

PROSPECTOR: You make enough money to buy your beans and bacon. Of course, nowadays it takes quite a lot of money to do that, but I can do it yet with that.

All those years of carrying the rock down the mountainside and pounding it and panning. And what does he have to show for it all?

PROSPECTOR: Some years, I got maybe four or five ounces; some years, six ounces. But the most, I think, was about ten ounces. And that was when gold was worst, eighteen dollars. So, you see, I wasn't making too much money, but I could live on it. Well, now, if it had been today and I had that kind of gold, look what I'd have had. Ten ounces of gold is four thousand dollars. Well, I didn't make that kind of money.

So, he's not rich, but he doesn't feel poor. He and his wife, Ruth, have enough to feed the cats and themselves and keep a roof over their heads.

PROSPECTOR: Well, yes, I've made it to a point of where we can get by good. I mean, we don't have to worry about too much of anything. Ruth and I are settin' as good as you'd want to be. [*Laughs*] But we have made it the hardest way that you can possibly make it. You just couldn't go any harder way.

When they tire of beans and bacon, he goes fishing with flies he ties himself. And the streams are richer in fish than the hills are in gold. In winter, he brings home an elk or a deer, and puts meat on the table. Then he gets back to the real business: finding gold.

PROSPECTOR: Oh, yeah, that one's got a lot of gold in it, too. Oh, yeah, that's rich rock.

Right next door to his claim, the Silver King and Red Fox operation has brought in heavy mining equipment and a new gold rush is under way. The price of gold has gone up so much in recent years that now it pays to spend a great deal of money mining it. A huge corporation has a better chance at riches than one man with a pick and a pan.

PROSPECTOR: Everybody figures that there's a big, rich claim here. And they have, ever since I can remember. They call that the mother lode. It isn't here. There's no such animal here. But there's about a thousand small mines here and they all produce; they've all got mineral in 'em. And then there's some that ain't never been found yet.

He could sell his mine, possibly for real money. But then he wouldn't have a mine anymore. And the rock still looks too good to him to sell.

PROSPECTOR: And if all the rock was like that little half-inch it'd be a billion-dollar mine, not a million. That'd be a rich mine.

So, like every prospector who ever pounded and panned in the West, he lives in hope. Perhaps he can get some money ahead. Perhaps he can buy some better equipment.

PROSPECTOR: And if I get a good mill set up, I might have to pay Uncle Sam some money. You never know. [*Laughs*]

He's still out here. We can't tell you where. We promised not to.

PROSPECTOR: I say don't tell hardly anybody that we got gold like this, because I don't want it all over. I don't want everybody to know it because they'll be coming here and driving me nuts. [*Laughs*]

Jackalopes

It is jackalope season around Douglas, Wyoming. Jackalope season roughly corresponds to the tourist season. Tourists are told of a rare and wily horned rabbit. [*There's one mounted in the window of the drugstore.*]

Only the most gullible of tourists could believe that there is such an animal, the offspring of a jackrabbit and an antelope. [*There's a jackalope mounted behind the desk of the Prairie Winds Motel.*] But the most gullible of tourists come through every day, of course. [*There's a jackalope on the wall at the truck stop.*] And when people in Douglas tell the tourists about the jackalopes, they're ready to go hunting. [*There's a jackalope behind the bar at the Water Hole Saloon.*] And if the tourists can't go to the jackalope, Douglas brings the jackalope to them. You can buy a bone china jackalope, or a jackalope T-shirt.

Not wishing to be taken in by a hoax, we went to Roger Welsch, professor of English and Anthroplogy at the University of Nebraska in Lincoln, and a jackalope scholar.

★ ★ ★

KURALT: What's the history of the jackalope? When was it first sighted?

ROGER WELSCH: Very recently. You know, it's very much like those ancient fish that they've just recently found in the ocean that they thought were extinct, or like

Democrats in Nebraska; they've only been found very, very recently. Now one of the curious characteristics, however, is that even though both parents are considered very timid and shy, the jackalope isn't shy at all. It's called the warrior rabbit, 'cause it can be very ferocious. It can be a dangerous animal, actually.

KURALT: A streak of violence in its nature?

WELSCH: Yes, especially in a full charge. From three hundred yards, it's very difficult to stop them, even with a buffalo gun.

Jackalopes mate only during lightning flashes, which is one thing that makes them so rare, of course. But some photographers with telephoto lenses have captured fleeting glimpses for postcards.

A local taxidermist, Ralph Herrick, will sell you a jackalope for thirty-five dollars. It is true that all of Ralph Herrick's jackalopes have an insouciant facial expression, as if they know something you don't.

KURALT: What other characteristics does the animal have?
WELSCH: Probably one of the most striking characteristics is its ability to imitate, like a parrot, the human voice. And people who are camping, or cowboys, frequently report having the jackalopes join in in the evenings when they're sitting around the campfire singing. Usually in the tenor line and in a voice that is often called unusual but not unpleasing.

There are those who don't believe in jackalopes. But that just makes people in Douglas mad, and you don't want to make people in Douglas mad. They are so fond of the animal that they've erected an eighty-foot fiberglass jackalope right on the main street. And they issue hunting licenses. I have mine. It requires the hunter to have an IQ of at least 50, but not more than 72.

"El Pipo"

(EL PASO, TEXAS)

Do we not all have dreams of glory? Breathes there a man who, in the moments before sleep, has not broken through the Dolphins' line for a touchdown or sunk the long putt on the eighteenth at Augusta or sailed the Atlantic? Hector Barragan, El Paso hairdresser, used to dream of fighting bulls. What makes Hector Barragan different from the rest of us is—he did it.

Five years ago, a little too old and a little too fat, he started taking lessons in a dusty, small bullring across the border in Mexico. He still practices there. In the meantime, Hector Barragan—or Hector Berrigan, as most of his customers know him—as American as you or I, has become El Pipo, one of the best known *banderilleros* at the Sunday bullfights in the border city of Juárez.

★ ★ ★

HECTOR BARRAGAN: I like bullfighting really. I shouldn't be in it, for the reason that I got five kids. You got to start that when you're about seventeen. I think I was about seventeen years too late. The bulls do teach you a lot about goals and how to motivate yourself though.

KURALT: I imagine.

BARRAGAN: Yeah, 'cause if you don't motivate yourself, you're gonna get it! [*Laughs*]

Most dreams of glory are safe because we don't take the risk of having them come true. Hector Barragan's come true every Sunday afternoon.

*[Bullfight fanfares and cheers
as Barragan walks into ring]*

BARRAGAN: When I start marching into the bullring, I very seldom see the crowd. You just glare up into the sun and you wonder sometimes whether you're going to get it that afternoon or not. I think the worst fear of any *banderillero* has is for him to really not be good.

As the young matadors perform their veronicas with the grace that is given by courage and youth, El Pipo, who is thirty-eight years old now, must wish that he had some of those years back. But if he is short on youth, he is long on courage. He has been injured five times, gored so badly last year that he was laid up for weeks. And yet, there he stands, *banderillas* raised high, and this is not a dream before sleeping.

> [*Barragan dances before the bull*
> *and plants his banderillas.*]

There is no accounting here for the handful among us who act out their dreams of glory. Maybe it's just this: that tomorrow morning at nine o'clock, this man, a little too old and a little too fat, will be back cutting hair in El Paso. Today, he is young, slender, and bold. Tomorrow, he will be Hector Berrigan again. Today, he was El Pipo!

The Cadillac Ranch

We were just coming over this little rise on Route 66, west of Amarillo, and I said, "Will you look over there? That looks for all the world like ten Cadillacs nose-down in a wheatfield."

So we stopped the bus and came out here and found that it was ten Cadillacs nose-down in a wheatfield. There they were, in a perfect row, tail fins resplendent against a Texas sky of blue. At first we thought maybe somebody might be trying to raise little baby Cadillacs. Then we thought maybe the farmer just parked them this way each year after he bought a new model. Then we thought we better ask whose wheatfield this is.

That's how we met Stanley Marsh the Third. He's in oil, cattle, banking, real estate, and art. It's his wheatfield and they're his Cadillacs. Stanley Marsh the Third came out to meet us wearing a mad-hatter hat with a Cadillac crest, and we knew we were in for it.

★ ★ ★

KURALT: When people say to you, "What are those ten Cadillacs doing out there in your wheatfield?" what do you answer?

STANLEY MARSH: Depends on who they are. When I get a chance, I lie to 'em. I tell 'em it's for an Elvis Presley movie or it's for Evel Knievel to jump over, or maybe it's the Caddy cult and it's the new mother church for a home religion. I tell 'em whatever strikes my fancy.

KURALT: Well, if I asked you, what would you tell me?

MARSH: Well, I'd have to tell you the truth. The truth is it's a roadside spectacular sculpture made by a group called The Ant Farm, architects from San Francisco. From 'forty-eight to 'sixty-four that was the American dream—the Cadillac fins. They're the American dream because they were so badly made and so cheap that after two or three years, anyone could have one.

KURALT: It must give you a proud feeling of proprietorship to own the only ten Cadillacs in a winter wheatfield in America.

MARSH: Absolutely. It's like owning Stonehenge. It's the most important roadside attraction of our generation.

KURALT: I see somebody stopped over there by the road now.

MARSH: Just some tourists, havin' a good time, takin' a look.

KURALT: And asking some questions of themselves, no doubt.

MARSH: Yeah, usually. They'll come wandering over in a little while probably. We'll tell 'em it's a windbreak.

Before it was all over, Stanley Marsh the Third has us over for supper and everything, and explained eloquently his theory of art. It was wonderful.

But we won't remember anything he said as long as we'll remember the sight of a cowboy herding steers out there where the tail fins grow, as the traffic heads west on Route 66, and the Texas sun goes down on the chromium bumpers of the American dream.

Gordon Bushnell's Highway

As highways go, it isn't much of one. It only goes thirteen miles through the woods and tamarack swamps. It's all overgrown now. But of all the roads we ever traveled On the Road, I suppose we feel most sentimental about this one. This little road has a story to it.

★ ★ ★

GORDON BUSHNELL: This is pretty good gravel in here.

We met Gordon Bushnell in this same place about this same time of year, August 1978. Gordon Bushnell always thought there ought to be a straight highway from Duluth to Fargo. About twenty-five years ago, he got tired of waiting for the state to build it. He decided he'd better just build it himself.

BUSHNELL: I'll tell you the reason I started digging. I had a pain in my side and I went to see the doctor and he said you've got to have your gallbladder taken out. And I thought, well, if I have my gallbladder taken out, I can't dig that ditch. So I better start and dig it before I have my gallbladder taken out. And I

started working, and the more I worked, the better I felt. And the pain went away and I haven't had my gallbladder out yet.

After meeting Gordon Bushnell, I thought maybe the best thing about Americans is that Yankee stubbornness and persistence against the odds. Here was a retired dairy farmer with nothing but a wheelbarrow, and a number-two shovel, and an ancient John Deere tractor, building a two-hundred-mile highway all alone. When we met him, he had worked on it for more than twenty years, winter and summer. He had finished nine miles. He had 191 miles to go. He was seventy-eight years old.

KURALT: There must be people who think you're crazy.
BUSHNELL: There's more than you think that think I'm crazy! My wife thinks I am. Maybe I am! But it's been a lot of fun just the same. There's fellas have retired—younger than I am—that go and sit down and listen to TV, and they're dead.

Gordon Bushnell kept hoping the state would see the wisdom of a straight road across Minnesota and take over the job from him, but the state never did. That was four summers ago.

Gordon Bushnell built his road log by log, and rock by rock, inch by inch, mile by mile, working on it utterly alone for twenty-five years. This summer, Gordon Bushnell died. We came out here on a rainy day to find his road already growing up in weeds, which of course led to long thoughts about whether he had wasted the last years of his life. But I remembered something he said on a sunny day four years ago.

BUSHNELL: You know, just to come out here some days and look and see what you've done, it seems to be reward enough.

So he didn't think all those years were wasted. And one other thing: now that he's gone, the state legislature, which would never build the highway, is impressed by what he did. The state senator from Sturgeon Lake and others have proposed that his road become the Bushnell Memorial Recreational Trail. Hikers on the trail may wonder some day who Bushnell was. Well, I'll always be glad I got to know who he was.

London Bridge

(LAKE HAVASU CITY, ARIZONA)

Here is a man wandering in the desert. He has a perfect right to do so. It's his desert. Robert P. McCulloch is a millionaire, a man who has everything, but his oil company, his land company, his motor company, his cars and planes and houses weren't enough. He wished, wistfully, for something more. And now he has that, too. What Robert P. McCulloch wanted was the London Bridge.

"We could put up some flagpoles here in my desert," he said, "and down there a fifth of a mile we could put up some more, and we could fit the bridge between them. That would look nice." So he wrote a check for two and a half million dollars, and he bought the London Bridge.

And that is how it happens that even now, beside the Thames, workmen are busy stacking the London Bridge

on a wharf, each stone numbered and coded. And freighters are plying the sea with cargos of granite. And in Long Beach, California, other workmen are stamping "Received" on bills of lading labeled "London Bridge." And here in the Arizona desert, Mr. McCulloch's little purchase is being delivered. Mr. McCulloch is as happy as a kid at Christmas.

* * *

MCCULLOUGH: Surely we were a little awed by how big the project would be, but particularly so when we went to London and went out on the bridge. It happened to be raining, and the bridge was black through years of all its weather, and it was so big that it scared us a little bit.

KURALT: And it was yours.

MCCULLOUGH: And it was ours and it had to be completed. Now, lots of people don't realize how big it is, but to put it in simple terms, it's a little longer than three football fields and almost as wide as one of them.

KURALT: And you're going to bring that whole thing over here by ship?

MCCULLOCH: We're going to bring it by ship, and fortunately we don't have to do it overnight because it's going to take them about three years to take it apart and us about three years to put it back together, hopefully in the right order.

KURALT: How much money is the London Bridge going to cost, the whole thing, the purchase, the transportation, all that?

MCCULLOCH: Well, our estimates are this: The purchase, as everybody knows, or lots of people know, was $2,460,000. We figure that it's going to cost about $350,000 for transportation and about another $3,000,000 to put it back together again. So in round figures we figure it will cost about $6,000,000.

KURALT: That's a pretty round figure, Mr. McCulloch. Is it worth it?

MCCULLOCH: I think it's worth it ten times over from every standpoint, and we certainly wouldn't send it back if we had a chance to.

There's no water under the London Bridge site yet, not even a mudpuddle, and there's been a bit of an argument with the Arizona water people about providing it. Various wise guys have suggested that, having pawned the London Bridge off on Mr. McCulloch, the English might now be able to sell him the Thames as well.

Robert P. McCulloch, owner of the London Bridge, doesn't even hear such gibes. He is developing Lake Havasu City hard by the bridge site, lots of lots are sold already, he figures the bridge will aid expansion, and there's plenty of room to expand.

So London Bridge is falling down, and the pieces are landing out here in the sagebrush. And Robert P. McCulloch is confident he's got himself a bargain. These are English stones, but the principle that brought them here is undeniably American—the principle that if you have five or six million dollars to spend, well, what you spend it on is entirely up to you.

Ball of Twine

Francis Johnson, retired farmer, lives in a house by the side of the road in Darwin, Minnesota. Like many rural Americans of his age and upbringing, he believes in thrift and conversation. The fact is, Francis Johnson has always hated to throw *anything* away.

★ ★ ★

FRANCIS JOHNSON: When I got a new pencil, I always hated to sharpen it. I wanted to save it, and my mother taught me not to waste anything. She was that way. She was so awful saving.

KURALT: Nobody could accuse you of wasting any string lately.

JOHNSON: No, not for the last twenty-five years. Twenty-eight years for that matter, and all.

When Francis Johnson started saving twine, he just couldn't help himself; he kept on saving it. His ball of twine is now thirty-eight feet around and nearly thirteen feet tall. It is the world's largest ball of twine. If Francis Johnson ever unrolled it, it would stretch from Darwin, Minnesota to the Gulf of Mexico.

KURALT: When did you think of it? When did you start?

JOHNSON: Well, I'll tell you. I started this in the first week of March 1950, the turn of the half-century. Twine was accumulating around on the farm there, and I said, "I'm going to tie it up in a ball." When the ball got a little bigger, then I heard about a man who had one on television. "Well, maybe someday I'll be on television, you never know."

Now Francis Johnson is on television, but that doesn't mean he can stop adding baler twine to that big ball. Owning the world's largest ball of twine is a heavy responsibility: the neighbors brag about it; visitors to Darwin are brought to see it. If Francis Johnson ever rests, somebody somewhere may come up with a bigger ball of twine, and then where would Francis Johnson be? So let this be a warning to compulsive string savers: this is where it all can lead.

JOHNSON: You don't have to be crazy, but it helps.

Bill Bodisch's Dream

(DURANGO, IOWA)

Bill Bodisch had a pretty little hundred-and-sixty-acre farm near Durango—a full corn crib, a full silo to see the stock through the snowy winter. That would be enough for most men. Not for Bill Bodisch!

For thirty years, he just hated farming. A nice small herd of yearling calves was feeding in his barn, but Bill Bodisch's dream was no longer corn and cattle. At the age of sixty-eight, he and his wife, Mamie, were preparing to leave their farm aboard a fifty-eight-foot steel yacht, which Bill Bodisch built in his barnyard.

Here is how much Bill Bodisch wanted to leave. He worked on the boat day and night for six years. He laid the keel by himself, bent the heavy steel plates of the hull by himself, welded them by himself, build the wheelhouse and deck by himself, installed the giant diesel engine alone. His single thought was to leave his farm and see the world.

Mamie was going with him. They've been together from the days when he dipped her pigtails in the inkwell. And now, if Bill was going to go around the world, why, of course, she was going with him. She had never been on a boat, except this one.

The boat is named *Cindy Marie*, after his granddaughter. Some days when the sun came out, Cindy Marie's grandfather stood at the helm, in the barnyard, running through the gears, taking her out of Monte Carlo, bound for Nice.

The lights above his head he made out of jelly jars. The running lights are big ashtrays—a red one and a green one. He made the boat entirely on the farm—and, what is even harder, shrugged off all the doubts of his farming neighbors.

★ ★ ★

KURALT: You're confident that the *Cindy Marie* is going to make it to the Mediterranean someday?

BILL BODISCH: Absolutely! I expect to be there with it, when it gets there. [*Laughs*] Certainly—not only there, but even go there, back, and then down the Horn of Africa and up into the Madagascaran coast and up in the Indian Ocean and around the Horn of India and down through Australia and New Zealand.

KURALT: Are you sure you're ready for this?

MAMIE BODISCH: Oh, yeah! I've been dreaming about it with him. [*Laughs*]

KURALT: You're not too old to start a trip like this?

BILL: I don't think I am. I just started living! [*Laughs*]

KURALT: When you pull this boat into Monte Carlo, I wonder if you'd send me a postcard?

BILL: I'll send you one—not only from Monte Carlo, but from Singapore, too! [*Laughs*]

Some days, Bill Bodisch went out to the barnyard just to watch the icicles melting off his anchor. He dreamed of this spring for thirty years. It's a big world. For some men, one hundred and sixty acres of it just aren't enough.

AUCTIONEER: Hey! Get a good flowerpot...how about a half a dollar for one? Half a dollar, half a dollar! Half a dollar he'll sell it to you, half a dollar. Half a dollar! Step right up!

And the day finally came for Bill Bodisch and his Mamie. They sold the farm. They stood in a crowd between the house and the barnyard and watched the accumulation of forty years of their lives auctioned off.

AUCTIONEER: Half a dollar. He'll sell it to you, half a dollar. Half a dollar, half a dollar! Half a dollar? Who said it? Fifty dollars? Three fifteen!

Good-bye to the hay fork and the scythe!

NEIGHBORS: Good-bye. Best of luck!

Good-bye to the cows! Good-bye to the cornfields!

The maiden voyage of the *Cindy Marie* took her, mounted on a truck, past rural scenes familiar to Bill and Mamie Bodisch since they were school kids together sixty years ago. As she neared the city limits of Dubuque, the kids from Resurrection Grade School turned out to cheer her on her way. And as she negotiated the narrow streets of the city, people stepped out of Victorian houses to stare at the unlikeliest of sights—a boat from Iowa and her master, who never before this day had captained anything grander than his Allis Chalmers tractor.

The launching, on the banks of the Mississippi, was anything but uneventful. Cindy Marie fretted over her inability to break the champagne bottle. [*Crying*] So her father stepped in to do the job. And soon after *Cindy Marie* was launched and underway to a big cheer and a puff of black smoke, suddenly the harbor was alive with other craft—a coast guard runabout, and then a big Mississippi River tug. All headed to the aid of *Cindy Marie*, which Bill Bodisch, in a disdain of channel buoys and an excess of enthusiasm, had driven hard aground on a sub-surface breakwater. Never mind! She was towed off with no damage to her hull and but little to her skipper's pride. And when we left Dubuque, Bill Bodisch was fitting out for the South Pacific.

We've heard from him since. He made it past Rock Island, Davenport, and Moline. They waved as he went past Hannibal, Cairo, and Natchez and out into the Gulf. He made it, not without some misadventures, past Mobile, Pensacola, and Port Saint Joe. He and Mamie and *Cindy Marie* are in Miami now, soaking up the sun. We won't be surprised if we get a postcard from Singapore one day.

5

SMALL TOWNS

*T*he sign on the bank said BANK OF ENGLAND. I thought, What is the Bank of England doing in a little town in the South? Then I realized what town we were driving through: England, Arkansas. Folks in Coy and Tucker, and as far away as Blakemore, Arkansas, joke about doing their banking at the Bank of England.

I haven't come across a small town yet that doesn't tell jokes on itself and its neighbors. Small towns, really small ones, are self-conscious about their size, sort of embarrassed that they've been there so long without becoming a state capital, or even the county seat. But often in small towns I feel a twinge of envy for people who have known one another since childhood and found a way to stay on, marry, have children, and grow old in familiar surroundings.

Some small towns I have returned to more than once. Sitting at Jean Byrd's kitchen table in Madisonville, Kentucky, or hitching a stool up to the counter of Arrol's Drug Store in Arcola, Illinois, or listening to the easy talk that goes on every night at the Golden Nugget in Boelus, Nebraska, I feel that I am at home somehow, in the natural center of the world, and that there can never be a good reason to leave. I hate getting to know small towns and then having to leave.

Small Towns

(SHELTON, NEBRASKA)

At Shelton, Nebraska, we stopped at a gas station and asked the man what the population was. He said, "Oh, about a thousand forty some-odd." He said it's the forty-some-odd ones that make things interesting around there. We went there to pay a visit to the local newspaper editor.

Like a lot of small-town editors, Douglas Duncan does all the jobs. He runs the press and sells ads and helps his wife, Jerry, with the layout. But what brought us to his office was something Douglas Duncan wrote and published in the *Shelton Clipper*, an index to the American small town, which is amusing because it's so true. "You know you're in a small town when——"

★ ★ ★

DOUGLAS DUNCAN: You know you're in a small town when Third Street's on the edge of town. [*Laughs*]

KURALT: I noticed First Street's pretty near the edge of town here.

DUNCAN: Yes, it is here. Right, right. Third Street makes us sound a little larger, though. We kind of like to sound big. You know you're in a small town when you don't use turn signals because everybody knows where you're going.

You know you're in a small town if you're born on June 13th and your family receives gifts from the local merchants because you're the first baby of the year.

You know you're in a small town if you speak to each dog you pass, by name, and he wags at you.

You know you're in a small town if you dial a wrong number and talk for fifteen minutes anyway.

You know you're in a small town if you can't walk for exercise because every car that passes you offers you a ride. I think of a retired grocer here in town who'd had heart surgery. We almost killed that fellow with kindness. He was supposed to walk several miles a day to build his heart muscle back up, and every car that went past tried to load old Ralph into the car and give him a ride back home. He's a nice guy and we almost killed him.

You know you're in a small town when the biggest business in town sells farm machinery.

You know you're in a small town if you write a check on the wrong bank and it covers it for you anyway.

KURALT: Could that really happen? [*Laughs*]

DUNCAN: It could, if we had two banks.

You know you're in a small town if you missed church on Sunday and the preacher sends you a get-well card.

You know you're in a small town if someone asks you how you feel and spends the time to listen to what you have to say. Now, that says a lot about a small town. We care about each other. And when somebody asks you a question like that, it's because they care. They're not trying to make idle conversation. I thank God for small towns and the people that live in them. It's a way of life. It's America as far as I'm concerned.

Doug Duncan knows his small towns all right. He knows this one anyway. It seems a fine one to me. The strength of the country doesn't come from New York and Los Angeles and Chicago only, of course; it also comes from Shelton, Nebraska, population one thousand forty-some-odd.

Coffee Cups

Early morning on Main Street, Arcola, Illinois. We stopped into Arrol's Drug Store, looking only for a cup of coffee. What we found was the heart of an American small town. Bill Klopfleisch, the manager of the lumberyard, was already there when we arrived, drugstore-quarterbacking yesterday's football game with Ray Holterman, the town clerk. Bill and Ray and one hundred and sixty other regulars at Arrol's coffee counter have their names painted on their cups. So before Bob Arrol serves you coffee in

the morning, he has to look to see who you are. He painted the names on nearly thirty years ago. He laughs and says he thought painting the names on would make it more interesting to wash the same old cups every day. The regulars come and go, and Fannie King, who helps out behind the counter, explains to a newcomer what you have to do to get your name on a cup.

★ ★ ★

FANNIE KING: You've got to drink a hundred cups.
CUSTOMER: A hundred cups.
KING: Then you've got to wait on the waiting list.

A hundred cups—that's five gallons. Pat Murphy, the town mechanic, drank his five gallons thirty years ago and won a crossed wrench and screwdriver on his cup. Once, when Charles Lindbergh got lost in the fog flying the mail from Chicago to St. Louis, he landed on a dirt road outside of town, and Pat Murphy helped him fix his engine and get going again—that was fifty-some years ago, and Pat Murphy is still more or less the town celebrity. A hundred and sixty-two cups on the wall and everybody up there knows everybody else. But you have to be from Arcola to decipher some of the names.

BOB ARROL: His name is John Clark, and when he went to grade school here he was called "Blackie"; and as corny as it may be, that's a black key. [*Close-up of black key painted on cup*]

Arrol's Pharmacy serves no food with the coffee, but on special occasions somebody goes home and bakes some cookies or cake for the regulars. Ma Bailey took one look at us taping all this and decided it was a special occasion.

MA BAILEY: Feel! [*She holds up cake pan for Kuralt to touch.*] Underneath.
KURALT: Oh, it's still warm!

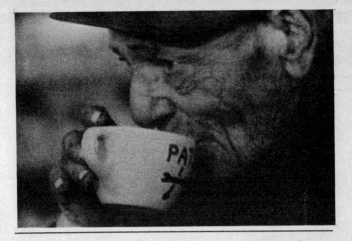

BAILEY: I went home and made those after I left here.

KURALT: Do you do this often?

BAILEY: I've been known to make three or four pans a day. And they don't last long. Who else wants a brownie? How many more?

Ma Bailey's brownies help the morning go by, and we began to wish—just for this morning—that we didn't have to travel on interminably; that we could stay in Arcola and enter into the talk about pheasant hunting.

CUSTOMER #1: I saw two cock pheasant all fall.

CUSTOMER #2: Is that right? Have you heard very many that did get them?

CUSTOMER #3: They're kind of scarce this winter.

CUSTOMER #1: Rough winter on them. They froze up.

And look forward to the big dance with Fannie and Bill.

CUSTOMER #4: You're going to the New Year's dance, aren't you?

KING: I don't know. I asked him last night, I said...

We wished we could stay and drink our five gallons and get a cup up there with our name on it, like Virge Roberts, the banker, or Bob Vogel, the tree surgeon, or Big Ben Shields, who was one of the first in town to volunteer for the Korean War, and whose cup still carries its star from those days. To have a cup with your name on it—it is such a small thing. But when you die, or leave town, they take your cup down from the rack at Arrol's Pharmacy, so if your cup is up there it means you're alive. The cups may not be such a small thing after all. They are a town register, and a history, and a confirmation that life goes on in a small American town.

Her Honor

(HERRICK, ILLINOIS)

Stand back please, make way for the Mayor! With her flashlight in one hand and her .38 revolver in the other, Mayor Maggie Conn of Herrick, Illinois, is on her way to work. The fact that she will be seventy-six on her next birthday doesn't slow her down any, as you will find out if you get in her way. Mayor Maggie is the law in Herrick, also Street Engineer, Health Inspector, Marriage Counselor, Fire Commissioner, and Dogcatcher. Before she became Mayor there wasn't any public water system in Herrick. Now there is, and heaven help you if you don't pay your water bill.

★ ★ ★

MAYOR MAGGIE CONN [*to the Town Clerk*]: Call them up and tell them that if they don't pay it by tomorrow we'll shut their water off. [*To Kuralt*] See, that usually gets them, that usually scares them, they get out and pay, see. That's about all of that. That's the job of being a water commissioner.

Maggie Conn was born in this town in 1895, but she ran away from home at eighteen and became a soft-eyed singer and dancer on the Orpheum Circuit, sharing bills with the likes of Jimmy Durante and Jack Benny under the stage name of Bobbie Adams. After two marriages went on the rocks, she came back to Herrick to be with her ailing mother, and now, going on seventy-six, she has found her great role at last. It's the same one Gary Cooper played in *High Noon*.

KURALT: I would think that some people would take advantage of a lady mayor.

MAYOR CONN: Not this one they don't. Nobody takes advantage of me. Listen, son, you fight the years of show business all by yourself the way I've had to fight through those ten years on Broadway amongst the gangsters and—ho, I love a good fight.

See this nice long street all that way down there? This is a beautiful drag-race place, and they just used it when I first took over. And so to stop them I used to come and park around that corner down there, and I had my gun and a flashlight, so I'd walk out in front of them and do this (blinking flashlight) and that means you stop whenever my flashlight goes that way. Well, they didn't stop. Then when they got to me I'd say, "Stop or I'll shoot," and if they didn't stop I shot, right through the tail end of their car, see. And if I hit the gas tank it's all right. That's how I stopped the drag racing on this avenue here.

Herrick was founded as a wild little town a hundred years ago, and its reputation hung on until 1965, when Maggie Conn got elected in a write-in vote, 151 to 2, and

set about calming things down. Mayor Maggie hates clutter even more than drag racing. As fast as Herrick's ornery beer drinkers clutter up the streets with beer cans, Herrick's ornery Mayor picks them up.

MAYOR CONN: We've got people here in this town, they don't care about cleanliness, they don't care about keeping anything nice. Those kind of people I just can't understand.

KURALT: Doesn't that discourage a mayor?

MAYOR CONN: Discourage—let me tell you something, son. There's been many a time that I sat here at this table and cried! I'd be so discouraged and so upset at the minds and the tempers of the people in this town that if I could pick this acre up and this house and put it in a suitcase, I'd be gone a long time ago.

KURALT: Well, why do you keep on being Mayor if its—

MAYOR CONN: They keep electing me! [*To child*] Hi, honey, got a kiss for me?

Exasperated as she gets with her town, Maggie Conn is proud of it, too. She's given up on a lot of the old folks, but she has high hopes for the kids.

MAYOR CONN: Well, what is it? Oh, a turtle!

And she's proud of the progress the town has made—like, for instance, the new—well, almost new, fire trucks.

MAYOR CONN: When I first came here we had one old fire truck. Somebody left it out in the cold and froze and busted it, so that was no good at all. So then we started in to build this firehouse, and the whole town built it—everybody came and everybody worked. We bought both of these firetrucks secondhand, fixed them up and painted them all up, the boys painted them; they put the names on them and all like that, and I'm mighty proud of them, because the whole town helped to do it. Everybody worked to buy these trucks. [*Spying an errant horseman*] See that? He rides on the sidewalk, he doesn't care where he goes, he thinks he's out in a forty-acre field, and—yeah, see, see, now he's going to go—now, wait a minute, you'd better not come up that sidewalk, brother, I'll be down there after you with a—

Maggie Conn, the pistol-packing Mayor of Herrick, gets paid five dollars a month, and the voters figure they've got a bargain. They keep her in, and she tells them where to get off.

MAYOR CONN: Now, let me tell you something. Don't you let that horse do anything in the middle of the street where I'm going to walk on it, see.
MAN: Okay, I'll tell him not to.
MAYOR CONN: Tell him not to *now*!

Boontling

We heard there was a lost valley in the California hill country, a remote place where nearly a hundred years ago the loggers and sheep ranchers made up a language of their own, partly just for fun, partly to confuse strangers. They still talk Boontling in Boonville, we were told. You can't understand 'em.

So we came to Boonville, and we couldn't understand 'em.

★ ★ ★

KURALT: Hello?
WAITRESS: Good morning.
KURALT: Nice day.
WAITRESS: Oh, it looks kind of peerlified, don't it? [*That means it looks like rain.*]
KURALT: Good hamburger!
WAITRESS: Thank you. We've got pretty good hot zeese [*that means coffee*] too. And not only that, but this place won't dehig you. [*That means you'll get your money's worth.*]
KURALT: It looks like a good apple crop this year.
MAN: Gatel crop good and plenty higs. Many kimmies and bahl dames come a long ways to buy ganos and Johnny Pete [*You're on your own here, reader, but watch out for that cider!*]

Even the local highway patrolman has learned to speak Boontling. He says he has to get along in the valley.

MAN: Did some posey tweed string a socker up there?
PATROLMAN: Arked his moshe.
MAN: Yeah?
PATROLMAN: Yeah.
QUESTION: String it bad?
PATROLMAN: Yeah. Strung it.

[*The preceding dialogue had to do with a hippie type wrecking his car*.]

As we drove around the valley, we learned that zeese means coffee, because an old-timer named Z.C. used to make his coffee so strong. A jeffer is a fire, because Inn-keeper Jeff Vestal used to light big fires. And Booner Jack June provided some further translations.

BOONER JACK JUNE: Well, a doctor is a shoveltooth.
KURALT: A shoveltooth?
JUNE: Yes, a shoveltooth. That was a doctor that had protruding front teeth. If you pike to the shoveltooth, why that's goin' to the doctor.
KURALT: Why do people go to so much trouble to speak a separate language in this valley to begin with?
JUNE: Well, I think you should go back and realize we were in a pretty remote area. If a brightlighter came in, you wanted to harp a little nonchness on him, you know.
KURALT: A stranger from the city, huh?
JUNE: Right. If he come in, it was just nice to be able to talk around him a little bit, you know, and—
KURALT: But you can still talk around brightlighters today.
JUNE: Oh, yeah, we can string 'em.

We wondered if the youngsters of the valley were pick-ing up the language from the old codgies. And I guess they are, because when we asked a wee tweed if he knew

"Tom, Tom the Piper's Son," this is what he answered.

WEE TWEED: Cerk, Cerk, the tooter's tweed
Strung his borp and shied
They gormed the borp and dreeked wee Cerk,
And he piked plenty greeneyed!

So Boontling survives. It may not always, but it does for now, and, as they say in Boont, a dom in the dukes is bahler than dubs in the sham. [*A bird in the hand,* etc.]

This is the telveef kimmey pikin' through Boont.

The Georgetown Telephone Company

(GEORGETOWN, MISSISSIPPI)

Making a telephone call in America today can take a little time. You have to say, "Operator, I'd like to charge the call to a billing code number in Area Code 212. The number is 555-4114. My name is K-U-R-A-L-T. I'd like to call Area Code 212, 555-4321, Extension 3613." In Georgetown, Mississippi, things are a little simpler. You just give the phone a crank and say, "Patricia, get me the drugstore."

★ ★ ★

MRS. PATRICIA BEASLEY: You want Georgetown Drugstore? The number is 8; shall I ring? Thank you.

Patricia is Mrs. Mallard Beasley, the operator for the eighty-five-phone Georgetown Telephone Company.

MRS. BEASLEY: Tommy, come here. What did you do? Listen, run in there and wash your hands for lunch. Run on.
TOMMY: No.
MRS. BEASLEY: Go on now.
TOMMY: They ain't dirty.
MRS. BEASLEY: Yes, they are.

The switchboard is in her living room. It has been in somebody's living room since about 1890 when the company was founded. There may be a couple hundred of

these little magneto-operated telephone systems left in America, but they are going fast. The Georgetown Telephone Company switches over to dial phones next month, and Mrs. Beasley will no longer be needed to say...

MRS. BEASLEY: Number, please. I think he's downtown, Juanita. Okay, good-bye.

KURALT: Do you know everybody on the telephone system?

MRS. BEASLEY: Yes, I know everybody here in town, yes.

KURALT: What kind of requests do you get from people?

MRS. BEASLEY: Well, a lot of them, you know, ask me to take messages for them, and they go and visit their friend and say don't ring me over here for the next hour or so, I'll be over at so-and-so's house, ring me over there. There's a little girl, Karen, she rings up, and she just says I want Grandmommy, so I just ring her grandmother for her. I just know who she is, you know.

KURALT: Karen won't be able to do that when the dials come in.

MRS. BEASLEY: No, I don't know what she'll do then.

Georgetown is eager to have dial telephones like all the rest of us; it is a mark of modernity, and every town likes to feel modern. But you wonder if Georgetown knows what it's giving up. Take Mr. L. D. Spell, down at Spell's Store, for example. He's been able to get by all his life without cluttering up his brain with the telephone numbers that clutter up yours and mine. If he wants to call his brother, for example, he does it with a twist of the wrist.

MR. SPELL: Hello, Patricia? Could I speak to Brother Rupert?

And when dial phones come in, Mrs. Bidwell Berry is going to give up a major convenience.

MRS. BERRY: Hello, Patricia? Have you seen Cathy?

In another month, if you want to call Elmer Knight's truck stop in Georgetown, Mississippi, you'll have to look up the telephone number. In the meantime, the number is 2, and if you can't remember that, Pat Beasley will connect you anyway.

People in Georgetown are all excited about the coming of dial phones. They haven't discovered yet that if you say to a dial phone, "Get me the truck stop," it doesn't know how.

Loving County

Loving County is the emptiest county in the United States. It covers six hundred sixty-nine square miles and has a population of ninety-one persons. That's about one lonely soul for every seven square miles. Loving County doesn't have many people, and it doesn't have much else.

★ ★ ★

MAN: There's no other county like this one; we don't have a cemetery, we don't have a road, we don't have nothing.

WOMAN: We don't have a hospital or a doctor or nurses.

MAN: We don't have no nightclubs, we don't have no big bars, anything to visit, we don't have no fancy restaurant.

There are no motels in the county. No movies, no newspaper, no radio, no TV, no pool hall, no bowling alley. No McDonald's. No Burger King, no Wendy's. No Kentucky Fried Chicken. There is one road in Loving County. Occasionally it brings a tourist—almost always somebody who missed a turn in Odessa and came here by mistake.

There is one town. It's called Mentone. It has exactly two businesses, Mattie Thorp's gas station, with a couple of pumps outside and a little store inside. It is the closest thing to a supermarket in Loving County . . . and Newt

Keen's tavern. If you've seen the gas station, and you've seen the tavern, you've seen all there is to see.

KURALT: If a stranger came to town and wanted to see the bright lights, though, what would you tell him?
J. J. WHEAT: Here in Mentone? I'd tell him to keep going on through, just don't slow up, just keep going.

J. J. Wheat is a character. He's also fabulously, unimaginably rich—because there is one thing Loving County *does* have: oil. J. J. Wheat's father, who was also J. J. Wheat, drilled for oil out here in the early twenties. Everybody said he was crazy. Then in 1924 his first well came gushing in, and everybody said he was the smartest man in west Texas.

KURALT: What was it that made your father believe that there was oil here when nobody else thought there was?
WHEAT: I asked him that same question two or three

times. I said, "Pop, whatever gave you the idea that there was oil over there?" And he says, "Oh, I just had a damn idea. Shut up." And that's all he ever said. [*Laughs*]

By the early 1930s, Mentone had two hotels and more than a thousand people. Then the Depression came, and the people went. The oil remained. That is why the one thing to see in Loving County is pumps, pumping. And that is why J. J. Wheat is driving around in a new Mercedes-Benz. Of course, he didn't always drive a Mercedes-Benz.

KURALT: You had those Rolls-Royces—
WHEAT: Yeah, and they ain't worth a damn. Sorriest car made. [*Laughs*] Yeah.
KURALT: You've switched.
WHEAT: I've switched to Mercedes and they're the best, I'll guarantee it. I just drive the hell out of 'em and they just keep a going. Mine average about nineteen miles to a gallon at a hundred mile-a-hour, and by gosh, them Rolls-Royces, they just tear up. Every two weeks I'd have to take it down and get something done to it. Besides, my dog didn't like the damn thing anyway. He likes this Mercedes a lot better.
KURALT: Why is that?
WHEAT: I don't know. He likes the back seat; it's a lower car, he don't have to jump so high to get in it.
KURALT: When you bought the Mercedes, you just walked in and paid cash, huh?
WHEAT: Yeah, I have three of 'em. [*Laughs*] Yeah—

J. J. Wheat grazes some cattle, too. He's hardly ever made any money on the cattle. But they have their uses.

WHEAT: Well, hell, goddamn, I got to have something to lie about for deduction. I can't just flat tell a black lie; I got to have a little room there to play in, you know. [*Laughs*] So that's it.

KURALT: So those three hundred cows are three hundred deductions walking around out there.

WHEAT: Just about. So is all these old fences, I rebuild 'em every damn year. And of course they want to know exactly what I spend on it. They can put a man out here with me, I'll put the son of a bitch to digging—[Laughs]—digging postholes.

You may be wondering, if there's all that oil in the ground, and J. J. Wheat has more money than he knows what to do with, why there aren't more people living around here. Well, there is something else that Loving County doesn't have. It doesn't have drinking water. It's true that sometimes, driving around, you think you see a little pond of water on the road, but it doesn't splash when you drive through. It's a mirage. If you want water to drink in Loving County, you have to truck it from someplace like Pecos, twenty-five miles away, at a dollar-twenty or so a barrel. Nearly everybody in Loving County spends a certain part of each day carrying water in a bucket for cooking and drinking. But nobody we met has any plans to leave.

WHEAT: I like it out here; I love every bit of it. I love the weather and the sunshine, and the sandstorms, the hailstorms, the rain, when we do get some, if we ever get any damn rain.

KURALT: How long has it been since you had any rain?

WHEAT: Soon be two years. Getting close to two years since we had any good rain.

KURALT: I just think that if I were as rich as you are, I might choose to live in Monte Carlo or someplace.

WHEAT: Well, I went through all that bull when I was younger, when I was able to. It wouldn't do me a damn bit of good if I was in Monte Carlo now and some of those places—all I could do was look!

So J. J. Wheat stays on, on the land that produces his millions. Getting along in a county that has no schools, no country clubs, no lawyers, no banks. No plumbers, no electricians. No carpenters, no dentists, no stockbrokers. No undertakers.

There's no unemployment in Loving County, no welfare, no budget deficit. No crime to speak of. There is a sheriff, Elgin Jones, and he has a jail, but there's nobody in the jail. There are fourteen other county employees, which figures out to one of six county residents with a county job. With so few people, and so many of them working for the government, you might expect the taxes to be something fierce.

Well, hardly. Think of what you pay in property taxes . . . and then think of what Edna Dewees pays. She has a nice house, four-car garage, about a hundred and ten acres of land—and her property tax bill last year . . .

EDNA: I think I paid four dollars and forty-seven cents taxes.

Residents don't pay taxes in a county like this; the taxes are paid by the big oil companies, with whatever they've got left after they pay J. J. Wheat his royalties each month. How it gladdens the heart of an old cattleman to see that machinery where the cows used to be.

WHEAT: That's a pumpjack there, that's the best cows of all, they really pay off. I wish I had a whole goddamn ranch full of them, just suit the hell out of me! [*Laughs*]

The pumps pump money, all day and all night. They are the most prominent feature of Loving County. Six hundred sixty-nine square miles, ninety-one people. No water to speak of. Not much of anything to speak of, except wide-open spaces and fresh air, and the beauty of the west Texas sunset. It is the emptiest county in the country. But at this time of day, J. J. Wheat likes to look up [*pumpjack churns away*] and admire the scenery.

American Names

We spend a lot of time in bus stations. When every place else in town is closed, you can still get a cup of coffee in a bus station. I don't know how long it's been since you've been in a bus station, but if you are in love with American names, you could be happy just sitting here all day and listening.

★ ★ ★

BUS ANNOUNCER: This will be the first call for the east-bound bus for Junction City, Harrisburg, Halsey, Brownsville, Crawfordsville, Holley, Sweet Home, Hoodoo, Sisters, Bend,——

Did you hear what that man said? Sweet Home, Hoodoo, Sisters, Bend? I suppose the names of Paris and London and Rome make some people's hearts beat faster. As for me, give me Sweet Home, Hoodoo, Sisters, and Bend.

BUS ANNOUNCER: Cheyenne, Denver, Dallas, Oklahoma City, Wichita, Kansas City, St. Louis.

"I have fallen in love with American names," Stephen Vincent Benét wrote. "The sharp names that never get fat. The snakeskin title of mining claims. The plumed war bonnet of Medicine Hat, Tucson and Deadwood and Lost Mule Flat." Oh, we know what you mean, Mr. Benét, we have been there too, to Bug Tussle and Granny's Neck and Hell-for-Certain, and we have learned that America's names tell stories if you will listen to them. Stories of hard times on the frontier.

Times couldn't have been very easy in Gnaw Bone, Indiana. Life must have been a little chancy in Cut and

Shoot, Texas. And probably not much better for the settlers who named Hardscrabble Creek in Oregon. But more common are the satisfied names like Humansville or New Deal or Fair Play or Enough. Or outright Chamber of Commerce names like Frostproof, Florida, which of course isn't really. Likewise, we found little competition in Competition, Missouri. And no excessive opportunity in Opportunity, Washington. But their founders *hoped* there'd be, you see. The Chamber of Commerce instinct is strong, but sometimes vain. One night we passed through what must be the smallest town in America, about three families, and named, of course, Jumbo.

Americans have always loved the names of faraway places. I mean, why name a town Stony Lonesome when you can name it Valparaiso? It's a safe bet that the namers of Palestine and Warsaw had never been to either place; they just thought those names sounded nice. And if those folks in Ohio who named their towns for Cairo and Lima

had ever been there, they wouldn't call them "Cay-ro" and "Lie-ma." The same goes for "CAL-lus," Maine, and "MAD-rid," Iowa, and "Vi-EE-na," Georgia. Faraway places with strange sounding names, which sound even stranger coming out of American mouths. And if Odysseus, that old Greek traveler, could have come as we did to this intersection in North Carolina [*sign pointing in different directions to Carthage and Troy, N.C.*], which way would he turn?

On we drove to Grubville, Missouri, where a traveler could always get a little grub. We had a Pepsi and a pack of Nabs there ourselves. And on to Limberlost Landing, Indiana, where limber Jim McDowell got lost in the swamps one day.

Some town names are just obviously the result of indecision or desperation. When they were trying to think of a name for one pleasant North Carolina community, somebody suggested why not call it this? Somebody else, why not call it that? Until one wise man said, why not call it Whynot? And indeed, why not?

"I have fallen in love with American names." So have we, Mr. Benét. All those places named out of patriotism, some of them, or convenience, or humor, or hope; all those places, all those lovely names. Sweet Home and Hoodoo and Sisters and Bend.

The Parking Meter

(LOOKINGGLASS, OREGON)

Lookingglass, Oregon, has a population of forty-two. Just in case you don't know where Lookingglass, Oregon is, there's a sign in town to straighten that out. Lookingglass is eight miles from Brockway, nine miles from Roseburg, and ten miles from Tenmile. All right.

Now, Lookingglass has aspirations, even as your town and mine. It has a phone booth, as of last year. It has a manhole cover, the pride of the town. But the thing that brought us to Lookingglass, the thing that has every other town in Douglas County buzzing with excitement and ill-concealed envy, is the latest acquisition. Lookingglass has a parking meter.

It is a fine parking meter, shaded by a locust tree, offering twelve minutes for a penny or one hour for a nickel, ticking away serenely in front of a forty-acre field. It's hard to overestimate how proud Lookingglass is of its parking meter. People ride by to look at it. Some people put a penny in it even when they have nothing to park.

Proudest of all is Norm Nibblett, who runs the 120-year-old Lookingglass General Store and is Mayor of the town.

★ ★ ★

KURALT: What made you decide that Lookingglass needed a parking meter?

NORM NIBBLETT: Well, for many reasons, but I looked out there, and there was a power drill with three

horses and then a guy drove up his pickup and parked out there, and I said, "Look at that mess out there; you know, we need some kind of traffic control." Right? So I was giving back change, and a guy said, "Let me have some nickels for the parking meters in Roseburg," and I said, "Hey, you know, *we* should have a parking meter." So we finagled around and started looking and finally we got one.

KURALT: Has it yielded a lot of money so far?

NIBBLETT: Well, not a lot of money, no. But for a parking meter, figure sixty cents, let's see, a penny a minute, that's sixty cents an hour. Six eights, four dollars, what is that? Twenty-three dollars. To make a long story short, twenty-three dollars.

KURALT: What are you going to do with the money?

NIBBLETT: Ah, the money is being used for civic improvement. We need so many things in the downtown area, and, because we've got rings on the parking meter for the horses, and basically a lot of horses use it, I thought that now we need a water trough.

If Lookingglass has a parking meter, can a streetlight be far behind? The possibilities of progress in Lookingglass boggle the mind. We sat there with Norm Nibblett for a couple of hours, feeding the meter and chewing the fat, and reflecting what a beautiful thing is municipal pride—until, finally [*expiration flag pops up*], it was time to go.

The Friendsville Foxes

(FRIENDSVILLE, TENNESSEE)

There's a sign on the wall of the Friendsville Academy gym that says, CHARACTER, NOT VICTORY, IS THE MOST IMPORTANT THING. Well, on that basis, the Friendsville Academy Foxes must have more character than any other team in high school basketball. They sure haven't had many victories.

They practice every day, they work hard, they stay in shape, they struggle. But for five long seasons, since February 6th, 1967, they haven't won a single game. The Friendsville Foxes have lost one hundred and nineteen straight.

★ ★ ★

PLAYER: Four years ago, Friendsville was ahead by one point, and an opposing player intercepted a pass, and they scored. And we drove for an easy basket, but it turned out to be the wrong basket.

PLAYER#2: Couple years back, my brother went to school here, and he played basketball, and it was the second year of this streak then. I thought it would be ended the next year, but it never happened. It's been going five years now.

PLAYER #3: Seems like everybody we play has a good game against us, seems that way. There was this team last year that didn't win any, and won against us. They lost all their games except when they played us. We really wanted to win that game, but it just didn't happen.

Put yourself in the place of Johnny French or Joe Housley or Bino Ingram, and try to imagine what it's like always to lose. Put yourself in the place of the new young coach, Rick Little. This is his first job in life, and not one of his players has ever played a winning game. Watch the practice shots arch toward the basket, and miss, and miss, and miss.

Friendsville Academy is a small Quaker high school and the Quakers believe, of course, that character, not victory, is the most important thing. But even the sternest elder would have to grant that this is getting ridiculous.

Now it is the following night at Lanier High School, thirty miles down the road, and the Friendsville Academy Foxes, with one hundred and nineteen straight losses behind them, take the floor against the Lanier Eagles. There is something poignant and touching in this moment. The Foxes are up for this game, coiled like springs. But Lanier is a much bigger school, and its players, at the other end of the court, look like giants. In the Quaker Bible, David slew Goliath, but in the real world Lanier controlled the tipoff and scored in the first four seconds to take the lead. We will spare you the suspense. It was never that close again.

They tried to win. They really tried to win. They exhausted themselves in the effort. They lost, 66 to 30. Number 120.

They dressed in silence and walked together through the empty gym to catch the bus back to Friendsville. Somebody said: "One of these days." Somebody else cut him off and said: "Saturday night." Saturday night is when they play their next game.

[*They lost that one to Copper Basin, 76–44.*]

Names, Names, Names

On the road in Savannah, Missouri, I stopped by Lowell Davis's house, because I'd heard he'd written a book.

Of course, nowadays everybody seems to have written a book . . . a diet book, cat book, or how-to-get-rich book. Lowell Davis never knew how to get rich. He had a hard life as a farmer and sign painter and small storekeeper. But he met a lot of people, and that's what his book is about.

His book is simply a list of everyone he has ever met, every single person he can remember. That's eighty-four years of remembering.

★ ★ ★

KURALT: How many names do you have in there now?

DAVIS: I believe I got 3584.

KURALT: Have you met some whose names you don't care to remember?

DAVIS: Yes, I do sometimes . . . but I put 'em down anyway.

The names are arranged in chronological order, grouped by all the different towns he has lived in. Sometimes he can't remember a name. But then, sometimes his wife, Hazel, can. They've been married fifty-seven years, so they've met a lot of the same people.

The book begins where it ought to. At the beginning.

DAVIS [*reading from first page*]: That's Seibert, Colorado, where we lived at that time, and this is—John Edward Davis is my father. My mother was Ida Housman Davis. Lola Davis Lash is my twin sister. Ed Whittle was a rancher and neighbor, Richard Whittle was his son, Dorothy Whittle his daughter. Mistress Whittle his wife....Mr. Alexander was another rancher neighbor....Goldie—she was the babysitter, and she lived at Flagler, Colorado....

The list begins there and goes on and on. Lowell Davis's book includes not only the names of people, but also a brief description of most of them...something to keep them alive in his memory.

KURALT: —says here, "Beulah Smith. Extra long hair."
DAVIS: Yeah—
KURALT: Is that what you remember about her?
DAVIS: Oh, yeah. Everybody remembers her for that. She was a kind of a little dwarf, she never got no more

than about that tall. Her hair reached clear down to the floor.

Everett Moss . . . he was a bad actor, he was expelled from school.

KURALT: Was he really a bad actor?

DAVIS: Well . . . no. Not to the other schoolmates, but to the teacher he was.

KURALT: "Dale Howard . . . Generous with his bicycle."

DAVIS: Yeah. He was a real nice boy. I didn't know how to ride a bicycle; I guess he didn't worry too much about it. He let me ride his bicycle whenever I'd want too—I never did have one myself.

KURALT: Well, he's a good one to remember.

DAVIS: Yeah . . .

And it's good to remember Charley Hall, who gave Lowell Davis his first day's work.

DAVIS: . . . and I followed that old mule all day for twenty-five cents.

KURALT: That was your first money that you ever earned?

DAVIS: First money that I ever earned. I should have kept it. I'd have twenty-five cents.

Most people have something memorable about them, like Herbert Walkernagle, whose motorcycle caught fire in the town square. Or Elizabeth Davis Odell, Lowell Davis's father's older sister.

DAVIS: . . . and when she was fifteen years old she and her sweetie got on one horse and rode to Memphis, Tennessee, and were married down there.

KURALT: No kidding. A one-horse elopement, huh?

DAVIS: One-horse elopement. She was fifteen years old . . . marriage turned out fine.

Not everything turned out fine, of course. Wilbur Tyler was killed by a hay baler. And many others in Lowell Davis's life are remembered for the terrible things that happened to them. One man who saved all his life to buy a house lost his savings and went insane. There is much heartbreak in here, and illness, and death.

DAVIS: J. Fred Terhune was the funeral director here and he had thirty-two funerals in the month of January, in 1918 . . . that's when they had the flu. It was awful. Thirty-two funerals in one month.

There are simple, homely entries. "John Tulloch, always sold sweet potato plants." And grateful entries, like the name of Chester Baum.

DAVIS: "Chester Baum, taught me to drive a car in 1915." Just like that one up there in the picture . . . 1912 Ford car.
KURALT: Did you take to it pretty easily?
DAVIS: Oh, yes. I didn't have no trouble. Worst trouble was getting it started, I was too little.

Once his friends and neighbors found out about this book, they kept asking Lowell Davis if he had any celebrities in it. Well, you know how it is. A small-town storekeeper doesn't meet many celebrities. Lowell Davis finally got tired of being asked about them.

DAVIS: So, I finally put down one that—that was really famous here. You see it?
KURALT: It says, "Jesus Christ, November 20th, 1917."
DAVIS: Yeah. yeah . . . That's when I was baptized.

One of Lowell Davis's neighbors, when he heard about the book, said, "Well, I suppose there are worse ways of wasting your time." But of course, it is not a waste of time. It is one man's way of summing up his life. In doing so, Lowell Davis has conferred a little bit of immorality on every man and woman who has come his way.

DAVIS: "Uncle Matt Hoover." He was a Civil War veteran

... and he served a long prison sentence as a prisoner of war.

KURALT: You mean he was a prisoner of the Confederates?

DAVIS: Yes, he was ... for a long time. But he was a highly respected old man and he lived to be a ripe old age.

Some names go way back. Some are as new as each new day. Whenever he meets somebody new, he writes the name on a piece of paper and later types it in.

Today, he's writing down the names of a camera crew and a television reporter.

KURALT: And it's Charles ... K-U-R-A-L-T.

That makes three thousand five hundred eighty-seven names.

The Mountain Eagle
—It Screams

(WHITESBURG, KENTUCKY)

It's a raw winter morning in Whitesburg, the very heart of Appalachia, and at this hour of the day none of the enterprises on Main Street are open—save one, the *Mountain Eagle*, and it is open to a fare-thee-well!

This is the morning the paper comes out. All week, Editor Tom Gish and his wife, Pat, work with very little help, but on Thursdays, Ray, Kitty, Ben, Sarah, and Ann Gish pitch in before school to make sure the *Mountain Eagle* gets down to the post office and out on the streets by eight A.M. The masthead of this newspaper says: THE MOUNTAIN EAGLE—IT SCREAMS, and three thousand six hundred subscribers along the roads and back in the quiet hollows, most of them poor peo-

ple, are waiting to see what the *Eagle* is screaming about this week.

There are nine thousand five hundred weekly newspapers in this country, and in some respects the *Mountain Eagle* could stand for any of them. Tom Gish has spent his week checking over the copy of Mrs. Mabel Kiser and his other rural correspondents who report the doings in the villages, Millstone and Hot Spot, Ice and Kingdom Come.

★ ★ ★

Thomas N. Bethell

TOM GISH: Is that A-M-M-O-N?

MRS. KISER: Yes, A-M-M-O-N. I didn't know his last name, and I had to call back.

"Dave Collier is a victim of rheumatism and not doing at all well," Mrs. Kiser writes. "The Ford Maddens are living good on Rock House Creek. They have a horse, a good milk cow, and two hogs to butcher."

But the Ford Maddens are the fortunate ones. This is America's rural poverty belt, and what Tom Gish has on his mind every week are more pressing things than neighborhood notes—things like food, and jobs, and housing, and the destruction of the land. This week, photographer Jean Martin has had her film confiscated and her life threatened after photographing strip-mining violations at a mine owned by Bethlehem Steel. The editor talks it over with the state Land Reclamation Office.

GISH: Well, one county official threatened to kill me a few years ago if I published an audit of his accounts. I published them. He did not kill me, needless to say. Then I get calls all the time telling me that I'm a Communist, that I ought to be chased out of the country, and then there's the variety that says that they're going to catch me out on the road and beat me up, and push me off the highway.

KURALT: Well, there is a tradition of violence around here. Doesn't that kind of talk begin to get to you after a while?

GISH: It does, except that I've had so much of it really, that I guess I've gotten so that I can't really respond to it anymore.

KURALT: Of course, you don't have to take it. You could move.

GISH: Yeah, but that would amount to a kind of surrender that I just can't do.

For Tom and Pat Gish, there is only one reward for the kind of life they have chosen. It has been the reward of weekly editors from the time of Ben Franklin and Tom Paine onward. It is the moment that the press starts, and the words come flashing out in multiples of a hundred and a thousand, under the bold masthead: THE MOUNTAIN EAGLE—IT SCREAMS.

[*Sometime later, the* Mountain Eagle *was firebombed. Tom Gish didn't miss an edition. The paper came out on time the next week, with the masthead slightly changed. It read: "The Mountain Eagle—It Still Screams."*]

The Sponge Fishermen

(TARPON SPRINGS, FLORIDA)

You drive into Tarpon Springs expecting to find just another small town on the Gulf Coast, and the first thing that hits your eye when you step out is a mural on the wall of a building—Perseus slaying Medusa. That gives you the idea: Tarpon Springs is not just another American town.

It is, really, a Greek town. The names on the storefronts are Greek; the shrine is to St. Michael, a patron of Greeks; the accents on the street are Greek; the tunes on the jukebox are Greek; and the aroma in the cafe where the jukebox plays Greek music is of lamb cooking on a skewer, and onion and oregano.

VENDOR: Shiskebob! You don't like, you don't pay! Shis- kebob! Souvlaki!

If you walk down the docks near the souvlaki stand, the pattern of sun and shadow on the old wooden boats transports you far away from Florida. The hull design of the boats is two thousand years old; unchanged since the golden age of Athens, and their purpose is the same now as it was then, to harvest sponges. Sponges are the reason for Tarpon Springs. They grow far offshore in the Gulf, as they grow in the blue water off Greece. Diving for them is a job for men. There are men among the Greeks.

Leave the safe harbor, as these men do, leave the land and the music behind, and you feel that the ancient spirit of the seafarers rides aboard the sponge boat *Kalymnos*.

She will be at sea for thirty days. The diver, Manuel Maillis, sits at the bow as the wanderer Odysseus must have sat, erect, unafraid, a king. Every two hours he dons the twenty-five pound shoes and the forty-pound helmet and takes his life into his hands and plunges into the sea.

When the boats return, the sponges go to a warehouse, where John Kalodoukas sits clipping them and pounding the rocks and coral out of them as he has done for twenty-five years since he left the boat himself. And the sponges are sorted and stored. *Zo-ofiton*, the ancient Greeks called them, half animal, half vegetable. The sponges go into the warehouse.

The spongemen go to the Port Said, to listen to the bouzouki play its ancient song, and to watch the dancer and her veils. Or they repair to a place where no woman may enter, the coffee shop of Nick Lazaros Kavouklis, to play the old game, *koumkan*, and to drink the black sweet coffee. Most of them are old men. One of the young-

est is George Billiris, whose father's father's father was also a sponge man.

★ ★ ★

KURALT: Why are you still here?

BILLIRIS: Because I don't believe anywhere in this country, or in this world for that matter, you can find a more exciting life, because it is definitely a life of its own, it's excitement, it's adventure. Here it's different altogether. There's a gaiety, there's an anxiety, there's sorrow—you lose men or men are hurt, as they often are—and you exercise, I believe, every

emotion that a man can possibly exercise, and these are all realistic, they're not false, there's no pretense, because it's a man's world. We live in a man's world and think as men. We do things with a certain amount of dignity and with the air of responsibility, and we maintain. So, to work around a group of men that think the same, act the same, feel the same, and still each man is his own man in his own right, I think that's worth a little bit more than the sign of a dollar bill.

The dancing at the Port Said goes on all night when the boats are in port. The oldest in the line of dancers is Charlie Karras, eighty-five, once a sponge man, and the youngest is Cleo Tsataros, eleven, the daughter of a sponge man.

As our bus carries us out of Tarpon Springs, back toward the superhighways of the other America, we leave with the conviction that it is a varied and miraculous country. The music of the bouzouki we carry with us.

Where Russians Can't Go

(INDIANA)

A Russian may drive down Route 129 in Indiana, but if he should happen to encounter a slow-moving tractor or combine on the road ahead, and swing out to pass him, he might be arrested and expelled from the country. Judging from the map, the center line of this highway is the dividing line between Switzerland and Ripley counties. Switzerland County is, according to the State Department, all right for Russian travel, but Ripley County, on the other side of the line, is out.

Indiana has ninety-two counties. Russians may not go to forty of them, and most other states have similar closed areas. This is called reciprocity; the Russians do it to us, so we do it to them. The State Department says if they'll let us go to Gorki, we'll let them go to Cleveland, but as long as we can't, they can't.

We decided we'd visit a place where Russians can go, Bear Branch, Indiana. If any Russians had been with us, they would have found Miss Norma Demaree just leaving Mr. Gridley's General Store with a bag of groceries. Neither Mr. Gridley nor Miss Demery have anything to hide from Russians, and would no doubt have been glad to visit with them. The Russian visitor to Bear Branch might learn a thing or two about grain storage up at Althoff & Wiesmann's feed mill, but nothing the State Department wouldn't be glad to have them know. He could learn something about American youth by watching Larry, Johnny, and Kenny Griffin playing basketball behind their barn. Specifically, the Russian could learn that Larry has an excellent set shot from fifteen feet out. So this is Bear

Branch. Any Russian may come here and Bear Branch would no doubt be glad to have him.

Bean Blossom, Indiana, on the other hand, is strictly off limits to Soviet visitors. No Russian may enter, as we did. No Russian may drive down the main street. [*Sign on church*: BEAN BLOSSOM MENNONITE CHURCH. STRANGERS EXPECTED] The charming sign of welcome to strangers on the Mennonite church cannot be seen by Russians, and so cannot apply to them, and across the road at Short's Country Market, if you're a Russian, the apples are forbidden fruit.

★ ★ ★

KURALT: What about you, Mr. Short? Would you object to Russians coming to Brown County?

SHORT: No, I've been all over the country myself, and I think it'd do some of them some good to see our part of the country down here, see how we live.

KURALT: Would you wait on a Russian who walked in to buy some apples?

SHORT: Yes, sir, we would, because we don't turn nobody down.

MRS. SHORT: We never stop to ask them what race they are; they're just customers to us, and all nice people.

KURALT: Do you think that Russians would be any kind of danger to Bean Blossom?

SHORT: No, sir, I don't. We have everybody here and it's a well-protected little town.

So that's the kind of world we live in, the kind of world in which a Russian may visit Bear Branch but not Bean Blossom, and when he sees a sign like this one up ahead [*sign*: RIPLEY COUNTY LINE] he must stop. It's not that there's anything in Ripley County that would jeopardize the security of the United States; it's just that the cold war of reciprocity has come even to Indiana.

The next town up this road is one which no Russian may visit, and it's too bad. It's a very nice town. Place called Friendship.

6

PASSING THE TORCH

I find myself drawn to old people. My friends back at the office kid me about this endlessly. They say I never do a story about a man until he has lost his hair and his teeth. Shakespeare explained this, as he explained nearly everything else: "What he [Time] hath scanted men in hair, he hath given them in wit." Old people are more interesting than young people, that's all. Most storytelling is remembrance, and young people don't have anything to remember yet.

Here is a fact, encouraging to me: Young people more and more are being drawn to old people, just as I am. The disaffected young of the sixties, who went into the country to escape the lockstep of the cities, have turned to their older farmer neighbors to learn the old skills, from canning to fence-mending to dealing with a colicky colt. Apprenticeship is coming back in such crafts as weaving and stonemasonry and glassmaking. At the side of many a practiced old woman quilter there is a young woman learning to quilt.

The kids are into computers, yes, but many of them sense that there must be more to the future than the knowledge loaded into silicon chips and stored in boxes—namely the knowledge, valuable beyond calculation, that is stored in the memory and hand and eye of one who has lived a long life, and is retrievable only by patient listening.

Blacksmiths

(SILVER DOLLAR CITY, MISSOURI, AND
SAVANNAH, GEORGIA)

Time was when Shad Heller worked alone plying the blacksmithing trade around the mines in Pennsylvania. Every mine had to have a blacksmith. Every farm town and shipyard buggy shop had to have one.

These days Shad Heller does his blacksmithing for an audience at Silver Dollar City in Missouri. It's mostly a youthful audience, and while it's safe to say most of its members have heard of a blacksmith, Shad Heller's probably the only one they've ever met.

★ ★ ★

SHAD HELLER [*to audience*]: In the mines, chain was most important. We liked to know we had a good weld because a man's life could depend on the chain. It's just right. That's a good weld. You can actually feel it go together there. Then we turn it over the other way, dress it down. Old-timers used to delight in welding a wagonwheel turn. Bet you couldn't find the weld!

As a general proposition, you could say that all blacksmiths are old men and that blacksmithing in America is a dying art. But one thing we've learned about America is: Beware of general propositions! Listen to this and you'll see what I mean.

HELLER: Now that's really getting cold. You see it doesn't work anymore so we've got to put it back in the fire. There's an old saying: There're two ways for a blacksmith to go to the devil, and one is to work on cold iron and the other is not to charge enough.

IVAN BAILEY: You know, an old blacksmith told me once that there are only two ways that a blacksmith can get to hell. And one of them is that he works cold iron and the other one that he doesn't charge enough.

Ivan Bailey is a young blacksmith, and not only does he know the same welds as Shad Heller, he knows the same stories. Maybe there's more continuity in American life than we thought. After a slow start, Ivan Bailey has founded his smithy in Savannah and found his own old-fashioned labor of love.

BAILEY: I worked as a night watchman in a slaughter-house during college. And I washed dishes. And as

Ivan Bailey

a child I picked berries in a berry patch in Oregon the way all kids do there. And then I had two years that I spent in a monastery thinking about what I wanted to do. Well, I thought about it so much I decided I didn't want to be a monk and that I wanted to do something that had to do with art. So I went to college and when everybody else was dropping out, I was beginning to get interested in metal.

When I was in Europe, I said to my professor there once, "Isn't it a shame that all this work, throughout the whole history of Europe, was just left to rust and go to ruin?" And he says, "No!" He said, "That's really great. That makes more work for *us*!"

As we watched Ivan Bailey at his work, we got to thinking how many times in our wandering we have found this theme repeated—the young craftsman who surpasses his master, the young woman who is better at quilting than her mother, the young couple who won't leave the farm.

One place our thoughts went back to is Millers Mills, New York. . . .

Ice Harvest

(MILLERS MILLS, NEW YORK)

Currier and Ives might have called the print "Ice Cutting on the Mill Pond." But it's not a nineteenth-century Currier and Ives. It's a surviving custom of winter in Millers Mills, New York. Millers Mills has been cutting the pond ice and storing it for use in the summertime every year since 1790. Elsewhere, this died out when refrigeration came in. Millers Mills still cuts the ice, out of stubborn recognition that refrigerators or no refrigerators, some old things are worth keeping.

There are grandfathers working here today who swept the snow from the ice for their grandfathers, a memory they value. They wanted their grandchildren to grow up with the same memory. The ice is loaded aboard a cart, which moves slowly from the pond and passes down the one lane of the village, carrying its burden of ice blocks and tradition. Phillip Brown, who died in 1846, cut ice on the pond in his day, you can be sure of that, and probably took part in hauling it up to the old icehouse behind the church. Today, that's Hank Huxtable's job. And, when the cart turns into the churchyard and arrives at the old shed, it's Hank's father, Henry Huxtable, and his uncles, Jim and Dave, and their old friend, Dalson Eckert, who build the blocks into tight layers, insulated by snow and sawdust, that will last until the ice of February is needed for the ice cream socials in August.

Listen to them talk, and you can learn something, some-

thing about cutting pond ice, something about agelessness and continuity in a small town.

★ ★ ★

MAN #1: It's a good community project.

MAN #2: It's kinda fun, gets everybody together.

MAN #3: There's not many things that communities do anymore, tryin' to keep together, a cooperative effort. It's good for us.

KURALT: You make it look pretty easy.

MAN #3: Well, we've been at it quite a while.

KURALT: How many years?

MAN #3: Oh, probably fifty.

KURALT: Have you had any misadventures?

MAN #1: Yes, we have. Had a team of horses fall through, and quite often, just one horse.

MAN #2: Yeah, we used to take a rope, tie it on the neck, chop the wing off and float 'em and pull 'em right out.

KURALT: Sounds kind of hard on horses to me.

MAN #2: No! It ain't.

MAN #1: Better'n leavin' 'em in the cold water!

At the end of the day, after the pond is cut, the people always come to the old Grange hall on the hill to sit down and talk about this year's ice-cutting and compare it with years past and tell old stories to their children and spend the evening all together. It is a celebration. Something difficult and worth doing has been done—again! There are kids there tonight who paid attention to the pond cutting and know how it is done. Their turn is coming.

Covered Bridges

(VERMONT)

Why did they cover bridges? Well, not to give young lovers a place to stop the buckboard and steal a kiss—not at all. They covered bridges to keep the roadway dry and to strengthen the structure and to make it easier to drive farm animals across the streams.

And who built the covered bridges? Our great-grand-fathers, who knew the uses of wood.

And we are letting them fall down. By flood and by neglect, America has lost half her covered bridges in the past twenty years. There are fewer than a thousand left.

And where are they left? Mostly in Pennsylvania, then Ohio, and Indiana, and Oregon, then Vermont.

Covered bridges still exist in New England because New Englanders cherish them so. Besides, they're attentive to what's written in the scriptures, and it's right there in Proverbs 22:28—"Remove not the ancient landmark, which thy fathers have set."

That is where Milton Graton comes in. Milton Graton never went to engineering school. But if you want to save a covered bridge, he's the man you call on.

The people who called on him the time we visited him were the people who grew up within sight of the Bedell covered bridge, across the Connecticut River between Vermont and New Hampshire. It was built in 1866, sagged in a flood a century later, and was scheduled for demolition two years ago. Its neighbors couldn't bear the thought. They started raising money. One man mortgaged

his farm. And Milton Graton looked at the workmanship in the old bridge and sighed and agreed to save it.

★ ★ ★

KURALT: Are you doing it the old-fashioned way?

MILTON GRATON: Yes, yes. Everything's done by hand power.

KURALT: Why do you do it that way?

GRATON: To make it fit the structure. If you look at the workmanship you don't have to be an ancestor-worshiper to admire the person who built it.

KURALT: Well made, was it?

GRATON: Oh, yes. Yeah, they were artists. The joints are good. They are joints that you can't get made today. It's gone. The workmen aren't here anymore. They're all in the cemeteries.

Well, not quite all. Milton Graton can make those joints as well as any workman of the past. And Milton Graton has a son who is learning. There are always a saving few who make the link across the river of time—the connection between the way we are and the way we used to be.

Tiger Olson

"This is the Law of the Yukon, and ever she makes it plain. Send not your foolish and feeble; send me your strong and your sane." There's a man who has lived in a cabin all alone for more than fifty years, who Robert W. Service might have had in mind when he wrote that piece of doggrel. His name is Tiger Olson.

Modern Alaskans mostly huddle together in cities. Tiger Olson will not. He prospects, hunts, fishes, and, as he's done every morning since 1918, cuts the wood to make his breakfast coffee.

★ ★ ★

OLSON [*chopping*]: This is a tough one, this is.

In the North, Robert Service said, "only the strong shall thrive." Then number Tiger Olson among the strong. The man who just split that log turned ninety last month. His home, Taku Harbor, is a remote place of great beauty, which even the rotting timbers of an old fish cannery seem to heighten somehow. He has one neighbor, a newcomer across the cove. His next nearest neighbor is twenty-three miles away, in Juneau. There are only a few of Alaska's pioneers left. Let Tiger Olson speak for all of them.

KURALT: You came from Montana?

OLSON: Yeah, Montana. Yeah.

KURALT: Why'd you ever leave Montana?

OLSON: Well, on account of that I had to work for somebody else all the time. I wanted to get out on my
own. Now, Montana had plenty of opportunities if
I'd have had intelligence. But I came up in this country here and trapped in the wintertime and in the
summertime I went prospecting. At the time I knew
to be a prospector you got to have intelligence, and
if you have intelligence you don't have to prospect,
but not having the intelligence I had to keep on the
prospect.

KURALT: Hasn't it bothered you to be alone all this time?

OLSON: No, sir, it's a mysterious thing with me. I am not
as lonely in the wilderness as if I'd been in the city.
There have been times in Alaska, seven, eight months,
I never see a human being. It never bothered me
whatever. The only thing—if I lived alone like that,
when I'd come into town, I'd become what they call
psychic. I'd meet people in Juneau, Skagway, Ket-
chikan, and I'd read their minds. I'd know everything
they think about. And if I'd took advantage of that
I'd been rich today. The curious thing about the human
mind, you look at a human being and you think he's
got a peace as calm as a river. And you look back
in his mind, it's a howling typhoon. You know the
storm that's going on back in the back of his mind.
And by living in the wilderness I was able to do that.
How I learned that is from the bear. When I meet
one of those grizzlies, or one of those wolves, I had
to know what he was thinking about, if he was going
to have me for supper, or have me for supper. See,
there's two meanings to that, too, you know. If I was
going to be the main guest or the main course. But
if I was to be the main course, something had to be
done about it now, not some other time.

KURALT: You never got married?

OLSON: Well, the reason I was never married, when I was young there was no woman on this earth. This was a tough place at that time.

KURALT: Do you believe in marriage?

OLSON: I believe in marriage, correct, but I come here too soon, you know, this country here, where there was no woman around.

KURALT: It must have been a pretty tough life, wasn't it?

OLSON: It was actually a tough life. You know what turned my hair white, don't you? The snows of many winters turned my hair white. Sleeping under windfalls, with the goddamn snow falling on you.

KURALT: That's positively poetic, Tiger. You haven't lived a sinful life, have you? You haven't had much opportunity.

OLSON: There's no opportunity for it, no, no. You got work here and you got to keep going, see. Oh, I take a drink once in a while, and that's about the limit.

KURALT: Alaska is changing pretty fast. Does it worry you what the effect will be of all these people coming up here?

OLSON: Actually, I am lucky that my sentence on this earth is just about over, because Alaska, from now on, is not going to be as fine as it was before. The oil fields haven't done us Alaskans a bit of good. The politicians want to spend the money to get a population of ten million in Alaska. The Senators, they go back to Washington, D.C., they want to go back there representing ten million people. The governors, the state representatives, they want to be representatives of ten million people. All that's on their mind is to get a population of ten million.

KURALT: Are you in favor of it?

OLSON: I am not in favor of that whatever. I believe in keeping Alaska the way it was.

When Tiger Olson goes, he won't leave much—an ax, and a chopping block, a water bucket and a pipe he laid to bring the water down from a mountain spring, an old boat beyond repair, a string of cork floats hanging on a tree. If you measure a man by how much he has earned or saved or built or paved, you might think of him as a failure. But in Tiger Olson's world, all the failures are dead and gone. He survived.

Ray Rouse

(FRIDAY CREEK, ALASKA)

Homesteading works this way. The government gives you one hundred and sixty acres of land, just gives it to you. Then you have to keep it. To do that, you have to live on the land most of the year. You have to clear at least twenty acres and plant it. The principal preoccupation of Alaska in this season is clearing land. Grown men are doing it, little children are doing it. By bulldozer and by hand, the spruce forests somehow give way to plowed fields, and America's new pioneers turn homesteads into homes.

But cutting a farm out of a wilderness was never easy. It wasn't easy in Tennessee, it wasn't easy in South Dakota, and out on the new frontier it's just as hard as ever.

We met a homesteader when we stopped for coffee at the Frontier Cafe in Palmer. He was back in the kitchen, cooking. What he was doing there was trying to make a little money. Ray Rouse, who three years ago was a discontented Pennsylvania tool and die maker, had learned what his predecessors of the last century learned—there's precious little money in homesteading. But even while he

cooks, Ray Rouse dreams of his one hundred and sixty acres in the hills. When we asked him if he'd show us the place, he was ready. He keeps his pack under the cafe's kitchen sink.

So that is how it happened that the next day we found ourselves aboard an unlikely six by six truck with no brakes, no lights, and no license plates, slogging up a logging road toward Ray's place. It's twenty miles, he said, and a little hard to get to. The first fourteen miles from town went all right; then the truck settled into a mud hole and we discovered that Ray's place was *impossible* to get to, at least that day. But it took a couple of hours of jacking up the truck and cutting cottonwood saplings to put under the tires before we made the discovery.

RAY ROUSE: Helpless without chains, a winch, in this kind of mud.

We left the truck there, on the theory that anybody who could take it could have it, and we walked back to the highway. But homesteaders don't give up easily. If they did, there wouldn't be any. We were back next day with Ray Rouse's friend, Vic Loyer, driving a weasel. The tracks came off only eleven times and broke only once.

VIC LOYER: Well, let's see if we can sneak up there aways.

We made the trip in six hours, which may be a record for that road, and reached Ray Rouse's homestead in early afternoon.

KURALT: It's beautiful.
ROUSE: That depends on how you look at it.
KURALT: How long did it take you to build it?
ROUSE: About two months. That's longer than it should take, but that's how long it took.
KURALT: Does this cabin keep you warm in the winter?
ROUSE: Oh, yeah. Well, it does, but when it gets about thirty below you get to feed the fire pretty good, pretty steady and quite often. You go through a cord in right short order. But it's nice; it's a lot nicer than I thought it would be. I kind of figured it'd just be black and white all the time, but it's not, it's green and black and white all the time.
KURALT: The mosquitos are pretty large and pretty numerous out here, aren't they?
ROUSE: Yeah, they come in giant size and giant squadrons out here. They say everything up here is big and we got lots more of it. I guess the mosquitos is one thing that's bigger, and we got lots more of them than most people.
KURALT: Do they bother you?
ROUSE: Yeah, in the summertime they get real thick, and they'll run you out of the house, and you get outside for a few minutes, and then they run you back in. But you have to live with them. I mean, they won't go away.

KURALT: They must be a lot of encouragements.

ROUSE: Yeah, well, I get discouraged every once in a while for a few days at a time, you know. I get mad, I'm going to shoot everything, burn the place down, run off, leave the country, but after a couple of days that wears off. I come back.

So there he is, at home, the new pioneer. We have a feeling Ray Rouse is not much different from the old pioneers. If you want to visit him ten years from now, you'll find him right here. But you'd better be prepared to pass a big six by six truck stuck in the mud on the way to his cabin. It may still be there, too.

The Woodworking Project

(HOPKINS, MINNESOTA)

You remember woodworking class. Woodworking class was where you made a set of bookends or a wooden trivet for your mother. Well, Woodworking 3, Al Peterson's class at Charles Lindbergh High in Hopkins, Minnesota, got tired of making bookends, so they made an airplane.

We were struck by the fact that pride of craftsmanship knows no age limit. This sleek and graceful plane was being constructed lovingly by students so patient and so intent that the occasional advice offered by Al Peterson and his assistant teacher, Al Schauss, seemed to come as an interruption.

★ ★ ★

AL PETERSON: You see, you got to consider we're gonna have another sixteenth of an inch of plywood on the top here, too.
STUDENTS: Yeah.

What was going on there was more than just a school woodworking project. It was an exercise in confidence. The kids knew they could do it.

PETERSON: They learned from my being able to show them my skills along with their learning new skills.
KURALT: What I want to know is, would you go along as a passenger on the first flight of this airplane?
PETERSON: If the FAA would let me, you bet I would.

And then, one rainy afternoon at Flying Cloud Airport near Minneapolis, FAA inspector Archie Newby signed a piece of paper, then handed it to Al Peterson. It was a Certificate of Airworthiness.

The Lindbergh band and cheerleaders and pom-pom girls all turned out, and the parents and kid brothers and sisters of the students in Woodworking 3, and North Central Airlines test pilot Lloyd Franke taxied "Experimental Aircraft N74LH-1974, Lindbergh High" right up to the crowd for a close look. It was painted in the school colors, maroon and gold, and it looked good.

[Radio exchanges: "Seven—Four—Lima—Hotel, is the runway clear of people now?" "Roger, it's clear." "Cleared for takeoff; right turn approved."]

"Cleared for takeoff; right turn approved"—and with

that matter-of-fact statement, Woodworking 3's year's work came rushing past the crowd.

[*Cheers at takeoff*]

PETERSON: There's something about building something and then going out and seeing it work. I'm a great believer in being able to build things that when you're done, you can take a look, stand back, and say: "There it is, I did it, and boy, look at it go!"

There it is. They did it. What do you remember from your senior year in high school? Not much, probably. Well, this is what Woodworking 3 will remember from theirs.

STUDENTS WATCHING FLIGHT: "Talk about your—" "Look at him!" "Ah!" "Gonna take off!" "Right! Beautiful!" "Now watch him, he'll take off." "He's really on his way!" "All right!"

[*Applause as their plane banks over field*]

Horseshoes

Behind the barn back in North Carolina, this is the way we used to throw horseshoes. [*Sound of horseshoe missing by a mile*] That's not the way they do it around here. [*The ringing sound of ringers*] Around here, if you can't make eighty-five ringers out of every hundred shots from a distance of forty feet, you might as well not show up, because you haven't got a chance.

This is the World Horseshoe Championships, a convention of the best barn-lot horseshoe pitchers who ever

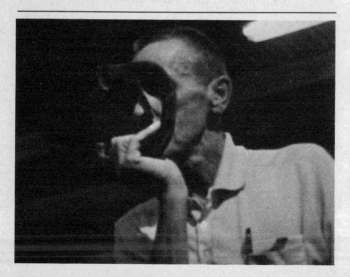

hustled a fellow farmer. They come mostly from places with names like Bremen and Plattsburgh and Arcanum—places where a man can while away an afternoon perfecting his style and listening to the satisfying plink of a drop-forged shoe encircling an iron stake.

Oh, they're good. They're real good. And some of them are legendary, like Elmer Hohl, a calm Canadian carpenter who is the defending champ, and Bob West, a lumbermill owner from Scappoose, Oregon, whose deadly aim is the talk of the tournament. And yet, none of these sharp-eyed old-timers is any better than a thirteen-year-old boy from right here in Eureka. Deadeye Williams, who competes at the under-sixteen-year-old distance of thirty feet, won the junior championship in 1971 and again in 1972 and was odds-on favorite to repeat, cheered on by his horseshoe-playing mother and father in the stands and his brother, Jonathan, and his sisters, Debbie and Cindy and Barbara, all horseshoe players.

But Deadeye lost his title, and who'd he lose it to? Another brother, twelve-year-old Jeff. Even when Deadeye and Jeff are just noodlin' around, as they were the day we met them, they still usually call out to the scorer, "Four dead," which means four ringers, and thus no points for either player.

★ ★ ★

DEADEYE: Four dead.

But, when it came to play for keeps, Jeff dethroned Deadeye, with the help of a fortuitous incident.

JEFF WILLIAMS: Well, he had a broken finger, and I beat him.
KURALT: How did he get a broken finger?
JEFF: I called him a name. He—
KURALT: What did you call him?
JEFF: I called him a girl.
KURALT: [*Laughs*] And then what happened?

JEFF: And then, he was ready to hit me, and then he said he wouldn't hit me, and then he hit me.

KURALT: And he broke his finger.

JEFF: Yeah.

KURALT: And the next day?

JEFF: The next day, he didn't win it.

KURALT: You won it.

JEFF: Yeah.

Thirty-four straight ringers is merely the stuff of daydreams for most farm boys, but it's what Jeff Williams did in fact. So he's the 1973 junior champ.

Youth was not served so well when it came to the grown-up championships. Foxy old Elmer Hohl, dueling tensely late into the night in a hushed arena, held off the challenge of nineteen-year-old Mark Seibold of Huntington, Indiana, to retain his title. [*The winning plink followed by cheers*]

Elmer was all smiles that night, but if he expects to remain the champ forever, he'd better think again. He knows about Deadeye Williams and Jeff Williams, but he may not know about Nathan. There is yet another Williams brother, you see. Nathan is seven. And one night we watched him march to the thirty-foot line, wind up with all his strength, and let fly. [*Another ringer, another cheer*]

The smart money in horseshoes is keeping an eye on Nathan.

Wooden Boats

We're a speedboat sort of country, as you must have noticed. We like going fast in fiberglass. In our time, in such a country, who would have the patience to build a great square-rigger out of sturdy oak? Well, to answer that we take you to the birch trees and the corncribs of lonely rural central Wisconsin. That's where we came across Ferd Nimphius, one of the last great craftsmen of one of the great historic crafts, building wooden boats capable of sailing the oceans of the world. Ferdinand Rudolph Carl Maria Nimphius cares not one bit about doing it quickly and efficiently. All he cares about is doing it right.

★ ★ ★

FERD NIMPHIUS: Now, this is a forty-seven-foot Banks-type schooner, the old-timer with a double cabin. You've got a step-up deck.

The schooner's name is to be *Christine Margaret*. Ferd Nimphius has been building her for more than two years. Doing it right takes time.

NIMPHIUS: There's all the best of construction all the way through, teak and mahogany, instead of having plywood. It's just like this, tongue and groove. These are all splined, all fastened.

Ferd Nimphius built a rowboat sixty years ago. He is still proud of that rowboat. He's been proud of every one of the one hundred and eleven boats he has built since. The schooner *Christine Margaret* is the one hundred and twelfth. The frigate *Red Lion*, identical to a Dutch man-of-war of the same name which sailed three hundred years ago, is the one hundred and thirteenth. Nobody taught Ferd Nimphius how to do this. He taught himself. The great joy in this enormous shed in the middle of Wisconsin is to watch him teach others.

NIMPHIUS: Go ahead. That's it.

He kids them.

NIMPHIUS: You're right on the line, too. Accidents will happen.

He praises them.

NIMPHIUS: You did a good job, I'm sorry to say.

He helps them.

NIMPHIUS: So, then, there's only a thirty-second difference in four pintles and that's—

Joshua Lee worked in television in Chicago. He decided
building wooden boats would be a more honorable occupation. And, of course, he's right about that.

Mike Allured was a math major at the University of
Colorado, looking for a calling. Out here in Ferd Nimphius's cold barn, he found it.

Earl Johnson was a fur salesman in the city. He used
to make a lot more money selling furs. But he'll never go
back to it.

Ferd Nimphius's own son, Alex, can already build a
wooden boat as well as any man alive, with one possible
exception.

NIMPHIUS: That's what I try to teach the young fellows.
First thing you do is do the thing right. Now, I don't
care just how much time you take, as long as you're
trying your best while you're doing it. Sometimes it's
hard to get that through their skull.
    They catch on. Boatyard will charge around twenty
bucks an hour. Now, we charge half of that, see, and
we do better work. I'd just as soon make less money
and feel satisfied and then the fellows feel better by
far that way, too.

There's a sign in Ferd Nimphius's cluttered office that
says, LONESOME? LIKE TO MEET NEW PEOPLE? LIKE A
CHANGE? LIKE EXCITEMENT? LIKE A NEW JOB? JUST
SCREW UP ONE MORE TIME. Quality, that's what Ferd
Nimphius teaches these young apprentices of his.

NIMPHIUS: The surprising part is they go along with it. Some of these, you see 'em with their long hair and whiskers all over the place—and by gosh, you kind of get the impression the first time you see them, Jesus, they look like they haven't washed for a while, you know. And you expect the work to be the same way. But no! I get those guys going and, by God, they'll do a good job. And they'll be honest.

So, there are all these long-haired young men from all over the country who have become a kind of family to the old man who never settles for anything but their best. Really, that's why they're here. He has seven children of his own. One of them, Barbie, the art major, is carving the figurehead that the frigate *Red Lion* will carry under her massive bowsprit.

You can't watch the patient craftsmanship that goes on her for very long without thinking: This is the best of worlds. This must be the fulfillment of Ferd Nimphius's earliest dream. No, his earliest dream, when he was young and single, was to sail away to Tahiti.

NIMPHIUS: I built a thirty-six-foot canoe-stern ketch, designed by McGregor, a ten-foot-six beam. I was going to sail around the world. She was built out of inch-and-a-quarter mahogany, Honduras mahogany over ribs that were on eight-inch centers. She was built like a brick privy.

KURALT: But you never sailed it around the world?

NIMPHIUS: No. It's too bad. My wife torpedoed me. That's where I met my wife, and I don't know. I got seven kids and no boat, but—[Laughs]

KURALT: Seven kids and no boat!

The boat has another owner now. The boat is in Tahiti, but Ferd Nimphius isn't aboard. So all this is the substitute dream, building boats on a farm hundreds of miles from the nearest ocean, boats for others to sail around the world, building each one as if it were to be forever his own. And in a way, each one is, forever.

NIMPHIUS: I really think it's worth it. It gives you a certain satisfaction yourself. Sometimes I've found the owner says, "Oh, that's good, that's plenty good," you know. But it didn't satisfy me.

KURALT: You've had owners willing to accept boats that you weren't satisfied with?

NIMPHIUS: Yeah, that I didn't think was right, no.

KURALT: So then what happens?

NIMPHIUS: Then as a rule they see it my way. Oh, sure. Why, in fact, I made a remark, "What the hell, you only own the boat; I'm building it!"

The frigate *Red Lion* left Sheboygan on Lake Michigan the other day and ventured out to see the world, her proud owner at the helm. He's just the owner. He knows she's Ferd Nimphius's boat in every beam and plank and fastening. She sails like a dream.

The Kite Flier

Ansel Toney is eighty-nine. He has lived with nature every day of his life and has learned to appreciate nature, as a farmer will. Ansel Toney knows the ways of the earth in his bones. He has come to know the ways of the wind as well. He's too old to be a full-time farmer anymore. And so where could a lover of nature turn?

Ansel Toney turned to a pleasure of his boyhood. Flying kites.

★ ★ ★

ANSEL TONEY: In the last two years I've started making kites for the kids. Just as a hobby. Just something to keep me from getting tired of life. Something to keep going. You can't sit down. If you do you're going to go right quick. At my age you know you just can't expect too many more years.

    Look it there, Charles.

KURALT: Listen to it sing!

TONEY: Yeah, that old string's like a fiddle string.

Ansel Toney comes out here between the wheatfield and the field of young corn every sunny day, and sends a kite up over the fields or over the drowsy town of Farmland. The kite is a signal to the children of the town, for whom he has made dozens of kites, to come and join him, to stand by his side in the fields and share in the wordless admiration of the wind.

His fame has spread far and wide. The kids come in school buses to hear him speak of kites that flew so long ago, they cannot imagine it.

TONEY: You want to have me take a big kite out?
CHILDREN: Yes.
TONEY: Good. Get out here in the sun. Here you are. You see, there's the kind of reels my daddy made me eighty-three years ago, when I was a kid six years old. You hold it right up here. Right—right in there. Now turn it. See, that's the way you wind your string

in. That's the way. Yeah. You've got on to it. You know how to do 'er now. Here's one of the little Delta kites.

BOY: My dog chewed mine up.

TONEY: Your dog chewed it up? Well, that's a bad dog wasn't it?

CHILD: Did you make it?

TONEY: Yes, I made it.

CHILD: How did you make it?

TONEY: Oh, just take the old sewing machine and run it up on the sewing machine.

KURALT: The sewing machine looks as though it has a little age on it.

TONEY: Yup. Sixty-seven years old. My wife bought it when we first got married. Nineteen-ten.

KURALT: Did you always know how to use it?

TONEY: Never used it before till two years ago. Started making kites and I had it all to learn. And it doesn't seem bad, but there's about as much to one as there is to a big combine on a farm, to operate. You've got to know how to handle 'em.

There's a knack to building a good kite. They won't fly if they're not balanced right. You can make two kites exactly alike in measurement and put 'em up, they won't perform the same.

[*To kids*] How's that, youngster? Come on, honey. Just straighten 'er up a little bit. Now let her go. Try it again.

[*To Kuralt*] I like this Delta kite the best of any of them. It's the most graceful. It just flies like an old sea gull up there, you know. Just kind of like he's flopping his wings.

This may seem to you an odd enterprise for a solitary man of eighty-nine in the middle of an Indiana cornfield. To Ansel Toney, a farmer all his life, the currents of the air are as intriguing and as abiding as the woods and the fields and the streams. The kite on the end of his string is an extension of life.

TONEY: The reason I like flying kites, you're always looking up. You're not looking down like you do when
you're playing golf or some of the other things. You're
looking up at that pretty blue sky. It's a beautiful
sight.

Strong Coffee

(PITTSBORO, NORTH CAROLINA)

Young Clark Jones used to come out to Miss Lula Watson's house near Pittsboro, North Carolina, to sing songs with her. They sang under a willow tree, which Miss Lula Watson planted when she was seventy, thinking it could be transplanted soon to her grave. Well, thirty-three years passed, the willow tree grew old and some of its limbs died, and there was Miss Lula Watson still doing fine at the age of 103. Hard work is what did it, she said. Hard work and strong coffee.

★ ★ ★

KURALT: You like coffee, huh?

LULA WATSON: Yeah, I like my coffee a hundred proof. Been drinking it ever since I was seven years old.

KURALT: Well, it doesn't seem to have done you any harm.

WATSON: No, it just made me dark. [*Laughs*]

I found Miss Lula Watson's wit to be at least as sharp as yours and mine, and her memory, at 103, maybe a little sharper.

KURALT: What kind of work did you do when you were young?

WATSON: Worked in the field. Plowed day after day, just like a man. Plant corn, chop cotton, cut wheat, cut

cordwood, split rails, and plow. I used to plow day after day.

KURALT: That's awfully hard work, though.

WATSON: Didn't seem hard to me. It was fun to me to jump on that old horse and ride back to the field and backwards and forwards. [*Laughs*] And I could pick my three hundred pound of cotton every day. And we weren't getting but thirty cents a day for work when I came along.

KURALT: Thirty cents a day?

WATSON: Thirty cents a day, honey, for hard labor. But we enjoyed it.

Miss Lula Watson always worked hard, and kept on working through her hundred and third year. She especially enjoyed going around to nursing homes, like Hill Forest here at Goldston. She felt that by singing songs and telling stories, she might help cheer up the old folks.

WOMAN: Miss Lula, if you had one thing that you could tell us to make us happy, what would it be, to make our life happy?

WATSON: Drink coffee.

WOMAN: Drink coffee.

WATSON: Hundred proof. [*Laughs*]

MAN: How long have you been singing?

WATSON: I've been singing ever since I was a child, but older I get the better I get. [*Laughs*]

When the roll is called up yonder, Miss Lula Watson will be there, no doubt, singing old songs and drinking strong coffee. In the meantime, when I met her she was earning her living by entertaining at the old folks' homes and, by the way, paying Social Security taxes on her earnings. She didn't mind that. She said she was going to need something to retire on.

WATSON: God bless you every day. Look sunny. Smile, honey. I hope you live and never die! [*Laughs*]

7

AMERICAN SUITE

You could close your eyes and stick a pin in a map of America and go to where the pin was stuck and find a story of the kind we look for On the Road. Some of my favorite stories have been about commonplace things—windmills, clotheslines, the things people use (welded chain, wagonwheels, old water pumps and cream separators) to hold their mailboxes up. In the section that follows, you'll find stories about a light bulb and a dead dog, for example. I left out the one about the swimming pig and the one about the Ohio butcher who could hold more eggs in his hand than anybody else. I had to leave out the penny-candy store and the tattoo parlor too, and the wildcatter, the mule skinner, the oyster shucker, the calliope builder, and the kid in Louisiana who could catch a grape in his mouth thrown from a distance of a hundred yards. (His problem was finding somebody who could throw a grape a hundred yards.)

What I'm trying to say is that there's a good yarn at every crossroads and in every city block. Some would say yes, but they don't all belong on the CBS Evening News, do they? Luckily for me, Walter Cronkite and Dan Rather never have said that.

Bag Balm

The Williams Company of Grand Rapids, Michigan, is not just any warehouse. It is a treasure house of snake oils and cure-alls and ancient tonics, keeping the rural pharmacies and country stores stocked with the patent medicines people want and need. These are the elixirs Grandpa swore by, still doing their healing work today.

Dr. J. H. McLean's Volcanic Oil Liniment for Man or Beast has stood the test of time, probably because it's so good for so many things: overexertion, fatigue, mosquito bites, stiff neck due to drafts, and "a convenient home liniment for livestock since 1841."

A number of other doctors have made their mark: Dr. Drake, Dr. Hubbard, Dr. Tichenor, and Dr. Pierce, with his Golden Medical Discovery. "Active ingredients: gentian root, grape root and blood root; aids digestion."

Dr. McLean couldn't resist putting his own picture on the bottle of his Tar Wine Compound. And Dr. S. Andrill Kilmer, similarly, a good-looking fellow, pictured himself on his Swamp Root: "aids the kidneys in their necessary work."

Some otherwise anonymous people of the nineteenth century survive into our time on the labels of these old medicines. Percy's Medicine has a picture of baby Percy. And since 1878, Grandpa's Wonder Pine Tar Soap has carried a picture of Grandpa. For many a year, many a family has sworn by Innerclean Herbal Laxative, but "none is genuine without this signature—Arnold Ehret."

There was a time when hardly anything went on a drugstore shelf without a man's signature on it. Since 1810, Edward Pinaud's own signature has appeared on his Eau de Quinine. Auntie Payne, "a medicine cabinet in a jar," carries the rather elegant signature of D. D. Williams, always has carried it. And no Barry's Tricopherous has ever gone on the shelf without the signature of A. C. Barry, the originator.

Speaking of Barry's Tricopherous, a lot of products have lasted down the decades in spite of or because of perfectly gaudy, hard-to-pronounce names: Glycerated Asafoetida; Occycrystine; Glycothymoline, Balsam of Myrrh; and Guadalupano Belladonna and Capsicum Porous Plaster, with a four-color picture of Our Lady of Guadalupe right there on every package.

They've been popular for generations: BQR, SSS, BGO, 666, and WDS, Wonderful Dream Brand Salve. Fat-Go, that's to take pounds off, of course. Wate-On, that's to put 'em on again. An amazing number of these products are designed to keep your teeth in: Rigident, Superhold, Dentlock, and Klutch. None of the products advertise that they make your teeth fall out and, presumably, none of them do.

Elsewhere, I know, they are splicing genes in the laboratory, and patenting miracle drugs, but most people don't need their genes spliced and don't want to fool around with the unknown. What they want is something tried and true—and good for what ails you. From all these cures and elixirs, let me choose just one example to show you what I mean: Bag Balm. It comes in a pretty green can; has been a heavy seller for most of the years of the century. And what is Bag Balm good for?

★ ★ ★

WOMAN: It is good for every sore. It is good for every cut.

WOMAN: It's the greatest thing for diaper rash there ever was.

MAN: It is one of the greatest healers—just the smell of it, just the odor is magnificent.

It is easy out in the country to find testimonials for Bag Balm. Those are some we heard. Here's another. [*Cow moos*] Bag Balm was invented, you see, and is still marketed as a soothing preparation for the chapped udders of cows.

FARMER: This is a product, Bag Balm, that I use on my cows for chapped teats in the summertime due to sunburn and also if they've got minor cuts and scrapes, it puts an ántiseptic over the cow's teat.

But one good use deserves an udder. People use it on themselves now, to the great satisfaction of its maker, John Norris, born and brought up and still at home in Lyndonville, Vermont.

JOHN NORRIS: Bag Balm was started in 1910 by my father. He bought the formula from a druggist in Woodsville and continued till I took over in 1934 and I've maintained the same formula and same design on the can up to the present time.

The company has grown and grown, until now it has four employees. They mix the lanolin and antiseptic and pine oil in the same proportions as first prescribed seventy-three years ago, and they fill four hundred thousand cans of Bag Balm every year to meet the nation's demand. How did it come to pass that human beings use Bag Balm?

NORRIS: Years ago, farmers' wives used to do a lot of milking, and they'd put Bag Balm on their hands to rub on the cow's udder and they'd find out how soft their hands stayed. So Bag Balm moved from the barn into the house.

Now you can find it in as many medicine cabinets as cow barns, that ubiquitous, gaudy green can.

NORRIS: The can was designed a long time before I was born, but I think it was a pretty good artist. The front of the can shows a cow's udder, which is the primary purpose of Bag Balm. The cover on the can shows a red cloverleaf and a cow's head, which is a very distinctive design and as much a part of Bag Balm as the ointment itself.

The ointment is used for just about everything, as documented in John Norris' company files. For itches, scratches, scrapes and rashes...

WOMAN: Frostbite, chapped lips, sunburn...

For lubricating wagon wheels and waterproofing boots...

WOMAN: I had a friend that said when his false teeth hurt him, he used Bag Balm underneath to take the soreness out.

It is also excellent, wrote a woman in Maine, for stopping her bedsprings from squeaking. Business has never been better, John Norris says, but he has one worry.

NORRIS: Well, the future of Bag Balm is the sixty-four-dollar question. Maybe my daughter will come up and run it, I don't know. If not, well, then, have to make some other arrangements, but I am very careful about whoever does it. I hope they'll try to maintain the same standards that my father and I've tried to maintain for, well, pretty near seventy-five years.

So, John Norris continues to test every batch of Bag Balm personally to assure that it never changes.

He is thinking of all the customers out there who depend on him.

[*Cow moos*]

The Livermore Light Bulb

(LIVERMORE, CALIFORNIA)

In 1879, Thomas Alva Edison invented the electric light bulb. Twenty-two years later, in 1901, they hung one of the newfangled gadgets in the Livermore, California, Fire Department, and turned it on. It's still there and still on.

The old bulb has been turned off almost never in seventy-one years. By today's standards it should have burned out 852 times by now, but clearly we are not dealing with today's standards. We are dealing with somebody who made light bulbs to last. The bulb, hand-blown, with a thick carbon filament, was made, apparently, by the Shelby Electric Company, which did not become one of the giants of the nation, for an obvious reason: they made light bulbs to last, and nobody ever reordered. One burns on, a memorial to Shelby Electric.

Needless to say, the bulb is accorded a kind of awesome respect by Fire Captain Kirby Slate and his men.

★ ★ ★

CAPTAIN KIRBY SLATE: We started out with this light bulb over at Second and Elm—that's the old fire station, that's where it was first put. Then it was taken from there and moved to here, and since that time the only knowledge that I have of it not working was when WPA was here in 1937, it was out for about a week.

KURALT: And you never turn it off?

SLATE: Never turn it off. Now, we have a switch on it.

But to my knowledge, no man has ever turned that switch.

KURALT: And better not?

SLATE: And better not, that's right.

KURALT: Do you sometimes have a fear that as you glance up at it, it's going to go out?

SLATE: Well, let me put it this way: I just hope that I'm not on duty when it goes out.

As the Livermore firemen went about their work, we stood around for the afternoon, just watching the old bulb burn, and thinking long thoughts about the planned and unplanned obsolescence which rules our lives. In a time when gadgets are forever falling apart or burning out or breaking up, it was kind of nice to spend a day watching a dusty, seventy-one-year-old light bulb just go on and on. If you're ever in Livermore and need reassurance, we recommend it.

The Grist Mill

There can't be a three hundred-year-old grist mill in mid-twentieth-century America, with a miller who opens the sluice gate to set his wheel turning to grind corn for his neighbors. Cornmeal and flour today come from General Foods and General Mills, not from Captain Frank Langrell, on Hunting Creek in Caroline County, Maryland. There can't be such a man or such a mill.

Standing here looking at it all, the millwheel and the millstream, and the mill, you get the feeling that when all this goes we'll be poorer as a nation. But of course there really can't be a mill like this in mid-twentieth-century America, so it's all going.

Captain Langrell is eighty-one now. When he dies there will be nobody to take his place. This mill ground corn for backwoodsmen and settlers in 1681, sold cornmeal to Washington's army, and is selling cornmeal yet. The Linchester Mill may be America's oldest continuously operated enterprise, and after sixty-five years of labor beside his millstone, Captain Langrell is surely America's most venerable miller, but there's no call for mills or millers anymore, and Frank Langrell knows it.

★ ★ ★

KURALT: What's going to happen to this mill when you're not able to run it any longer?

FRANK LANGRELL: She'll be tore down, tore down, I guess, like a lot of others.

KURALT: There's no young man looking forward to taking over this mill?

LANGRELL: No, no, I don't know. I don't know. Take a mill like this today, a fellow couldn't really raise a family on the profit you get out of it today, but years ago, why, you could do it. It was a good living.

Sometime during the Industrial Revolution, the great gears of the Linchester Mill were changed from wood to iron, but very little else has changed here since the 1600s. Of course, such a place cannot exist; the day is coming, sooner or later, when the sluice gates will be shut and never opened again, when the waterwheel will stop for good, and the ceaseless rumble of the millstone will give way to silence. We will be poorer. If the developer who buys the land has a sense of history, he may name a street Linchester Mill Road or Langrell Drive.

Worm Grunting

The casual passerby through Sopchoppy, Florida, watching Jim Rozier at his daily occupation, would surely think he'd taken leave of his senses. But no, he's just doing what a lot of people do around Sopchoppy, grunting for worms.

[*Rozier rubs truck spring across top of wooden stake.*]

Jim Rozier's skill with a piece of iron and a hardwood stob sets up a vibration in the earth that Sopchoppy earthworms find extremely disagreeable. To escape it they pop to the surface, there to become fish bait.

★ ★ ★

KURALT: What's the stob made out of?
JIM ROZIER: Well, this here one made out of sweet gum I got here, and most people use hickory.
KURALT: It has to be either sweet gum or hickory?
ROZIER: Right.
KURALT: And what's the iron you're using?
ROZIER: It's a piece of old truck spring, regular spring.
KURALT: Can people actually make a living at this?
ROZIER [*with a big smile*]: I do!

It turns out that dozens of people make a living at it around here, and it's not a bad living. A couple of hundred dollars a week is not an unusual income for this unusual occupation.

It's the early bird who gets the worm, as we all know, so the hours just after dawn are worm-grunting time in Sopchoppy. In neighboring counties of the Florida panhandle this is known also as worm twiddling or worm scrubbing, and it is thought that square stobs or triangular stobs work best. Sopchoppy is contemptuous of these deviations from the round stob and truck spring which pay off here to the tune of more than thirty million earthworms a year. We spent a long morning in the woods and we'd never have believed it if we hadn't seen it.

A couple minutes' work by an experienced worm grunter might yield as many as fifty or sixty worms in a thirty-foot circle. Then, on to another spot. Five hundred worms to the can, and the cans fill up fast. By eleven o'clock in the morning, people are reassembling at trucks scattered all through these woods, and by noon the trucks are rolling in to Myron Hodge's bait store, where Mr. Hodge pays $6.25 a can. He repackages the product in paper bags full of sawdust, and every morning he fills a lot of paper bags. Within twenty-four hours, at smaller bait stores all over the South, these worms will be enticing fishermen, and

shortly thereafter, they'll be enticing bass. It's big business.

MYRON HODGE: Well, I guess a year of business—in this area—it'd be about two hundred and fifty thousand dollars' business a year.

KURALT: Really, that much?

HODGE: Yeah, in this Sopchoppy community. Course there are other counties. I don't have that much, but me and all the other dealers together.

KURALT: That's really something. Why do people go out in the woods to grunt worms? Why not just grow them in their backyards?

HODGE: Oh, they can't—they can't grow this kind of worm. This worm will only grow in the woods.

Therefore, do not scoff at worm grunting. After all, you probably thought that the way to get worms is to go out in the woods with a shovel. Hah! Shovels are for kids, and amateurs, and others who have not mastered the truck spring, the black gum stob, and the sensitive touch.

Busted Flat in Baker

(BAKER, CALIFORNIA)

Let's say you're driving home to California from Las
Vegas. And let's say you're broke. And let's say you've
been driving ninety miles through the desert with nothing
to look at but that hot sand and the gas gauge, which is
riding on empty. Well, when you see the sign that says
BAKER, naturally you take the exit. Baker is at least somewhere in the middle of nowhere: a hot, dusty string of
gas stations where a busted gambler might figure if he can
talk fast enough he can talk himself into a tank of gas. It
turns out that this is exactly what thousands of busted
gamblers figure every year.

Bob Kennedy, who works in one of the filling stations,
says Baker must be the fast-talking capital of America.

★ ★ ★

KURALT: What sort of things have you been offered down
the years?

BOB KENNEDY: Oh, watches, rings, all sorts of jewelry.
Clothing, tires, tools—you name it. If it's been made,
it's been offered. They come out with some ridiculous things.

KURALT: But they get you to pump that gas first—

KENNEDY: Oh, yeah.

KURALT: —before they admit they're broke.

KENNEDY: Oh, yeah.

Bob Kennedy has lost track of the number of old cars he has taken possession of in return for a bus ticket to Los Angeles. And gas station owner Ken George has a gaudy collection of clocks and watches and guns and radios that used to belong to motorists headed home from Vegas.

KEN GEORGE: Stories change from gettin' robbed, losin' their wallet or people just come out and tell you the truth. "Look, mister, I've lost my money in Vegas. Could you loan me two dollars and somethin' worth of gas?" You know, and of course, you get so many of these people comin' through, pretty soon you start asking for collateral.

KURALT: What kinds of collateral have you been offered?

GEORGE: Huh! Well, there's been cases where even people's kids have been offered as collateral.

KURALT: It strikes me that, living in Baker, you could pick up a bargain from time to time.

GEORGE: Well, yeah, you can pick up a bargain from time to time, but what is a guy gonna do with six or eight bowling balls when we don't have a bowling alley? Heh!

To operate a gas station here, as Bob Kennedy and Ken George and all the others will tell you, is to run a hockshop in the desert. The Las Vegas winners, of course, never slow down. They zip past the exit on the Interstate, humming a happy tune.

The losers stop at Baker.

Burgers

America is infinite and various. The infinity shows up on our odometer. As for variety, we have found that on the road at lunchtime we can choose from all kinds of—hamburgers.

★ ★ ★

WAITER: A Tacoburger and an Islandburger and a side of fries, yes, sir.

Americans have eaten forty billion hamburgers in just the last year, give or take a few hundred million, and on the road you tend to eat more than your share. You can find your way across this country using burger joints the way a navigator uses stars. Where are we now? [*Sign in window:* MITEY MO-BURGER] Missouri, of course. But there is mo' and mo'. [*The signs flash by as Kuralt ticks them off.*] We have munched Bridgeburgers in the shadow of the Brooklyn Bridge, and Cablecarburgers hard by the Golden Gate, Dixieburgers in the sunny South and Yankee Doodle Dandyburgers in the North. The Civil War must be over; they taste exactly alike. And which lovely mountains are these? [*Sign:* SMOKEYBURGERS] Count on it: a burger stand will tell you, while blocking your view of the Great Smoky Mountains!

[*Sign:* CAPITOLBURGER *with U.S. Capitol dome in the background*] We had a Capitolburger—guess where. [*Sign:* HAVE A PENTABURGER] And in the inner courtyard of the

Pentagon, so help us, a Pentaburger! The free world may be lost.

WAITRESS: Hippoburger with a Bippieburger, well on the Bippie, medium rare on the Hippo.

[*Sign:* GURNEYBURGER] Gurney Campbell, of Johnson City, Tennessee, couldn't resist naming his burger for himself. [*Signs flash past:* OLIVERBURGER, BUDDY BURGER, MURRAYBURGER, CHUCKBURGER, BEN BURGER, JUANS-BURGER] We have also consumed burgers from the grills of guys named Oliver, Buddy, Murray, Chuck, Ben, and Juan. It begins to get to you after a while. [*Kuralt talks faster and faster as we see these signs.*] We've had King-burgers, Queenburgers, Miniburgers, Maxiburgers, Tuna-burgers, Smithfieldburgers, Baconburgers, Wineburgers, Heavenly Burgers, and Yumburgers. Yum, yum. In Inde-pendence, Kansas, we lunched on Papaburgers, Mama-burgers, and little teeny Babyburgers. Then there was the night in New Mexico when the lady was just closing up and we had to decide in a hurry. "What'll it be," she said, "a Whoppaburger or a Bitta-burger?" Hard to decide.

WAITRESS: I still have a Frenchburger coming.

The Acropolis of burger joints is probably the Hippo in San Francisco, home of the Nudeburger, Stripburger, Bippieburger, Italianburger, Joe's Burger, Mushroom Burger, Bronxburger, Terryburger, Russianburger, Tahiti Burger, Onionburger, Tacoburger, Smorgasburger, Continental Burger, Frenchburger, and so on ad infinitum to hundreds of strains and mutations.

WAITRESS: Decided what you'd like?
CUSTOMER: Myerburger for the two kids.
WAITRESS: One?
CUSTOMER: Right, I'm going to split it. And a Bippie-burger for her, well done.
WAITRESS: One Bippie, well done.
CUSTOMER: Right. And I'll have a Mushroom Burger.

But this is not merely a local phenomenon. The smell of fried onions is abroad in the land, and if the French chefs among us will avert their eyes, we will finish reciting our menu of the last few weeks on the highways of America. [*He starts talking fast again as we see all these signs.*] We've had Grabbaburgers, King-a-Burgers, Lottaburgers, Castleburgers, Country Burgers, Broncoburgers, Broadway Burgers, Broiledburgers, Beefnutburgers, Bellburgers, Plush Burgers, Primeburgers, Flameburgers, Lunchburgers, Top Burgers, Plazaburgers, Tastee-Burgers, Dudeburgers, Char-burgers, Tall Boy Burgers, Golden Burgers, 747-Jet-Burgers, Whizburgers, Niftyburgers, and Thing Burgers!

[*Camera pans desert . . .*] One day in the desert I had a vision—that the last ding-dong of doom had sounded, that the land was empty, and that the last American had left only one small monument to mark his passing [*. . . and we see a lonely sign bearing one word only:* BURGERS.]

The Balloon Man

(MEDFORD, MASSACHUSETTS)

This is an American success story, the story of Frank
DelVecchio, the Italian immigrant who worked hard and
saved for his two sons so they could go to college and
become successful so they wouldn't have to do what he
does for a living. You know the story. What Frank
DelVecchio does for a living is sell balloons.

★ ★ ★

KURALT: What year did you begin selling balloons?
FRANK DELVECCHIO: Well, let's see. I got married in
    1928, and two years later I started to go out contin-
    uously. So that would be around 1930.
KURALT: That means you've been selling balloons every
    year for fifty years?
DELVECCHIO: Oh, I must have sold a lot of balloons.

Frank DelVecchio has sold a lot of balloons around
Boston, and probably has given away just as many. Work
hard, make friends, that was the idea. Save money. Make
sure the two boys don't have to sell balloons for a living—
fifty years of hard work.

KURALT: In the beginning you didn't have helium?
DELVECCHIO: Oh, no. My God, at the beginning, the
    balloons were homemade balloons. The rubber was
    so heavy, and in order to get it started to inflate we

had to blow with our mouth. The minute I started to blow one, to get it started, my eyes would pop out. My ears would start to ring, and it would get red around here and my eyes would start to tear. I said, "My God, how long am I going to have to do this?"

Fifty years, that's how long.

CHILD: Can I have a balloon?
DELVECCHIO: Yes, if you smile.

It was all for the kids, the kids who always clamored for the balloons, and the two kids growing up at home.

BOY: I need a blue one, because mine—
DELVECCHIO: Now, wait a minute. I just gave you two. Now, you tell your sister to come here. I just gave you two balloons.
BOY: That is—no. For me, because my other one flied away.
DELVECCHIO: Well, you bananahead, I told you to hold

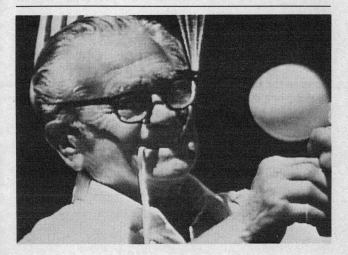

it tight. Will you hold it tight? Tie it around your neck, will you?

FRANK DELVECCHIO, JR.: As a kid, I observed and worked with my father, and I used to get annoyed with him because he would spend simply too much time with a customer, when there were other sales to be made. A balloon would break, and he'd replace it. The little kid would come by, and he'd bend down and tie the string around the child's wrist so he wouldn't lose it, whereas some other balloon peddlers would sell another balloon if the child lost it.

JOE DELVECCHIO: It's very hard work and I remember, for the first twenty years of my life, my father always saying, "Joey, go to college so you don't have to be a balloon man."

That was the whole idea of Frank DelVecchio's life, and it worked. Joe was graduated from the University of Massachusetts and won his master's degree. Frank, Jr., was graduated from Tufts and the Harvard Law School. Both got good government jobs. So, what do you think has happened, after Frank DelVecchio's fifty-some years of hard work to keep his sons from becoming balloon sellers?

They've become balloon sellers. Joe quit his government job to create Balloon Bouquets in Washington, and has expanded to New York, Chicago, Los Angeles, Philadelphia, San Francisco, half-a-dozen other cities. Frank, Jr., runs the Boston branch in his spare time and his wife, Marian, helps make deliveries. People call up and order balloons for birthdays, bar mitzvahs, and fancy balls. They sell hundreds of thousands of balloons. Balloons are going to make the DelVecchio boys rich men.

"Kids!" says Frank DelVecchio. "What are you going to do about kids who don't listen to their old man?"

Scholar of the Piney Woods

(BANKS, ARKANSAS)

Eddie Lovett lives at the end of a long dirt road in the piney woods of Arkansas.

There wasn't much to see when we got there: a couple of unpainted houses, the beginnings of a garden enclosed by a broken-down fence. But one thing we didn't expect: a shack with a tin roof, bearing an inscription: HIC HAB-ITAT FELICITAS—Here lives happiness.

You'd expect the man who lives here to be a dirt farmer, or maybe a self-taught carpenter, a doer of odd jobs. And Eddie Lovett is all of those. Then how to explain that inscription in Latin over his door? Well, because Eddie Lovett—who never finished high school, and who lives with his children in near poverty out in the woods—is also a formidable scholar. He has a library: a lifetime accumulation of thousands of books which he reads day and night. They have transformed the unlettered son of a sharecropper into an educated man.

★ ★ ★

KURALT: What are you reading right now?

LOVETT: I'm reading space—about the great astronauts. I writes them pretty frequently; they writes me. And I admires their courage because I am a amateur, self-taught astronomer myself. I've sat on rooftops of barns many nights. That's what I'm studying right now. I am studying space.

Didn't study last night 'cause I worked up to two thirty this morning, trying to get this place halfway presentable for you all to try to make pictures of it.

KURALT: How much time do you spend reading each day, now?

LOVETT: Out of twenty-four hours, I average twelve of them reading.

KURALT: Are you a fast reader?

LOVETT: Not too fast. I'm a slow, steady reader. I ponders as I go along.

KURALT: What about literature? What about fiction?

LOVETT: Well, I don't like that too well, but one of my writers I like—I like James Baldwin. I likes him. He's good. I don't like all of his books, but I like some of them: *Go Tell It on the Mountain, The Fire Next Time*, things of that nature. I like some of that.

KURALT: Who are your favorite authors?

LOVETT: Oh, Lord! They're too numerous to name. But I will name a few. Oh, Lord!

René Descartes, the great French philosopher—"I think therefore I am."

And Socrates! Now, Socrates, you know, he really didn't do any writing. He's known as the father of logic, even if he didn't do any writing.

I am a lover of literature and a lover of knowledge.

Of course, Shakespeare, to my way of thinking, he's the greatest of them all—William Shakespeare. I got the complete works. I have it right here in forty volumes. I think he was the greatest that ever lived. That's in my judgment. Now, some people think otherwise.

KURALT: But what good has all this reading done to you? You're still living out here in the piney woods.

LOVETT: Well, you know, a man is happy wherever he loves and I love to read. I like to be quiet. And the country is about the best place that I can find quietness to read and study and research like I desire. And I think that it's doing me—particularly my children—a lot of good because the truth to tell, I'm really living for my children. I want to set good examples for them. And the only way I can get my children to do things that I would like for them to do constructive, I have to set the example.

I don't think I've lost anything by gaining knowledge, because I've been told by my father and also by other people throughout the world that man's greatest enemy is his ignorance. And so by me pondering in my library, researching, I have declared war upon my ignorance. And the more I learn, the more I learn that I need to learn, and the more I learn that I *don't* know. And I aspires to drink very deep from the fountain of knowledge.

Eddie Lovett steps to the door of his library each afternoon to watch his children come home from school. He gave the children names he discovered in his reading: Joanna, one of the women who discovered Jesus' empty tomb; Enima, a name suggested by Nietzsche; Yuri, for

Yuri Gagarin, the Russian cosmonaut. He says his children are his greatest happiness. It pleases him that they all like to read nearly as much as he does, and that while he hasn't been able to give them much, the knowledge that they'll always have the library is a deep satisfaction to him.

LOVETT: Children maturing—great! They'll be men and women someday.

HIC HABITAT FELICITAS—here lives happiness.

The Spiveys

(BLACKFOOT, IDAHO)

This is the Spivey family of Blackfoot, Idaho. What's your name?

★ ★ ★

CHILD #1: Berry.
CHILD #2: Zerry.
CHILD #3: Perry.
CHILD #4: Cherry.
CHILD #5: Terry.
KURALT: Is that all?
MRS. SPIVEY: No, we have four more. One's in the Marine Corps, and two are visiting their grandparents and one is babysitting.
KURALT: What are their names?
MRS. SPIVEY: Jerry, Sherry, Merry, and Kerry.
KURALT: Mr. Spivey, how did this happen?
MR. SPIVEY: Well, we started off as a typical American family, two kids. We had Jerry and Terry, and then we had Sherry. Then we had Merry, and we thought it would be cute to make it rhyme, so we spelled it M-E-R-R-Y, and then, when my wife the following year was on her annual vacation up in the maternity ward, she had a little girl, and we didn't want to name it Sue, or something that didn't rhyme, and she'd grow up thinkin' we didn't love her, so we named

her Kerry, and then the next year, another one, and on and on and on.

KURALT: Can you name them all?

MR. SPIVEY: Chronologically: Jerry, Terry, Sherry, Merry, Kerry, Cherry, Perry, Zerry, and Berry.

KURALT: What's your name?

MR. SPIVEY: Joe.

Butterflies

Early spring is the time of the year the Monarch butterflies migrate north from Pacific Grove, where a couple million of them have spent the winter, and raise with their departure all kinds of troubling questions for man, who outweighs them but can't outsmart them.

In the first place, Monarchs are confused by radio, television and radar waves, and destroyed by atomic fallout, fertilizer, insect sprays, air pollution, and the construction of housing projects on their breeding grounds, so how do they survive at all? In the second place, when they leave Pacific Grove, they fly as far as two thousand miles into Canada, through storms and across mountains and deserts, sometimes even across oceans, though they are as fragile as feathers. How do they do it? In the third place, these butterflies do not live long enough to return to Pacific Grove, but next fall, their Canadian-born offspring will come to the very same trees their parents are now leaving. By what miracle of navigation do butterflies, who've never been here, find their way each year? Good question to ponder next time you start feeling like the master of all you survey.

I put some of the questions to one of Pacific Grove's more ardent butterfly admirers, Mrs. Shirley Bass.

★ ★ ★

KURALT: What is the basis of the affection between Pacific Grove and butterflies?

SHIRLEY BASS: Well, it dates back to Indian times. According to folklore, the Indian children reputedly said a lovely chant every fall. When they saw them, the great golden horde of butterflies, they said: "They have come, they have come, bringing peace and bringing plenty." And we still think they're a sign of very good luck and good fortune. Besides that, they're nice to watch, they're lovely. They're fragile and they're beautiful. And they're ubiquitous in the gardens.

KURALT: And it's a dire offense to harm one?

BASS: Five hundred dollars and six months in jail. This is a city that loves fragile, beautiful creatures, and we protect them by law, by ordinance.

KURALT: How do they know where to come back to?

BASS: Miracle.

KURALT: Nobody knows?

BASS: Nobody knows. It sort of gives you faith that things are going to go on and on, some sort of continuity that we can't understand, and yet it's delightful to contemplate.

To the credit of Pacific Grove, it knows that it's got some kind of miracle on its hands here, and as a small town will, it celebrates its miracle on private walls and public streets. We found a bulky statue to the Monarchs and, so help us, a wreath, bidding them farewell. We even found a little girl, Lisa Henderson by name, caught up in the spirit of the season, seeking not to molest butterflies, but only to meet one. She never really did, but she shouldn't feel too bad about that; the Monarchs don't reveal themselves to grown men with doctorates in biology either. They are bright, diaphanous mysteries, very hard to get to know.

The Park

(RENO, NEVADA)

Reno has never been known for early risers, but this is 7:30 on a Friday morning and all these people have been up since way before dawn. They are standing around a surveyor's table in the middle of a vacant lot in a largely black neighborhood. This has always been a vacant lot. These people are going to turn it into a park, with grass and walkways, and trees shading the walkways, and basketball courts for the kids, and benches for the old folks. They're going to do it free, and they're going to do it fast—in forty-eight hours flat. There goes contractor Tony Taormina's son Chris out to check a surveyor's stake, and the work is on.

[8:30 A.M.] Now two thousand tons of topsoil, which came free, is being spread by big front-end loaders which were contributed, operated by heavy-equipment men— union men, not used to working for nothing. They're working for nothing.

[9:30 A.M.] Dozens of people are working out here together now. They are people who never met before today. They are black and white, rich and poor. They have nothing in common except this: they all think this vacant lot ought to be a park.

[12 noon] They need a ditch here. Bill Brooks, a school custodian, and Lonnie Feemster, an unemployed kid, and Manny Ruiz, a roofer by trade, are digging it. A man named Hartage, eighty-four years old, who came by to watch, picks up a shovel and gets down in the ditch himself; he says he needs the exercise.

[2 P.M.] People are still coming from all over Reno to pitch in. I have the feeling that something extraordinary is happening on this vacant lot. Guy Smith, a black mechanic making wooden forms for pouring concrete, has the same feeling.

★ ★ ★

KURALT: What are you doing right now?

SMITH: Well, this is a form for a double tennis court that should be in before dark, we hope. This is one of the things people say is impossible, but we're going to prove that we can do it. You know?

KURALT: Well, you have the kids sawing away!

SMITH: Yeah, this little Red here [*indicating youngster*], he's become a little kinsman of mine, this little fellow here. He was up bright and early this morning, said he'd be out here and give me a hand, and you know, he's going to make a pretty good carpenter before the day is over!

KURALT: Suppose he's ever used a saw before in his life?
SMITH: Well, I don't see any fingers missing. By tonight, he just might be a confirmed carpenter.

Throughout the long day, Red, who is Lem Lewis, keeps sawing as if everything depended upon him alone.

[5 P.M.] Almost lost in this crowd is a slight, pretty woman named Pat Baker. The whole crazy idea of building a park in two days was hers. The night after Martin Luther King was killed, she sat up late, thinking she had to do something. The difference between Pat Baker and most other people is that after talking to her employer, the Sierra Pacific Power Company, and to people in this neighborhood, and to tough-minded contractors she'd never met before, she was able to figure out a thing to do. Her idea became everybody's idea, and Pat Baker is watching her dream happen out here in the sun.

[Saturday morning, 10 A.M.] By now it's not a vacant lot anymore. The park is here to be seen in outline. Now Coast Guardsmen, Marines, Seabees, are giving their day

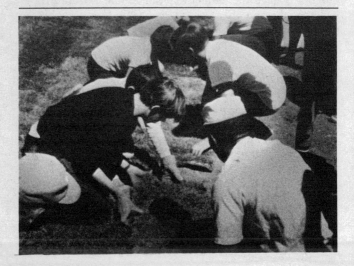

off to this. A little girl named Donna Snow plans to work here all day doing what she can do—bringing a bucket of water around to anybody who's thirsty.

[Saturday midnight] Saturday night in Reno was always a time for bright lights and action. In this corner of town, big spotlights at the corners of the lot are the bright lights, and people planting grass are the action.

[Sunday 9 A.M.] MAN ON BULLHORN: Let's get all the sod off the sidewalk and finish planting it! We're going to turn the sprinklers on. Watch out, you'll get soaking wet!

And now there's a park here, with grass and walkways and trees and basketball courts and benches, just as they said there was going to be when they started two days ago. Reno had what it took. What it took was working together.

[Sunday 2 P.M.] It's Sunday afternoon and the neighborhood has turned out to admire what has been done and to dedicate the new park and name it. They name it Pat Baker Park.

PAT BAKER: Thank you. This was a great big black-and-white thing, that's what it was. A great big black-and-white thing.

A black man, leaning on his shovel after it was all done, said, "This is the best thing that has happened since I came to Reno fourteen years ago."

He didn't mean the park. He meant building the park.

Blackie

We were going somewhere else, like all the other traffic on Illinois 16, when we noticed what looked like a grave beside the highway. Funny place for a grave, so we stopped and asked around.

It turned out that this place, which is just a crossing of country roads, has a special meaning for the people around here, because of something that happened here once. It was a long time ago, the summer of 1965, when a little dog showed up, a little black dog who seemed to be lost. Bill Stiff, whose family farm adjoins the road, was ten years old then; probably it was Bill who first called the dog Blackie.

★ ★ ★

BILL STIFF: Nobody can fully explain why he was here. But I've always theorized that he was dropped off or left or something. And he just stayed here and was waiting for his master to return. That's all I can figure.

HELEN PARKES: He definitely was lost. He would sit and watch. He would get up on the bank and watch each car, and you could see him. He'd turn his head as a car went by.

Helen Parkes is editor of the weekly paper up the road at Oakland.

PARKES: Often I saw him on this island, between the roads here, and just sitting there, kind of watching the traffic, and, apparently, waiting and watching for someone.

The summer went by and the fall came, and Blackie kept his place here at the crossing. People around here worried about him, what with winter coming on, and more than one family tried to adopt him.

STIFF: All the neighbors and everything brought food out here. I remember one Thanksgiving, there was more turkey bones here than anybody could ever imagine. They were stacked up high.

KURALT: And he stayed right around here?

STIFF: Yeah. He didn't leave. He wouldn't leave. I think that unless some motorist hadn't killed him, I don't think he would ever have left. I really don't.

That's what finally happened, of course. On an icy morning in early February, Blackie was struck by a car and killed.

He was just a lost dog, and it all happened a long time ago. It's hard to explain the impression Blackie made on the people around here; hard to explain why all these years later, the kids still take turns mowing the grass and keeping the place cleaned up. Maybe the explanation is in what they wrote on Blackie's grave marker:

BLACKIE,
Feb. 6, 1966.
Know Ye Now True
Loyalty & Love

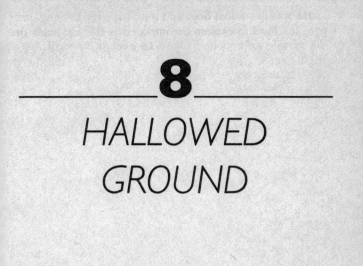

8

HALLOWED GROUND

*I*n 1976, the Bicentennial year, Izzy and Larry and I traveled to every state to record a moment of history from each of them. We ended the year exhausted by the trip and awed by the country. We had seen it all before, but that year we really thought about America—its beginnings, it expanses, and its wanderers westward: the con men, cowpunchers, and wishful thinkers; the schoolmarms, soldiers, and sodbusters; the preachers and the politicians. American history is gaudier than a dime novel and a lot better reading, and the places where it happened are mostly still there to be seen. If you go to some of these places early in the morning, say, when there's nobody else around and think what happened there, they'll give you the shivers.

Rogues' Island

It's hard to find, lost in the seedy sidestreets of a big city. But if you want to see where the raucous give and take of American democracy really was born, you have to come to this small urban park. In the wilderness of 1636, there was a spring on the spot, and a troublemaker named Roger Williams, kicked out of Puritan Massachusetts and fleeing for his life, stopped running here. He wanted to live in a place where you didn't have to believe what the government told you to believe. And when he considered what had brought him to this place, he knew he had a name for it—Providence.

Then as now, Rhode Island was just a little place, twenty-five miles across, but the colony put it right into its first code of laws that within these twenty-five miles, "all men may walk as their consciences persuade them." That was Roger Williams' idea, 150 years before the U.S. Constitution got around to saying the same thing.

Well, it was freely predicted the idea would lead to chaos. And it did. These old streets were soon filled with every kind of screwball, all arguing with one another.

With the steeple of the church Roger Williams founded behind him, Professor William McLoughlin of Brown University gave it to us straight.

★ ★ ★

KURALT: I should have thought that the other colonies

would be proud of Rhode Island for its religious diversity.

PROFESSOR WILLIAM MCLOUGHLIN: Oh, no, no, that's happened since the Revolution. At the time, Rhode Island was a scandal and a disgrace. The ideal in the colonial period was to have a well-ordered, well-regulated community with uniformity of belief and conformity of practice. And this place was known as "Rogues' Island." It attracted people who couldn't get along in decent society. All the bad rubbish drained into Rhode Island, and since we were at the bottom of New England, that seemed to make sense.

Well, it was called the licentious republic. And in the period called the Critical Period, the Rhode Islanders were looked upon, even by the other states in the new nation, as a rather outrageous example of what happens when popular democracy goes too far.

"Don't tread on me." It was a South Carolina flag, but it was a Rhode Island sentiment. We found the flag flying outside the old Touro Synagogue. The Jews started a congregation in Newport in 1658, and it's still there, worshiping in the oldest synagogue in America.

See, Rhode Island was a mess, but it was a democratic mess, long before the idea of democracy occurred to anybody else around here. It sounded good to the Jews.

It sounded good to the Baptists, too. Today, every town has a First Baptist Church. Rhode Island has the *first* Baptist church, with a congregation that goes straight back to 1638.

Freedom of conscience is so old in America that we've forgotten where it began. Every one of us who listens to the cantor on Friday night or sings "Faith of Our Fathers" on Sunday morning or kneels with a rosary before a statue of the Virgin Mary or who never goes to church at all ought to remember that religious liberty, the separation of church and state, the whole idea of the sovereignty of the people, started here.

The early Rhode Islander was disrespectful and disreputable, always fighting about something. Today they've put him on a pedestal. The figure atop the capitol dome is called the Independent Man. He can see the whole state from up there, the first state to be disrespectful and disreputable and free.

Independence Hall

"I say let us wait." John Dickinson of Pennsylvania stood in this hall, July 1st, 1776, and begged the Continental Congress to be reasonable. "The time is not yet ripe for proclaiming independence. Instead of help from foreign powers, it will bring us disaster. I say we ought to hold back any declaration and remain the masters of our fate and our fame. All of Great Britain is armed against us. The wealth of the Empire is poured into her treasury. We shall weep at our folly."

John Dickinson was not a timid or frightened man. He was a great old Quaker patriot, and he had a good argument. At the moment he spoke, British grenadiers were sweeping down from Canada, British guns were bombarding Charleston, and just ninety miles away an incredible British armada was entering New York harbor—five hundred ships carrying thirty-two thousand troops, the best army in the world. That army could march to Philadelphia and take this building and arrest this Congress any afternoon it chose to do so. So John Dickinson pleaded, "Let us not brave the storm in a paper boat."

The delegates paid him respectful attention. John Adams and his cousin, Sam, hot for independence, impatient with the delay, sat listening. Thomas Jefferson sat back in the corner. He had already written the Declaration of Independence. It spoke his thoughts. Beside him, old Benjamin Franklin, also silent, his mind made up.

But every mind was not made up. Pennsylvania and

South Carolina were opposed to independence; Delaware divided; New York undecided. All through the spring into the summer they had sat here and wrangled, their tempers growing hot with the season. Young Edward Rutledge of South Carolina had said of John Adams and the New Englanders, "They will bring us ruin. I dread their low cunning and those leveling principles which men without character and without fortune possess." And John Adams had said of Rutledge, "Rutledge is a perfect bobolink, a swallow, a sparrow, a peacock, excessively vain, excessively weak."

Now, Rutledge and Adams and the rest listened to John Dickinson speaking gravely from the heart: "Declaring our independence at a time like this is like burning down our house before we have another."

It was John Adams who rose to his feet. He was not John Dickinson's equal as a speaker, and everything he had to say he had said before. He never said it better than on that July afternoon: "We've been duped and bubbled by the phantom of peace. What is the real choice before us? If we postpone the declaration, do we mean to submit? Do we consent to yield and become a conquered people? No, we do not! We shall fight! We shall fight with whatever means we have—with rusty muskets and broken flints, with bows and arrows, if need be. Then why put off the declaration? For myself, I can only say this: I have crossed the Rubicon. All that I have, all that I am, all that I hope for in this life, I stake on our cause. For me, the die is cast. Sink or swim, live or die, to survive or perish with my country—that is my unalterable resolution!"

That night, John Dickinson went home, put on his militia uniform, and rode away to join his regiment. He could not vote for independence, but he could fight the British. That night, Edward Rutledge changed his mind. South Carolina would not stand in the way of unanimity. That night, Caesar Rodney, a man dying of cancer, rode through the night on horseback in a storm to Philadelphia to cast the deciding vote for Delaware. And so, when Secretary Charles Thomson called the roll on July 2nd, of the twelve colonies voting, all twelve voted for Independence. It was done. What remained was the declaring it.

The next morning, July 3rd, an anonymous note was found on President Hancock's table. It said, "You have gone too far. Take care. A plot is framed for your destruction, and all of you shall be destroyed." It suddenly occurred to them that there might be a lighted powder keg under the floor; there was an uproar. There were volunteers to search the cellar. Then crusty old Joseph Hewes of North Carolina stood up to say, "Mr. President, I am against wasting any time searching cellars. I would as soon be blown to pieces as proclaim to the world that I was frightened by a note."

Without searching any cellars, the Continental Congress proceeded to a consideration of the Declaration of Independence. They're immortal words now, but of course they weren't when Charles Thomson read them for the first time: "When in the Course of human events . . ." And for two days Jefferson sat back in the corner and fumed as they all toyed with his masterpiece. "Did we really have to call the King a tyrant quite so often?" They changed some of the "tyrants" back to "King." "Did we have to bid the British people our everlasting adieu?" They struck that out. And Jefferson's mightiest passage, his denunciation of slavery, that was struck out, too, at the insistence of Georgia and South Carolina. Jefferson wrote elsewhere, "Nothing is more certainly written in the book of fate than that these people are to be free."

But finally, all the cuts and changes were done, and what remains was a document still noble enough to inspire the tired delegates and bold enough to hang them all. It was read through one more time to the end: ". . . And for the support of this Declaration, with a firm reliance on the Protection of Divine Providence, we mutually pledge to each other our Lives, our Fortunes and our sacred Honor." There was one final vote, and President Hancock announced the result with the use of a new phrase: "The Declaration of the United States of America is unanimously agreed to." There was no cheering, no fireworks;

not yet. The delegates simply walked out into the night of the Fourth of July thinking their own thoughts, some of them no doubt remembering what John Dickinson had said: "This is like burning down our house before we have another." Others hearing Tom Paine: "The birthday of a new world is at hand. We have it in our power to begin the world all over again."

John Adams walked to his boardinghouse to write a letter to a friend. "Well," he said, "the river is passed. The bridge is cut away."

The Most Contentious Little Town in North America

(JONESBORO, TENNESSEE)

Jonesboro, Tennessee's oldest town, stands quietly in the late autumn sun. It's all so peaceful now. Hard to believe that this was once the most contentious little town in North America. That was just at the end of the Revolutionary War, when North Carolina, which had ambitions to be a civilized place, took one look at its western possessions, filling up with rough characters wearing buckskins and fighting Indians, and decided enough was enough. So the state of North Carolina said to the brand new American Congress, "Tell you what we're going to do. We're going to give North Carolina west of the mountains to you." The brand new American Congress said, "Thanks, just the same. But we've troubles enough already and what we don't need is a bunch of backwoodsmen living in a wilderness."

People around here, left with no government, decided they'd better start one. And right here, on this spot, they did. As far as they were concerned, it was the fourteenth state. They named it for Ben Franklin.

The state of Franklin convened itself in the courthouse, right where today's courthouse sits, and elected Colonel John Sevier as governor. Sevier's state should have been a success. And it would have been if Sevier's constituents hadn't turned out to be the most headstrong, unruly, rough and tumble, ungovernable lot who ever tried to form a government. They fell out into factions and threw one another bodily out of the courthouse. They appointed competing sheriffs to arrest one another. They sent one another to the old graveyard above town with muskets and pistols. And it didn't help a bit when a blustery young lawyer came riding into town spoiling for a fight, an ambitious troublemaker named Andy Jackson.

Jackson, who lived here, to Colonel Robert Love—"You, sir, and all your family are a band of land pirates!"

Colonel Robert Love to Jackson—"And you, sir, are a damned long, gangling, sorrel-topped soap stick!"

Colonel John Sevier—"Andrew Jackson is the most abandoned rascal my eyes have ever beheld!"

Jackson, in a newspaper ad—"Know ye that I, Andrew Jackson, do pronounce, publish, and declare to the world that his excellence, John Sevier, is a base coward and poltroon." They fought it out on the street, with sword and cane.

With other opponents, during and after the days of the state of Franklin, both Sevier and Jackson fought it out with guns. Then there was the time down here at the Chester Inn . . . But let Paul Fink, the Jonesboro historian, tell you about that.

PAUL FINK: Well, Jackson came here to hold court, and he was just so ill that he had to be helped off his horse and put to bed over there in the Chester Inn, now still standing. And when a lot of Sevier's friends heard that he was ill, they gathered around on the outside and there was a lot of talk going on: they'd bring Jackson out and tar and feather him. Well, some of Jackson's friends heard that and they went to him and said to him, "We can sneak you out the back door. They're going to come in here and get you." Well, Jackson was never a man to run from anything. He said, "Nope, I won't do that." He said, "Bring me my pistols. Load 'em and lay 'em on the bed." They were laid there, and then he sent the message out to the mob. It said, "I'm ready to receive you at any time you wish to wait upon me, and I only trust that your leader will lead his men rather than follow them." Well there wasn't any tar-and-feathering. [*Laughs*] I guess nobody was a candidate for the honor. So things quieted down then. Not exactly nice, quiet individuals we had here at the time!

Those nice, quiet individuals finally cleared out of Jonesboro. The state of Franklin failed of admission to the union by one vote in the Congress. John Sevier left town to become six times Governor of its successor, the state of Tennessee. Andy Jackson left town to become war hero and President. Half the people in Jonesboro claim relation to one or the other of them. But let me tell you something: Jonesboro's been a lot quieter town since they left.

Noah Webster's
Little Book

(WEST HARTFORD, CONNECTICUT)

A man was born in West Hartford in 1758 who was so excited by being an American that he showed all the rest of us how. He gave us, more than any other man, an American style, an American culture, an American education, and that most priceless of gifts, an American language.

Before he was twenty-five, he wrote a little book. Before he died, it had sold a hundred million copies, and nearly every American who could read had read it. He gave it a long title, but people called it Noah Webster's blue-backed speller.

★ ★ ★

DR. JANE DORGAN: "Democracy."
STUDENT #1: D-E-M-O-C-R-A-C-Y.

Noah Webster's little book came out at a time when even illustrious Americans like George Washington spelled pretty much as they pleased. The next generation spelled the way Noah Webster told them to.

DORGAN: "Property." It was Noah Webster's property.
STUDENT #2: P-R-O-P-E-R-T-Y.

And when Dr. Jane Dorgan and her students from

 ON THE ROAD WITH CHARLES KURALT

Bridlepath School put on a spelling bee in Noah Webster's kitchen, the words came from the blue-backed speller.

STUDENT #3: F-E-S-T-I-V-A-L.

The kids come from all kinds of backgrounds, from all over the country. That they can agree that there is a right way and a wrong way to spell and pronounce words—that is the work of Noah Webster. He was the first to insist on an American language. He was the first to teach American history. He was the first great American newspaper editor. This Yankee schoolmaster wanted us to give up European ways and become a new nation, and he wanted us to do it his way. And we did.

West Hartford historian Nelson Burr:

NELSON BURR: Webster—let's put it quite frankly—is not the kind of a person out of whom you manufacture a popular hero. I mean, he wasn't a military hero; he wasn't a great sportsman; and so on. He was primarily a scholar, an author, an intellectual, and I think this is one of the reasons why to a large extent the American public hasn't appreciated him as much as he should be appreciated. If you want to put it crudely, he was an egghead. And he was not always too diplomatic in handling people.

KURALT: A little contentious.

BURR: Contentious. One American literary historian, Vernon Parrington, even calls him "the laborious and truculent Noah" in one of his books. And if you got into a controversy with Noah Webster, it would be well for you to do your homework, because, otherwise, he might cut you up and throw you away. He was a formidable man. He had a very powerful, formidable intellect that just worked full-time.

Webster learned his first words as a child in the parlor of the Webster home. He never forgot any of them. He buried himself in words. He spent twenty-five years of his life, working alone and by hand, to put seventy thousand words into one book, his masterpiece. He called it, proudly: *An American Dictionary of the English Language*.

The book and its legitimate successors—leaving aside its many illegitimate successors—established the standards of the language we speak today. We still look it up in Webster's.

There are words enough in the book even to describe its author—"versatile," "passionate," "humorless," "rigid," "indefatigable" . . . "ingenious" Noah Webster.

The National Road

(CUMBERLAND, MARYLAND, TO VANDALIA, ILLINOIS)

People travel far too fast to read milestones nowadays. And whenever you find one, you can be sure it's a very unimportant road. But when one particular milestone was planted 150 years ago, it was on the most important road in America. The road started one mile back in Cumberland, Maryland. And it went—west.

The road was a dream of Washington and Jefferson's; and John C. Calhoun made a great speech in favor of it. He said, "Let us conquer space." The space he meant was not from here to the moon. But in 1817, it might as well have been. It was from Cumberland, Maryland, clear to the Illinois frontier. And they built it with mattocks and axes and paving stones. They actually built the thing west to the river town of Wheeling, and west to Zanesville, and west to the prairie village of Columbus, Ohio, and west across the Wabash. It was the longest, straightest road in history and a marvel of the world. They called it the National Road.

We stumbled upon a few miles of the old roadbed in Ohio; a few cobblestones, a few massive old abandoned bridges. And we thought we better show you these things now, because before long there might be nothing left to show you.

Already the road is a nearly forgotten part of the American romance. This incredible road, which carried so many peddlers and paupers and preachers and politicians west to the new America; and carried so many poor families in battered wagons from worn-out farms west to a second chance. Ideas went west, mail and newspapers; and in fancy stagecoaches, Jenny Lind and P. T. Barnum; and in groaning Conestoga freight wagons, calico and iron and whiskey and gunpowder—all the things it took to build a country. The National Road brought Henry Clay east from Kentucky and Abraham Lincoln from Illinois.

You mustn't imagine that it was just a road. It was an Appian Way, sixty-six feet wide for six hundred miles. "A finer road," an English traveler said, "than the highway from London to Bath." It must have been impossible for travelers on this highroad through the wilderness to imagine that anything would ever take its place. In places, the route of the National Road is now called U.S. 40. In places, it is called Interstate 70, our new National Road, on which the thunder of the big diesels drowns out the creaking echo of the Conestoga wagons.

But in quieter places, the vacant windows of shuttered general stores still reflect the pathway of the original road. A handful of the fine old taverns—which once watered the horses and brandied the gentlemen—still stand. The one on Mount Washington in Pennsylvania is remembered as unusual: its landlady was civil and her husband was sober.

Nobody reads the mileposts anymore; great green signs have taken their place. And the traffic roars up the hills past the old tollhouses with their quaint list of charges: "For every chariot, coach, coachee, stage, phaeton or chaise with two horses and four wheels, 12 cents." Today's chariots pass without reading or paying.

We just wanted to show you this much before it's too late. If you go slow enough and look hard enough, you can still find traces in the weeds, the last faint traces of the road that made us a nation.

A Stop on the Trail

If you pick your way among the young cottonwoods and old rattlesnake nests along the face of a cliff in Wyoming, this is what you find: men's names, carved here long ago.

[*Reading from sign chiseled into cliff:*] "JOHN A. MATHIS, JUNE 10TH, 1856. BORN HENRY COUNTY, KENTUCKY, DECEMBER 15TH, 1837." A nineteen-year-old boy, a long way from home. [*Sign:* JED. HINES, OHIO CO., KENTUCKY, JUNE 1, 1864] And in time came Jedediah Hines, from Ohio County, Kentucky. [L. E. PRESTON, BELLEVUE, MICHIGAN, JULY 29TH, 1864] And in time a man named Preston from Michigan. And in time came thousands, each yielding to the urge to carve his name on Register Cliff.

Who were all these people so far from home? Of course, they were the pioneers. The wagon track that leads past the Cliff was called the Oregon Trail.

Wyoming was a place of passage, a kind of alkali hell to be got through. You can still read the signs of the getting through, all these years later. The Oregon Trail is a faint path through the sagebrush, leading westward toward the mountains. It is a hard climb over rocks, westward. It is deep ruts in soft stone, carved by wagon wheels rolling west. Those wagons were so heavily laden with the hopes and belongings of people who knew they were never going home again that they left an indelible mark—the sculpture of their wheels, upon Wyoming.

The trail follows the rivers as far as the rivers go—the

North Platte into Wyoming, and then the Sweetwater—
and passes beside a granite outcropping the immigrants
called Independence Rock. By the time they reached the
rock they had a thousand miles of desert behind them and
a worse thousand miles of mountains ahead of them, and
no true American could resist climbing the rock with a
hammer and chisel to say, "Look, I got this far! I was
here!" [*Sign carved in the rock:* W. GANNON. 1858]

If you wanted to get across the Sierra before the bliz-
zards, it used to be said, you'd better get to Independence
Rock by Independence Day. [J. J. HUGHES, JULY 4, 1850]
You were right on time, Mr. Hughes. [JOHN BECK, IOWA,
JULY 4, '62] So were you, Mr. Beck. [M. McKEE, E.
MOODY, NEW YORK, JULY 9, '53] You were a few days
late, McKee and Moody, but you had come a long way.
[MILO J. AYER, AGE 29, 1849] You were a forty-niner,
Milo Ayer, bound for the goldfields, I imagine. [W. HANKS,
ILL. 1860] Did you see the war coming, Mr. Hanks? Is
that why you left Illinois? [H. HART, MAY 24, 1865. GEOR-

GIA] Did you lose your farm in that war, Mr. Hart? Is that why you left Georgia?

From 1841 until they finished the railroad in 1869, through the three middle decades of the nineteenth century, the wagons rolled through Wyoming along the Oregon Trail. Register Cliff and Independence Rock give rise to long thoughts about those people, those failed farmers and dreamy-eyed gold seekers and hopeful young families who passed here so long ago. Three hundred thousand of them endured this trail, almost none of them prepared for the heat and hunger and misery of it, for the sake of whatever they were hoping for in Oregon or California, places they had never been and had no good idea of. Wherever they had come from, when they got where they were going, they had one experience in common—Wyoming. But Wyoming tells us so little about them.

[*Sign:* J. R. HORNADAY, AGE 19 YEARS, 1 MONTH, 9 DAYS] What happened to you, J. R. Hornaday? Did you make it across the desert and across the Divide? Did you grow to manhood in some lush valley of California? Are your great-great-grandchildren happy tonight in Bakersfield or San Jose?

There is nothing here to tell us. All you left in Wyoming was your name.

Place of Sorrows

(LITTLE BIG HORN, MONTANA)

This is about a place where the wind blows and the grass grows and a river flows below a hill. Nothing is here but the wind and the grass and the river. But of all the places in America, this is the saddest place I know.

The Indians called the river the Greasy Grass. White men called it the Little Big Horn. From a gap in the mountains to the east, Brevet Major General George A. Custer's proud Seventh Cavalry came riding, early in the morning of June 25th, 1876, riding toward the Little Big Horn.

Custer sent one battalion, under Major Marcus Reno, across the river to attack what he thought might be a small village of hostile Sioux. His own battalion he galloped behind the ridges to ride down on the village from the rear. When at last Custer brought his two hundred and thirty-one troops to the top of a hill and looked down toward the river, what he saw was an encampment of fifteen thousand Indians stretching for two and a half miles, the largest assembly of Indians the plains had ever known—and a thousand mounted warriors coming straight for him.

Reno's men, meantime, had been turned, routed, chased across the river, joined by the rest of the regiment, surrounded, and now were dying, defending a nameless brown hill.

In a low, protected swale in the middle of their narrowing circle, the one surviving doctor improvised a field hospital and did what he could for the wounded. The grass covers the place now and grows in the shallow rifle trenches above, which were dug that day by knives and tin cups and fingernails.

Two friends in H Company, Private Charles Windolph and Private Julian Jones, fought up here, side by side, all that day, and stayed awake all that night, talking, both of them scared. Charles Windolph said: "The next morning when the firing commenced, I said to Julian, 'We'd better get our coats off.' He didn't move. I looked at him. He was shot through the heart." Charles Windolph won the Congressional Medal of Honor up here, survived, lived to be ninety-eight. He didn't die until 1950. And never a day passed in all those years that he didn't think of Julian Jones.

And Custer's men, four miles away? There are stones in the grass that tell the story of Custer's men. The stones all say the same things: "U.S. soldier, Seventh Cavalry, fell here, June 25, 1876."

The warriors of Sitting Bull, under the great Chief Gall,

struck Custer first and divided his troops. Two Moon and the northern Cheyenne struck him next. And when he tried to gain a hilltop with the last remnants of his command, Crazy Horse rode over that hill with hundreds of warriors and right through his battalion.

The Indians who were there later agreed on two things: that Custer and his men fought with exceeding bravery; and that after half an hour, not one of them was alive.

The Army came back that winter—of course, the Army came back—and broke the Sioux and the Cheyenne and forced them back to the starvation of the reservations, and in time, murdered more old warriors and women and children on the Pine Ridge Reservation than Custer lost young men in battle here.

That's why this is the saddest place. For Custer and the Seventh Cavalry, courage only led to defeat. For Crazy Horse and the Sioux, victory only led to Wounded Knee.

Come here sometime, and you'll see. There is melancholy in the wind and sorrow in the grass, and the river weeps.

Henry Ford

(GREENFIELD VILLAGE, MICHIGAN)

He was a farm boy, thirteen years old. He didn't know anything about watches. But his friend Albert Hutchings had a watch that wouldn't run. The farm boy persuaded Albert to let him look inside. He sat down at a shelf beneath a window of the farmhouse, and, with a pair of tweezers he made from one of his mother's corset stays and a little screwdriver he made from a shingle nail, he figured out that watch and—he fixed it.

When Albert Hutchings' watch started ticking, the world was changed, because the farm boy wasn't interested in farming anymore; he was interested in wheels and machines.

America had always had more than her share of boys like Henry Ford and has yet—boys who don't care about school or their father's line of work but who love machinery.

Watches and clocks just happened to be the first machinery Henry could get his hands on. Henry Ford worked in a foundry, in a streetcar plant, in an engine works. Summertimes, he took jobs with a steam sawmill gang and a steam threshing crew. Wheels—wheels that moved—iron on iron. Gears and valves and rockers and pistons and turning wheels were becoming an American religion, and among the devout communicants was Henry Ford.

And so, when the gasoline engine was invented, of course he mastered that, too. And of course he made it run a carriage on the road, always sending his friend Jim Bishop ahead on a bicycle that summer of 1896, to warn other drivers to hold their horses. And that is how a new sound was heard in Dearborn, Michigan.

[*Sound of early car going by*]

Henry Ford didn't invent the automobile, but he did invent one in particular. People laughed at it, but when Henry parked it, he found he had to chain it to a tree or a lampost to keep those same people from trying it out.

He kept tinkering with the car. He improved it, in a major way, nineteen times over the years. The twentieth time, he called it the Model T.

He went out and sold fifteen million of them.

Of course, the Model T changed everything. It gave us mass production, mass mobility, an industrial elite, the motorcar that could be afforded, the motorcar as a right of birth. It gave us traffic jams and parking lots and paved streets and billboards and air pollution. It gave us the Sunday drive and the Sunday driver. It gave us suburbs and supermarkets.

But it is useless to hail or condemn the coming of the automobile. It is this way: There were boys in the land who did not care for farming or schooling, who cared only for wheels and machines. There was one named Edison in New Jersey, and two brothers in Ohio named Wright, and one in Michigan named Ford. Similar boys have returned from the moon, and who knows where they may go next?

In the Henry Ford Museum at Greenfield Village, there are hundreds of thousands of exhibits and one most visitors overlook.

It is the one that promises the inevitability of the automobile. It goes back to Henry Ford's youth. It is Albert Hutchings' watch.

Mother of Exiles

Whom do you think about when you think about New York? I think about her. [*We look up at the Statue of Liberty.*]

I think about her, and Igor Sikorsky and Igor Stravinsky and Mother Cabrini and Father Flanagan, and all the other eyes and minds who have looked up to return her gaze. I think about her face, and about theirs. [*Photographs of immigrants*]

Their faces are familiar, of course. Under the fur hat, under the babushka, those are our faces. We came from the world, and our port of debarkation was New York—seven blond boys admitted, to go to Kulm, North Dakota; seven farmers from the plains; seven soldiers lost to the Kaiser.

In the earliest days, there was no United States Immigration Service. We came to New York, and it was New York that took us in. John James Audubon, John Peter Zenger, John Jacob Astor—all came. Anybody came who could afford the fare. New York said welcome.

New York even prepared a place of welcome, the first in the world. Castle Garden, at the tip of Manhattan, was first a fort; then a music hall; then, from 1855 to 1890—it had a high vaulted roof on it back then—a receiving station for immigrants.

This was the way into America. One day in about 1860, a boy named Karl came walking down this passageway and out into the light and looked up and saw New York.

This was my great-grandfather. His name was Karl Kuralt. Whatever your name is, chances are fair that your great-grandfather made the walk down this passageway, too. Nearly eight million people, the great-grandparents of quite a lot of us, stepped into America right here.

Sixteen million more came to Ellis Island. Immigration began to get restrictive about then. You could get turned back for having the wrong political opinion or having the wrong color or being too old or too ill. There was heartbreak and injustice in these halls. But most made it in— Hannah Arendt, Charlie Chaplin, Knute Rockne, Felix Frankfurter. They carried our greatness in their baggage.

We are all immigrants. Even American Indians came here from someplace else. New York is a celebration of our diversity. A long way from Georgia, an even longer way from China, a Georgia boy got his name written in Chinese on a banner over Mott Street.

[*A Jimmy Carter banner hangs in the breeze.*]

This is the authentic picture of New York City. And this is the authentic sound—in Orchard Street on the Lower East Side:

JEWISH SALESMAN: On you, the hat looks wonderful.
BLACK CUSTOMER: Wait a minute, man. Don't rush me.

It is no tight little island, this New York. It is the original site of the raucous American miracle, the place most of us started out from, and to which, merely by walking in its streets and looking into its face, we can come home to.

Here, Emma Lazarus wrote in 1883:

Here at our sea-washed, sunset gates shall stand
A mighty woman with a torch, whose flame
Is the imprisoned lightning, and her name
Mother of exiles.

Town Meeting Day

(STRAFFORD, VERMONT)

This one day in Vermont, the town carpenter lays aside his tools, the town doctor sees no patients, the shopkeeper closes his shop, mothers tell their children they'll have to warm up their own dinner. This one day, people in Vermont look not to their own welfare but to that of their town. It doesn't matter that it's been snowing since four o'clock this morning. They'll be in the meeting house. This is town meeting day.

Every March for 175 years, the men and women of Strafford, Vermont, have trudged up this hill on the one day which is their holiday for democracy. They walk past a sign that says: THE OLD WHITE MEETING HOUSE— BUILT IN 1799 AND CONSECRATED AS A PLACE OF PUBLIC WORSHIP FOR ALL DENOMINATIONS WITH NO PREFERENCE FOR ONE ABOVE ANOTHER. Since 1801, it has also been in continuous use as a town hall.

Here, every citizen may have his say on every question. One question is: Will the town stop paying for outside health services? The speaker is a farmer and elected selectman, David K. Brown. And farmer Brown says yes.

★ ★ ★

DAVID K. BROWN: This individual was trying or thinking about committing suicide. So we called the Orange County Mental Health. This was, I believe, on a Friday night. They said they'd see him Tuesday after-

noon [*mild laughter*], and if we had any problems, take him to Hanover and put him in the emergency room. Now I don't know as we should pay five hundred and eighty-two dollars and fifty cents for that kind of advice.

They talked about that for half an hour, asking themselves if this money would be well or poorly spent.
This is not representative democracy. This is pure democracy, in which every citizen's voice is heard.

JAMES CONDICT: We will vote on this before we go to Article Four. All those in favor signify by saying "Aye."

PEOPLE: Aye.
CONDICT: All opposed.
PEOPLE: Nay.
CONDICT: I'm going to ask for a standing vote. All those
    in favor stand, please.

It's an old Yankee expression which originated in the
town meeting and has entered the language of free men:
Stand up and be counted.

And when the judgment is made, and announced by
James Condict, maker of rail fences and moderator of this
meeting, the town will abide by the judgment.

CONDICT: There are a hundred votes cast—sixty-one in
    favor and thirty-nine against. And it then becomes
    deleted from the town budget.

This is the way the founders of this country imagined
it would be—that citizens would meet in their own communities to decide directly most of the questions affecting
their lives and fortunes. Vermont's small towns have kept
it this way.

Will or will not Strafford, Vermont, turn off its streetlights to save money?

CONDICT: All those in favor—
MAN [*shouting*]: —Paper ballot!—
CONDICT: —signify by saying—
MAN [*shouting*]: —Paper ballot!—
CONDICT: —"Aye."
MAN [*shouting*]: Paper ballot!
WOMAN: What?
MAN: That's my right, any member's right at a meeting—
    to call for a paper ballot.
CONDICT: Is that seconded?
WOMAN: I'll second it.
CONDICT: It's seconded.
MAN: It doesn't have to be seconded.
CONDICT: Prepare to cast your ballots on this amendment.

If any citizen demands a secret ballot, a secret ballot it must be. Everybody who votes in Vermont has taken an old oath—to always vote his conscience, without fear or favor of any person. This is something old, something essential. You tear off a little piece of paper and on it you write "yes" or "no." Strafford votes to keep the streetlights shining.

There is pie, baked by the ladies of the PTA. There are baked beans and brown bread, served at town meetings by Celia Lane as long as anybody can remember. Then a little more wood is added to the stove and a dozen more questions are debated and voted on in the long afternoon. What is really on the menu today is government of the people.

Finally came the most routine of all motions—the motion to adjourn.

CONDICT: All in favor signify by saying "Aye."
PEOPLE: Aye!
CONDICT: All that oppose.
PEOPLE [*much louder*]: Nay!
CONDICT: Then we don't adjourn, and the Nays have it.

It is heady stuff, democracy. They wanted to go on enjoying it for a while in Strafford today.

When finally they did adjourn and walk out into the snow, it was with the feeling of having preserved something important, something more important than their streetlights—their liberty.

9

Seasons

*I*f I were able to work things out just right, I'd spend every January in New Orleans getting myself up to fighting weight for the year to come. I'd have beignets and strong coffee for breakfast every morning at the Café du Monde, oysters for lunch every noon at the Acme Oyster Bar, and whatever they were serving at night at Le Ruth's, La Provence, or La Riviera.

By February, I'd have to leave because Mardi Gras arrives in February and I don't like big parties. So every February I'd wander slowly along the coast through Mobile and Pensacola and Tampa until I got to Sanibel Island and spend the rest of the month there reading under a palm tree, with special attention to the page one stories in the St. Petersburg Times about the snow and slush in Chicago and New York.

In March, I'd mosey along up to the Okefenokee to give my regards to the 'gators and the iris and the ibis and then settle down in Savannah to watch the azaleas bloom in the Bonaventure Cemetery.

April, certainly, I'd spend in Chapel Hill, North Carolina. I am a Tar Heel born and a Tar Heel bred and when I die I'm a Tar Heel dead, as we say in Chapel Hill, and April is North Carolina's glory, the month of daffodils and dogwood blossoms and soft breezes from the south. I'd go to Chapel Hill in April and imagine myself young again.

I'd give my May to the Bay and the foghorns. San Francisco is our most beautiful city, no doubt, and May is the month the fog rolls in under the Golden Gate and pours down the hills into the city streets and swirls inland, making ghostly the cedars of Point Lobos and the wind-bent pines of Point Reyes. I love that coast in May.

By June, I'd be ready to see blue sky again, and I'd go to Oregon to find it, around Newport where in June the wild roses grow at the edge of the fir forests and the meadows are filled with daisies.

In July, I'd go straight to Ely, Minnesota. There, I'd rent a canoe and paddle it slowly north into the boundary waters, away from all pavement and neon. They don't allow motorboats there; they don't even allow planes to fly over. So the loons make the loudest sound.

I'd spend August in Rockport, Maine. One day I'd give to the annual antique show, one day to a sail on a schooner, and one day to the Shakespeare play up the road at Camden. The other twenty-eight days of August, I'd sit still, contemplating the perfect harbor of Rockport, Maine.

Right after Labor Day, I'd go to West Yellowstone, Montana. There, on every remaining day of September, I'd stand in a different trout river—the Firehole, the Yellowstone, the Madison, the Henrys Fork—trying to learn how to fool a trout with a little bit of floating fur and feather. (I have been trying to master this deception on these rivers for many years and may never become good at it. But September in the Yellowstone country is a glorious time and place to try.)

Spring starts at the Okefenokee Swamp and moves north; fall starts at Derby Line, Vermont, and moves south. So I'd come south with the fall, right down Vermont Route 100 through Westfield, Waterbury, Warrens, Weston, Wardsboro, Wilmington. The crimson and gold of October in Vermont is so stunning that you can't remember from one year to the next how beautiful it is, which makes Vermont a shock to the senses every fall.

November I'd spend in San Antonio walking along the river and soaking up sun and sangría in the sidewalk cafes. A hundred other cities could have made their riverbanks as joyful as this, but only San Antonio did it.

I'd want to be in New York City for December. The great old lady looks a little shabby the rest of the year, but in December she dresses up and puts a garland of white lights in her hair. One year, somehow, I missed seeing the ice skaters gliding round and round at the base of New York's Christmas tree and felt I had missed Christmas.

That's my year. You'll notice I haven't done any work at all. I've *never spent a year anything like this one, of course; these are bits of many years pieced together. I realize it's a year that wouldn't suit everybody; some North Dakotans find February appealing right there at home. But if there are any idle rich among us who can spend twelve months as they choose, and choose to try this itinerary, I say to them: Damn you for your good luck. And send me a postcard once in a while.*

Sugaring Time

(JACKSONVILLE, VERMONT)

It happens every year. As surely as the sun climbs in the April sky, the snow will melt, the streams will start to flow, the sap in the sugar maple trees will run again, and there begins the old ritual of the New England spring. On a thousand Vermont farms, it's maple sugaring time again.

George and June Butler work together on their farm in Jacksonville, Vermont, collecting the sap that has dripped into the buckets overnight. No man planted these maples; they grew wild. This annual harvest is all the sweeter for being a gift from the trees.

★ ★ ★

GEORGE BUTLER: Think that it takes at least forty years for a tree to get ten inches, which is the minimum diameter at the butt to tap. A tree like this has to be at least two hundred, maybe two hundred fifty or even three hundred years old.

KURALT: I suppose it's sweetened a lot of people's pancakes over the years.

BUTLER: Well, I guess so. I don't know whether it sweetened any of the Indians' or not, but some of the trees that have been cut down actually show the tomahawk cuts, where Indians tapped them before the white man came.

KURALT: You know, hard as this work is, you give me the impression that you enjoy it.

BUTLER: I certainly do. I wouldn't do it for money. It's the fun of it, the real joy of being in the woods, because after being cooped up all winter, to be able  to come down and take part in this great festival of nature, of spring, it's a great experience. You get in the sugar house, and the steam comes, and you boil; the sap bubbles, the wood crackles, it's a great thing. I mix in the slabs along with the hardwood, because the hardwood gives it a little staying power, and the resin in the softwood gives it the very hot heat.

KURALT: Smells good.

BUTLER: That's the one thing you can't get on your equipment. You can get color and you can get sound, but you can't get smell, and the aroma is the thing. Maybe it's the osmosis of the sap getting into your system, but there is just something about it that makes old-timers who've sugared want to sugar.

See there, it's the lightest color, it's Fancy. This is A, this is B, and our syrup is Fancy syrup. This is unusual, so late in the season, to be Fancy.

KURALT: It's the best?

BUTLER: It has the most delicious bouquet. Light color, light flavor, and I think you'll agree that it's—

KURALT: Oh, ho, it's superb. It's really wonderful.

BUTLER: But it's fun. It's essentially fun. And it's healthy. There's a romance about it. It's part of the romance of America, and it's part of vanishing America. And each year there are fewer taps set. I like to do it because I enjoy it. I enjoy the hard work.

KURALT: But fewer and fewer people enjoy all that hard work?

BUTLER: Well, unfortunately, that's true. But also, it's very healthy. Now, I don't have any pot. When I came up to Vermont, thirteen, fourteen years ago, I weighed two hundred pounds. After sugaring, I knocked off forty pounds of lard. And I've stayed down. Healthy! The work is good for you!

It is spring in Vermont, and here is how you can tell: The birds are back; every animal, wild and domestic, is released from the grip of winter; and the ping of the sap of maple sugar trees is heard in tin buckets on every hillside.

In another week, the sap will stop flowing. But by then the sweetening for summer's pancakes will be safely in tins. For that we can thank the trees, and the Butlers, who work so hard among the trees, to celebrate the season.

Fourth of July

(CHARLOTTESVILLE, VIRGINIA)

How did you spend the Fouth of July? Did you sleep late, watch the ball game on TV? Will you even remember, this time next year, how you spent the day? We spent the day with some people who will remember. They met on the lawn of Monticello, Mr. Jefferson's house—Kenyans and Koreans and Hungarians, Czechs and Chinese— eighty-seven people from twenty-four countries. They heard their names called.

★ ★ ★

CLERK: Romeo Olivas, Nina Cullers, Cleo Ferris on behalf of Jennifer Rose Ferris.

They stood there, while facing Mr. Jefferson's porch and a District Court judge. They raised their right hands and they said a few words.

JUDGE: Renounce and abjure...
ASSEMBLED: Renounce and abjure...
JUDGE: ...all allegiance and fidelity...
ASSEMBLED: ...all allegiance and fidelity...
JUDGE: ...to any foreign prince...
ASSEMBLED: ...to any foreign prince...
JUDGE: ...potentate...
ASSEMBLED: ...potentate...
JUDGE: ...state or sovereignty...
ASSEMBLED: ...state or sovereignty.

And they became citizens of the United States. A lady from the DAR gave each of them an American flag to take home. As we stood there, watching their faces, we felt a kind of satisfaction, not for them but for all the rest of us. The United States got a transfusion of good blood today. There came Miss Marcelle Hark Moses from Lebanon, and Mrs. Nadya Garfein from Israel. There came Dutch and Indonesians, Indians and Pakistanis, Germans and French—people who have historically hated one another, now compatriots—two Cubans, one Japanese, one woman without any country at all until today. "How do you feel?" one man asked his wife. "I feel reborn," she said.

How did you spend the Fourth of July? Patricia Lam will remember how she spent it, and Zakia Noorani, and Rosito Abellera, and Ronnie Wheeler, and Francis Chow. They came up the hill to Mr. Jefferson's house Korean, Kenyan, Filipino, German and Chinese, but they're Yankee Doodle Dandies now, real live nephews of their Uncle Sam, reborn on the Fourth of July.

Pumpkins

(SECURITY, COLORADO)

Pumpkins are mostly for kids. We forget about the delights of the jack-o'-lanterns and Halloween as we grow older. This is about a couple of old-timers who never forgot.

Nick and Tony Venetucci have grown rich farming outside Colorado Springs. But they weren't always rich.

★ ★ ★

TONY VENETUCCI: I come up the hard, rugged way, and I'm glad I did. I'm glad I have. It's made a man out of me.

And not just a man, but a good and generous man; and anything you can say of Tony Venetucci goes also for his brother, Nick. But who are all these kids running through the Venetucci pumpkin patch? They are the schoolchildren Nick and Tony Venetucci invite out to the farm every fall to pick the pumpkin of their hearts' desire.

We watched Ladonna Bearden, six years old, dance across the furrow toward the one—out of so many thousands—that she had identified from afar as the perfect pumpkin. We watched Andy Salazar, six years old, pump-kinless among those who had already found their pump-kins, bump along, studying the ground until he, too, found bright orange fulfillment. We saw pumpkins rejected, not once, but twice; and pumpkins chosen, sometimes very big pumpkins chosen by very little kids.

Pumpkin fields have many lessons to teach the city kids fresh off the school bus, and one is that pride sometimes goeth before a fall. [*Little girl trips and falls under weight of huge pumpkin*.] Another is: If at first you don't suc-ceed, try, try again. [*She struggles to pick it up again*.]

We watched a certain amount of pumpkin envy. It seemed that with the discovery of a nice pumpkin comes the gnawing fear that your classmate has found a nicer pumpkin.

CHILD: I got an even bigger one.

We watched all this and then asked Tony Venetucci why he and Nick do it.

TONY VENETUCCI: We love it. We love to have these

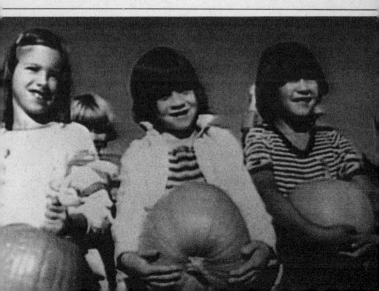

youngsters. And a lot of these youngsters, what you see out here now, they'll never forget this all the rest of their lives. Well, look at the thrill they're getting out here. Look at them, they're going wild!

There are thousands of schoolchildren around Colorado Springs. This year Nick Venetucci, who does the growing, grew thirty tons of pumpkins just to give away to them.

KURALT: Well, there's certainly no shortage of kids out here.

NICK VENETUCCI: No. And the population's growing. Kind of looks like I'm going to have to plant more pumpkins next year, don't it?

And so, this goes on from year to year, this harvest of joy in the fields of two old men who never let the joy of childhood escape them. And every year, the teachers line up the kids in the fields for photographs of the big day, which Tony Venetucci hopes they will always remember. Click! Some of them will keep this picture until they are old. Happy Halloween.

Turkey Trot

If you talk turkey, turkeys talk back. Turkeys are—how can I put it—not too bright. Ah, but they are numerous on the broad range around Cuero, Texas, and the community must celebrate what it has.

Every year, in the crisp fall days before Thanksgiving, Cuero celebrates turkeys. Well, what would you do if you had to make a big deal out of a dumb bird? First, you would import a phalanx of fiddlers, to play ceaselessly the municipal anthem, "Turkey in the Straw."

MAN: On your mark... Get set...

Since turkeys were made to gobble, not gallop, there is not exactly a thrill a minute in a turkey race, but you have to go with what you've got, remember, and Cuero's got turkeys. After an eternity there are winners, and turkey trophies, which self-conscious boys accept on behalf of their puzzled birds.

Then you would have a parade, which moves along a trifle uncertainly, because of the unpredictability of its leading participants, five thousand turkeys marching down Main Street.

It is difficult to describe how dumb turkeys really are. Suffice it to say that the organizers of the Cuero turkey trot dread rain on parade day, because of the tendency of turkeys to tilt their heads back to drink, and then to forget to tilt them forward again, thus drowning right there on

Main Street. The sun shone this year and the parade went off with decorum, but they haven't always, as J. D. Bramlette remembers.

★ ★ ★

J. D. BRAMLETTE: In the old days they was really in a mess because the birds were not domesticated. They were just wild turkeys raised on the range, and they ate acorns that fell on the ground. They weren't fed like our turkeys today are.

KURALT: So they were a little wilder when they got to Main Street, I imagine.

BRAMLETTE: Very much so, because when they saw the crowds of people, they became excited, and over the tops of the building and up in the trees they went, and this was a three-day job, to put them back into the flock and get them down to Cudahay Packing Company, where we were going to take them to market.

The sobering fact is that if there were no Thanksgiving there might be no turkeys, and if there were no turkeys there might be no Cuero, Texas. So while we all give thanks on this holiday, Cuero gives most deep and heartfelt thanks that once a year the nation takes all these dumb birds off its hands.

Coming Home

(PRAIRIE, MISSISSIPPI)

A long road took nine children out of the cotton fields, out of poverty, out of Mississippi. But roads go both ways, and this Thanksgiving weekend, they all returned. This is about Thanksgiving, and coming home.

One after another, and from every corner of America, the cars turned into the yard. With much cheering and much hugging, the nine children of Alex and Mary Chandler were coming home for their parents' fiftieth wedding anniversary.

★ ★ ★

GLORIA CHANDLER: There's my daddy. [Gloria rushes to to hug him.]

Gloria Chandler Coleman, master of arts, University of Missouri, a teacher in Kansas City, was home.

All nine children had memories of a sharecropper's cabin and nothing to wear and nothing to eat. All nine are college graduates.

Cooking the meal in the kitchen of the new house the children built for their parents four years ago is Bessie Chandler Beasley, BA Tuskegee, MA Central Michigan, dietician at a veterans hospital, married to a PhD. And helping out, Princess Chandler Norman, MA Indiana University, a schoolteacher in Gary, Indiana. You'll meet them all.

But first, I thought you ought to meet their parents. Alex Chandler remembers the time when he had a horse and a cow and tried to buy a mule and couldn't make the payments and lost the mule, the horse, and the cow. And about that time, Cleveland, the first son, decided he wanted to go to college.

ALEX CHANDLER: We didn't have any money. And we went to town; he wanted to catch the bus to go on up there. And so we went to town and borrowed two dollars and a half from her niece, and bought him a bus ticket. And when he got there, that's all he had.

From that beginning, he became Dr. Cleveland Chandler. He is chairman of the economics department at Howard University. How did they do it, starting on one of the poorest farms in the poorest part of the poorest state in America?

PRINCESS CHANDLER NORMAN: We worked.
KURALT: You picked cotton?

NORMAN: Yes, picked cotton, and pulled corn, stripped millet, dug potatoes.

They all left. Luther left for the University of Omaha and went on to become the Public Service Employment Manager for Kansas City. He helped his younger brother, James, come to Omaha University, too, and go on to graduate work at Yale. And in his turn, James helped Herman, who graduated from Morgan State and is a technical manager in Dallas. And they helped themselves. Fortson, a Baptist minister in Pueblo, Colorado, wanted to go to Morehouse College.

FORTSON CHANDLER: I chose Morehouse and it was difficult. I had to pick cotton all summer long to get the first month's rent and tuition.

So, helping themselves and helping one another, they all went away. And now, fifty years after life began for the Chandler family in a one-room shack in a cotton field, now, just as they were sitting down in the new house to the ham and turkey and sweet potatoes and cornbread and collard greens and two kinds of pie and three kinds of cake, now Donald arrived—the youngest—who had driven with his family all the way down from Minneapolis. And now the Chandlers were all together again.

ALEX CHANDLER [*saying grace*]: Our Father in heaven, we come at this moment, giving thee thanks for thou hast been so good and so kind. We want to thank you, oh God, for this, for your love and for your son. Thank you that you have provided for all of us through all these years. [Mr. Chandler begins weeping.]

Remembering all those years of sharecropping and going hungry and working for a white man for fifty cents a day and worrying about his children's future, remembering all that, Alex Chandler almost didn't get through this blessing.

ALEX [continuing grace]: In Jesus' name, amen.

And neither did the others. [Family members wiping tears away]

The Chandler family started with as near nothing as any family in America ever did. And so their Thanksgiving weekend might have been more thankful than most. [*Chandler family singing "I'll Fly Away"*]

"I'll Fly Away" is the name of the old hymn. It is Mr. Chandler's favorite. His nine children flew away, and made places for themselves in this country; and this weekend, came home again.

There probably are no lessons in any of this, but I know that in the future whenever I hear that the family is a dying institution, I'll think of them. Whenever I hear anything in America is impossible, I'll think of them.

Santa Claus

(CALIFORNIA)

KID: I want a color TV.
SANTA: Color TV?
KID: And a pony.
SANTA: A pony?
KID: A baby doll.
SANTA: A big baby doll. What else would you like?
KID: An inchworm.
SANTA: An inchworm?

Listen, being Santa Claus isn't all visions of sugar plums and ho ho ho. For one thing, it's big business. An outfit called North Pole Santas, Incorporated, is supplying hundreds of Santas to department stores nationwide this year, and each Santa gets an instruction booklet full of advice, like: "Sometimes children will ask for a baby brother. This is strictly not your department. Try to keep kids from breaking out sobbing and becoming semi-hysterical. Omit the ho ho hos; it may frighten children." The trouble is, it's not always easy to go by the book.

★ ★ ★

KURALT [to child]: Would you like a candy cane? Would you like a candy cane?

At Serramonte Shopping Center in Daly City, Califor-

nia, I took a short turn behind the whiskers myself, and discovered that children may like the idea of Santa Claus, but a lot of them find the real item terrifying.

At Mervyn's Department Store in San Pablo and here at Serramonte we watched two experienced employees of North Pole Santas, Incorporated: Richard Allen, a recent PhD in theology, and Paul Chernock, an aspiring opera singer and recent kibbutz worker in Israel. Both of them earned their two seventy-five an hour, I'll tell you that.

FIRST WOMAN: Tell him about the car you want.
SECOND WOMAN: The car, honey.
FIRST WOMAN: 'Cause his reindeer are waiting for him.

The man who sends these Santas to the firing line, and the man who wrote the book, is the head of North Pole Santas, Charles Rose.

CHARLES ROSE: I think the biggest problem, and you

wouldn't think of this as being a problem, is making the child feel at ease, making the child not be afraid of this man with these white whiskers and beard and so on, because the child cannot really see the whole face, and sees the Santa in costume. He's awfully scared and frightened. So Santa has to make the child feel at ease.

Mr. Rose makes it all sound so reasonable, like a general before the battle. But out here in the trenches, Gina won't smile.

MAN: Aren't you a good little girl? Can't you smile big for Santa? No? Come on, Gina.

And Aaron won't speak.

MAN: Can you tell Santa what you'd like for Christmas? Huh? Can you tell Santa what you'd like for Christmas?

And Scott won't do anything.

WOMAN: Hey, Scotty. Scotty, listen. Lookit.

And the stubborn nonbelievers abound.

WOMAN: He's the real Santa.
KID: You're sure a skinny Santa Claus.
SANTA: I feel pretty fat to me.
KID: Real skinny to me.
SANTA: Yeah, my knees are. See, I've always had skinny knees.

And the flashbulbs. Oh, those flashbulbs.

WOMAN: Everybody say cheese.
SANTA AND KID: Cheese. Cheese.

We have it straight from the lips of Jolly Old Saint Nick. It is all right with him if you omit the hot chocolate on the hearth this Christmas Eve. After eight hours of this, six days a week, he could do with a stiff double scotch instead.

The Toy Fixing Man

(CEDARVILLE, CALIFORNIA)

Every year at this time, hundreds of toys are left at the Modoc County Courthouse for any kid who wants them. Only one man can do a thing like that, of course— St. Nicholas. Around here, St. Nicholas wears boots and a battered cowboy hat and a two-day growth of beard. His name is George Wilcox. And if he looks more like an old sheep rancher than Santa

Claus to you, that's because he used to run sheep on seven hundred and eighty acres at the head of Deep Creek, near Cedarville. Seven years ago his doctor told him the sheep had to go, so George Wilcox sold off the sheep, sold off the acres, and started looking around for something to do. This is it.

Every day for seven years, George Wilcox had fixed a toy. Some days he's fixed two or three toys. Days when he gets tired of fixing toys, he makes toys from scratch. He says that what he knows about is sheep, not toys, but he flails away with hammer and pliers and paint and glue until he's got it about right. He does it all day, every day. The yard between his house and his shed, littered with the broken playthings of this whole remote corner of California, looks like some kind of nightmare version of *Babes in Toyland*. George Wilcox says to him it's beautiful.

★ ★ ★

KURALT: Why do you go to all this trouble, work so hard all year to give kids toys?

WILCOX: Well, I don't know. Did you ever look at it this way, that if you had a child and you didn't have the money to give him a toy, you'd feel kind of let down? Christmas to a kid without a toy, well, that's kind of a poor thing. I mean, when I was a kid, we didn't get very many toys. If we got a new shirt or a bag of candy, well, that was quite a lot. We were poor but we was never allowed to know we were poor, and that's the way I've been most of my life. I've been poor but I just never let people know it.

KURALT: Well, you're rich in junk toys now.

WILCOX: Yeah. It makes me rich in my feelings, too, for the simple reason is that some little kid is going to have a nice Christmas.

In a corner of the dining room, Mabel Wilcox, who has also been ill this year, does her best to make dresses for the dolls that her husband has repaired.

They had to ask two neighbors with pickup trucks to help them deliver this year's toys to the courthouse. There were five bicycles, eighteen tricycles, ten red wagons, sixty-five dolls, and four hundred sixty-seven toys of other descriptions—all of them shiny, bright, and good as new.

George Wilcox acknowledges that it's been a year of hard work with no pay, but he says it's easier than sheep ranching, and there wasn't always a lot of pay in that either. He says he thinks of this as a privilege.

Afterward, I remembered that's how those others felt too—those earlier shepherds who came with the wise men, bearing gifts.

The Christmas Tree

(DELTA, COLORADO)

Trees just do not grow up here on the high plateaus of the Rockies—everybody knows that. Trees need good soil and good weather and up here there's no soil and terrible weather. People do not live here. Nothing can live up here and certainly not trees. That's why the tree is a kind of miracle.

The tree is a juniper, and it grows beside U.S. 50 utterly alone, not another tree for miles. Nobody remembers who put the first Christmas ornament on it—some whimsical motorist of years ago. From that day to this, the tree has been redecorated each year. Nobody knows who does it. But each year, by Christmas day, the tree has become a Christmas tree.

The tree, which has no business growing here at all, has survived against all the odds. The summer droughts somehow haven't killed it, or the winter storms. When the highway builders came out to widen the road they could have taken the tree with one pass of their bulldozer. But some impulse led them to start widening the road just a few feet past the tree. The trucks pass so close that they rattle the tree's branches. The tree has also survived the trucks.

The tree violates the laws of man and nature. It is too close to the highway for man, and not far enough away for nature. The tree pays no attention. It is where it is. It survives.

People who live in Grand Junction, thirty miles one way, and in Delta, Colorado, fifteen miles the other way,

all know about and love the tree. They have Christmas trees of their own, of course, the kind of trees that are brought to town in trucks and sold in vacant lots and put up in living rooms. This one tree belongs to nobody and to everybody.

Just looking at it makes you think about how unexpected life on earth can be. The tree is so lonely and so brave that it seems to offer courage to those who pass it—and a message. It is the Christmas message: that there is life and hope even in a rough world.

About the Author

Charles Kuralt appears regularly on the CBS EVENING NEWS and anchors the CBS News broadcast, SUNDAY MORNING. "I was a real reporter once," he writes, "but I was not suited for it by physique or temperament," so, in 1967, after several years reporting for CBS News from every corner of the world, including Vietnam, Latin America, and the North Pole, he decided to "wander around the country and do some feature stories." He and his camera crew are wandering still, having logged more than a million miles, and in the process, won a host of honors, including two Emmys and two George Foster Peabody Awards. In 1983 he was named "Broadcaster of the Year" by the International Radio and Television Society. Charles Kuralt is the author of two previous books, TO THE TOP OF THE WORLD and DATELINE AMERICA. Born in North Carolina, he makes his home in New York City—when not "on the road."